Stark Raving Mab

Stephanie Caye

1

"You're definitely getting better, Jude." Diana poured a shot of tequila into my waiting glass.

"Maybe I'm not cut out for surfing." I snorted at the platitude, rubbing the rising goose egg on the side of my head. "Lying on the sand is more my beach speed."

We clinked glasses before throwing back our shots, but the tequila just made me thirsty. That deviation from the warm, numbing rush of alcohol felt like being betrayed by an old friend.

Not a new experience for me, actually.

"Sometimes you have to try something more than twice to improve at it," Diana chided.

"Twice is once more than I usually try." She was right, though—she'd been surfing for years, having grown up here on the west side of Vancouver Island. She was full of stories about sharks, jellyfish and riptides and even had a pale scar on the back of her left hand from some kind of stinging coral to prove her dedication to the sport. Only last weekend had she managed to get me—from land-locked, rural Ontario—out into the chilly Pacific waters on a waxed board for the first time.

Even though Tofino was known for year-round surfing, late March wasn't supposed to be the best time for beginners. Still, I'd figured I couldn't fail, since 'good balance' was basically my defining trait. I'd been looking forward to impressing Diana.

Something about the unpredictable, roiling waves, or maybe the saltwater stinging my eyes had thrown off my Faerie groove, though. I'd had trouble digging into my powers last weekend out on the water and again today.

I still felt an echo of the waves on my body, even slouching here in a second-hand wooden chair in the kitchen of our tiny, warm apartment a kilometre and a half from the beach.

"We'll try again next weekend, if it's calm." Diana played with the tequila bottle's cap for a moment as if debating pouring another shot. Instead, she craned her neck to check her phone screen nestled in its waterproof case, then screwed the cap back on. "I've gotta shower and head out."

"You're back on Thursday?"

"Probably." My roommate sighed and ran a hand back through her tight black curls, which were punctuated by fading pink highlights. "If Mrs. Davis goes late, I'll probably stay over another—"

I didn't hear the end of the sentence. Searing pain hit the top of my head. It sizzled down through my skull and into my neck like lightning. A distant, strangled cry echoed back to me. My own voice.

When the agony sparked out, I lay on my back on the hard floor, exhausted.

Oh, no, not the floor—the *ceiling*. Our cramped apartment spread out below me—my shot glass on its side on the kitchen table, Diana in her chair with her head tilted back, eyes wide . . .

Another jolt shot through me and normal gravity caught up.

I dropped like a stone. New stinging waves of pain swept through my knees and elbows as I hit the floor, but unlike the lightning in my head, this felt more normal—to be expected for having, you know, fallen three metres onto the hardwood.

With a huff, I rolled onto my back and unfolded my arms. I couldn't help studying the ceiling. Had my sparking, splayed body left some kind of charred impression, a shadow on the white plaster?

Nothing.

My motion snapped Diana out of her frozen state. She fell to her knees beside me, prodding my body for injuries.

"Don't move. Does anything feel broken?"

"No." Despite her warning, I sat up on my aching elbows, testing my muscles.

"Have you ever had a seizure before?" She touched my face to examine my pupils.

"What? No!" Startled by the word, I shoved her hands away with more force than I'd intended.

"You spasmed, fell out of the chair and . . ." Her eyes flickered to the ceiling, then her head twitched slightly as reason seemed to erase my little gravity trick from her memory. She gestured to the floor instead. "You fell," she finished, "shaking. It looked like a seizure to me."

"I just got a little dizzy." Nausea rolled through me hard enough to make me flop back over onto my side in case it brought up the tequila. My skin blazed with sudden heat and a distinct, unpleasant buzzing—a sustained electricity that mimicked how I felt being around other Faeries, only magnified ten times.

Diana tried to stop me when I made a second attempt to get up, but when I growled at her, she gave in and helped me toward the sofa.

I sank back against the cushions, shoulders tensing as if I could shrug off that unnerving Faerie tingle. The nausea had passed, but my nerves still felt distantly raw, like a layer of my skin had been torn off and I was still half-numb to it.

"We should go to the hospital," Diana said. "I'll get the car."

"No!" I protested. "I'm fine! I don't need a hospital!"

When Diana gave me her sternest look, I struggled to come up with some explanation that didn't involve my Faerie heritage. That had to be what had caused my little gravity blip and doctors were only going to find the low iron in my blood strange. Convincing them that I wasn't dangerously anemic—that it was actually normal for me because I'm half-Faerie and my body can't handle too much iron—would be a lot of lying I didn't feel up for.

Not to mention that I definitely didn't want my name showing up in the government health system.

"Probably just some water in my inner ear," I stammered. That was a thing, right?

Diana frowned, jaw clenching as she chewed over her protests. Finally, she shook her head, black and pink curls bouncing.

"I'm calling in sick for you," she said.

"Who died and made you queen?" The command annoyed me.

"Call it a compromise," she shot back. "You say no hospital. Well, I say no running around. We're both mildly annoyed."

"Fine," I muttered, trying to ward off the uncomfortable shift in my stomach. I'd already taken the morning off from stripping hotel beds and scrubbing toilets to indulge Diana's desire to teach me to surf. Missing my afternoon shift in the hotel's laundry room wasn't going to endear me to my boss at the resort.

Still, my body ached from the pounding surf. The pain in my head had turned into a dull throb down the centre of my skull that was starting to trickle into my temples. The idea of the sweaty, humid laundry room, the loud whirring and thumping of industrial washing machines, brought my nausea back with force.

"Maybe I should stay," Diana started.

"Don't be ridiculous." I kept from wincing as I jerked my head up to meet her gaze. "We can't both skip work.

Plus, you get paid more. I promise not to stroke out while you're gone."

She gaped at me, caught somewhere between amused and aghast, then threw her hands up in an 'I can't even' gesture.

"I'm holding you to that," she warned.

I drew a finger twice across my heart in an x, giving her my most earnest expression. I liked Diana's company but I didn't need her mothering me, especially when whatever had just happened probably had some kind of shitty, magical explanation. She couldn't do anything about it, and I'd left anybody else who might be able to help behind in Toronto five months ago.

As soon as Diana disappeared into the bathroom at the back of the apartment, I got gingerly to my feet. I took a drink of water from the kitchen faucet, rinsed my mouth and then took another long sip and swallowed, daring my stomach to bring it back up.

I lingered a moment, head bowed and elbows resting on the stainless steel sink. The static sound of the running water calmed me. That jolt of pain preceding my not-seizure had been instantaneous, a tap at the top of my skull searing down through every vein. Like nothing I'd ever felt before. The tingle of goosebumps still shivered intermittently across my arms, though the sensation was muted now. I studied my bronze skin to make sure it wasn't glowing or anything weird.

I'd run from everyone I knew who might have been able to explain this. Abe, a part-Faerie hybrid like me and a healer, could probably have put his big hands on my head and mended whatever was wrong. At the very least, he could have read me empathically to diagnose the problem.

My aunt Miranda would have even more powerful healers at her disposal, and libraries of knowledge about Faerie crap.

I could probably find some way to contact them—try to force my way into the Faerie safehouse or shout into a mirror until they showed up—but I didn't want to start that ball rolling if I could help it. Calling the Faeries into my life had only ever made things worse—made *me* worse.

2

When Diana emerged from her bedroom fifteen minutes later, wet hair pulled back and an overnight backpack slung over one shoulder, she quizzed me halfheartedly to gauge whether I'd admit defeat and ask her to stay. I could tell her mind was already on the births that would be starting to happen, hours away, around the island. My roommate was a travelling doula. I didn't know exactly what she did, but I knew she had more important things to worry about than me.

Once she'd left, I gave in and embraced the day off work and the empty apartment. I made some instant ramen, stirring in two flavour packets and foregoing my usual fried egg on top, then filled a large glass with water. I curled up on the sofa again in hopes that the food and hydration would ease the headache and the prickling energy in my skin.

When I turned on the TV, I found a soapy medical procedural I might normally have enjoyed, but I didn't want to think about hospitals. I flipped channels until I came to a movie I'd already seen. With the warm afternoon sunlight coming through the windows and the chatter from the TV, I finished my lunch and managed to doze until a sudden, new sound in the room woke me.

I opened my eyes and started at the shadow of giant wings on the floor. Twisting around to find its source, I saw what looked like a giant, pale green moth on the outside of the window. It beat its wings against the screen, casting the larger-than-life shadow.

Sliding off the sofa, I crossed the room to peer at it. Its wingspan was the width of both my hands side-by-side. I'd never seen anything like it, but I was still a newbie to the west coast rainforest fauna. As I got closer, it freaked out, throwing itself against the screen with what seemed like suicidal angst.

"Hey," I said despite myself. "Quit it." What was a moth doing out in the daylight, anyway? Was it strong enough to tear through the screen? "Scram."

Someone knocked at the front door and I jumped, heart racing. *Spooked by a moth. A new low.*

I debated staying silent and ignoring the visitor. It was probably just a tourist looking for the rental property on the first floor of our duplex. The landlord had only included an outside photo of the house in his listing, so more than one person had gotten confused and come upstairs upon arrival, looking for the lock-box.

When the knock came again, I straightened my tank top and ran a hand back through my hair. There was no peephole in the door, which I'd always hated because it went against my natural paranoia. I could have peeked out through the side of the curtain on the front window, but that wasn't stealthy.

I opened the door to an unfamiliar man on the wooden, second-floor porch. Dark-skinned and a good six inches taller than me, he wore black trousers and a pale blue shirt, a little professional for the neighbourhood—for the laid back resort town in general, actually.

Before I could say a word, he went down on one knee, bowing his head low.

"Vacation rental's downstairs," I managed, studying the muscular shoulders under the tightly stretched blue cotton.

"My name is Eli." He didn't lift his head. "I was sent with a message for Judith."

Hearing my full name sent an icicle through my chest. Nobody used that except my father.

Fuck.

"It's Jude," I said, voice more strangled than I'd intended. I hugged my arms to my chest, suppressing a new set of unpleasant goosebumps. "Would you just get up?"

Eli hesitated then straightened up again, still avoiding my eyes.

"The Ubran contacted me this afternoon," he said. "They apologize for being unable to come across themselves—"

"That's okay. I don't know who 'they' are."

He paused, startled, studying the door frame to my right as if that might hold the answers.

"My Lady Jude." He tripped a little over that title, which did sound pretty stupid. "I'm afraid I'm the bearer of bad news."

"That's all I ever get."

Eli finally met my eyes with a pair of pale yellow ones. That unnatural gaze clinched my ninety-percent certainty that he was Faerie, then he shot it to a hundred by announcing:

"Your aunt, the exalted Mab, has died."

The words hit me like a fist to the stomach. I stared at him, trying to remember how to breathe.

"The Mab is dead." Eli bowed again. "Long live the Mab."

"Nope," I said—and slammed the door.

3

"Knock, knock?" A tinny tap came at the trailer door, then the latch clicked open. Marianne Nguyen poked her head in. Her expression darkened when she recognized the trailer's sole occupant, perched on the tiny, uncomfortable sofa with a notepad on his lap and several decrepit books spread around him.

Daniel Cain wasn't thrilled to see her either.

"Where's William?" Marianne's insistence on calling the wealthy, American asshole who'd all but kidnapped them both by his first name, as if they were colleagues, turned Daniel's stomach. She called the man 'Mr. Leshe' to his face.

"He had to take a call." He didn't elaborate—everyone in camp knew that when William Leshe took a call, he hopped into his glossy, black SUV and went racing around the empty desert. Leshe had this whole trailer to himself as a private office and sleeping space—the only one in the dig camp who did—but he apparently preferred to be in motion while he negotiated business.

"I'll wait, then. Nice and cool in here." Marianne's tone was snide and accusing as she mopped sweat from the back of her neck with a handkerchief. Her clothes were streaked with reddish dirt. The substance had found its way into everything at the dig camp.

Daniel didn't dignify her comment with a response. She knew that the only reason he'd been given access to the trailer for a few hours was because of the books around him and the shard of stone tablet he was currently working to decipher. They required a climate-controlled environment and Leshe's private sanctum was the only place for miles with air-conditioning. Most days even its generator struggled in the blazing Arizona heat.

He turned his attention back to the stone tablet on the table. When he made the mistake of scratching off a hard speck of dirt to double-check the form of one of the carved letters, Marianne said, "You ought to be wearing gloves."

She was right, and it was a complaint Gracie would have made. Daniel had to fight off a sharp pang thinking of his sister. She would have resented the sloppy protocol, but if she'd been the one to who'd woken handcuffed to a hospital bed, then been forced to work for an arrogant, cagey millionaire, she'd have known there were more critical concerns than artifact handling.

"Amateur," Marianne muttered. "There are *two* members of my team who'd have finished this by now."

"Well, send them in—I could use some research assistants." It wasn't worth reminding her that both of those people had already been given first look at the tablet and come up puzzled, but Daniel couldn't help adding, "Unless they're as duplicitous as your last one."

"I only hired Tess on Grace's recommendation." Marianne looked affronted at the mention of the woman who had betrayed them both to William Leshe and his organization. Probably not a coincidence Tess Foster wasn't even here on the dig—she'd obviously worked her way up in the world since last fall.

Marianne looked toward the door, muttering under her breath. Daniel couldn't hear the word but he didn't need to—she'd already said it to his face a handful of times since they'd been forced to work together.

I'm the traitor, sure, he wanted to tell her. *But I'm not the one running after William Leshe and his magic-seeking cronies like a lapdog.*

He didn't bother. Staying alive in this place meant keeping Leshe happy. The surfeit of men with guns in camp obeyed his commands, so everyone else did too. Only Marianne seemed willing to pretend that she was content with the situation, probably because it won her more freedom and respect than the other ex-Consilium forced labour. *She* didn't have an armed escort walking her daily from her tent to the tunnel and back, standing half a metre away from her at the crude pit toilets.

She also hadn't tried to escape Leshe's grip three times in the last five months, though. The permanent guard detail was marginally better than the dark, solitary cell Leshe had used as punishment for Daniel's transgressions before they'd all been hauled out to the desert to dig.

As if her thoughts had gone the same way, Marianne folded her arms across her chest and mused, "I'm surprised to find you in here alone. Maybe I should call a guard over."

"They know where I am." Daniel lifted a finger to point out the streaming webcam that sat exposed on the shelf above him, and Marianne huffed, startled.

"You might have warned me," she muttered, shifting nervously. She seemed to be thinking back over what she'd already said, probably making sure she'd been deferential enough even in her boss's absence.

Daniel hadn't actually tested this camera to see if it was really in use, but if nobody was actively monitoring him on it, then somebody would inevitably be standing sentry outside the trailer. Someone in Leshe's employ was always watching.

"Have you placed the discrepancies in the tablet yet?" Marianne studied the open books around him and then eyed the piece of broken stone. "Age? Regional dialect?"

"If I had, I couldn't tell you." That was half for the satisfaction of pissing her off and half for whoever might be listening on the other end of the camera. They weren't supposed to be talking together without Leshe present.

Before Marianne could snap a response, they both tensed at the heavy rumble of an engine—a vehicle pulling up to the trailer. Marianne twitched, clearly debating between being found waiting unasked-for in her boss's private sanctuary or caught emerging from it.

She hadn't made up her mind by the time the latch clicked again and the aluminum door opened.

"Having a party in here?" William Leshe sounded annoyed as he took in the space.

"We should be—that's what I came to tell you." Marianne deftly turned the subject. "We've reached a set of doors. We're still cleaning them up, but it's already clear there are symbols there, some kind of message."

"Fantastic." Leshe brightened. "Show me." He swung the door open and stood back to let Marianne pass in front of him, then hesitated.

Daniel realized he had Leshe's full, piercing attention.

"I haven't finished," he said, indicating the half-legible stone piece on the table. He resented being forced to submit to this asshole, but he still couldn't help the desperate curiosity that had taken hold around the actual work.

"That's not important anymore." Leshe dismissed a week of study with a wave of his hand. "I need you focused on the real prize. Didn't you hear the professor? She found doors, and there's writing on them."

He glanced to Marianne to add, "I'm betting it's not in English."

"It's not," she agreed reluctantly.

"And that's the whole reason *you're* here, right?" Leshe reminded Daniel. "Rather than in prison up in the Great White North?" His chipper tone amplified the threat underneath.

Apparently. Daniel didn't say the word aloud. Sarcasm was always the wrong tack to take with the volatile American.

Probably only ten years older than Daniel's own twenty-nine, the other man's face had been surgically smoothed to an almost computer-generated sheen. It was made more jarring by the perpetually condescending expression he wore, which should have created more lines around his eyes. Even accompanied by a mop of thick, reddish brown curls that seemed to have been scalped off a precocious cartoon child and a trim, athletic figure, Leshe looked older than he probably was.

Daniel still hadn't figured out his endgame. Leshe's reassembling by force the remains of the Consilium to pinpoint and excavate a tunnel in some godforsaken corner of the American desert could have been driven by pure ignorance or curiosity. Maybe a simple lust for untapped power or magic. Still, the last few months had given him the distinct feeling it was for a more malicious purpose.

"It would be a hell of a waste of resources to have to go out and hunt your sister down now," Leshe mused. "If you were bluffing, I mean, when you assured me you knew everything she did and more, so we didn't need her—?"

Marianne gave a derisive snort but Daniel ignored her, shoving the notepad off his lap so he could get to his feet. He hated every twitch in his muscles that pushed him into acquiescence, into following orders, but he had no choice. Gracie was safe out in the world somewhere right now. Leshe and his agents hadn't caught her yet, even though she'd ostensibly been the one person in the pool of remaining Consilium agents that he wanted, due to her background in archaeology and her focus on the Wild Hunt.

She and Ted were deeply in hiding—they had to be. Still, Daniel wasn't about to pit their admittedly impressive skills in going to ground against Leshe's shockingly vast network of resources.

"Good." Leshe flashed a toothy smile as Daniel joined him at the door. "No use shaking the team up now, right? Not when we're on the precipice of such a lucrative dis-covery."

"Lucrative how?" Daniel dared to ask.

The other man's smile only widened. "Let's find out."

4

I THREW THE DEADBOLT on my front door and stalked across the room as a tentative knock came again. I couldn't breathe. My chest felt tight, amplifying the sudden, rushed pounding of my heart.

Miranda was dead. The Mab was dead.

My aunt had been a distant cousin in the royal Faerie family. She'd gotten kicked up in the line for the throne when the palace had been decimated by human adversaries in a big battle a year ago. The crown always went through the female line, so since Miranda had no kids of her own, as her closest female relative—maybe the *only* one—I'd automatically become her heir.

But *I* couldn't be the *Mab*.

The polite knocking at the door turned to a pounding fist.

"I don't wish to break this down." Eli's voice carried through the wood, low and terse but deadly serious.

I gritted my teeth to keep from daring him to do it. Diana would be furious if she got home to find the front door kicked in. With a growl, I crossed the room again and unlocked it, yanking it open to repeat, "No. Find somebody else."

"W—what?" Eli hesitated, brow furrowed.

"I can't be the Mab," I said. "I'm only half-Faerie and I used to work for the Consilium. I'm an enemy."

"Your Highness—"

"Do *not* call me that."

"Then . . ." Eli started to look lost.

"Jude."

He balked. "I can't."

"It's my name."

"But you're . . . you're the Mab and respect needs to be maintained, even in—"

"I'm not the Mab," I said again.

Eli stopped, dropping his hesitant respect to gape at me in amazement. "Yes, you are," he said. "The power has already passed to you. I can . . . I can sense it."

"*That's* what the seizure was?" Maybe this wasn't a conversation to have on the outdoor landing in a crowded neighbourhood. "Inside," I said, stepping back to let him in. He didn't seem like a guy who did well when given options.

After he'd entered and closed the door, I paced the living room, running a hand back through my short hair. "What happened to Miranda?"

"I'm not privy to that information." Eli stood in front of the door, shoulders straight, hands clasped behind his back like—of all things—a soldier. His earlier cool had returned.

Another chill went through me—maybe a touch of grief mixed in with that disbelief. The last time I'd seen Miranda, she'd been trying to co-opt my womb to carry a more suitable heir. No—the absolute last time I'd seen her was when she'd forbidden me, through a mirror, from going to save my human friends from a murderous Faerie cult. I'd smashed the glass and gone anyway.

"I'm not qualified for this," I said, trying to keep my voice from trembling.

"Your blood says differently, ma'am."

I shot him a dirty look for the ridiculous term of address and he looked toward the window to ignore it. "The Ubran will cross over as soon as possible," he said, "but I was warned it could take twenty-four to thirty-six hours here before the ban on travel is lifted."

"What's the Ubran?"

When Eli realized that was a serious question, his expression melted into one Abe had given me each time I'd revealed the depths of my ignorance about Faerie politics. Everyone always assumed that my supernatural DNA made this information magically appear in my head.

"The council of advisers that serves under the Mab," Eli finally said.

"So these guys are like the Parliament? They can hold onto Faerie for a while until they find themselves another queen, right?"

"That isn't how it—" He took a sharp breath, then his tone turned distant and formal again. "I haven't got the authority to speak on these matters. I was only sent to protect you."

"*Protect* me?" My pride itched under my skin. "Who are you, anyway? Why'd they send *you*? Why not somebody I know?" It hadn't occurred to me that this could be a trap, something shady. Probably should have thought that through before I let him in.

"I was stationed in this world," Eli answered, "and the Ubran are unable to cross over. The portals are restricted and all travel's been suspended. I didn't ask them why they chose me."

Operating without all the information. No questions asked. It did sound bureaucratic. Maybe it *was* legit. After all, I'd had the seizure and my skin was still humming. A little more now that Eli was in close proximity.

"Why's travel suspended? Was Miranda murdered?"

Not like it would be the first time a Mab had been assassinated, or even the first time in the last few years. A bunch of Consilium agents had managed to get through the portals somehow last spring and taken out Miranda's predecessor and her whole Court. From what I'd heard, they'd used some kind of bomb.

But the Consilium was gone.

"As I said, I don't know." Eli's voice thinned. "We should go somewhere safer," he said, glancing to the large front window. "This apartment has two, probably more entrances—" He craned his neck to see into the bedrooms, looking for more windows. "—and is situated in a populous area."

"Pass," I said.

Eli clenched his jaw, though I wouldn't have seen that if I hadn't been looking hard. He was pretty good with the stone face.

"Your safety is the first priority of the realm," he said. "You are currently without an heir. Should something befall you, the power would—"

"What? What would it do? Disappear into the air and liberate the peasants in Faerie?"

"There are no peasants," Eli scoffed, fighting not to glower at me. "And I don't know what would happen to the power, but I'm sure it would be disastrous."

"It always is." I sighed. "Look, I feel safe here, and I'm not letting you herd me off somewhere—I don't even *know* you."

"Your Highness, allow me to speak freely?"

"When was I stopping you?"

"If I wanted you dead, you would be dead."

"Big talk." I fixed him with a steady gaze, challenging the boast.

He met my eyes and disappeared.

I blinked, searching for any outline of his body in the space where he'd just been. Then I concentrated on looking through glamour, thinking past what my eyes saw and fixating on what I expected to be in the spot.

Nothing changed. I'd seen a Faerie turn into water vapour, but there'd always been a little shimmer as a giveaway. Pixies burst into glitter that was visible. Even chameleons—lesidhe—could be picked out of their camouflage if you looked hard enough.

Breath teased the hairs on the back of my neck. It took all of my willpower not to spin around and punch him. Heart racing, I stepped forward, then turned as calmly as I could to see that Eli had moved respectfully back.

"Fine," I said, voice still a little tight. Invisibility was a new one on me. "You have my permission to protect me."

I dropped onto the sofa in what I hoped was a cool, collected way but probably looked more like a collapse. From there, I stared out the window to the house across the street. Bright, blue sky shone above the shingles but the angle of the sunlight had changed to late afternoon while I'd been dozing on the sofa.

Maybe eight hours ago, I'd been sitting on a board in the ocean with Diana, getting pummelled by waves and everything had made sense. Now some random guy had come to tell me I was the Mab and had the seizure to prove it.

Nausea washed over me again and I pressed a hand to my warm cheek. Miranda had manipulated me and jerked me around. Always more concerned with my womb than me—with me producing a royal heir to keep the line going. I couldn't remember any time we'd been in the same room and not argued.

And now she was dead. How was I supposed to feel about that? What was I supposed to do?

My phone buzzed in my back pocket, startling me. Not a call, but an alarm. I pulled it out to dismiss the noise and took a look at what I'd meant to remind myself.

Monday at five p.m. Industry Night at our local bar, Pacific Slim's. Probably zero chance of convincing Eli to take a field trip for three-dollar well shots and dollar pizza. The muscles in my legs itched to get me upright, make a break for freedom. Eli could go invisible, sure, but how fast could he run? Maybe I could make it out of this tiny trap of an apartment and the hell away from here.

My phone screen turned off automatically, leaving me staring at my dim reflection. I didn't look like a queen—I looked like a grouchy chick with a bad haircut. I'd cropped my dark curls short when I'd gotten to Tofino, and they brushed my jawline unevenly.

"A moth wouldn't have had anything to do with Miranda's death, right?" Behind me in the reflection, I caught sight of the window where the giant insect had been beating its wings, trying to get in.

"A . . . what?" Eli straightened.

"Earlier—just when you showed up—there was this huge, green moth beating against my screen." I watched his expression and concluded, "I guess it was just—"

"The Archduke."

I hadn't thought I could possibly feel worse, but here it was, a new low.

"Last time I checked, the Archduke was a jackass, not a moth," I muttered.

Eli gave me a quick, razor-thin smile.

"It's a message."

"It didn't—" I hated the uncertain words about to pass my lips. "—*say* anything?"

When he shook his head, I concluded, "Oh, so one of those messages I'm just supposed to *know*." I sighed. "Do *you* know what it means?"

"I wouldn't presume."

Eli wouldn't and I didn't want to. My brain had absorbed all the new information it could take for the day. Maybe for the decade. On top of everything else, I did not have the energy to consider the smug Faerie Archduke.

I shoved myself to my feet and retrieved the tequila bottle from the cupboard above the sink. Last time I'd drunk tequila, I'd become the Mab, but I was willing to risk it.

"You want a drink?" I asked over my shoulder.

"I don't drink, Your Highness."

"Just Jude, okay?" I sighed, pouring a shot for myself. "Pretend I passed an edict or something."

"Yes, Y—" He caught himself but still didn't say my name.

I turned, glass in hand, and found him contemplating the tiny apartment. His expression seemed more dubious than critical, something beyond calculations of how to defend the place.

"It may be tiny and not easily defensible, but it's home," I quipped.

He flinched, startled at having been caught.

"I'm just surprised," he said, "given all the trouble you went through to hide. I'd expected something . . . grander." He winced. "I didn't mean—"

"Don't worry, I'm not going to toss you in the dungeon. What do you mean *trouble*? It was, like, three buses and a long train ride to cross the country."

Eli eyed me with a hint of uncertainty, as if trying to suss out whether I was being genuine again.

When I raised my eyebrows to urge him on, he said, "No one's been able to locate you since last fall."

"What?" I'd been lifting the shot to my lips but I paused. "What do you mean?"

"Mages, trackers, spies—no one could determine your location. The last place they found any trace of you was just outside Calgary."

It had been a harsh night at the beginning of November last year when I'd told Abe not to find me. I'd told my father to disappear. Then I'd headed away from Toronto by bus, aiming westward. The buses had gotten complicated, so I'd gotten a coach ticket on the cross-country train. I hadn't actually tried to hide at any point—hadn't done anything but keep moving to prevent people from finding me. I didn't know how to do more—I didn't know magic. I didn't have power beyond my Faerie ability to manipulate gravity.

Going north through Ontario around the Great Lakes then west across the prairies, anxiety had gnawed my insides. I'd expected to see Miranda in the reflection of somebody's blank cell phone, or have my father stride down the aisle of the moving train. I'd waited and dreaded the tingle of a nearby Faerie.

So—now that I thought about it—how the hell *had* I gotten off the Faerie radar and stayed that way for the last five months?

I threw back the shot of tequila, letting it infuse me with a warm flush.

"If nobody could find me, how did you?" I asked Eli.

"I don't have the official story," he answered, voice annoyingly measured, "but from what I've gathered, you just . . . turned up suddenly when your aunt passed. Like a beacon in the fog."

"Could it have been Miranda?" I asked. "Covering me? Hiding me? Secretly?"

"Perhaps." Eli sounded dubious. "I didn't know her, but I'm not sure why a Mab would—"

I didn't hear the rest, because it struck me who would have been likelier than Miranda to blur my existence from the rest of the Faeries. My fucking father.

Joshua definitely had that kind of power. If he'd done it, though, it hadn't been to protect *me*. The alcohol lessened the choking surge of fury and revulsion that typically came with thinking about my father, but it did nothing for the tight paranoia that flooded in.

I started to set my glass down, then realized that Eli had gone still, his eyes on the front door.

Footsteps creaked on the wooden stairs outside, coming up toward us quietly but quickly.

5

"Isn't it beautiful?" Marianne gazed proudly upon the treasure she and the others had uncovered. She stood flanked by her three dig assistants and seven armed guards—Leshe had hauled everybody in camp down into the tunnel.

A door frame was set tightly into the earthen walls. The heavy double doors themselves appeared to be the same pale stone as the frame, covered in elaborate carvings still half-caked with dirt.

"Perfect," Leshe whispered, reaching out to touch the stone with a surprising reverence.

Even holding semi-automatic weapons, the guards' eyes moved anxiously, waiting for something to leap out from the shadows that the hastily rigged, battery-operated lights cast on the dirt walls.

They didn't like it down here any more than Daniel did.

Despite his misgivings, he couldn't help moving closer to examine the find. The square blocks that made up the frame were each small enough to hold in two hands. They all bore different glyphs, but holes gaped in each corner of the rectangle like missing teeth. Four blocks had been removed—not recently, since the holes were half-full of earth. The door had been buried like this, missing pieces.

He touched the closest carving and brushed away the remaining chunk of dirt. Though not a match to his own alphabet, the letter was familiar. It was long and delicate, curling at the ends. Faerie.

"It looks the same as what's on that tablet you've been puzzling over," Leshe said.

"It's not," Daniel said. "I mean, it's the same language but these aren't runes. They're pictograms, like . . . road signage." He recognized maybe half of the glyphs as he moved down the frame. His training was more in the written language but he'd encountered a few of these symbols in his Consilium work.

"Can you read it?" Leshe asked.

"Stop. Danger. Closed. A different, more exciting icon for danger." Daniel moved his finger from one pictogram to the next, reading down the row and relaying the translations with a heavy dose of cynicism.

Marianne snorted, still standing with her arms folded across her chest even though her assistants had busied themselves setting up photography equipment.

"Of course *he'd* say that," she muttered.

"Can *you* translate it?" Daniel snapped.

Her withering glower spoke volumes but she answered anyway, in a curt, chiding tone. "You know that I can't."

"Then shut the fuck up." The expletive was as close as he could come to expressing the helpless hysteria that had started to boil in his chest.

Marianne recoiled, inordinately offended. Before she could snap back, Leshe glanced over his shoulder at her and paralyzed her attention.

"Open it."

She froze, mouth half-open. Recovering quickly, she scrambled to argue, "After we photograph it, surely—"

"No need." Leshe made a quick gesture and sent what had ostensibly been, until now, Marianne's assistants scrambling. "Get it open."

"But—"

"What's the rush?" Daniel asked, keeping his tone calmer than he felt. "Can't wait to face two different types of danger?"

"Pretty insistent, don't you think? It's clearly subterfuge, meant to scare us off." Leshe eyed the stones with a sour, dismissive expression.

Daniel didn't waste his breath arguing that he'd never come across anything indicating that Antagonists—Faeries—had either worried about or guarded against humanity cracking their language. There was no reason for them to have faked this.

"This find needs to be documented at each step," Marianne broke in, speaking slowly and gingerly even as her tone turned more desperate. "It's unprecedented and we *must* proceed carefully to ensure that nothing is lost." Her eyes darted to Daniel for backup.

He took more petty satisfaction than he should have in giving her a slight shrug and stepping back. Leshe wouldn't listen to either of them. He'd warned Marianne already, in the scant few minutes they'd gotten alone to talk, that Leshe was after something dangerous, that this wasn't an archaeological mission with any academic value.

She hadn't wanted to listen. She'd preferred to pretend this was some extension of the Consilium, some altruistic—or at least capitalistic—task that would bring her renown. Then she'd fallen back on the most tired of excuses, calling Daniel a traitor to an organization that hadn't existed for over a year. Hard to have sympathy for her now.

With the workers hurrying to rig a set of explosives, Leshe moved back down the tunnel and sank into a crouch, brushing dirt from his khaki trousers. The position looked uncomfortable and was pointless if he was trying to stay clean. Everyone in the tunnel was already coated in the reddish dirt they'd been digging in for the past four hours. For the past eight days.

Daniel didn't feel easy enough to sit, but he hovered against the wall beside the other man again to stay out of the way.

Marianne flitted around her assistants, hissing and clucking, glancing back every few seconds as if she thought she might change Leshe's mind. She didn't protest again as she joined them in moving around the far corner of the tunnel to avoid flying debris. She yanked the bandana around her neck up to cover her mouth and nose like a mask, the action reminding Daniel to do the same.

With all of them crowded together, awaiting an explosion, the guards had dropped their defences. Daniel realized he might be able to get one of the guns away from them, but he had no experience with weapons of that calibre. What would he even do with it—take Leshe out?

And if there was nothing behind the door? Or whatever *was* there wasn't worth killing to keep it locked up? Killing and then dying, since there was no way he'd manage to shoot Leshe without taking fire himself.

He dismissed the idea. Once the doors were open, he could better judge a plan of action. And there was always the chance that whatever was concealed back there would kill all of them anyway.

"Fire in the hole!" A woman, one of Marianne's assistants, detonated the explosives with a handheld remote. Protected by the curve of the thick wall as they were, the noise was loud enough to make several people jump but too muffled to linger in their ears. The temporary scaffolding above their heads shook, raining dirt from the hatched ceiling of wooden boards.

Should have added a cave-in to the list of our possible, spectacular deaths.

But whoever had done the dig planning had been competent. The planking held overhead and the tunnel kept its shape. A cloud of smoke drifted out at them and Daniel lowered his head, shielding his eyes. Two of the guards who'd been blessed with goggles of some kind used tiny battery-powered fans to help usher the smoke and dust out toward the tunnel's opening, half a kilometre back.

One of the guards turned on a battery-powered lantern and, at Leshe's urging, took the lead. Two others followed, their guns at the ready.

Leshe didn't wait to let them secure the area. He started forward, gesturing for the rest of the party to follow.

The doors had been reduced to a pile of rubble on the threshold, but somehow the frame was undamaged. While a few of the assistants and guards hauled the larger pieces of stone out of the way, Leshe gestured to the first guard to duck inside. His swinging the lantern around showed them that the space inside was definitely wider than the tunnel. The floor was smooth, beige stone—the same as the door.

Once the threshold was clear of the largest pieces of debris, two other guards ducked inside and turned on their lanterns. The additional illumination allowed a dim glimpse of perpendicular walls. The room was built of larger stone blocks than the ones in the door frame, though they still had runes carved into them at intervals. The light of three lanterns didn't reach all the way to the far end. Did it even have an end? The looming darkness brought a wave of vertigo crashing over Daniel, as if he were standing at the top of a cliff. His instinctive fear of heights swamped him, freezing the muscles in his legs.

In the inky blackness ahead, something took shape. He couldn't quite make sense of it, a wisp of—not smoke, something more solid. Something winding through the darkness. Something with teeth.

"Wait." He startled himself when the word came out of his own throat. He hadn't realized he'd moved away from the wall, reached the doorway.

He'd spoken too softly. The rest of the party either didn't hear or ignored him, Leshe and Marianne pushing forward at the head amidst their guards and assistants.

Someone bumped into him from behind. Daniel managed to spin and see the last guard, the only other person who hadn't set more than a foot across the threshold.

"Where the hell did the lights go?" the other man muttered. His face was drawn, gun lowered as he studied the room ahead of them.

He was right. The lanterns had gone out. The doorway was empty and dark, lit only by the lights strung behind them in the tunnel. The rest of the party had disappeared, but their footsteps still echoed distantly inside. They couldn't be that far ahead, maybe around a corner . . . ?

But Daniel hadn't *seen* any corners in his initial view of the space.

Sudden gunfire and shouting erupted from the darkness. Daniel and the last guard scrambled backwards, out of the chamber and into the tunnel. The noise echoed as if it were occurring simultaneously right beside the doors and much further away.

In the ensuing, ringing silence, Marianne lurched through the doorway and collapsed across the threshold.

Daniel almost leapt forward to grab her hands and drag her out, but something stopped him short. Her eyes had gone dull, her lips frozen in a grimace that showed her teeth. She seemed to shimmer for a second.

It wasn't right. It wasn't Marianne.

The guard shoved past, intent on helping her, but Daniel grabbed his shoulder. Despite the warning shrieking through every part of him, he couldn't put it into words fast enough.

"Don't," was all he could manage.

The other man shrugged him off and clasped the hands of the corpse, readying to pull her to safety. He only managed a startled grunt as both he and the body were yanked back over the threshold.

They disappeared almost instantly into the inky darkness. No shouts, no sounds of dragging or scuffling.

Daniel stumbled backwards and lost his balance. He rolled onto his stomach and grabbed the gun the guard had dropped. He'd learn to use it fast if anything came out through the void beyond that rectangular, stone frame.

Nothing stirred around him.

After several agonizing, silent seconds, he got to his feet. When motion still triggered nothing from the doors, he removed one of the lanterns from the tunnel wall. Holding it in one hand and the gun in the other, he crept to the threshold. The light extended maybe half a metre into the gloom.

He crouched and rolled the lantern inside, giving it just enough lift to land it as far as possible without breaking. It stopped three or four metres inside, the light dimming briefly, then blazing again.

Nothing new. The room was still made of pale, stone blocks and the light didn't extend to the far wall. There was no indication of other people inside: no bodies, blood or dropped weapons. Not even footprints in the reddish dirt scattered across the stone floor.

Daniel's stomach lurched suddenly, and he realized he'd slid the toe of his boot across the threshold. He inched back, but it was like pushing through tar, creeping away from a ledge that beckoned with a new, sickening intensity.

It was easier as he straightened up and managed a full step away. The co-mingling of vertigo and dread subsided the further he got from the door. He searched the tunnel for anything that he could use to cover the gaping doorway. Maybe he could build a wall with the pieces of rock left over from the blast? He didn't have the skills to rig up the remaining explosives and just bring the whole tunnel down, bury the doors again.

When he glanced back at the doorway, the lantern had gone out.

6

"STAY THERE." ELI USHERED me back with one hand, moving toward the door like a wary tiger. He disappeared as he reached it, in the same moment the footsteps outside stopped.

I snatched up the empty shot glass and yanked a drawer open to rifle for the sharpest knife I could find.

The sound of keys in the lock stopped me short.

"Wait," I started, spinning as the door swung open to reveal Diana, her overnight pack slung over one shoulder.

I only caught her eyes for a moment before Eli materialized directly in front of her.

He grabbed her and swung her inside, kicking the door shut behind her. Shoving her back against the wall, he kept both hands wrapped around her throat to cut off her protests.

"Eli!" I snapped, rushing forward. "Stop, that's Diana!"

My startled roommate slapped his arm weakly, struggling for breath. Eli froze, eyes roving around the room before returning to me. Then he released Diana and backed off, leaving me to dart to her side and catch her before she crumpled.

Throwing Eli a glare over my shoulder, I snapped, "What the *hell*?" He couldn't possibly consider a human a threat to me, could he? How weak did he think I was?

He continued to study the apartment with his chin tipped up slightly, wearing a puzzled, uncomfortable look.

"I'm sorry," he said, voice distant. "I thought I felt—" He looked back to Diana and narrowed his eyes, then dismissed whatever he'd been about to say with a curt shake of his head and went back to peering into the corners of the room as if he'd missed some threat hiding there.

"This is Diana," I said. "She lives here. Don't assault her."

My roommate sucked in a breath as the colour came back into her face. "Do you want water?" I stammered. "I'll get you water."

"No," she managed, rubbing her throat. "I'm okay. Just . . ." She spit out a soft, maybe hysterical laugh. ". . . what the actual fuck?"

"That's Eli. He's, um, protective."

"He just *appeared.*" She wrinkled her nose as she stared past me into the apartment, her brain trying to put things together in a way that made sense. Her shoulders slumped and she let her backpack fall to the ground. "Right in front of me, like out of *nowhere*—"

"He was, uh—" A knock at the front door cut me off. My skin itched in the familiar, magic-sensing way, tickles of electricity slithering through the hair on my arms.

It felt somehow comforting this time, though. Abe was outside. How the hell did I know that?

I got to my feet but Eli beat me to the door with an inquisitive look.

"It's okay," I said. "It's Abe." It was like I could pick out his specific scent, but with magic. Abe felt warm and worn, sunlight on a polished wood floor. Someone else was with him, cool and smooth, salt and pine. Ilse? I hadn't seen her in months—how come I was so certain she was outside?

Eli opened the door cautiously.

"Abe!" I tried to dart around my bodyguard but he blocked me, keeping his back to me. For such a wiry guy, he held his ground like a brick wall.

Fine, I'd go around him. I turned gravity and bounced off the ceiling to come down in front of him. Somehow I moved in slow motion and 2x speed at the same time. My movements felt smoother, easier than they'd ever been. I rarely planned out shifting my gravity but I usually did have to consciously think about switching directions. This time, though, my body had just executed each turn, floor to ceiling to floor, in one fluid motion.

Before I could marvel further at that, strong arms wrapped around my shoulders. Relief I hadn't expected flooded me as I pressed my face into the soft flannel of Abe's diamond-patterned button-down.

He hugged me tight. For an instant, I wanted to just stay there in his warm, comfortable embrace.

Pulling away and indicating the ceiling, I demanded, "Did you see that? Is that Mab shit?"

A grin split the cowboy's weathered face under his wide-brimmed hat, but before he could give me an answer, a sharp voice came from behind us.

"Jude, what the *hell* is going on?"

Diana. Shit.

I turned and gestured Eli aside to face my roommate, who stood beside the sofa with her fists clenched. Her eyes pleaded with me to explain, make all of this make sense.

"How did you—" She indicated my trajectory to the ceiling and back again, then seemed to give up and flung a hand toward Eli instead. "How did he just *appear*?" Eyes darting to Abe, she finished, "And what's with the hat?"

"It's, uh—" I wracked my brain for a good answer, but I was just too tired to lie. With a sigh, I indicated them each in turn. "Eli can turn invisible. Abe's a healer, for the record, and Ilse's a water sprite. Hi, Ilse."

"Your Highness." She bowed deeply, hovering beside Abe.

"Don't do that," I started, as Diana squawked, "Your *what*?"

I met my roommate's stunned eyes to finish, "They're Faeries. I'm their queen. It's all a misunderstanding."

7

I BRACED MYSELF FOR an eruption but Diana only snorted, taken aback. Abe gave me a look of amazement tinged with disapproval.

"That is—not what I expected you to say," Diana murmured.

"I know. Come in, guys." I gestured to Abe and Ilse, then told Eli, "Let them in. They're friends." Then I turned back to Diana. "Do you remember seeing me on the ceiling this afternoon?"

"I don't know what I saw." She folded her arms stubbornly across her chest and glared at the floor.

Behind me, Eli shut the door as he asked Ilse and Abe, "Are either of you armed?"

"Just my razor wit," Abe returned in his familiar drawl. Eli made a grunt of dismissal that didn't sound as amused.

"I don't—" Diana started, then shook her head and raised a hand to her temple. "I don't know what to say?"

"Yeah, it's a lot." I should have walked it back, denied everything and lied. Still, as I glanced back to see my bodyguard roughly frisking Ilse, shorter than all of us and built like a ballerina doll, I figured Diana wouldn't buy that either.

Eli had already cleared Abe, apparently, and the cowboy tugged the cuffs of his shirt back into place around his wrists. He was dressed with his usual Western affectation in jeans, boots and his brown cowboy hat, which he'd swept from his bald head as he entered.

"What are you guys doing here?" I asked him. Part-human like me, Abe wouldn't be allowed through the portals to Faerie, so he wouldn't have been caught up in the travel ban.

"Heard the news a few hours ago." Despite the faint, encouraging smile still on the cowboy's face, strained creases around his eyes reminded me that he'd been much closer to Miranda than I had. He and my aunt had been friends and colleagues for years.

He went on before I could interrupt with condolences. "I'd been camping out in the desert and found Ilse here waiting for me when I got back to my motel." He gestured to the water sprite, who stood with her hands clasped together in front of her.

I hadn't seen Ilse since last summer, but she hadn't changed—petite and demure, with skin several shades darker bronze than mine and vivid violet eyes. The black of her soft, sleek curls faded into a noticeable blue at the roots of her hair.

"How did you get across?" I asked her. "I thought the portals were closed and there was some ban—"

"Miranda sent me to find you, before—" She stopped and swallowed the words delicately, then continued in an even tone that sounded too unbothered. "Unfortunately, I'd only made it to the safehouse when the travel ban was enacted, so I was stuck for some time. I'm very sorry I wasn't here for you."

"Ilse, it's fine." Her apology made my stomach shift unpleasantly. "I don't get it—why did Miranda send you across?"

"To assist you, in case she succumbed to her injuries."

"What injuries?" Another short knock at the front door cut me off. I was still the closest one to it, and it didn't occur to me not to yank it open, expecting to tell off somebody who'd come to complain about the noise.

The words died on my lips. My father stood outside. He'd traded last winter's long, wool coat for a beige trench that made him look like a character in a bad film noir. Both his pale skin and the silver in his reddish hair gleamed under our porch light.

Eli tried to shoulder past me to forcefully evict him, but I didn't need assistance. I started to fling the door shut.

"Judith, I need to speak to you." Joshua caught it, slamming it against me so that it knocked both Eli and me back.

No way was this asshole forcing himself into my life again.

"Not now," I snapped, swinging a fist at my father's face. "Not ever."

I wasn't close enough to strike him, but heat and force shot down my arm. Joshua flew backwards out the door like he'd been sucked back by a tornado, disappearing over the wooden balcony.

I looked down at my hand, startled by the ripples of warm power that still clung to my skin. What the hell? I'd never done anything like that before. It had felt like when I shifted my own gravity, except . . . aimed at somebody else? Instead of manipulating my body in the world, I'd manipulated the world around another body.

Reluctantly, I crept forward onto the wooden patio and peered over the railing. I hadn't heard Joshua hit the ground. He probably hadn't, at least not on his ass the way I'd have liked. No doubt he'd flipped gravity in that casual, better-practised way of his and come down on tiptoe like some kind of dancer.

He stood on the sidewalk below, brushing himself off as he glared up at me.

"I don't give a damn that you're the Mab," he growled. "You're going to listen to me."

"Nope." I turned to go back inside the apartment, shutting the door and locking it with as much force as I could.

Then I sagged back against it. My body didn't feel tired but my brain was spent.

Joshua had a ridiculous amount of power, just in case I needed *that* after me again. In the twenty-plus years since he'd run out on my pregnant mom, he'd developed mage abilities—strong magic honed sharper than the normal, gravity-defying power he'd been born with.

At least I apparently had some kind of new Mab power to counter that.

"I don't know if I can wield *The Force* again." I threw out the reference with a heavy dose of sarcasm, studying my hand again in case I'd missed some kind of otherworldly blue or green glow emanating from my skin.

"You can," Eli said with certainty. "But we shouldn't stay here. I would prefer somewhere easier to fortify."

"The house," Abe said, nodding toward the pantry—the nearest door that didn't have a psychopath on the other side.

"You love that stupid house," I muttered. "But, yeah, fine, let's go."

Ilse pulled the door beside the oven open. It usually led to our shallow shelves of ramen and canned soup. Now it opened into a larger front hallway done up in ugly yellow wallpaper dotted with trees.

We'd all queued up by the door, all but Diana. She still stood by the sofa, gazing into the Faerie safe house with quiet shock.

"You can't stay here," I said. "It's not safe."

"Why not?" She eyed me.

"Joshua's out there."

"Who's that? Another *Faerie*?"

"My father. And yes. He's killed my friends before so I'm not leaving you here."

"He's—" Diana's expression changed, eyes widening as terror followed by uncertainty flashed across her face. She jerked her chin toward the unfamiliar foyer waiting beyond our normal pantry. "Where is that?"

"Faerie safe house."

"Can I . . ." Diana hesitated, her eyes on the open door. She snapped her gaze to me, looking pained, as if she didn't want to ask what she was about to ask. "Can I come back? From there?"

"Yes." Relieved that it hadn't been a harder question, I added, "Any time you want. It's just a house that's, um, hidden."

"In our pantry?"

"For now."

"Has it—" She seemed to reconsider her question and finished, "—*always* been in our pantry?"

"No."

Diana nodded slowly, then gave me a sidelong glance.

"You'd better be for real," she said, before following me through the door.

8

ONCE WE WERE ALL through into the Faerie house's foyer, Diana and I both let out sighs of relief, though probably for different reasons.

The door had only been shut a few seconds when it swung right back open again.

Eli swept me behind his body with practised efficiency, and everyone else retreated further into the house, taking half-defensive positions. Abe took charge of Diana, shouldering in front of her.

Whoever entered said a word in the sing-song Faerie language. While I couldn't resolve the syllables, it seemed like expletives had the same tone in pretty much any tongue.

I stood on tiptoe to peek over Eli's shoulder and saw three men take defensive positions around the door. A fourth man—probably the one who'd spoken—stepped inside.

Eli dropped his shoulders, relaxing, but kept his body between me and the newcomers.

"Your Highness." The powerfully built blond man stopped inside the doorway and bowed his head to me. Even bowing, he towered over me. He must have been over six feet tall. He wore an expensive suit and carried a briefcase. "I am Karl, representative of the Ubran."

"It's about time," I said over Eli's shoulder, which prompted my bodyguard to step aside.

40

"We were unfortunately unable to come any sooner, Your Highness."

"Who's 'we'? I only see one of you. Or are these guys *Ubran* too?" I nodded toward the men flanking him.

"Though one speaks alone for the seven," Karl said, "our consciousness is shared. We are a collective, your Highness."

"So, 'he/him' or 'they/them'?"

A flash of confusion crossed his face.

"As Your Highness wishes."

"I wish to know what you prefer." I gritted my teeth, swallowing my first impulse to snap at him.

"It truly does not matter. We are not human and have no interest in the distinction."

"Fine. 'They/them' it is." Seemed easier, given Karl was using the plural already. "Can we get back to this tomorrow?"

"No." They tried to hide the flash of incredulity across their features. "It's imperative that we speak to you now."

"Worth asking." I glanced over my shoulder, meeting Abe's eyes and then telling my roommate, "Dee, can you go with Abe? Maybe the kitchen?" That was to the cowboy, who nodded, trying to gently steer Diana backwards. "Abe makes great flapjacks. And he could probably whip up a stiff drink too."

I hoped so, anyway, because I was going to need one next. I turned back to the man containing my seven advisers.

"What happened to Miranda?"

"Perhaps somewhere more private." Karl gestured to a room off to our right. I didn't remember it being there before.

It looked like some kind of formal dining room, with a shiny, expensive-looking, oval wooden table and eight chairs. I flipped a switch on the wall and brought the chandelier to life, but it didn't do much with the dark red walls and heavy wood panelling.

Karl followed me in. All of their guys stayed in the hallway, but I beckoned for Ilse and Eli to join us. No way was I dealing with the Ubran alone, and Abe already had his hands full with Diana.

I figured it was my right to take the chair at the head of the table, furthest from the door. Ilse sat in the chair on my right and Karl settled to my left. Eli shut the door and remained standing beside it.

"Talk," I prompted.

"We regret to inform you that your aunt's death was a tragic accident," Karl started.

"Accident?" I balked. "Are you sure? Do Mabs usually go out in 'accidents'?"

"Given your disappearance and presumed death, your aunt believed it critical that she take a new heir," Karl said.

When Ilse made a small noise, Karl added, "She waited as long as she reasonably could for news of your continued existence." He cast a brief, disapproving eye at the water sprite. "Unfortunately, if the ritual to name a new heir is pursued while a living heir exists, the results are often fatal. Such was the outcome of your aunt's ritual."

"You're saying Miranda tried to take a new heir, but since I'm still kicking, it backfired and killed her?"

"Killed both of them," Ilse agreed quietly.

"It was thought that your aunt might recover from her injuries," Karl added, "but as you know, her reign ended this afternoon."

I deflated in my chair. Miranda had tried to replace me. I couldn't even be angry with her, because she'd thought I was dead, and on top of that, I'd have loved being replaced in this particular instance.

I tried to keep my face blank as I studied Karl's. Were they being straight with me? Ilse was going along with this story, but I vaguely remembered Abe making some comments last summer about how Miranda *wasn't a Mab everybody wanted.* Could I really have been that well hidden, or could this 'accident' have been some kind of inside job?

Pretty stupid one if so, since it got my half-human ass plopped onto the throne.

"Your Highness," Karl said, going on as if they'd given the requisite moment of silence for my ill-fated aunt. "There are a good many *other* things we need to discuss that—"

"Pick two."

Ilse gave me a sidelong glance that told me I was supposed to be more polite, but I pretended not to see it.

Karl hesitated, either offended or narrowing down their options. Finally, they said, "Your aunt's death was sudden. You're no one's choice for Mab, including, we've heard, your own. You're half-human and that presents a significant problem. But the most troubling thing is that you have no heir."

"I'm not popping out a kid," I said.

"No." Karl agreed a little too quickly. "That's not necessary."

"Miranda seemed to think it was."

"As I've said, if a living heir exists in the bloodline, the line can't be transferred." They paused. "But at this point, given you have no relatives, you can attain an heir without giving birth to one. You can name a successor, designate someone to your bloodline. *Adopt* a daughter, as it were."

The information took a moment to sink in and had a new edge this time. Miranda could have solved all of her problems by just having me killed at any point last year. Why hadn't she?

Not relevant now.

"It's imperative that you take an heir as soon as possible," Karl added.

"Why?"

They studied my face the way Eli had each time I'd asked a stupid question, before finally circling back to the realization that I didn't intrinsically know their customs, news cycle and politics.

"Because the line must continue. There must always be a Mab. Your power holds the foundations of the world in place."

I considered demanding an *actual* explanation for that poetry, but I was flagging and pissing off my royal advisers didn't sound as fun as it normally might have.

"I guess you've got somebody picked out, huh?" I asked.

"We've gathered several excellent candidates for your consideration." They produced a set of manila folders stuffed with papers from their briefcase. The Faerie Court clearly hated digital records as much as the Consilium had.

I flipped the first folder open and had to blink at the uniform, black characters for a few seconds before realizing it wasn't in English. It was in Faerie. *Typed* Faerie. They had computers over there.

Well, there was magic, so why not technology? As hard as I tried to rationalize it, it was still weird. "I can't read this," I said.

"Of course." Karl winced, looking flustered for a hot second as they reached for the folders. "We apologize, Your Highness. We'll have them translated immediately."

"Take your time. I'm not reading them tonight." I had to stifle a yawn.

"This is a *critical*—"

"I know," I interrupted, "but I've had a shit day, and you probably have too, so can we just take the night and regroup tomorrow? We're all safe in the magic house for the time being, right?"

Getting to my feet, I went for a more authoritative approach. "I move that we adjourn for tonight. And, as the Mab, I second it. Motion passes. To be continued."

Karl stared at me, dumbfounded, and I seized on their silence to move to the door. They stood hastily and awkwardly and gave me a bow.

Ilse and Eli scrambled to follow me out.

In the hallway, I took a look at the three guys still standing near the door. Karl's security; their problem. I didn't have the energy to issue any more orders. At least, not without a drink in my hand.

Ilse followed me to the kitchen and Eli stayed outside the door.

"I gave Diana a bedroom upstairs." Abe sat alone at the table. "She was exhausted."

"Aren't we all," I said. "Where's the back door?" Every other time I'd been here, there'd been a door beside the sink that led to the backyard visible out the window but non-existent when you actually stepped outside.

"The house has been manipulated to fortify it," Ilse said. She nodded toward the hallway to indicate the guys Karl had brought with them.

Great. The house layout was apparently as changeable as what you could magically pull out of its drawers and cupboards. I shouldn't have been surprised, but I wished somebody would give me a full rundown on all the tricks.

"Miranda got to have a back door," I argued.

"Miranda had an heir," Ilse returned.

"What actually happens if I die without an heir?"

"It hasn't happened in thousands of years."

"So, what? Nobody knows? It might be fine?"

"Apart from you being dead?" Abe asked dryly.

"Fair point," I conceded. "Though I don't think Karl and the Ubran would be too broken up about that part. Who's to say they won't take me out once I adopt a daughter and they have their living heir?"

"That is unlikely," Ilse said.

I waited for her to add something more reassuring. She didn't.

9

DANIEL EYED THE WAITRESS several tables away. He was either going to have to slip out of the bar while she wasn't looking, or else explain to her that a secret agency run by an insane—and now probably deceased—millionaire had frozen all of his accounts and credit cards. Thus, he had no way to pay for the three glasses of Scotch he'd already downed to erase Marianne Nguyen's dead eyes from his memory, or the fourth currently in his hand. It was nearly last call.

He hadn't been able to drive any further. He'd dozed off at the wheel twice before arriving in Phoenix. After getting out of the tunnel, he'd gone through the empty camp and found the keys to one of the cars, as well as broken into the lock box where Leshe had kept his wallet and phone as a precaution against his running away. The phone wasn't charged and didn't have signal since he hadn't used it or paid for service for months, and the wallet hadn't contained anything useful.

He'd found an American twenty dollar bill in one of the other wallets in the lock box, and that had been enough to get him a burger and a shower at a giant truck stop three hours ago. He'd ditched the car upon reaching Phoenix, so Leshe wouldn't be able to find him with it.

But Leshe was dead. Had to be dead.

"I almost didn't recognize you with the beard." Someone sat down in the empty chair at his tiny table.

Daniel flinched, startled, and then scrambled to his feet when his new companion's face came into focus.

"Sit down." Joshua seemed to be trying for amiable but his tone still rang as menacing.

Daniel found himself back in his chair. His body had complied with the command without the decision passing through his brain.

"How?" At least his voice still worked. He tried again to get up, but his muscles didn't respond. "You couldn't do this last year." Because if Joshua had wielded this type of compulsion last fall, the fight at the house in Switzerland would have been over a lot sooner.

"One could say I picked it up from Revelle." The older man made casual reference to the wraith who had used similar paralytic magic on him last November. "I've played with it a little over the last few months," he added. "As it turns out, it costs significantly less energy to control an inebriated human, so drink up."

The command forced Daniel to finish the last of his Scotch so quickly that he nearly choked.

"Stop," he huffed through a raw throat. He waited for Joshua's expression to become haughty or amused, either disdaining his human weakness or delighting in exploiting it.

Instead, the older man studied him, unnatural green eyes vivid with a new, sudden interest.

"Where have you been?" he asked.

Daniel bit back a caustic response that would probably only get him hurt.

Joshua leaned forward, keeping their conversation contained and taking a closer look in one motion. "You've been somewhere—" He hesitated, searching for the word before settling on, "—*enchanted*. Recently. Explain."

"Fuck off." Daniel tried again to leave the chair.

When Joshua slammed a hand down on the table, the accompanying shudder through his body rattled his teeth.

"Very well." The old mage lifted a hand to signal the waitress. "I expect with one or two more drinks, I can order you to confess every thought you've ever had. We'll just have to experiment."

"A cave in the desert." Daniel stammered the words through frantic, cold panic. He couldn't give the Antagonist more control over him. He'd been stupid to stop here, stupid to drink, stupid to think he might be safe.

The answer made Joshua lower his hand, so he added, "Not a cave. Some kind of underground chamber. There were doors."

"Doors?"

"Stone doors. Heavy ones. Leshe dynamited them open."

"This is a name, *Leshe*?"

"A man. William Leshe." Daniel's muscles had come back under his control enough to let him slump back against the chair, so he did. He tried to take some control of the conversation too. "How did you find me?"

Last fall, he'd exchanged the magical incantation in his head for the vial of his blood that the Faerie Court had collected. That was supposed to have been the only way the Court had to track him. Joshua wasn't necessarily with the Court, though, and clearly had access to heavier magics than they usually trafficked in within the human world.

"I tried to approach Judith this evening with some critical information, but she wouldn't hear me out. Already drunk on the power of the crown. I've gleaned from past experience that she'll listen to me with a knife to *your* throat, so here we are. Though, to be honest, now I find myself much more intrigued by your desert doors."

"Drunk on the power of . . . *what*?"

Joshua backtracked, lips twitching in something that was almost a wan smile as he realized where Daniel had gotten lost.

"My sister is dead," he said. "Judith is now the Mab."

"She's—" Daniel couldn't get the words out. How would that even work, *Jude* being the Mab? She was half-human. She couldn't pass through the portals.

"Sort of makes you want another drink." Joshua searched the room as if considering calling the waitress again.

"Not with you here, no." Daniel seized the moment to bolt again, but his companion made a quick gesture with one hand and his legs folded, nearly depositing him on the floor. He had to grope his way back to his seat using the table for balance. He sagged into it, feeling dazed and spent.

No one around them seemed to have noticed his stumble. Joshua had glamoured them, hidden them from the rest of the room.

"You're worn out," the older man said. The haughty, superior tone Daniel remembered from last fall crept into his voice and Joshua seemed to realize it at the same moment.

Trying again—and failing—to sound friendly, he said, "Just tell me what's happened to you. Perhaps I can assist."

That word, wildly inappropriate in relation to any action the old mage might *ever* take in his regard, made Daniel choke on a laugh. The only *assistance* he could imagine this creature offering him was a quick death.

He resisted the urge to simply put his head down on the table and give up, check out. Let the mage get fed up and kill him or walk away or . . . anything, really.

Joshua regarded him expectantly, but the crease between the Antagonist's brows deepened by the moment, indicating that his patience wasn't infinite.

"I don't suppose you know that fable about the frog and the scorpion?" Daniel finally asked.

The older man hesitated as if the question were a trap. Then he conceded, "You'll find that I have more instinct to self-preservation than a scorpion."

10

I woke up with a headache. I didn't know what time I'd actually fallen asleep—time was probably different in the magic house, anyway—but I'd conjured a bottle of whisky out of the kitchen cupboard before staking out a bedroom. I'd had more than a few pours while figuring out how to summon a television into my room, and I felt them.

I rolled off the bed and accidentally kicked the bottle as I stood up. I hadn't put the cap back on and it soaked into the carpet. I managed to right it on the bedside table. The idea of taking over a bathroom and showering sounded heavenly, but Diana was somewhere in this house, probably terrified.

When I opened the door to my room, Eli nearly fell backwards into me.

"Sorry." He bolted to his feet, rubbing the back of his neck.

"I wish you'd taken a bed," I said. "The Ubran's got guys downstairs."

"I just closed my eyes," he insisted.

"Whatever. Is Diana up?" I crossed the hall to the door Eli had pointed out the previous night, where I'd peeked in and seen her curled up in bed. I knocked gently on the door and then pushed it open.

Diana sat cross-legged on the bed. She relaxed when she recognized me.

"What are you doing?" I asked.

"I wasn't sure I could, like, leave," she admitted.

"You're not a prisoner."

"Okay." Not her most convincing tone.

I came inside and shut the door behind me. Diana moved over to make room for me on the bed. A plate of toast sat untouched on her nightstand.

"Abe bring that up?" I asked.

"I found that—" Diana sounded quietly mystified, "—in the drawer here." She indicated the nightstand.

"Were you thinking about toast when you opened the drawer?" She'd probably unknowingly conjured it up from the house.

"Yes." Diana frowned at the plate. "I'm starving."

"So eat the toast."

"I don't know how long it's been there."

"I'm betting it's pretty fresh." How was I going to explain all of this to her? "Give it here." At the prompt, she passed it to me and I took a bite from one piece. It was dry and unpleasant, but then, I'd never really liked toast. "You didn't want jam with this or something?"

"I didn't want—?" She started to repeat my words, then stopped. She leaned forward to run her hands through her dark curls and pulled them away from her face. "I'm so . . . I don't think *confused* covers it. I thought I'd wake up and this would all have been some weird-ass dream." She snatched the second piece of toast off the plate I held and studied it. "You think I made this toast happen?"

"I know you did. You must have really wanted it. I didn't know it'd work for a hu—you."

Diana caught my awkward correction.

"You're not human?" she challenged. "You're a—what, a *Faerie*?"

"I'm half-Faerie. My mom's human. My dad's Faerie. It's a separate world that's sort of over-top of ours, or actually it's joined to ours like—" I'd intertwined my fingers around the toast to demonstrate and stopped. "Abe's so much better at this explanation."

"Abe is . . . who?"

"The cowboy."

"With the hat." Diana's eyes narrowed as she remembered, "Everybody kept calling you *Your Highness.*"

"Yeah, I'm the Faerie Queen."

"Should have asked you for more rent."

"It just happened yesterday. I *am* actually broke," I assured her. "I'm still the same person you know. Everything I told you before about myself is true. I'm just also part-Faerie and can walk up walls."

"So, a lie of omission," Diana muttered, messing with her hair again.

I slid off the bed and pulled a hair tie from the nightstand drawer. When I offered it to her, she looked to the drawer, then reluctantly took the elastic and wrestled her curls into a ponytail.

"Is there a beginning you can start from?" she asked.

"There is but I don't think it's going to help."

"Give it a try." Diana tentatively took a bite of her toast, then grimaced. "You're right, this needs jam or something."

When I pointed to the drawer, she shook her head. "No, I'm good." She lifted a finger to the ceiling. "Start with this 'walking up walls' thing. Show me."

I slid off the bed and went to the far wall, where I turned gravity with ease to put my feet down on the perpendicular plane. I moved up it and stepped onto the ceiling, my clothing remaining settled around my body like I was still upright. The ceilings in the house weren't very high, so my head was less than a metre from the carpeted floor as I regarded Diana upside down.

She climbed off the bed and stood in front of me, studying my feet on the ceiling, the way my hair and clothes followed the rules of my own gravity.

"How do you do it?" she asked.

"I don't know." I'd never really thought about it, at least not in a way I could express in words. "I just . . . take a step. I guess I think about it a little, like, turning the world around me. How do *you* think about walking?"

Someone knocked at the door and I flipped gravity to spin and land on my feet beside Diana. She flinched, studying me with wide eyes.

"Your Highness?" It was Ilse at the door. "I can't really hold Karl off any longer."

"Damn it." I'd almost forgotten about the mess waiting for me downstairs.

The door opened a crack and Ilse peeked in. When she saw Diana and I both awake and upright, she pushed it open wider. She held a stack of clothing.

"I imagine you'd like to change before your meeting," she said.

"What's wrong with what I'm wearing?" I glanced down at my t-shirt and jeans. Yeah, I'd slept in it but the t-shirt didn't even have a logo printed on it. One of my nicer ones.

Ilse pressed the clothes into my arms and I unfolded the green thing on top. "This is a dress."

"Is that not what female humans prefer to wear in formal situations?" Ilse blinked. "Miranda almost always wore dresses and skirts."

"I'm not Miranda."

"Even so, I don't think you should attend a meeting in denim, and I believe this colour will suit you."

"Right. Then I'll paint my toenails and start calling myself 'Judy.' " I held the dress back out to her with a firm finality.

When she refused to take it, I draped it over her shoulder, then immediately added the next thing on the pile: a pair of pantyhose. I'd never actually seen any in real life. "Definitely not with these. My mother doesn't even wear these anymore."

"Your Highness, this is important." A note of exasperation slipped into her tone.

"First, Ilse, it's just Jude. No 'Your Highness' or any other titles." I fixed her with a firm gaze. "I need you to call me Jude or I might lose my mind. Second, I haven't worn a dress since I was seven and I'm not putting one on for *Karl*."

"Very well." She sighed and gestured me out into the hallway.

Downstairs, I found Karl still holed up in the dining room. They'd taken a chair in the middle of the table, the same spot they'd chosen last night, and sat writing something. A stack of papers sat to one side and they had a vanity mirror propped up beside them, which was probably the equivalent of an office phone to the Faerie realm.

When I entered, they got to their feet and bowed their head.

"Your Highness."

"Hi, Karl." I hesitated. "Should I call you something else? I don't want to leave anybody out."

"Karl is fine," they said, giving me something that was almost a smile. They gestured to the seat at the head of the table.

Once I'd made myself comfortable, they sat back down too.

"Our last meeting didn't go as we had hoped," they said. "We've realized we were rather pushy and wanted to apologize."

"It was a stressful day," I agreed. When their concerned expression didn't change, I added a tentative, "Uh, you're forgiven."

"You are very gracious, Your Highness. Since you value forthrightness, there is a topic we must broach."

"Shoot," I said. When Karl paused like they didn't understand the word, I amended: "Go ahead."

"We understand that you may not trust our motives." Karl met my eyes. "We wanted to assure you that we accept you as the rightful Mab, as much as all of us may not like the situation. No member of the Ubran would lift a hand against the Mab. Your life is sacred."

"That's . . . good to hear," I managed, surprised. Had Ilse told them what I'd said last night? She didn't seem like the gossiping type.

"You're not from our world, and you know few people there," Karl continued. "It's only natural you should feel some trepidation."

I didn't like having them tell me how I was feeling, but I managed to bite back the response that I didn't need a group therapy session right now.

"We realize that there will be a necessary building of trust between us," Karl finished. "We are open to doing so and hope you are as well." The smile they gave me was clearly not something they'd practised much, but it was more genuine than the smirks and disdainful looks I'd received from them so far.

"Yeah," I agreed. "I'm in. But I want to know what happens if I die without an heir."

Karl's smile turned a little brittle. "Why would you need to know that?"

"Mostly because you're trying so hard not to tell me."

They hesitated, looking lost for a moment, then took a deep breath.

"The Mab's power is tied to the foundations of our world," they said. "In circumstances when a Mab has died with no heir to continue the line, the stories say the earth rebelled and tore itself from beneath the people's feet. The air filled with pestilence and plague and the water turned sour and unfulfilling."

Okay, unpleasant. A little dramatic, though. I certainly didn't feel powerful enough to hold foundations together and keep water fulfilling. On the other hand, I *was* half-human.

"So, you believe these old stories?" I prompted.

"We'd rather not discover the truth of them."

"Better safe than sorry, huh?"

"That's an apt phrase, Your Highness." Karl took a breath. "It's also the reason we must insist you remain sequestered here, under protection, for the time being. The transition of power after your aunt's death has upset . . . some factions at home."

My advisers had really buried the lede by starting with that apology about their pushy behaviour last night.

I tensed. "Somebody's coming after me? Who?"

"There have been no direct threats," they assured me, "but until we're certain that there are no lingering resentments—"

"From *who*?" I pressed.

"The family of the presumptive heir who was killed yesterday are . . . unhappy." Karl winced, as if recognizing that the word couldn't possibly do the situation justice. "It shouldn't concern you, Your Highness, we only mean to—"

"Wait, but you said my life is sacred," I interrupted. "Me dying without an heir fucks up the world—broken foundations and bad water, remember?"

"There are those who would prefer a broken world to a Mab—" Karl stopped, chewing over their words, and then finished in a tersely deferential tone, "—such as yourself."

"Right." I sat back in my chair. Faeries really had a nasty superiority complex when it came to humanity. Fuck them.

"We've had the dossiers translated." Karl's voice lightened as they changed the subject. "If you would look over them at your earliest convenience." They passed a set of pristine manila folders to a man standing at attention beside them, who brought the files the two steps down the table to me.

"How many candidates?" I asked, tapping a fingernail on the hefty stack.

"Three. Any would be a prudent addition to your lineage."

"I'll check them out over breakfast, then." I started to get to my feet, but Karl leapt up, bowing their head slightly as if to stop me.

"Your Highness," they said, "there are a few other things we must discuss."

11

"FOR MY FIRST ORDER, I want cushier chairs in that dining room." I dumped my armload of manila folders onto the kitchen table. My back ached from what must have been two hours in an uncomfortable wooden chair, listening to Karl's mind-numbing list of goings-on in the Faerie realm.

"Sounds easy enough." Abe scooped an omelette off a pan on the stove and passed the plate over to me.

"Karl wants to get me tutors." I eyed the kitchen chair and decided I'd eat standing up. Before forking the first piece of fluffy egg into my mouth, I added, "Full-time lessons in Mabbing."

"You have a lot to catch up on," Ilse said.

"Doesn't royalty just delegate and spend their time waving off balconies? I'd probably only need to practice my wave for an hour, tops. Save a lot of time on the tutors."

"This isn't a joke, Jude." She frowned at me.

"You try living it," I shot back. Poking at my omelette with my fork, my thoughts returned to the question that had spun dizzily in my brain last night until enough whisky had finally sent me to Dreamland and washed it away.

"So, why'd Miranda waste her time trying to pressure me into getting knocked up when she could have just had me snuffed out and picked anybody else she wanted?" I asked.

They'd both known my aunt better than I had, maybe they had some ideas.

"What a cruel question." Ilse stiffened. "You were all she had."

You're our blood, and we can't lose anymore of it. Miranda had said that to me when I'd confronted her about our family connection. She hadn't deigned to *tell* me, of course—I'd had to suss it out on my own because she thought it more important to manipulate me into action than explain our relationship.

"Miranda never expected to be Mab," Abe added, "any more than you did."

"We wouldn't be if the Consilium hadn't blown the rest of the family to hell," I muttered, my shoulders prickling. Their tones said I wasn't being fair to my aunt, and maybe they were right. Still, she and I had been at odds for the whole time I'd known her—she'd strong-armed me into going after Aubrie for her, hidden our family ties, lied about her history, then popped up a few too many times to convince me I had a duty to the Faerie crown that involved my uterus. Made it hard to give her the benefit of the doubt.

Except that she hadn't had me killed. So I guess that counted for something.

"I wonder which 'daughter' she wanted," I muttered, casting a resentful look over the manila folders. I couldn't help but shift uncomfortably, remembering the conversation with Karl last night. "I guess it would have been her second choice anyway."

"I don't know why you'd wait until now to care what Miranda wanted." Ilse huffed a sigh and left the room. I'd never actually seen the unfailingly polite water sprite get angry before. It made me feel like an ogre.

"She just wants to help you," Abe offered, probably reading the guilt that had splashed over me like a rogue wave.

"She wants to help me be queen," I said. "I want to help me *not* be queen."

"You might give it a little more thought."

"*They* don't want me to be queen." I thumbed backwards to indicate Karl and, in fact, the whole of Faerie. "They won't even let me into the world I'm supposed to be running." I didn't bother to mention the ones who'd rather watch their world crumble apart than accept me.

"That could change."

"It won't." I finished my omelette and set the plate in the sink as I ran a glass of water. My morning's headache had receded a little with the food but still twinged at the base of my skull.

"Jude." Ilse was back in the kitchen doorway. "You have a visitor." She said it like she knew I wouldn't like who it was.

I followed her into the hallway.

"Crap," I said aloud.

"It's hardly a palace." The creature who presented as a well-built, Asian man in a stylish and undoubtedly expensive suit pretended he hadn't heard me. Most of the human world would have recognized him as Declan Raj, lead guitarist for the wildly popular alternative rock band Broken Brooms. The Faerie world knew him as the Archduke.

Either way, he was powerful and I was supposed to be nice. I'd struggled with that since I'd met him last year.

"I'm keeping a low profile," I answered, glad he hadn't used my new title. Anything he called me was going to seem mocking and piss me off.

He stepped closer and bowed his head slightly—an even less enthusiastic bow than Karl's.

"I hope you're settling into your new position," he said.

"It's great. How are you? Finding enough new psychopaths to bankroll, I hope?" He'd been the one to give my father a swanky hideout last fall for his bloody work attempting to raise and destroy a powerful Faerie ghost.

That ended our banter. A muscle in Declan's jaw twitched in annoyance but he got to the point.

"I'm here about our debt." He shot a glance to Karl's goons by the door. "Could we speak privately?"

"Thirsty to cash in your favour, huh?" Since Karl was still using the dining room, I gestured the Archduke towards the living room.

He stood back to let me enter first, as I said over my shoulder, "Sorry there's no—"

The word *door* didn't make it out of my mouth as he pulled shut a heavy wooden door that this room, to my knowledge, had never had before.

Rather than marvel at that, I sat down on the rickety sofa in front of the window that looked out onto a fake, sunset-drenched street. "You ditched the dreads."

Declan's hair was short now. The last time I'd seen him, he'd been sporting dreadlocks, as well as a few more piercings than he had now. Did he still have the spider-webs of colourful tattoos on his biceps or had all of that been erasable human glamour? He'd dressed up too, in a grey suit with a blood-red pocket square.

"The band's on hiatus," he said. "I'm experimenting with a bit of an image change."

"Sounds fun. Sorry, I didn't mean to make friendly conversation. What was with the moth?"

"That's what I came to speak to you about: the message conveyed in the moth. It's a rather archaic tradition, and I knew you wouldn't understand it—"

"Then why send it?"

"It's *tradition*," he stressed with a sigh. "It signifies the proposal of a union. The Mab needs a consort. My blood-line and status positions me as the obvious choice."

If I hadn't already been sitting, I'd have needed to grope for a chair. The word 'obvious' clearly meant something different to him.

He swept on, "That will give you license to adopt Saskia. In a union such as this, both parties would be expected to present important gifts to one another. As mine, you will take my daughter as your heir."

"Hold on!" I snapped. "I haven't even agreed to this bullshit and you're already dictating what I'm going to give you as a *wedding* present?"

"I am laying out the terms of our bargain," he returned, voice mild but somehow still condescending.

I bit my tongue before saying something I'd *really* regret.

"I'm not thinking that far ahead yet."

"You should be. Your reign needs legitimacy. You're an anomaly, an *outsider*." He smiled as if he knew exactly how the word sounded. Had he been talking to Karl? "A union with me would calm anxious minds at home and ensure the stability of the realm. It would also give you a proper heir in Saskia."

"Veto," I said. "Pass. What else you got?" Being only half-Faerie, I wasn't bound to the weird, metaphysical rules about bargains like the full-bloods were. A Faerie who broke their word lost their magic. My word, like that of most humans, meant absolutely squat.

"We didn't agree on a veto option." The Archduke sized me up. "A Mab who breaks her word is no Mab. I should raise an army against you."

Would that make me the first Mab to start a war on her first day on the throne? Ilse wasn't going to be happy about that.

"However," the Archduke continued, "given your admittedly. . . *murky* knowledge of our customs, I will deign to accept this breach gracefully."

Bullshit. He'd known when we'd made the deal that I could wriggle out of it with no supernatural consequences.

"This means, of course," he added, "that our previous deal is void and you will surrender your terrier to me now."

I stared at him for a confused minute before remembering that had been his patronizing nickname for Daniel. I'd only agreed to this favour last year after Danny had punched Declan and the pissed-off Archduke had been demanding his head in return. What the hell kind of weird flex was it now?

"Daniel's not even *here*," I protested. "I haven't seen him in months."

"I shouldn't have trouble locating him."

The snide tone made me grit my teeth.

"This would have gone a lot quicker if you just said either I marry you and make your kid my heir or you'll kill Daniel," I snapped.

"That would have been crass and untrue. When you kill a human, their blood stops flowing. It's wasteful."

My eyes darted to his crisp, crimson pocket square. As a redcap, he fed on human blood, collecting it in some magically-imbued article of clothing—I didn't know the details and I didn't really want to. Defensive anger washed through me at the memory of Saskia holding her sharp, bone-coloured dagger, bleeding a college student at the party last year where I'd met her.

I wasn't about to let that be Daniel.

"Is this some kind of stupid Faerie honour thing?" I made my voice withering. "Has it just been eating at you for months now that a mere human managed to sucker-punch you and lived to tell the tale?"

The Archduke stiffened like I'd either gotten it right or I'd offended him further—Faeries tended to be really petty like that—but he went on to correct me like he hadn't heard it.

"It's a political union, not a 'marriage' in your human sense."

"But there's probably a ceremony that we seal with an official roll in the hay?"

"Humans and their strange customs. Don't you find hay rather . . . prickly?" He gave me a haughty look. "There is no need for any sort of copulation to establish our union, merely a contract. Should you wish to add such an addendum, I will consider the petition."

What a romantic.

But I wasn't going to keep the crown any longer than I had to, and the Faerie Powers That Be—Were?—wouldn't let me into their world, so it wasn't even like Declan and I would have to go to parties together or anything like that.

Plus, I wouldn't have to read any of those heavy files Karl had given me in order to choose a successor. They might be pissed, but they *had* stressed how critical it was for me to find an heir.

"Fine," I said. "Let's get hitched."

12

ABE RINSED THE BREAKFAST dishes in the sink, conjuring up soap and a sponge. He could have let the house swallow them back up dirty, but the warm water and repetitive motions of the chore helped put him at ease.

The house felt odd, and it wasn't just the strange, brusque Court guards. It had really only been a year since he'd first set foot in the place, since Miranda had learned of its existence as a Court safehouse and started using it. Since then, he'd been here without her plenty of times, especially after she'd moved permanently over to the Faerie realm to run things, but somehow he still associated her presence with the spot.

Would be nice to pretend she was still over there, just out of sight, but try as he might, he knew better. Miranda was gone, torn irrevocably from both worlds, and now he was the last of the old guard still standing.

Funny, since he'd always thought he'd be the first to go. He was part-human after all, and full-blood Faeries tended to live longer than his kind. But years spent on guerrilla campaigns to undermine both the Faerie Court and the Consilium had taken its toll, turned all his old friends against each other and split them up before death had time to do its thing.

Everybody but him and Miranda. Having her off in the Faerie realm calling the shots hadn't broken their amity, but it had changed the dynamic—she hadn't needed his participation anymore, hadn't relied on him. No use for a part-human healer when you had dozens of the real thing at your royal disposal.

He'd been left to his own devices more and more over the last few months, with fewer requests for assistance coming from the palace, and he'd seized on it, making a new hobby of venturing out into the desert on his own, hiking or camping. He liked the solitude, the straight-forward work of quiet survival—no immediate danger screaming at him, no enemies to vanquish—and the satisfaction of a strong fire, a hot meal, a few tough crossword puzzles and the open sky.

It wasn't in his nature to be alone, though. His powers were for aiding others. His grandmother, his parents, they'd built a tight community based on mutual reliance, on helping others. After the Consilium had ripped that apart, he'd tried to do the same with Miranda, Joshua, Aubrie and the others, but it had never really caught. Their work had necessarily been more about cutting down obstacles than building around them.

This new Court seemed like more of the same. It made him wonder if he could even be useful here. His thoughts circled back to the way Jude had hugged him last night—her tight, grateful embrace and her relief to see him. He hadn't been missed in a long time.

And he'd missed her too.

Speak of the devil—the new Mab stormed in, a thundercloud of roiling reds and purples surrounding her head. She bee-lined for the empty spot on the wall where the back door had been, then stopped short with a growl. Her anger and frustration condensed into tight ringlets shot through with a pinkish thread, a defensive edge that flickered as it frayed and rewound.

"How do I get the door back?" Jude snapped.

"No idea," Abe admitted, then ventured, "Where you headed?" to distract her before she tried smashing her way through the window above the sink.

"Anywhere but here." The smoke of frustration smoothed out into calmer waves that tinged green around Jude's body as she studied the space.

Abe saw her intention a split second before she pressed one hand flat against the wall and pushed. A rectangle the size of a door swung out from the plaster.

A cadre of guards came spilling suddenly into the kitchen from the hallway, brandishing weapons and barking orders. The one in the lead stopped, bowing low to Jude.

"Your Highness." His voice was terse and surprised.

"Don't mind me, just popping out for a coffee," Jude said.

"Your Highness, you can't—"

"Leave?" Jude drew herself up in some affectation of authority. "You're telling your *queen* she can't leave?"

"It's not safe for you outside this fortress." The leader didn't back down. His tone verged on patronizing and Abe winced when Jude's anger flared, flooding her body with a deep crimson.

"Jude." Ilse had threaded her way gracefully through the packed bodies to the front of the crowd. Her voice was calm and quiet and the use of their queen's human name seemed to startle the guards into silence.

It worked on her sovereign too.

"They're only doing their jobs—protecting you," Ilse said. "If you require a sojourn, we can arrange it. It will just take time to work out the logistics. In the meantime, may I make you some coffee here?"

"Coffee's not the point, Ilse," Jude muttered, but she slammed the door shut and the wall snapped back into place.

Ilse nodded the guards out with a practised efficiency and then guided Jude to a seat at the kitchen table. Resting her hands on Jude's shoulders, she began to massage them.

"No, I don't—" Jude stopped, her expression turning dreamier. "Wow," she murmured. "That's, uh—that feels really good. How are you—?" She jerked away, whipping her head around to glare. "Are you *feeding* on me?"

Ilse didn't flinch. Water sprites fed on human anxiety and fear, replacing it with a calm, blissful state that, in their natural habitats, usually resulted in their victim drowning.

"I'm siphoning your stress," she said. "Merely applying my powers to aid you. I assure you I take no sustenance from it."

"Well, quit it." Jude rolled her shoulders, sighing as if in memory of the pleasure the sprite's soothing touch had brought, then steeling herself with a brief head shake. She added haltingly, "Please," and slipped out of the chair to put more distance between herself and Ilse.

Then she yanked the nearest drawer open and pulled out a pad of paper and a pen, starting to write at the counter.

"What's that?" Abe asked.

"List of people I care about. People someone could use to hurt me." Jude paused, considered, then muttered, "Right, Mom." She stared at the list again. "There's, like, six people on here. That's not too bad."

"Most people might be more disappointed by a low number," Abe ventured, trying to feel her out.

"Most people didn't just become queen of a world full of predators looking to twist their arm for favours."

"The Archduke," Abe said, the answer snapping into place. He'd felt a powerful Faerie presence and recognized it in hindsight. "What does he want?" There wasn't much he could think of that would ruffle Jude like this.

"A game I'm not playing." She set the pen aside, body tense. "But he's probably not going to be the last person that tries it. I'd like to be prepared."

She set the list on the counter and took in both Abe and Ilse to continue, "Last year Joshua said he'd done something to my mom and me after he left us—a binding? Have you heard of it? It keeps a Faerie from hurting a human unless the human strikes first?"

"Reflection," Ilse said. "It's a type of spell that protects by mirroring back the harm visited on its target."

"Old magic," Abe added. "Never seen one in the wild. Heard they're tricky."

Jude's expectant look pushed him to explain further. "Best I understand, they rely on malice—*intent* to harm. Meaning accidents aren't covered and someone in precise control of their emotions could probably slip it."

"I'm not worried about Vulcans," Jude said, "just Faeries."

Ilse glanced to Abe and started to ask, "What's a—?"

He gave her a slight shake of his head to say it wasn't important.

"Do either of you know how to find out if the one on my mom is still active?" Jude asked.

"Yes," Ilse said.

"How long will that take?"

"Yes, it's still active," the water sprite amended. "You mentioned your mother this morning and that prompted me to check on her to be certain she hadn't been targeted."

Jude looked startled. "I didn't mention her."

"When you enlightened me about the dated human clothing I brought you, you said, 'my mother doesn't even wear these anymore.'"

After a moment of baffled amazement, Jude risked a glance at Abe to gauge his reaction. Finally, she said, "Thank you."

"I try to anticipate needs." Ilse bowed her head slightly.

"Do you know how to make them, then?" Jude asked. When Ilse said nothing, she turned on Abe to add, "Cast them? Whatever?"

"Beyond my pay grade, darlin'," he said. "You'd need a mage."

"The Ubran know mages. Think they could make me some?"

"Imagine they could."

"Whether they *would* likely depends on who it's for," Ilse put in delicately.

"This guy, for one." Jude inclined her head toward Abe.

A rush of affection flooded him and he couldn't help smiling at her earnest effort.

"Doubt I'm human enough," he said, and Ilse's brief shake of her head confirmed it.

"Damn." Jude nodded, chewing on a fingernail. He could see the emotions flickering across her face, working her way up to something. Finally, she conceded, "Well, Daniel definitely is."

There it was. Abe chastised himself for not guessing sooner—that bristling, protective defence in her anger should have tipped him off.

"That's what the Archduke pulled, huh?" he guessed.

"Yep." Jude's jaw tightened. "He wants to be my consort."

"He's proposed to you?" Ilse's violet eyes widened.

"*Proposed* is too charming a word for what he did," Jude said. "Marry him and make Saskia my heir, or he's going after Daniel."

Abe managed to murmur, "Well, hell," but couldn't come up with anything further. If he'd just been quicker to intervene last fall, to keep Jude from flippantly making a bargain with that bastard Raj—

He'd been exhausted, sure, still bloody and bruised from Joshua's torture, running on fumes and anger just like Jude had been. Desperate for information, desperate to get the hell out of that viper's nest of a hotel.

He still should have stepped in, though, stopped her. Should have kept them from going to Raj in the first place, protected her.

"I'm sorry, darlin'," he said quietly.

Jude gave him a dubious sidelong look.

"Danny's safe," she said. "He went off with Grace and retired or whatever. I'm not letting Declan drag any of them back into this bullshit just to mess with me. Can I bind him without knowing where he is?"

Ilse's body had gone rigid but Abe still couldn't read her emotions. He eyed her, then answered Jude, "You'd have to ask Karl."

"Great." The breath and fight seemed to go out of the new Mab.

"Maybe you should give this 'consort' business a little more thought," Abe ventured. Jude's tendency toward split-second decisions wasn't going to do her any favours on the throne. This one, especially.

"Oh, I already agreed. Declan's probably picking out flower arrangements and drawing up paperwork." Jude tried to sound optimistic as she added, "Maybe Karl will forbid it."

"The Ubran would never forbid you anything," Ilse said. "And the Archduke is a suitable, if surprising, choice."

"You ought to talk to Saskia before you go through with this." Abe tried again. "See if she's somebody you could live with turning the worlds over to."

"What does it even matter?" Jude frowned at the space where the back door had been. "I'm not one of them, not Faerie. They don't care what I think—I'm just a game piece to push around the board until it benefits the most powerful jackass. Aubrie got *that* part right."

Her flip, bitter words made Abe's heart hurt. He couldn't stand seeing her on the verge of giving up already, letting the scheming Court machinations bulldoze over her.

"Never considered you easily pushed," he said. He kept his tone light, but the words landed like stones, the way he'd known they would.

Anger flashed in Jude's eyes and he expected her to lash out, snap something at him. Instead, she seemed to draw further into herself, then she turned and stalked out of the room.

Damn. Abe winced. He'd meant to piss her off, but maybe he'd done more harm than good.

Ilse seemed to think so.

"You should take more care not to upset her. This is a delicate time."

"Jude's not delicate. You can't treat her like a china doll," Abe said. "And if we're being honest, I don't love watching you manage her."

"Manage?" The water sprite blinked uncertainly, not much for the subtleties of human hedging.

"Manipulate," Abe amended, gentling his tone to blunt the accusation.

"I merely meant to steer her from trouble." Ilse pressed her lips together, the edges turning up as if she'd swallowed an uncharacteristic laugh. "But if you feel I'm manipulating her, perhaps you should aim the projectile."

Abe studied her face, trying to suss out where they'd lost each other, then realized,

"The idiom you're looking for is 'take a shot.'"

"Noted." She took the correction with her usual grace.

He couldn't help admiring her total lack of egotistic self-defence. Miranda had loved this woman, taken her into her confidence for years. He hadn't always agreed with his long-time friend's decisions—especially of late when she'd become the Mab—but this one seemed well-considered.

Sudden, hurried sounds from the hallway outside the kitchen got their attention. An army of heavy footsteps headed upstairs, fast.

Ilse went to the doorway, presumably to find out what was going on, but Abe already had a good idea. Exasperation washed through him.

The Mab was on the move.

13

"Hey." I slipped into Diana's room without knocking because she'd left the door cracked.

She was sitting on the bed, surrounded by piles of new clothing and shoes. It looked like designer stuff.

"I just wanted to try it out," she said, looking a little guilty as she shoved the bedside drawer closed and kicked off the platinum three-inch heels she was wearing.

"And I love that for you, but we need to go." I surveyed the room, cataloguing the furniture to determine the heaviest piece we could reasonably push up against the door. Probably the bed—the tables on either side weren't wide enough to block the whole door frame and wouldn't provide enough heft to hold it shut.

Diana got to her feet, eyeing me as I put my shoulder against the bed frame to give it a shove.

"What are you doing?" she asked.

"Barring the door so we can get out of here." The wooden frame and mattress slid a few centimetres across the carpet under my weight. "Help me, would you?"

She didn't move. "Can't you just, like, magic it?"

Good point. I stepped back, trying to remember how I'd made the hot power shoot down my arm when I'd tossed Joshua off our balcony. I'd been jittery with rage then too, so at least I still had that going for me.

Who the hell did Abe think he was, piling all this shit on my shoulders? He wasn't the one getting tugged in three directions at once, being told simultaneously that he was in charge now and also that he wasn't worthy to be in charge. I was the most powerful person in the room and yet I was supposed to follow every else's instructions?

Fuck that. Fuck the Faeries and the Court and the crown. Fuck the power, even. I'd already told Declan he could be my consort, that Saskia could be my heir. They had my consent and they could run with it—take over the palace, play politics, get all that shit done without me. I'd just disappear again—if nobody could find me, then nobody could drag my ex or my mom or any of my friends back in front of me and cut them to make me bleed.

I sucked in a breath to steady my heart, calming my anger as I considered how to lift the furniture. I needed to be more careful here than I had with Joshua—quieter. I felt like an idiot holding my hands out and concentrating on an invisible link from them to the bed, but I managed to lift the thing a few centimetres from the floor and guide it toward the door.

Then I faltered. The bed slammed down on the floor, loud enough to echo in the room.

That made Diana relent. She propped a shoulder against it and helped me shove it the rest of the way. Fatigue crept through my muscles, not from the physical exertion—more like a drain from the magic I'd used.

I wasn't sure I had the energy to create another door like I had downstairs, so I went to the window instead. The other side of the glass showed the same calm, sunset scene that the front windows downstairs held. It looked like a car was just turning the corner at the end of the manicured, suburban street.

I rested my hands on the sash and tried to focus again, the way I had when I'd knocked the door out of the kitchen wall downstairs.

"Your Highness?" an unfamiliar voice came through the door. Somebody tried the knob.

Diana hovered beside me, chewing on her lower lip. "Are you sure you should—?"

I cut her off by yanking the window up to reveal the cool darkness of Tofino outside.

"I'm sure," I assured her, nodding her through first.

When the knocking started, she didn't hesitate to fold herself through the window. I followed as gracefully as I could, but I still tumbled over the ledge as harder blows began to rain down on the bedroom door.

Diana stopped short outside, startled by our change of venue, but I didn't wait to slam the window shut and cut us off from the safehouse. We'd emerged onto the second-floor balcony outside our own apartment—from Dee's view, it looked like we'd crawled out of our own front window.

"Okay, that's weird," she observed, then, "What are we doing here? I thought it wasn't safe."

"We're not staying, just getting your car." I added awkwardly, "if that's okay."

"You're the queen," she concluded, but her tone started to veer a little further away from 'entertained' into uncertainty.

"I don't suppose you've got your keys?" I'd left mine back in the safe house, along with my wallet, and hadn't had the foresight to duck back into my bedroom for them before launching our escape plan. At least I had my phone in my back pocket.

"They're inside." Diana tried our front door, even though we both knew I'd locked it from the inside last night to keep Joshua out.

I snatched up a plastic pot full of dirt and a dead plant. It had been beside the door for months—neither Diana or I were gardeners, must have been the landlord's. Burying my fist in the dirt, I used the pot to protect my hand as I landed a shattering blow to our front window.

Diana squeaked in surprise and the sound of breaking glass made us both flinch, but the neighbourhood remained quiet. I had no idea what time it was here—the sky overhead was dark and clear, glittering with stars. It was hard to tell through the tall trees that populated the street, but there seemed to be some light in the east.

I used the pot to knock the larger, sharper pieces of glass out of the window frame, then climbed inside.

"You might want to, uh, get your things?" I offered, once I'd opened the front door to her. "Quick, though."

"We're really doing the prison break, huh?" Diana hesitated on the doorstep like she might argue, then nudged the backpack she'd dumped inside last night. "Overnight bag's already packed."

"You don't want the rest of your stuff?"

Her eyebrows disappeared beneath pink curls. "Are we not coming back?"

"I don't know." I probably wasn't, now that every Faerie in the world knew where to find me, but Diana might be able to. She wasn't really involved in any of this. Well, she hadn't been—until I'd dragged her in. "How about I drop you and your car at your mom's?"

If I remembered correctly, Diana's mom was in Nanaimo, where there was a ferry terminal that would take me back over to mainland BC.

"She's in Hawaii for the winter." Diana shook her head. "The house is rented out."

"Well, we'll think of something, but I don't think you should stay here." I tried to keep my voice calm. "At least not right now."

"I guess I'll grab a couple more things." She moved past me and disappeared into the bedroom. I didn't want to leave the door in case somebody came after us, or in case Joshua was still hanging around.

I finally relented and shut it, then took a whirl through my own bedroom. I dug an envelope of cash from under my mattress, then grabbed two t-shirts, an extra pair of jeans and some socks and underwear along with my toothbrush and phone charger. I stuffed it all into a brown paper take-out bag from the kitchen, then met Diana at the door.

She'd added a half-full duffel bag to one shoulder along with her overnight pack on the other, and she brandished her car keys as if to say she was ready.

"I'm driving." I snatched them out of her hand. "That way nobody thinks you kidnapped me if they catch up."

"Nobody thinks I *what*?" Her protest rang behind me as I headed back out onto the balcony and pounded down the stairs.

I couldn't help but stop once I'd reached the car. I faced her across the roof before I unlocked the doors.

"You don't have to come," I said.

"Hell if I'm letting you flee a bunch of Faeries on your own," she returned.

"It's not my first rodeo," I assured her, but she didn't back down, so I unlocked the doors and we both climbed in.

It had been a minute since I'd been behind the wheel, but driving was a skill that came back instinctively, like riding a bike, right? Not that I'd done *that* in years either. I guided the sedan down the street.

Tofino was nestled at the end of a peninsula on the west side of Vancouver Island, and there was only one road in or out—Highway Four. We'd take it inland to Port Alberni, then east to Nanaimo.

"I feel like you should probably fill me in on all your Faerie backstory," Diana said quietly, as we cleared the edges of our barely-stirring downtown. There were a few other cars on the road, and one of the cafes was open, catering to the fishermen, seaplane pilots and other early risers. I'd been right about the sunrise—the sky was definitely lightening ahead of us.

"I don't know where to start."

"Explain it like I'm five."

Was there any way out of this, any way of not having to introduce Diana to my bat-shit insane world? She had been good to me. She'd taken me in when my expected housing in Tofino had fallen apart. She'd become a friend. I owed her.

I took her sarcastic request to heart. "I didn't mean for any of this to happen, and I'm sorry."

"Five-year-old me is calling bullshit."

"On which part?"

"You skipping the actual explanation."

I settled on telling her about my introduction to Faeries. Seemed like as good a beginning as any. I told her about learning I could shift gravity as a teenager, about being recruited to the Consilium. About working for them to keep predatory creatures out of the human world. I glossed over the harder stuff—conspiring with Aubrie, killing Alan, my three-month coma. I left out Daniel entirely. He wasn't somebody I could explain yet.

I skipped over the bulk of what had gone down in Montreal five months ago with my father and the vicious, heart-stealing mages and tailored the truth a little to finish with my running away across Canada to escape Miranda. Not a complete lie.

Despite leaving out so much, my long story got us all the way down the peninsula to the intersection near the Pacific Rim Park Visitor's Centre and the good poke shop, where Highway Four took a hard left inland.

"Are you okay?" Diana asked, voice still gentle.

"Yeah." I didn't know what else to say, how to explain. The house had gotten too small and claustrophobic with Eli, Ilse and all of the faceless guards hovering around me, reacting to my every move. Not to mention Karl's laundry list of chores and classes, and then Declan—

The memory of his smug smile made my fingers tighten on the steering wheel.

I couldn't be the Mab.

14

Daniel blinked awake, initially aware of a sharp pain in his temple. Since he didn't actually remember getting stabbed in the head, it was probably due to the stale, faintly smoky taste of Scotch on his tongue. All of his muscles protested as he sat up, but he managed to lift a hand to shield his eyes from bright light. He'd fallen asleep on an uncomfortable sofa . . . somewhere.

It looked like a hotel room. Like a hotel *suite*, in fact. The sunlight streamed in through floor-to-ceiling picture windows to one side, illuminating an unfamiliar city skyline. Far in the distance, something blue glittered—a large body of water.

Not Phoenix, then. At least he was far enough from the windows that his usual vertigo stayed at bay. Facing the height with his head throbbing like this might have made him pass out again.

"You're awake." The double doors to what must have been the bedroom opened. "Finally."

At the sight of Joshua standing casually in the doorway with a mug of coffee, Daniel stumbled to his feet. The sudden motion made him queasy but he ignored it.

"Wait," the older man started.

Daniel hesitated at the command then realized his limbs were still under his own power. Joshua didn't seem to be able to control him this morning. He dashed for the door, colliding with it in his haste. He fumbled to undo both locks, then yanked on the handle.

It didn't budge.

Blood pounding in his ears, he double-checked the lock and pulled the handle again. Still nothing.

A sharper nausea washed through him and brought weary resignation. He swallowed bile, turning to face Joshua, who still stood in the bedroom doorway.

"Where are you planning to go, exactly?" the older man asked, in a tone that still seemed too mild. "You yourself told me last night that you have no accessible finances to your name, no transport and, at this moment, no means of communication." He punctuated that by holding up Daniel's phone.

Daniel patted his pocket despite recognizing it. He didn't remember saying any of that aloud but it came back to him. They had talked for an unpleasantly long time last night after leaving the bar and coming here, Joshua asking questions and Daniel compelled to answer.

He still couldn't remember exactly how they'd gotten here, though, or where *here* was.

"You're out of your depth," Joshua said. "You always have been. Your former organization was as well, but they, at least, had the strength of numbers." He tipped his head as if to concede the point. "You, however, are alone. Only alive now by luck and the beneficence of more powerful people. The former has clearly run out and the latter is waning."

He took a sip of his coffee before finishing, "It would be unwise to leave."

The bleak assessment wasn't wrong. Still, Daniel couldn't help snapping, "I'll take my chances."

"Short-sighted and wilfully ignorant. You're more like your father than I realized."

"And you're a patronizing asshole."

"But I haven't been wrong yet." Joshua snorted. "Take your chances? You'll have *no* chance. Judith has become a powerful force, and it's common knowledge that she's fond of you. I'm undoubtedly not the only person who's realized you'd be a useful hostage. You should be grateful I got to you first—I have reason to keep you in one piece. Coffee?"

It took Daniel a moment to realize the last word had been an actual offer. He spun again and banged both fists hard against the door, shouting, "Help! Fire!"

"No one outside can hear you," Joshua said. "Obviously." He walked to the armchair beside the sofa Daniel had vacated and sat down. "But yell if it makes you more comfortable."

Threats Daniel could take. Insults, fine, but the old mage's bored condescension frayed his last nerve. His muscles twitched to lash out, to take a swing at Joshua, but he was too far away to make contact.

It wouldn't matter anyway. Joshua could lay him out without blinking.

He slumped against the door, keeping one hand on the knob and scanning the room for a weapon. Maybe the spell sealing the door would wear off if Joshua were unconscious. Better yet, dead.

Half a dozen empty coat hangers hung in the open closet beside him, and a luggage rack was folded against the back wall, but neither of those presented as helpful. The coffee pot was the only thing that seemed feasible to wield, especially if it were actually glass and he could break it, but it was across the room.

"How did we get here?" he asked.

"Through a curtain. Are you going to stay at that door all day? We have places to go."

"We don't!" Daniel snapped.

"Then you're no longer interested in learning where it is you were yesterday? Your desert doors?" Joshua paused to give his words time to sink in.

"You know?" The question came out before Daniel could stop himself.

Rather than answer, Joshua reached into the minibar and withdrew a bottle of water. He held it up then rolled it across the floor, saying, "This is sealed. I haven't tampered with it. You should drink it."

The water bottle hit Daniel's boot but he didn't reach for it.

"Drink it," Joshua said again. "You've proven more interesting than I anticipated, and I don't relish the idea of hauling you around after you collapse from dehydration." He sighed, as if disappointed in himself, then ran his fingers along the row of tiny liquor bottles in the minibar's door. "I think you'll prefer that to my alternative."

Goddamn it. The thought of Joshua forcing liquor down his throat, controlling him like a wraith again, filled Daniel with cold dread. After passing out on the uncomfortable sofa, each ache and strain in his body from the last week in the tunnel had made itself more acute. He wasn't going to get far like this.

He broke the seal on the water bottle and downed half of it. Then he lowered himself to the floor, back still against the door, and waited to see if it would kill him.

When it didn't, he fixed Joshua with a weary look and challenged, "So, where was I?"

"The Lower Halls." The older man's eyebrows twitched. "You shouldn't have been down there. No one should be. It's exactly what I predicted would happen."

He continued, as if having the conversation with himself, "But I'm more interested in *why* you were there, which—we established last night—you don't know. That's another piece of this maddening puzzle."

"Stop. Go back. What is that place—the Lower Halls?"

Joshua hesitated. "A prison."

"For?"

"Something intensely dangerous that you never should have sought out." The mage exhaled through his teeth and turned his eyes to the window again.

"I was dragged there against my will," Daniel snapped. "I wasn't *seeking* anything!"

"You *led* them there." The older man's voice became charged as his expression darkened. He retrieved Daniel's phone again, brandishing it with a picture clear on the screen. He'd charged it somehow overnight, gone through it, found . . . what was that?

Reluctantly, Daniel moved closer to see the screen better. It took him a moment to remember what the photo of the grainy stone tablet meant. He'd taken it last November, a photo of a printout from a Consilium folder Gracie had been going through. Before she'd left.

"I don't know what that is," he said.

"Of course you don't!" Joshua snapped, shoving the phone back into his own pocket. "But you gave it to them. *And* a copy of the grymoire, so conveniently translated!"

Shame flooded Daniel. Gracie had been right in fearing that the dangerous information could fall into the wrong hands. They should have burned the damn spellbook.

"Leshe went through my apartment," he protested without conviction. "He took those. I didn't *give* them to him."

"That you had them in the first place is damning enough," Joshua growled. "Fucking Consilium—always collecting, always dabbling. Never could leave well enough alone."

He punctuated the last word by flinging his coffee mug at the window. It hit hard enough to shatter.

The coffee pot and three empty mugs a metre away exploded in unison.

Daniel fled back to the door, clawing at the knob. It turned but the heavy wood still didn't move. He sucked a ragged breath, expecting a shock of agony at any second, the pain of Joshua lashing out.

The room had gone silent, the air charged and heavy. With no other choice, he turned, tensing for a fight he wouldn't win.

Joshua gazed at the stain his coffee mug had left on the reinforced glass, then rolled his shoulders slowly. The gesture seemed to shake off the moment of black fury that had just surged through him.

Finally, he sighed heavily. "As I was saying," he said, voice disturbingly calm and composed again as he met Daniel's eyes, "you opened the box, so you will help me close it."

15

The twisty, two-lane highway remained quiet and empty as I drove. The sun rose ahead of us but the dark, heavy rainforest pressed in around the road, keeping things shadowy. The trees broke occasionally to offer a stunning view of a sparkling mountain lake but I barely saw it, fighting a lead foot that could only lead to trouble. There seemed to be a yellow sign every fifty metres warning me to slow down—not that I needed them, with all the hairpin curves, but the tension in my muscles urged me to hurry.

Ahead of us, something moved onto the road. Diana gasped and I blinked, taking my foot off the accelerator but not yet willing to hit the brake. Was it real? Had a long, spindly tree draped in moss just slid, upright, into the middle of the highway?

My fingers tightened on the wheel, intending to swerve around the single figure, but then more dark shapes crowded onto the road, lining up to make a barrier. I had no choice but to slow down and stop. Helpless rage bubbled in my chest. How had they found me so goddamn fast?

"Run them over." A sudden voice came from the back-seat.

I nearly smacked Diana's forehead with my own as we both whipped around to see a shimmering form lounging on the upholstery behind us. I blinked hard to dispel the glamour obscuring our uninvited passenger and then found myself glaring at Saskia.

The Archduke's daughter stretched languidly, like a cat. The graceful motion gave me a glimpse of her long, silver sword lying across her lap. She usually wore her signature weapon strapped to her back, glamoured so nobody knew it was there. The backseat didn't give her much room to use it, but she probably had her dagger on her too.

"What the hell are you doing back there?" I snapped.

"These assholes," she said, nodding to the group that had moved to surround the car, "are related to that unfortunate girl your aunt killed yesterday. They want payback."

I gritted my teeth when something tapped on the window beside me. Dim memories of getting pulled over as a teenager contributed to my glower as I turned to face a pair of giant, hooded eyes peering out of bushy branches.

My skin tingled, electrified by the tree-like Faeries. The one outside my window lifted what looked like a lichen-crusted hand and made a cranking motion, miming rolling down a manual car window.

Diana made a small sound in the back of her throat, reminding me that I wouldn't just be risking my own life committing vehicular Faerie-slaughter. She gripped the door handle so tight her knuckles went white, matching the pale scar on the back of her hand.

"Go," Saskia pressed under her breath.

I didn't trust the redcap, but another glance in my rearview mirror showed that she'd coiled her body to one side, gripping her sword tightly in one hand, prepared to burst out through the rear door. She was ready to fight.

That made up my mind. I slammed a foot onto the accelerator. The tires squealed on the road but the car didn't move forward. The tree creatures had seized on my hesitation to immobilize it somehow.

Something shattered the window beside my head. A thick, rough branch darted in with more grace than I'd expected, trying to wrap itself around my throat. I shoved my body as far back in the seat as I could, flooring the gas pedal again. The car swung dizzily to the side and the tires screamed once more on the pavement.

Behind me, Saskia shoved her door open, slamming it into the leafy body beside my window and knocking the wriggling branches away from my face.

"Run!" I shouted to Diana. She was half a step ahead of me. already pushing her door open.

I followed suit with a shout intended to draw attention to myself as my roommate hauled ass off the road and into the forest. She disappeared from my view when the dark forms blocking the road all moved to intercept me.

I swung myself up on top of the car with ease, out of the grasping, wooden fingers of the four—five?—creatures that vied to reach me. On the ground to my left, Saskia moved like a vicious dancer, fighting two others with both her long, gleaming sword in one hand and the short dagger in the other. Both weapons were already stained with blood, so dark green it looked black.

"Hey!" I shouted. My voice rang across the empty road, swallowed up into the heavy, non-sentient forest on either side of us. I *was* the fucking queen here. "What the hell is going on?"

The largest one, who'd shattered my car window, glowered at me, growing in height to reach mine atop the car and meet my eyes directly. A booming growl issued from its mouth, but whatever accusations it spat at me weren't in English.

"False one!" a smaller, mossier creature to the right hissed. "Deceiver! Your blood shall run for our lost kin!" Its rapidly branching arms dug into the metal near my feet with an ungodly screech that made me want to clap my hands over my ears. One appendage shot up through the roof, curling the metal like a can opener and narrowly missing puncturing my left foot.

Guess we're not talking this out, then.

I drew gravity into my core, gathering it into a sucking black hole, then took a leap from the roof of the car. The extra mass let me come down like a ton of bricks on the big Faerie in front of me, my legs extended to plow through its solid midsection. Branches snapped under me and the thing gave a bloodcurdling shriek of rage as it broke apart.

I pulled back as I landed to keep from driving my feet into the concrete, then kicked gently through the flurry of twisted wood and sticky blood.

Beside me, Saskia seized the opportunity to cut the legs out from under one of her stilled adversaries, then plunged her dagger into the trunk of the other.

The remaining creatures drew together like an army of tall, spiky shadows, feathered with leaves and pine needles. The heavy, earthy scent of decaying leaves overpowered me as I swung a fist. My blow glanced off a dark, wooden limb and my knuckles stung, but I managed to catch a softer, fleshier side of the Faerie with the back of my other hand and was rewarded with a pained grunt.

I took another wild swing, concentrating on the electric buzz of the power under my skin rather than the velocity of my hands. I tried to toss the creatures away from me without touching them like I had Joshua. My power fizzled and my nearest opponents only turned their heads, wincing. I hadn't even reached the ones a metre behind them.

It was enough to create a small opening, though, so I somersaulted through the swinging boughs. Sharp, prickly needles scraped my skin and I didn't manage the full flip, pushing off the ground instead with both hands into a messy cartwheel. Swinging my legs over my head, I slammed my boots into the tough, shaggy body of my nearest adversary.

Feet back on the ground, I plunged into the woods beside the road and made for the wide trunk of a huge redwood up ahead, shifting my gravity again in an instant to reorient the world ninety degrees and put me upright on the trunk.

I sprinted up the wide bark like a road. Could trees climb trees?

Turned out, sort of.

A heavy cord-like tendril snaked around my ankles, snapping my legs together and sending me sprawling forward. Something caught me before I could smack face-first into the redwood's trunk.

Bark scraped my skin raw as the branches or roots around my ankles hauled me back down the tree. My captor swung me away from the trunk when I was still several metres up, dangling me upside-down over the forest floor. The motion would have been dizzying if I hadn't spun the world around my head to find an equilibrium. At least that power still came easy.

"Hey!" I went for broke, banking on its sense of Faerie community as I shouted, "If you kill me, it'll throw your world off-kilter!"

"You care nothing for my world." The thing was directly below me, dark eyes gleaming.

"The *fuck* I don't!" I wanted to laugh. It was usually the other way around, haughty Faeries not giving a shit about the human world. *Touché, Tree Monster.* "Look," I said, trying to flex my ankles and loosen whatever was binding them, "this whole thing is a misunderstanding. I didn't *mean* to be hidden, and I didn't want Miranda to die, or your kin . . . person. I'm really sorry that happened—you have *no* idea."

"I need no idea," the tree growled back. "Your begging shall engender no mercy."

"*Begging?* Hang on, Treebitch, I am *not—*"

Below me, the dark, shaggy shape cracked with a sound like a gunshot.

"I shall consume your frail body and absorb your power," the voice grunted. "I shall ascend in my sister's place and the lineage will be satisfied." It started to spread and widen into—was that a mouth?

Full of sharp, splintered, wooden fangs.

Before it could lower my thrashing body into its gaping jaws, silver glinted in the patchy sunlight and Saskia appeared on the ground. Her sword sang through the air, slicing my captor's body in half. Not cleanly—there were a lot of splinters.

As the tree Faerie collapsed in two ragged pieces, the branches around my ankles loosened suddenly. I flipped gravity as I fell, managing to land on my feet, but I still resented the sideways stumble I had to take to stay upright.

"Where are the rest?" I demanded.

Saskia pulled something from her pocket and began cleaning the blood and splinters off her sword in a calm, irritating manner.

I gaped at her. "You took *all of them* out?"

"Yep." She wasn't wearing her red tuque today, or her red socks. The blood-soaked object that sustained her powers must have been disguised as something new. Maybe the rag currently soaking up greenish-black tree creature blood from her weapon.

"Did you set this up?" I demanded.

"Excuse me?" She stopped the motion to glare at me through narrowed eyes. "Because I'm better armed and better prepared, you think I *rigged* some half-assed assassination attempt? For what?" She scoffed and went back to her sword, muttering, "Just say 'thank you' and move on."

I had to dig my fingernails into my palms to keep from swinging a fist at her. If being rescued by this smug, bitchy redcap was the worst thing that happened today, it would still be too much.

"How long were you playing urban legend psycho in the backseat?"

"I don't know. How long had you been driving?" She replaced her sword in the glamoured hilt on her back and gave a heavy sigh before deigning to explain, "My father insisted I request an audience with you. I reached your little fortress to do so just as a considerable number of soldiers were attempting to batter a bedroom door down, so I made an educated guess and went back to your little human hovel." She gestured in the direction of the road, indicating Tofino. "When I found you packing, I just broke into the car that smelled the most like your apartment. You're *very* predictable."

You too, I wanted to say, because that dig was obviously meant to bait me. The thought of Saskia skulking around outside the apartment while Diana and I had been hastily stuffing our lives into luggage made my skin crawl.

Damn it, where was Diana? I shoved past Saskia and stalked back to the road to be certain she wasn't lying. A bundle of inert Faeries lay scattered across the road, looking like wind-blown trees. Six in all—the one I'd smashed as well as the others I'd counted surrounding us before, minus the hungry one in the woods.

"Diana?" I called, edging past the bodies and the ruined car. Roots extended under the chassis, probably wrapped around the axles. "Dee?"

I'd just reached the opposite edge of the road when something shifted in the trees and Diana's pale, drawn face appeared from behind a bush. She hadn't gone far. Luckily, the tree people hadn't been interested in a random human.

It had been stupid to bring her along with me on this ridiculous escape, but it wasn't like I could have left her back at the house either. Maybe I should have just wised up and stopped trying to make friends. Seemed like they either ended up with their hearts ripped out or chased by tree monsters.

"Are you hurt?" I asked.

She hesitated, then got upright slowly, testing her limbs to check.

"I don't think so." She blinked rapidly, still looking shell-shocked, then gingerly picked her way through the shrubs to meet me at the edge of the road.

"We should return to your fortress," Saskia called, standing beside the car.

I wanted to cuss her out, punch her, make her draw her sword and fight me, but I couldn't. She'd saved my ass.

"How do we get *back*?" I challenged. "There aren't any doors around here."

"I see four doors." Saskia nodded to the ruined car, where three of the said doors still hung open. "Five if you count the trunk, I suppose."

16

After Saskia opened the car's rear passenger door to the bright foyer of the safehouse, I took the lead back through. I didn't want to go back to the house, but the car was useless with its axles wrapped in thick, rigid roots and there wasn't anywhere to walk—we weren't close enough to a town yet to have any luck begging at somebody's house, which would probably be a vacation home anyway. Who knew if there were more angry trees out there in the woods?

After folding awkwardly through the small opening that should have let me slide into the car's back seat, it was jarring to find myself on my hands and knees in the familiar foyer of the safe house.

I got to my feet, coming face to face with Karl, Eli and Ilse. My advisers looked furious and Eli was stone-faced. Ilse wrung her hands. Abe hung back, separate from a second-string cadre of guards. Even though they'd clustered to one side, they were clearly itching to get me away from the door.

The cowboy paled when he saw me and started to move my way. His expression made me aware of the throbbing scrapes and cuts dotting my arms and the ache in my ankles, but I turned to help Diana crawl through the doorway.

Almost as soon as I hauled her through and helped her to her feet, her eyes rolled back in her head. Her legs folded and she crumpled.

"Dee!" I squeaked, managing to catch her. Saskia, coming in behind her, shot up to help me, and Abe darted in too. He put a big hand on the side of Diana's face, probably reading her as I stammered, "She said she was okay, she said—"

"She's fine. Just fainted." Abe slipped an arm around Diana's back, lifting her weight off me.

"*Just*—?" I started.

"Overwhelmed, I'd guess." The cowboy was trying to sound reassuring.

"Can you wake her up?"

"You think that's a good idea right now?" He lifted her into his arms, letting her head loll against his shoulder. He'd finally started to sound annoyed, probably more at my running off than Diana's condition. Maybe at both—one had led to the other, after all. "I'll settle her upstairs," he said tersely. "Get her some rest."

"Your Highness, this behaviour is unacceptable," Karl snapped.

"Don't scold her like a kid who snuck out after curfew," Abe drawled.

Even though he was technically on my side, the words still made me bristle.

"Talking *about* me over my head is patronizing too," I couldn't help pointing out.

The cowboy looked chastened, but still annoyed. I half-expected him to snap back at me, but he took a deep breath and gave me a slow nod. "You're right," he said. "Sorry, darlin'."

"*Your Highness*," Karl corrected him, punctuating each word with cold precision.

"Abe can call me whatever the fuck he likes." I spun on my so-called advisers. "I gave you that option too but you wanted to keep the stick up your ass."

Huffing a noise of surprise, Karl drew themselves up to their full height so that they could glare down their nose at me.

"It is not *proper* to—"

"I think the Mab can make her own decisions about what's proper," Ilse broke in. Karl turned on her and they started to argue.

Abe seized the moment to head upstairs with Diana. Saskia had slunk across the room to lean against the wall. I met her eyes and she gave me a sly, amused grin. At least somebody was enjoying this.

"Regardless." Karl raised their voice to speak over Ilse's objection. "It was not only foolish to flee this way, but *selfish* when there are those out there who would—"

"What?" I challenged. "Eat me to absorb my power?"

Karl snapped their mouth closed, something more than anger flickering in their eyes.

"That's ridiculous."

"Tell that to the sentient tree that tried to pop me in her mouth like a Skittle."

"Such beliefs are deeply misled," Karl said in a tight voice, maybe a hair's breadth from sounding chagrined. "To become the Mab by . . . *consuming* the—it's impossible." They shook themselves out of the shock, going on, "We are truly sorry you went through such an experience. This is why we must insist that you remain safely *here*. This dwelling can be manipulated to make it exactly as you desire, as comfortable and pleasing as possible."

"Yeah, it's a great little prison," I agreed.

"If you would prefer to cross the portal to Faerie, that can of course be arranged, but—"

"Ugh. No." I winced at my instinctive reaction, realizing too late that it wasn't just insulting to Karl and the Faerie soldiers clustered around me, but probably to Ilse and Eli too. If I didn't rein myself in, I was about to have a couple fewer allies in this hallway.

"Fetch a healer," Karl told one of the soldiers.

"Abe—" I started to say, but Karl added sharply, "A *real* healer."

Catching sight of my probably murderous look on Abe's behalf, they added hastily, "Your friend is busy caring for the unfortunate human—you wouldn't want to tax his abilities. We have other healers easily accessible."

"Fine." I felt like a traitor, somehow. Not like Abe probably even *wanted* to heal me after how I'd ditched him and run off. Again.

The thought of Diana's bloodless, shaken face on the side of the road and the memory of her unconscious body in Abe's arms twisted my guts harder. I couldn't keep this up. I couldn't be Mab.

But I clearly couldn't just run away from it either. The vicious tree creature's dig about me not caring about her world wormed its way inside my head.

"You," I told Saskia. "Let's talk."

17

Daniel kept his distance from Joshua as the older man made a gesture, running his hand down from above his own head and sweeping it to his feet in a quick straight line. He used both hands to part what suddenly looked like a fabric drape that matched the colour of the beige wall exactly. Blinding white light shone from the opening.

"This is a curtain," Joshua said, as if speaking to a child. "We used it last night."

Seeing it made Daniel's heart race. He had a vague, queasy memory of walking through it, as Joshua had said.

"It's merely a rift in the fabric of space that compresses the distance between two points," the mage prompted.

"Oh, is that all?"

"It doesn't even pass beyond the boundary of this world. You travelled further stepping into that house of Judith's."

"That looked like a house. This looks like an empty void."

"I will be sure to amend the aesthetics for future trips." Joshua's hand connected with Daniel's shoulder before he could protest further, shoving him roughly through the tear in the world.

He didn't fall. There was no loss of control, no sense of vertigo. One instant, he was in the hotel suite and the next he stood outside somewhere. He blinked against the rush of daylight, trying to make sense of it. They'd emerged into the middle of a scruffy yard that hadn't been mowed recently, in front of a wooden-shingled house surrounded by trees.

He turned to look back where they'd come from, but the curtain was gone. A wooded neighbourhood stretched behind them, houses on large lots with trailers and kayaks in the driveways.

Joshua started down the gravel driveway in front of them and Daniel took a step back, seizing on his lack of attention to bolt. As soon as he spun to run, he butted against an invisible barrier. He put a hand out to test it, swallowing to suppress the desperate anger that made him want to punch it instead.

"This is tiring," Joshua said from behind him. "I thought we had an agreement."

"You dictating a term and forcing me to follow it isn't 'an agreement.'" Daniel gave up on another argument he wouldn't win. "Why are we here?"

"To find out why you were in the Lower Halls."

Someone here in this mundane neighbourhood knew where he'd been? What he'd been used in service for down in that cave? How?

Joshua's certainty was too enticing not to follow, but Daniel still hated every step he took trailing the older man around to the back of the house.

A resounding clang of metal on metal grew louder as they came down the driveway. They reached a deep, grassy backyard lot with a large, covered forge set on a clean patio of paving stones. Coals glowed orange in the centre of a raised brick oven. On an anvil to one side, someone worked hot metal.

Joshua waited in the driveway for the person to stop moving a chisel. At first, Daniel thought it was from some bizarre politesse, but then he noticed the pile of scrap metal sitting near the bellows.

Iron. Joshua was keeping his distance on purpose.

The blacksmith straightened up, pushing a pair of safety goggles back over short, grey hair to reveal a pinched face. She presented as female, despite narrow hips and broad shoulders. Her skin was dark and her muscular arms gleamed in a sleeveless shirt. She wore heavy, heat-proof gloves, but no other protective clothing.

Her eyes widened as she took Joshua in.

"You wicked fucking man!" A faint accent, maybe British, grew stronger with each word. She clutched the chisel in one gloved hand, advancing on him. "I thought you were dead! Again!"

"Not yet," Joshua returned. "Still."

He danced back to avoid the short, sharp weapon in the same moment that she swung it, but the woman didn't let that faze her.

"You absolute *bastard!*" she snapped. "Pop up at my door after fifteen years, short out the electricity in my whole neighbourhood, cry on my shoulder just to vanish again?"

"I didn't want to cause you more trouble until I had to, Bel."

"As if you've worried a day in your life about someone other than yourself." She kept her hand clenched around the chisel like she might take another swing.

"Could we speak inside?" Joshua nodded toward the back door of the house.

"I'm not inviting you in for tea, not after last time," she scoffed, then gestured to the driveway. "Piss off, you *and* your friend."

"Hostage," Joshua corrected.

The woman stilled, narrowing her eyes. She darted a glance to Daniel, as if expecting him to protest. When he didn't, she shook her head like she didn't want to know anything that might implicate her further. Gesturing again to the driveway with the metal chisel, she concluded, "Right, then. Continue to piss off."

"He's recently been to the Lower Halls," Joshua said.

The woman's breath hitched. Her eyes moved to Daniel's face again as if she might find something there to prove the claim.

"You've *been* there?" A note of awe entered her voice.

Before Daniel could answer, Bel shook her head, changing her mind as she waved her free hand. "No," she said. "No, I don't care."

A third change of heart made her grit her teeth and about-face again. "What were you doing down there?"

Half-expecting her to interrupt again, Daniel looked to Joshua to gauge the conversation. He resented the impulse immediately and Bel seemed to notice.

"Do you have a spell on him or something?" she asked Joshua.

"Not at the moment." The older man sounded amused.

"I don't know," Daniel answered her earlier question, interrupting the conversation that had started to move past him like he were a piece of furniture. "Why I was there, I mean."

Bel snorted, shaking off her heavy gloves and fishing into the pocket of her jeans to produce a half-smoked joint and a lighter. She wrapped a glove around the metal chisel and tucked it under one arm.

"The Lower Halls aren't somewhere you just end up *accidentally*," she muttered, setting the spliff between her lips. "Especially human." She cupped a hand around the lighter, then inhaled before giving him a proper once-over and asking, "Who are you?"

"My apologies." Joshua broke in to do the introductions. "Isabel Furst, Daniel Cain."

The casual levity on the woman's face vanished. She didn't go so far as to take a step back, but she seemed to take Daniel in with new eyes. Her lip curled into a sneer, somewhere between fear and disdain.

It had been a while since he'd seen that look, since he'd gotten it regularly. The all-too-familiar suspicion stung the way it always had, but he took it head-on.

"I guess you knew my father," he said.

"Yes, I've had the pleasure." Bel spun back on Joshua to demand, "When did you join the bloody Consilium?"

"The Consilium is gone," he said.

"That's not what I heard." Bel took another drag off her joint and exhaled thoughtfully.

Before Daniel could demand exactly what she meant by that, she raised her eyebrows and concluded, "Well, I guess it's tea after all." Still carrying the lit joint, she headed toward the back door, stopping to dump the chisel onto a table at the edge of the patio covered in rags and other tools.

When Joshua followed her, Daniel tried to grab the weapon. It burned his fingers, so he snatched up a rag to wrap around the base. Even through the fabric, the metal weapon with a wider, sharp edge on one end was still uncomfortably warm. He was almost within swinging distance of Joshua when the other man turned with a suddenness that made him bounce back on his heel.

"That won't go well for you," Joshua warned.

Daniel swung anyway, but Joshua dodged with preternatural grace. His hand closed around the chisel's handle and he yanked it out of Daniel's grip. In another instant, he had one hand around the back of Daniel's neck and the hot chisel tip burned under Daniel's jaw.

"If you're finished," Bel called from inside the house behind them, sounding mildly annoyed.

Joshua raised his eyebrows to press the question.

"Yes," Daniel growled.

Joshua released him, tossing the chisel aside with an easy grace before he strode into Bel's kitchen. He shook out his burned hand as he went, but he was breathing harder than usual. The manoeuvre had winded him. It had to be the proximity of the iron in the yard.

That was something, at least, since Daniel had no choice, once again, but to follow him.

18

INSIDE THE SMALL, CLEAN kitchen, the first thing Bel did was take an electric kettle from its base and fill it with water from the tap.

"The only reason to go to the Lower Halls," she said, as if their conversation had never been interrupted by the attempted attack and change of scene, "is to free N'ellaphalen thrace."

She pronounced the initial consonant of the word more like a musical note than a letter, but couldn't quite tap the Faerie pronunciation like a native. "That seems unlikely, though," she finished, putting the joint back to her lips as she set the kettle on its base. "You're human. What could you get from them?"

"What are 'they'?" Daniel pressed his fingers to the stinging burn under his chin, digging back into his memory to try and find the words she'd used. That first short note she'd half-sung made whatever it was a proper name, or a title. "A—the?—guest?"

"*Ellaphalen* is more like an 'uninvited' guest." Despite the correction and the heavy irony in her tone, Bel looked mildly impressed with his translation. "The Incomparable Guest is what most of my scarce literature called it in English, though I prefer 'The Visitant.' I think that's what the Consilium used. It doesn't have the nice, pejorative slant, but it's simpler."

When she noted that her explanation didn't seem to have made anything clearer, she tossed out the bullet points: "Ancient entity. Dangerous, powerful, terrifying—the usual. Why were you down there if you didn't know what—?"

She stopped again mid-sentence, exhaled toward the open, screened window above the sink and answered her own question, "You didn't go alone. How many?"

Daniel thought back, struggling to count the people he remembered from the tunnel. He'd clocked the guards daily but the other workers had sometimes fluctuated by the hour, depending on whether Leshe brought in a load of temporary workers from some nearby town.

"I think there were thirteen of us," he concluded. "But only twelve went into the, uh, the chamber."

"Thirteen sounds like a sacrifice."

"A sacrifice to what?"

"Our Visitant is old school—think ancient gods. Probably not going to help you unless you give them something to start with, gain their favour with a little blood or life energy. At least that's how I understood it." Bel shook her head. "Everything I know is theoretical. But theoretically, this is bad."

"How do you know any of this?"

"I wondered how long it'd take for you to demand my credentials."

"You weren't Consilium?"

She'd known his father, but she hadn't spoken about the organization as if she'd belonged to it.

"I prefer rogue scholar." She grimaced. "And in answer to your original question, let's just say that an idiot in love can be quite the force to be reckoned with." With a glance to Joshua, she added, "But I'm only one of those three things now."

As if realizing that she hadn't helped her case, she addressed Daniel again, jerking her chin toward the old mage to say, "*He* disappeared fifteen years ago. I went looking for him. Everywhere I could look."

She included Joshua again. "I was probably the only one looking for you who considered the Bie'lelhii—"

"You were the only one looking for me at all," Joshua murmured.

"I think I'll skip the tea for something stronger." Bel's voice cracked. She opened a cupboard to her right and pulled out a bottle of whisky. She added a glass to the counter, then glanced over her shoulder in offer.

"No, thank you," Joshua said, and Daniel shook his head, the scent of the alcohol turning his stomach. He couldn't drink around Joshua. He might never drink again.

"How did you even find the place?" Bel asked, pouring two fingers into the glass and then adding a third. "I researched it for years and I never got close."

"Leshe had a map. William Leshe, the man who took us there." Daniel paused, but Bel didn't seem to recognize the name. Leshe had gotten wealthy in pharmaceuticals, from what he'd been able to dig up during some off-hours when his research wasn't being monitored, but wasn't a public figure. How he'd known about the Consilium or Faeries—or these 'Lower Halls'—was still a mystery.

"Where did he get a *map*?" Bel murmured.

"The Shadowed Mab," Joshua supplied. "She knows the location. This fool gave them the key to reaching her."

When Daniel realized Joshua meant him, he started to protest, but the older man cut him off. "Check your phone."

"I don't *have* my phone."

Looking irritated, Joshua dug the device from his pocket and brought up the same picture he'd shown that morning, the photo of the document from Gracie's folder.

"That's a map?" Bel squinted at it.

"The tiny symbols form a code which allows a penitent safe passage into the Bie'lelhii."

"It was on a tablet that my—that the Consilium dug up in India." Daniel felt a weight of exhaustion settle on his shoulders. The words felt too defensive, like a frantic excuse.

Joshua clearly agreed.

"Typical," he sneered. "Always digging up things that should have been left alone."

"Maybe they shouldn't have been dumped over here like garbage!" Daniel snapped.

"Who?" Bel interrupted, forcing their attention back to her. "*Who* maybe tried to make a sacrifice to the Visitant imprisoned in the Lower Halls? Who went to the Bie'lelhii and somehow coerced a location from the mythical Shadowed Mab?"

"*Mythical*," Joshua repeated bitterly. "Perhaps if you haven't been imprisoned by her."

"Or nearly sacrificed to raise her," Daniel agreed.

Bel's gaze ping-ponged from one man to the other with her eyebrows raised, then she took another drag off her joint. She waved a dismissive hand at Joshua, saying, "Yours I know." Then she prompted Daniel, "Someone tried to raise Our Enduring Lady?" She put a dry twist on the epithet.

Joshua answered first: "Some mages summoned her out of the Bie'lelhii and hid her between the worlds several months ago."

"*Some mages* led by you!" Daniel wasn't about to let him write himself out of that story.

The electric kettle beeped but Bel didn't seem to hear it, staring dumbfounded at Joshua.

"The Lady could only be destroyed once she was made corporeal," Joshua said in a terse, defensive tone. "I meant to prevent *this very thing* from happening: some idiot using her to find the Lower Halls."

Rather than go further into his motives, he moved on with a sniff of annoyance. "Is that all that's necessary to deal with the creature in the Lower Halls? A sacrifice?"

"I just said thirteen *sounded* like a sacrifice," Bel managed, still taken aback. "I'd guess after so long you might need to send in a snack to wake the Visitant up. But I assume it would want to be freed. Tea bags are in the pantry there."

The non-sequitur threw Daniel until he realized that she was indicating the open door behind him. As the closest one to it, he assumed the direction had been aimed at him.

Inside, he found a small room, not just the set of shelves he'd expected. He tugged the light chain above his head. Large cardboard moving boxes had been stacked along the floor under the shelves, but otherwise it looked like a regular kitchen pantry. He scanned for anything resembling a box of tea bags, even though he doubted at this point that any of them would be partaking.

Something caught his attention—something shoved into a back corner of the top shelf, surrounded by half-used candles. It was taller than the other lumps of wax, but still looked somehow like it belonged there. Its squat, irregular form matched the other candles, but it shimmered as he focused on it. He had to blink a few times to be certain it was even real.

He reached for it, fingers curling back instinctively like touching it might hurt. Finally gaining the nerve to close his hand around it, the glamour of the misshapen candle dissipated, leaving smooth, cool stone.

It was almost too large to hold in one hand, the same pale colour as the stones around the door in the Lower Halls. The bottom of the diminutive stone obelisk had been carved with a familiar-looking pictogram, though it had a drip of wax running through it, supplied no doubt by the neighbouring candles.

Daniel traced the pictogram with his finger the same way he had in the tunnel, only this time scratching off the daub of wax. He didn't know this one, but his memory returned to the empty spots around the door in the Lower Halls, the dirty holes gaping like missing teeth.

"What's taking you so long?" Joshua snapped, appearing in the pantry doorway.

When he saw the stone in Daniel's hand, his eyes went wide. Face drained of colour, for once the old mage looked stunned.

"Oh, hell." Bel's voice came from over his shoulder, along with another exhaled puff of smoke. She elbowed her way around Joshua to snatch the stone from Daniel's hands. In the same movement, she shouldered Joshua into the pantry along with him and slammed the door shut, locking it.

"Bel!" Joshua spun to pound on the flimsy wooden door. Given the powers he'd demonstrated multiple times in the last day, he should have had enough force to splinter it without even trying, but his fists landed weakly.

Daniel backed as far as he could into the walk-in pantry to give Joshua room to batter the door, but the close quarters felt painful.

"You didn't tell me he'd see through glamour!" Bel snarled, voice strained as she dragged what sounded like a chair across the floor outside and wedged it under the door knob.

"You said the keys were lost. Irretrievable."

"It's only *one* of them!" Bel snapped. "It's harmless!"

"That is *not* harmless." In the harsh light of the single overhead bulb, Joshua looked older than before, gaunt. He took a deep, shaky breath and a step back from the door, then slashed a hand down.

The gesture put Daniel on guard for the curtain they'd walked through earlier. He anticipated the blinding white light, but nothing happened.

"Damn it!" The old mage made the gesture again, then tried a third time with both hands. He snarled in the direction of a cardboard box that sat on the floor under the lowest shelf, then pressed his back to the door and sank into a crouch.

Daniel flipped the box lid open. It was full of stacked iron rods—probably the type of thing Bel melted down in her forge out back.

"I'm sorry." Her voice came again from beyond the door, adding offhandedly, "Kind of. But I can't have you running off and telling the Court—or your *William Leshe*, whoever that is—about this key. At least not before I dispose of it."

Her voice faded at the end of the sentence, footsteps retreating. A sound like the back door opening and shutting. After another few moments, the distant rumble of a car engine came through, then receded into silence.

19

I REALIZED TOO LATE that I should have brought Saskia's file into the little interview room I'd created. Then I'd have had something to do with my hands instead of just shifting awkwardly in the plush, overstuffed chairs while we stared at each other.

Karl had seemed to immediately understand the reason for my heart-to-heart with Saskia, so once an unfamiliar woman had healed the bloody cuts and scrapes on my exposed skin with only a modicum of the usual pain, he'd shooed Eli and the guards away before making himself scarce too.

I hadn't wanted to stare at Saskia across the big, dusty living room full of its uncomfortable antique furniture, so I'd put Karl's boast about the house to the test and tried creating a new room in the elongated front hall. It wasn't that hard, actually. I just envisioned a cozy spot between the living room and the stairs where we could talk and Saskia couldn't draw her sword too easily. It ended up looking a little like an old-fashioned train compartment, something I'd seen in a movie, maybe. Or something the house liked.

"Why do you want to be Mab?" I asked.

She had the decency to look surprised, so I added, "We both know why your dad sent you here to talk to me, right? So, let's do this. Why do you want to be Mab?"

"If we both know why he sent me, then we both know this isn't a job interview," the haughty redcap scoffed. "You have no choice in the matter."

"I have a choice," I corrected, leaning back. "It's just a shitty choice. I wanted to get a better idea of just *how* shitty."

Saskia darkened, tucking a piece of her sleek, black hair behind her ear. Then she sighed, crossing one leg over the other and clasping her hands around the top knee to give me a breezy answer.

"For the power, of course. And the parties. In anticipation of your next dull question, my strength is my exceptional skill with a sword. As for weakness, why, I'd say human blood."

"*You've* been on job interviews?" I couldn't picture that. Mostly because I couldn't imagine Saskia attending to the boring, frustrating details of human life. "What, did Daddy kick you out of the hotel once as a life lesson or something?"

"I've experimented with a series of human experiences." She sat straighter in her chair. "It's intriguing, sometimes, to experience what these creatures do to pass their limited time drawing breath."

"Human cosplay."

"Oh, I don't dress up."

"Don't you?" I gestured to her pretty, oval face and the full-figured body that sported two arms and two legs. I didn't know what redcaps looked like without glamour, but Saskia was definitely dressed as human today.

That won me a quick, half-roll of her eyes, but the little twist of a smile didn't leave her lips.

"Got any plans to subjugate humanity to your capricious whims if you become Mab?" I asked.

"When," she corrected me. "And I have no plans to *yield* that subjugation, if that's what you mean."

"This is my world," I said. "I know it's just a fun little playground to you, but people matter. Humans matter."

"I agree. Their blood is fantastic."

Her annoying snark rang painfully familiar. I hated it.

"This world is a precious resource," Saskia said, conceding to my frustration. "Faeries who take too much, go too far, they're dealt with. We have laws and judgments too, you know. Or maybe you don't. In any event, we've survived for centuries in your world, unknown save by a very . . . *observant* few. This isn't a new situation."

"It is for me," I said, without meaning to. I couldn't wrap my mind around ethical rules to hunting humans, around permits and punishments. Around this being my life now.

"Jude, I don't know what you want me to say." My name off her lips startled me, especially in the almost-laughing manner she said it. She hadn't called me 'Your Highness' like everybody else, and it didn't feel like a slight. Despite hating her on principle and history, I couldn't help but appreciate that.

"I have no nefarious plans where humanity is concerned," Saskia said. "Nor do I expect to be Mab for some time yet. Your life is sacrosanct. You're safer now than you ever were as the heir. The power is in your blood."

"Didn't stop the tree people," I pointed out. "And flattery's not going to win you any points."

"As if I would." She levelled a frown at me, insulted.

"You want a drink?" I needed something to help me focus, to slow my mind, dull the unexpected anxieties that warred to take priority. Sitting here asking stupid questions and letting a manipulative redcap lie to my face wasn't going to cut it.

"Oh, yes." Saskia sat forward in her chair. "Martini, please."

"Fuck off." I snorted a laugh, leaning forward in my chair to open the cupboard at the bottom of the table beside me. I debated a moment, then pulled out a bottle of tequila and two shot glasses. I uncorked the bottle—never any liquor-store plastic wrap on these bottles in the Faerie safehouse—and started to pour.

Saskia pursed her lips, cocking an eyebrow. "Shots? Really?"

"You can sip if you want, princess."

She groaned, but accepted one of the glasses brimming with clear liquor. Holding it gingerly in her hand, she asked, "What's your preference? Cheers? Santé? Şerefe?"

"Bottoms up, bitch."

She gave me that one, clinking her glass against mine before throwing it back. I had to fight the part of me that wanted to be impressed as I hoisted my own. The burn of the alcohol and sweetness of the agave hit the back of my throat and I stifled a sigh of relief.

"Could have used a lime and salt." Saskia frowned at her empty glass. "My turn." She raised her voice and sang something that caused the door to open.

Eli peeked in, his gaze going to me. I gestured awkwardly to Saskia, and she gave a couple of lilting scale runs in Faerie language to make some demand I couldn't understand. My bodyguard showed no emotion being ordered around, though his eyes did dart back to me long enough for me to flash what I hoped was an apologetic look.

As soon as he'd closed the door, Saskia turned back to me. "You should get a more extensive staff. I suppose he'll do tending bar for now."

"He doesn't even drink," I said, still uncomfortable not only at her casually ordering Eli around, but the way he'd just given in.

She shrugged. "Then he'll delegate."

"Do you have a staff?"

"Occasionally." She twitched, as if bracing herself for further interrogation on that point, but I already knew she was a little rich girl. Of course she had a staff—she'd probably had everything provided to her her whole life.

"What was that last one, anyway?" I struggled to remember and pronounce the last toast she'd given. "Şerefe?"

"It's Turkish."

"Why?"

"Because you're Turkish."

"No, I'm not. My maternal grandmother was Turkish. I'm Canadian."

"What do Canadians say, then?" Saskia leaned forward, resting one elbow on her knee.

"I don't know. Probably 'cheers' or 'santé.' What do Faeries say?"

She sang a few notes back to me that sounded a little like. "*Ooh-hoo-sharah.*"

"Seriously?" I frowned at her.

"Yes."

"Well, you can add this to your notes about humans: it's weird to know the ethnicity of somebody's grandparents in polite conversation. I guess that means you've got a file on me?"

"It only seemed fair." She sat back in her chair with a shrug.

"I didn't read yours."

"Of course not." A shadow flickered across her face, almost too fast to catch, but her tone soured. "Why *would* you?"

"Give me the rundown. I'll compare for lies later."

"What do you want to know?" She sighed heavily. "My mother died in childbirth, as many of our species do. I have no siblings. I was raised in privilege. I've moved between worlds my whole life, as my father's business interests and my own hobbies dictated."

"Tell me about your mother."

"Did you miss the bit where I never met her? My father doesn't talk about her much."

A sharp knock sounded at the door then it popped open without awaiting a summons. A new man arrived with two small, icy martinis on a silver platter. Eli had, in fact, delegated.

He offered one to me first, then to Saskia, then finally slipped out and left us alone.

"No olive, huh?" I eyed the tiny, perfect drink in my hand.

"Never in the first martini." She tilted her glass toward mine. "*Ooh-hoo-sharah.*"

"Are you making me swear? Or say something stupid? Because I can have you killed."

She laughed, a sparkling, genuine thing that probably came from that first tequila shot. It made me brace myself, then try to repeat her tones.

"*Ooh-hoo-sharah.*"

Saskia toasted me and we both sipped our martinis. "It's gin in a fancy glass," I concluded, but took another sip anyway, savouring the freezing bite. "Go on—your dad doesn't talk about your mom."

"Are you asking about him or about me?"

"Mostly you. If you let some weakness about him slip, though, I'll take it."

"I'd be the first to admit that he can be . . . abrasive." She studied the fingernail of her free hand on the carved armrest of her chair. "I understand that. We're both stubborn, both certain we're right. Often, he is, but on the rare occasion that he is not, he doesn't back down gracefully. It takes some finesse."

"You're so sure he's not the one finessing you?"

She returned an expression of such familiar disdain and skepticism that I could almost feel it melting onto my own face.

We sat in silence for another minute or so before she said, "I don't like you much. And I don't think you like me. However, I'm not your enemy. Don't get me wrong, I would enjoy that, but circumstances have conspired to render it impossible, and I believe I've more than proved it today."

"Do you *want* to be Mab?" The sharp pricks of anxiety had melted away and my skin was starting to feel pleasantly warm. The question had been buzzing in my chest for a while and it would have escaped me with or without the lubrication of alcohol.

Saskia hesitated, lips half-parted as if words had come to her automatically but she'd managed to rethink them.

"Yes." When she caught my surprised look, she added, "You have this stupid, romantic notion that only someone who shuns power is worthy of it. It's ridiculous."

Before I could protest, she continued, "I relish the idea of experience, the new and rare. The throne is a position few can ever aspire to."

"You can't cosplay at being Mab."

"Isn't that what you're doing?" She paused to let that sink in, then continued, "Don't take this the wrong way, but I will be a better Mab than you are."

"Is there a *right* way to take that?" She was probably correct, though. She knew the rules, the customs. She'd grown up in Faerie *and* in the human world. She could walk in both. Raised, presumably, by her tricky bastard of a father, she could definitely navigate Faerie politics. Whether she could navigate my world was the question, much less whether she could keep it safe.

She'd certainly saved *my* ass today, anyway, taking out six tree creatures to my one. I'd distracted the last one, though—maybe we could split that one.

It was probably the tequila and gin shots—sorry, martinis—talking, but she seemed sincere. Saskia had never struck me as the type to lie or scheme like her father—she just laid out her desires and made them happen. Why the hell did I want to adopt this bitchy, dilettantish mess of daddy issues as my daughter and heir?

For one thing, she was *here*—it would be so easy. I'd be at least fifty percent off the hook on this whole Mab situation. A voice in my head that sounded too much like Abe's warned that that probably wasn't the best thing to base my choice on.

But he wasn't the one chained to a throne. If I adopted Saskia, Karl and the others would no doubt be happy to shower Mab responsibilities on her. She was a full-blood Faerie, a skilled warrior from a fancy, noble family. She was the queen they wanted. They'd probably be glad to put me in their rearview, magical Mab power or not.

As if she knew what I was thinking, Saskia slouched back in her chair and nodded to her empty glass.

"What's next?"

20

"Move," Daniel said. The sharpness in his tone made Joshua glower at him, but the older man deigned to slide to one side and give him access to the pantry door. It opened inward, but he didn't know how strong the lock was and it wouldn't budge with the chair wedged under the knob outside. Trying to ram it from this side wouldn't do any good, at least not without some supernatural strength like Joshua's.

The mage had huddled into the furthest corner from the boxes, knees pulled to his chest, forehead resting on them, like he wanted to put all the distance he could between his body and the boxes of iron. He lifted his head just enough that Daniel could see his eyes. Their normally disturbing electric green had been dulled by the proximity of the poison.

"You're enjoying this, I suppose," he said.

"Not even a little." Daniel turned his attention to the door's hinges. They were on the inside, accessible. They'd been painted over, but with a flat-head screwdriver and a hammer, or their equivalents, he might be able to pry the pins out. "You didn't feel the iron in here?" he challenged. "You didn't keep your distance?"

"Bel's got iron all over this property."

"Then why did we come here?"

Joshua laughed, a bitter, hollow sound in the small space, and leaned back against the shelf behind him, knocking a box of granola bars to the floor.

"I'd have thought you better-versed in the inevitable conclusion of misplaced trust by now," he murmured.

"Well, I don't just sit around and wallow in it," Daniel shot back.

The older man didn't rise to that needling, so he turned to search the pantry shelves for something he could use to knock the hinge pins out. He took more care rifling through the items now that he knew Bel might have hidden dangerous objects among the mundane ones.

"What does it do?" he demanded. "That stone? Obviously it goes into the door frame of the Lower Halls and—what?"

No response.

Leshe and his team hadn't needed the stones to walk into the chamber, and Daniel himself had stepped into it and out of it. They were all human, though. Maybe the stones only had to be in place for Antagonists to enter? Or for the creature locked inside to exit?

"How did Bel glamour it?" Daniel persisted. Peppering Joshua with questions would either eventually win him an answer or else piss the old mage off enough to make him blow the door off the pantry. "Isn't she human?"

"Human like you."

"Meaning *what*?"

"You've dabbled too much in magic, cursed yourself with a second sight." Terse irritation fused through Joshua's voice. "Had there recently been a proper Mab in power, you'd already be dead. Bel's done the same, cultivated a grasp of Faerie magic."

"Why's she not *dead*, then?" Daniel rifled through the canned goods on a bottom shelf, testing for the heaviest one to use as a hammer.

"Because she's nobody to the Court. She kept her head down and didn't make a habit of showing it off—making wards and breaking glamour, like you and your mother."

"What?" Daniel flinched, dropping a can of tomatoes.

"That ward you made had Maggie's fingerprints all over it."

"You knew my mother?" Joshua had intimated that before, last fall, when he'd encountered the ward on Daniel's door. Daniel had found the instructions for the protective spell buried in his mother's notebooks of paranoid nonsense. The ones she'd kept in the years spent dragging her children from place to place in a muddled, terrified haze, always running from something.

He'd always assumed that something was his father. Maybe not.

"You're lucky you take after her." Joshua's statement wasn't really an answer. "Otherwise I'd have dispatched you immediately."

"So, you liked her?" Daniel pressed. "You were, what, friends?"

"Friends." Joshua echoed the word with distaste. "With the Ferryman's issue? Hardly."

"What's a Ferryman?"

"She was smart not to tell you." The older man's tone changed, taking on a strange hint of nostalgia. "Smart and brave, Maggie. Betrayed her own people—her own family—for Miranda and me." He quieted, ruminating on his words before concluding, "She was a good woman, before she lost her mind and married that fanatic who fathered you."

The Antagonist's sneer stirred a pang of loyalty for his father that Daniel hated.

"You've got the order wrong," he said, bracing himself to dive to one side in case that set the mage off to free them from the pantry.

The huddled form in the corner only hissed a sound that was part laughter and part frustration.

"Given her choice of partner, my sequence of events is more believable."

He wasn't getting angry or any closer to freeing them. Talking in circles around the past wasn't going to accomplish anything. Maybe the iron would be more helpful. Daniel gingerly opened the top box and rifled through the metal pieces, looking for something narrow enough to hold against the hinge pin so he could hammer it out with the can.

"Who made the sacrifice to the . . . the Visitant?" He stumbled on Bel's preferred term to avoid trying to pronounce the Faerie words. "You know or you've got a suspicion."

"Not who—*what*." Joshua hesitated as if he might not say more. Finally, his voice dropping to a reluctant growl, he muttered, "Humans have called it many things. Puer mendacem, twin stranger, fetch, changeling."

"None of those are real." Daniel tucked the smallest piece of iron from the box under his arm. It was too large for his purpose of breaking out of the closet, but he wanted to keep a weapon handy.

"Correct," Joshua murmured. "They're folktales in the fictional cosmology of your deceased collaborators. But she—*it*—is real."

"Then how is your 'changeling' any different from a regular shapeshifter?" That won him a contemptuous look that reminded him of the one his father had often given him when he'd dared to speak out of turn.

"This creature doesn't just *mimic*," Joshua said, voice thin and brittle. "It *becomes*. It *is*. A mere shapeshifter can appear as an ogre, as a bird, as a—a mushroom. But even in such forms, it wouldn't have the strength of an ogre, the grace of a bird in flight, the poison of a fungus. This creature, though, *becomes* those things, in all attributes. When it takes a form, it can be unrecognizable from the true version. It has spent centuries becoming anything it likes."

And it just gets crazier. Daniel tried to bite back his skepticism, to keep Joshua talking.

"The thing's immortal?"

"In practice, not by design. Whether she began as a shapeshifter or a healer, I don't know, but she's combined them. She can survive a fatal injury by turning herself into someone else who isn't injured. No other healers—no other shapeshifters—can do that."

"How do you know? You've seen her do it?"

"I thought I'd killed her," Joshua muttered. "Before I knew what she was."

A sound came from the kitchen, glass breaking. The distant creak of the back door's hinges filtered haltingly through the pantry.

Joshua twitched in his amorphous huddle and then raised his head with a low growl.

Given that reaction and his own palpable unease, Daniel doubted it was Bel returning. He pressed himself back against the shelves as a grinding sound signalled the chair being torn from under the knob outside.

The wood splintered around the lock as something yanked the door directly backwards. Daniel stumbled back, nearly colliding with Joshua, who had swept to his feet with more speed than he'd demonstrated in the last thirty minutes.

"Leave," the mage hissed at the three hulking forms who stood in the gaping doorway, back-lit by the sunlight streaming through the kitchen windows.

Daniel expected them to attack Joshua, but instead one of the figures reached in and fingers closed around *his* upper arm like a steel vice. He lost his grip on the piece of iron as the intruder yanked him out of the pantry and tossed him across the kitchen.

He caught himself against Bel's counter, turning to see two men and one woman in nondescript black attire. Their faces were blank—bored, even—but one man raised a phone in his hand and angled it at Daniel, tapping the screen. Had he taken a *photo*? Why?

Without waiting to find out, Daniel broke for the door. He didn't make it more than two steps before burning pain ripped through his left leg. His muscles gave out, sending him to the floor in a heap, but he barely felt the jarring impact because a fist smashed into his face. Another blow from the side drove his head harder into the laminate.

Then the pain was gone, leaving him cold and dazed, gasping on the floor. Quiet footsteps crossed the kitchen and someone hauled him to his feet. One person held him upright and another pinned his arms, securing his wrists with zip-ties. They worked briskly and without comment, as if he weren't a living thing they were manhandling, just an object they meant to bundle up.

He managed to look down at his leg. No blood on his jeans, no tears in the fabric—no wounds. His face didn't hurt either. His vision was fine. The stunning pain had vanished as quickly as it had flooded his body.

His captors didn't seem to have claws, and they hadn't been near enough to punch him once he was on the floor. It couldn't have been them attacking because he'd *known* the pain. He'd remembered each twinge intimately the moment they hit—the burning agony of an Antagonist's talons slicing through the back of his leg last summer, Jude's wild, furious punches rattling his skull the winter before that.

Time had blotted out the details from his memory, but *something* had just brought them rocketing back into his body with visceral clarity, disjointed and out of order, then made them disappear just as quickly.

Daniel looked to the man holding the phone, realizing with a jolt that a thin, black cord snaked from the bottom of the phone into the mottled skin at the man's wrist, where it seemed to join the large vein there.

"That is *my* hostage," Joshua broke in, voice thin with annoyance. There was no real threat in his tired, half-hearted effort.

Daniel grunted a wordless objection as the captor behind him threw some kind of dark hood over his head, then his stomach dropped when the man told Joshua, "The Archduke will compensate you."

21

After two more fancy snifters of whisky—my choice, procured from the cupboard in the room without calling in any assistance—Saskia and I were both sunk deeply into our seats, pleasantly buzzed and actually getting along.

"Tell me about your power," I said. "What's drinking blood get you?"

"I don't *drink* blood." She grimaced. "I draw part of my life essence from it, through contact with my—" Another foreign word I didn't know. Probably meant her tuque. Or socks—or whatever form her talisman took. "It's a sacred ritual with a strict code of ethics," she finished.

"Thralling people into giving you their blood. Very ethical."

"You're being wilfully reductive." Her eyes narrowed. "Yes, there are bad actors on my side. More, in fact, as the Mab's power has waned in the last year, but—"

"You mean, without strong leadership to tell them not to, Faeries will slaughter humans for all their worth? I'm shocked."

"Hypocrite."

She wasn't wrong. I was resorting to simplistic, human-centred arguments I'd definitely picked up at the Consilium. Blame it on the whisky. Or the tequila, or the martini—there was a familiar song in there somewhere. Why had tossing back drinks felt like a good idea for this interview?

Because when did it not?

"We don't *slaughter*," Saskia muttered. "That's just ludicrous. I've never killed a human. There would be no point. Most of them are perfectly harmless."

"You tried to hack *my* head off with your sword the first time we met," I returned. After I'd interrupted her feeding on a dazed human last Halloween, she'd stalked me to the bus stop afterwards, intent on murdering me in an alley.

"You're not human," she pointed out. "And that was territorial, plus you impugned my honour." A pause, then she added archly, "Had I known that you would eventually ascend to the position of Mab, I would have acted differently."

"So, if I make you my heir, are you going to try and assassinate me?"

"Are you serious? We went *into battle* together."

I kept from repeating the key word in surprise. I was sure she didn't mean today, given she'd done most of the work. She had to mean last year, but going up against the small contingent of rogue mages and one half-trapped, pissed-off Shade Queen didn't constitute an actual *battle* in my mind. I couldn't escape the memory of Saskia drawing her blood-letting dagger and her long, graceful sword and rushing terrible odds as my ally, though. Her zeal for running headfirst into the fray had endeared her to me then, and again today.

"We did that for different reasons," I said. "You went to please your father. I went to save people I care about."

"If you only ever fought side-by-side with people who shared your motives, nothing would get done."

"Sounds like a solid way to run a kingdom."

"It wouldn't serve my purposes to assassinate you." Saskia deflated in annoyance. "I have things to do before becoming Mab, things to wrap up. I'd guess I'm booked at least two years out. I *might* be able to set up an assassination at that point but I can't imagine it would be my best effort."

I had to fight not to reward her sarcasm with a laugh. Pithy, smart—she probably *would* be a better Mab than me. So why did it still feel like I'd be turning a flock of sheep over to a wolf?

"I know you haven't chosen me of your own free will." Saskia's voice quieted, and I snapped my attention back to her, startled. "Whatever my father's holding over you, I'll see that he stops."

"That's the whisky talking."

"It's the tequila, actually. You believe I went into battle at your side just to please him? Battle is the only place where I can win on merit alone."

That felt like a cheap, last-ditch effort to trap me. Poor little rich girl just wanting to achieve something on her own, without relying on her father's money, power, reputation or arm-twisting manipulation.

But uncertainty niggled at me.

"Just so we're clear," I said, "you're offering to go up against your father for me?"

"I'm offering to handle the situation," she said coolly, "as someone better practised in dealing with him."

"And what happens when there's a 'situation' between us that you can't *handle*? Divided loyalty is never a good time." Aubrie came into my mind without warning. His pitting my loyalty to him against the Consilium had almost wrecked me, not to mention everybody else in his way.

"That should never happen once you're joined as consorts," Saskia returned. "My father's as loyal to you as I am. You're the Mab."

"He threatened to raise an army against me a couple hours ago."

"It was probably just a bluff."

"Right." I got to my feet, wanting suddenly to escape and talk to Abe. Maybe Ilse. Maybe even read those thick files Karl had given me. Saskia hadn't raised any *new* red flags, but I still wasn't sure I could bring myself to make her my heir.

When we emerged from my little den, Eli was beside the door. He fell into step behind me but I barely noticed, biting back a frustrated growl.

Declan waited for us in the foyer, reclining in a distinctly throne-like chair he must have created, reading his phone.

"How did your meeting go?" He got to his feet, tucking the phone in a pocket.

"Fine," I said, as his daughter politely understated, "Well."

"Excellent." His enthusiasm made me flinch. I cringed further when he focused on me to add, "I've brought you something."

"Me?" Fear flared in my chest. "I don't think I—"

"You'll grant me a great boon by agreeing to adopt my beloved Saskia as your own," he continued. "I wanted to be sure I reciprocated appropriately." He gestured toward the antique-ridden living room closer to the front door.

I shot a glance at Saskia to gauge her reaction. I didn't want her to know what was going on, but on the other hand, I didn't want her to *not* know. If someone was going to stab me in the back, they ought to at least know why they'd brought the knife.

She looked just as baffled as I was. Great.

22

My stomach flip-flopped as I followed Declan into the living room where he and I had argued earlier. Saskia didn't follow, and neither did Eli, but I'd have bet he took up the same position outside the door.

Inside, on the rickety sofa, a person sat huddled forward with their arms pinned behind their body. A dark, fabric hood had been pulled over their head.

"What the hell?" I started.

As if he hadn't heard me, Declan strode to the sofa and yanked off the hood with a theatrical flourish that made my stomach twist.

Daniel winced against the sudden light, blinking rapidly as he jerked away. The force of his movement rattled the rickety sofa under him. He looked dazed and overwhelmed, sporting maybe a week's growth of beard, with his dark hair mussed from the hood. His t-shirt was torn at the neckline too, probably from whatever fight had landed him here.

Rooted to my spot, my brain screamed to do a hundred things at once: throw my arms around him, break the bonds around his wrists, apologize, shout at Declan, pummel Declan with both fists—

"As I said, finding your pet was no difficulty." The Archduke gave me a brief, mocking bow.

"I didn't *ask* you to—"

"Consider it a wedding gift, according to your human custom." His shit-eating grin helped my shock give way to bitter understanding, then anger. I almost missed his chiding followup: "I would be remiss, however, if I didn't advise you to invest in some training. Your lack of control over his feral aggression is frankly astonishing."

"I'll *show* you fucking feral." Daniel lunged to his feet.

"Proving my point with both hands tied behind his back." Declan didn't flinch, holding his ground with his usual self-important condescension. He smirked at me. "I'd be happy to lend a strong hand if you prefer—"

"Get out!" I managed to choke the words out around the fury that had built in my throat, just barely keeping myself from launching a fist at his smug face.

"The reunion's made you emotional." He stepped toward the door, deftly out of my reach. "I understand."

As soon as he'd left the room and closed the door behind him, I rolled my shoulders to slough off my intense desire to punch something. My fury seeped back into the general anxiety that had been buzzing in my stomach for hours. Calmer, in full position of my faculties, I had to face Daniel.

"Hi. Sorry. Fuck." I managed my reactions in quick succession. Then I fumbled through the desk beside the fireplace and yanked the first drawer open to find a blade I'd willed into being.

Daniel was still facing the door like he expected it to open back up and an army to sweep in. He flinched when I took the knife to the plastic bonds around his wrists. Then he looked at me warily, like he wasn't quite sure I was real.

Affection swelled in my chest, but I tried to stifle it. I rifled through my brain for some acceptable explanation and settled on, "This wasn't my idea."

"Did he say 'wedding gift'?"

Fuck my actual life.

"No." I regretted that. "Yes." Jaw tight, I managed the truth. "Declan called in that favour I owed him."

Daniel winced, rubbing the red marks ringing his wrists. It wasn't just the pain—he clearly remembered the situation that had forced me to make the bargain with the Archduke in the first place. The situation *he'd* caused.

I opened my mouth to make excuses, to absolve him and place the blame squarely on myself. *I didn't make that deal to save you. I just didn't want Declan screwing with me.* But that was a lie. Daniel already knew it. I'd made the bargain with that smug asshole to save his life.

"He, uh, showed up just about the second I became Mab," I finished weakly.

"That's true, then?"

"That I'm the Mab? Seems like it's gone on too long to be a nightmare." I bit back an inappropriate laugh. "Where'd *you* hear it?"

"Joshua."

My father's name made my heart stutter in my chest. A flood of questions strangled me, but I managed to cough just one up.

"How?"

Daniel grimaced. "It's a long story."

"Well, there's no Internet here, so I've got time." When he didn't rise to that, I couldn't hold back. "Did Joshua come after you at the hospital?" Guilt swelled like a lump in my throat. "I *told* him to leave you alone. Wait, did he—? Have you been with him since November?"

"No." Daniel didn't sound as relieved about that as he should have been. He looked distracted and uncertain as he studied the room around us. "No. He just showed up last night."

"Why?"

"He said he'd get an audience with you if he—if I—" He stopped with a sharp intake of breath, as if simultaneously embarrassed by and resenting the answer he'd left off.

"He's right," I admitted. A dozen emotions squirmed in my guts. It took all of my willpower to keep from closing the distance between us and folding my body into Daniel's. He probably wouldn't appreciate that after having been kidnapped, blindfolded, bound and dragged into my presence, but I still wanted to do it.

I'd left him in a hospital in Toronto last fall, unconscious. Recovering from the emergency surgery that had repaired the hole in his stomach that Gordon the mage had stabbed through him merely to reach me. I'd walked away from him before he woke, thinking that would be better—give Danny a fighting chance at a normal life without me and the dangerous Faeries in my orbit. I couldn't let somebody go through him again to get to me.

So much for that.

"It's good to see you," I managed.

"You too." His tone didn't quite match the naked, honest desire I'd been hoping for.

We both tensed at a gentle rap on the door.

"Jude?" Abe's voice sent relief shuddering through me.

I crossed the room and pulled it open just enough that I could see out, in case he had other company with him. Just Eli, who still stood with his back to the wall beside the door, pretending not to listen.

"Thought you'd want to know—" Abe started, then stopped, eyeing the narrow opening we faced each other through. "What's going on?"

I pushed the door a little wider.

Surprise wasn't usually in the cowboy's repertoire but he did a double-take when he saw my unexpected guest.

"Well, damn." He looked from me to Daniel and back again. "How'd, uh, this happen?"

"Declan's being a creep," I muttered. "As usual." I didn't want to rehash the grinning bastard's cheerfully backing me into a corner. It would just make me angry all over again. "I have to have a quick convo with Karl," I told Abe. "Can you play host for a minute?"

I pushed the door wider and poked my head out to make sure Declan wasn't hanging around the foyer behind Abe, waiting to gloat some more.

Besides Eli, only one guard lingered by the front door. No Declan, no Karl, no Saskia. Perfect.

"Eli, can you go announce me to Karl?" I hated the request, but I didn't want to explain Daniel's presence to my bodyguard, who was sure to have questions.

"As you wish." That felt like a dig at me for letting Saskia boss him around, but I ignored it in favour of my more pressing anxiety.

Once Eli had disappeared into Karl's office, I gestured for Daniel to follow me.

He stopped short in the doorway. He looked around the foyer and understated, "You've redecorated."

Something in the flat certainty of his voice indicated that he'd been in this spot before. He'd been in the basement, that I remembered. A sadistic siren had tied him up down there and tortured him last summer. I'd gotten him out in one piece, but we hadn't escaped this way. No—we had, last fall. I'd used the house to transport us from the cave where Joshua had trapped us to Daniel's apartment in Montreal.

"Yeah, it's a fortress now," I concluded. "But the kitchen's still normal, and Karl doesn't really go in there." I had to fight to keep from taking his hand, twining my fingers through his to reassure myself that he was real. He was really here.

"Who's Karl?" He seemed reluctant to ask.

"He's a lot of people," Abe muttered. The joke didn't land for Daniel, of course, but I appreciated it.

"The Ubran," I added. "My seven royal advisers rolled up into one human-shaped burrito. Uh, not literally."

Beginning to feel giddy with anxiety—a feeling I was *not* used to—I added, "Go with Abe. I won't be long. Then we'll . . . figure something out."

23

In the dining room, Karl was still working on paperwork. Why the hell was there so much paperwork in Faerie? Was it just because of me, or did all Mab changeovers merit this much bureaucracy?

"Thanks, Eli," I said, as my bodyguard shut the door behind me to leave me alone with my royal advisers, who were already on their feet. "Got a minute, Karl?"

"Of course, Your Highness."

"Can you just call me Jude?"

"We would prefer not to."

"Fine." I wasn't going to argue too hard since the next words out of my mouth were, "I need a favour."

"It is never a mere favour to fulfill your command; it is our pleasure. We are at your disposal."

That should have made me feel better about what I was about to ask, but it didn't.

"My father mentioned he'd done something to me and my mother—a binding. Can you make one? For a human, I mean? Like, to keep them safe from Faerie interference?"

"If you wish." Karl's tone was guarded but if I'd offended them, they didn't show it.

"What do you need?" I expected them to demand a name, a pint of blood, a precise latitude and longitude, maybe some rare herb that only grew on a mountain in Bulgaria.

Instead, they blinked and bowed their head, turning it slightly as if listening to someone behind them.

I waited a minute, not knowing whether I was supposed to say anything else. "Karl?"

No response.

After another minute of weird silence, I leaned in and slowly waved a hand to get their attention.

Karl snapped their head back up to meet my eyes and we both jumped, startled.

"Our apologies, Your Highness," they said. "Seven voices and only one conduit to you can make for . . . delays. It's something we're working on."

They were arguing in their head. Great.

They continued smoothly, "We require nothing more than your will and the name of the human."

"You don't need blood or . . . or hair or fingernails or something?"

"Bindings are old, heavy power, beyond mere contagious magic. It's dependent only on your will and a modicum of your own power."

"Wait, it uses *my* power?" Joshua hadn't mentioned the rules.

"The spell draws its initial spark from your magic, yes." I'd half-expected Karl to be snide explaining this to me, but their tone was neutral, informative. "You're merely the catalyst. Once cast, it takes on its own power."

"And if I die?"

"The binding would remain unchanged. Nor can you break it yourself."

That tracked with what Joshua had indicated, at least. My mind raced to unearth more questions, more caveats and gotchas.

"So there's nothing . . . nothing I need to get?" I stammered. "No potion I need to—?"

"No quests nor subterfuge." Karl eyed me. "You wouldn't be the first Mab who wanted to protect a human

. . . companion. Is the person in question here in this house?"

The touch of flatness in their tone indicated that they already knew the answer, but it was nice of them to pretend they didn't.

"Yes," I said.

"That helps narrow things down considerably. I'll need the full name, written in your hand, then I will deliver it to our royal mages, who will cast the binding."

"How long does that take?"

"No time at all. They are always on call for you, and need merely see the note written in your hand through a mirror."

Karl produced—of all things—an index card and a pen, and presented them to me. "Full name," they prompted. "As complete as you know it. You'll need to put your intention to protect into each letter."

"My what?"

"Your intent. Your desire to shield this individual from harm."

What was my intent? The jittery, sick feeling of guilt I got when I looked at Daniel—the certainty that I owed him something I'd never be able to repay? The unbidden swell of desire that tightened my lungs, the desperation to be closer to him? The cold terror that clenched my stomach at the idea of having him disappear again?

All of the above, probably.

I put pen to paper and wrote: *Daniel Andrew Cain.* I'd seen his driver's license once last year, when he'd been paying for our drinks or something. It had only contained his middle initial and I'd been certain at the time that the 'A' stood for Alan. That would have fit his father so damn well, bestowing his own name as an inescapable part of his son's rather than giving his egotism away so blatantly by fully designating a junior version.

But, no, Daniel had corrected me when I'd asked. He'd seemed relieved in the same way I'd been, laughing it off in an unconvincing way. He'd told me that, as the oldest child, it had fallen to his sister to take that hit: Grace Alanna.

Where *was* Grace, anyway? Had Joshua hurt her? Threatened Riley or Ted to get to Daniel? I'd need to get three more bindings made. I didn't know Riley's middle name.

Better see if the first one even takes. Relax.

I half-expected Karl to balk as they accepted the card and read the name. I braced myself for their refusal, but they just gave a brisk nod and said, "It will be done immediately."

"Thanks." The word didn't feel adequate, and at the same time it made Karl twitch, like I shouldn't have deigned to use it.

"It is our pleasure to serve," they repeated.

24

"You're bringing to mind that saying about a long-tailed cat in a room full of rocking chairs," Abe remarked.

"A cat in a what?" Daniel's attention was fixed on the blank wall where Soren had created a basement door so many months ago.

"Never mind." Abe winced at the memory despite himself. "You hungry?"

"No."

Normally, he tried to keep from reading others' emotions too deeply. Sometimes he couldn't help it, though. Here he had to chalk it up to both a healthy mix of curiosity on his own part plus Daniel's inability to tamp down the flood of uncertainty, anxiety and raw fear that kept washing through him in waves.

"You don't believe that nonsense about eating and drinking in Faerie, do you?" Abe knew he'd hit the nail on the head as soon as he said the words. "Gettin' stuck here if you do? Nah, I've eaten and drunk plenty in this kitchen and never had any problem stepping out that door whenever I please."

"Well, you're . . . you," Daniel said, shoulders still drawn uncomfortably in.

"A good-looking, rule-breaking rogue?"

"Not human." The younger man gave him a weary look, indicating that the sarcasm wasn't appreciated.

"Human enough, believe you me, for hexes and spells to work on me." Abe pulled out a chair at the table and gestured to the one across from him. "You look like hell, son."

"Don't—" Daniel winced, reconsidering before finishing in a strained, halting tone, ". . . call me that. You don't have to act like—" He sank into the chair on the other side of the table. "We're not friends."

"And *this* is how I find out?" Abe feigned surprise.

His corny humour finally made a dent. Daniel fought back a smile, then his eyes darted back to the empty kitchen wall beside the refrigerator. He seemed to realize his fixation a second later because he aimed his gaze at the window over Abe's shoulder.

"Jude's really the Mab?" he finally asked. "How does that work?"

"Not too well, so far. You know our girl—she's not exactly Miss Congeniality. And the Court's got no idea what to do with her either. I expect they'll work it out, eventually."

"And she's . . ." Daniel hesitated, not wanting to speak the words. With another sharp breath, he forced himself on. "She's *marrying* Raj?"

"That's a new one on me too," Abe muttered. "What I understand, though, this consort thing's not much like marriage over here. More like a, uh, business partnership, I guess. Miranda hadn't taken a consort yet. I don't know much about it."

"I'm sure Raj jumped on the opportunity."

"A snake quick to strike, I'll give him that." Abe kept his voice low. With the Ubran and palace guards here, these walls had more ears than they ever had before.

"Can you let me out of here?" Daniel lowered his voice too, as if the same thought had struck him. "This house, this . . . plane, whatever it is?"

"Ubran took all the doors away. Not sure I can leave myself." Abe regretted the clumsy attempt at commiseration when it won him a dark, dubious look in response. "No use running," he conceded. "Raj'll find you if he wants to."

"How? You gave me my blood back."

"Blood only helped 'em find you faster. There's other spells, more complicated ones. Beyond my capabilities."

"So you lied to me." Daniel seized on the answer with a surprising ferocity.

"You wanted your blood back and I gave it to you." Abe bridled his annoyance. "*And* got that incantation excised from your head before it killed you. Or killed somebody else." He waited while the other man's initial resentment faded into a weary acceptance.

"Can you read Raj?" Daniel asked. "Why am I here? Is it just to fuck with Jude?"

"I don't read minds," Abe reminded him patiently. "But I can wager a guess why he's interested in you. You broke his thrall."

"I didn't—"

"I watched you do it."

The Archduke was well-trained in hiding his emotions from empaths, but Abe had caught a sudden flash of amazement—and anger—right when Daniel had fought his way out of the trance back in Singapore last November.

Raj had shut it down immediately, played it off and resumed mocking Jude. The situation had escalated from there and Abe had forgotten it himself, given the battle and carnage that had followed.

"Don't know if he didn't expect that sort of reflex from a human or just not from a compatriot of Jude's, but either way, it surprised him," he added. "Man like that doesn't like to be surprised."

"*What* reflex?" Daniel demanded. The insistent denial woven into the question made Abe frown.

"Breaking a thrall's not *standard* for humans," he said.

"Am I still human?" The younger man slumped back against the back of his chair, looking defeated.

"Far as I can tell."

"Joshua said I'd cursed myself with a second sight."

"Wouldn't trust a word that asshole says." It was Abe's turn to tense. He managed to keep his voice from lowering to a growl. "Where'd you see him?"

"He came after me before Raj did."

"What for?"

"Same reason."

A lie. Hesitation and anxiety twined with a thread of guilt. Maybe not a complete falsehood, but not the whole truth.

"Are you reading me?" Daniel asked.

The blunt question sent uneasiness prickling along Abe's shoulders. Given their recent topic of conversation, it felt extra loaded.

"Little bit," he admitted. "Can't help it. Was that just a paranoid guess or did you—" He wasn't sure how to phrase it. "—feel something?"

"An *educated* guess," Daniel corrected dryly. "What would I feel?"

"Don't rightly know. I've got no experience with this 'second sight' business." Abe sighed. "You want to get some sleep? Bedroom's upstairs."

"No." Daniel flinched. There was probably some other Consilium proscription again falling asleep in the land of Faerie too.

Abe almost pointed out that the younger man had already been unconscious for hours in this house when Soren had captured him last summer and it hadn't affected his ability to come and go. But that wasn't really true, and anyway, Daniel clearly didn't need the reminder.

"So, the plan's just to sit here quietly 'til something kills you?" he concluded. When he got no answer but a half-hearted glower, he concluded, "As plans go, I've heard worse. Though not many."

"What plans?" Jude's voice, a note too cheerful, startled them both. She entered the kitchen, shutting the door heavily behind herself like she meant to keep something out, then bee-lined for the nearest cupboard. She sat down a moment later with a bottle of Scotch and three shot glasses.

Abe waved her off and to his surprise, Daniel did too.

"Seriously? It's the good stuff." Jude held up the bottle as if he hadn't noticed the label.

"No. Thanks." Cloudy dread flooded the younger man as he shook his head.

When Abe felt Jude's baffled gaze dart to him, he gave what he hoped was an almost imperceptible shake of his head.

"Suit yourselves." She didn't press the issue, but still poured herself a glass of amber liquid with a defiant flourish.

Her emotions spiked in bursts around her too-easy movements. Evasion. She'd done something she didn't want them to know about. It lit on her like a beacon, the mix of sharp, yellow anxiety, greyish-pink shame and a sickly greenish flare of . . . maybe hope? Odd combination.

The colours dulled after she threw back the liquor in one gulp. Slouching against her chair, she looked to Daniel. "Let's hear this 'long story' about how you ended up running around with Joshua, then."

25

"I DON'T KNOW WHERE to start." Daniel tightened his fingers to stifle the twitch that made him want to reach for the Scotch bottle. He could smell the familiar, peaty scent and practically feel the warm numbness it would produce on his tongue.

"Beginning's always a classic," Abe offered.

"Where's Grace?" Jude asked.

"I don't know." The question sent a pang through him and the answer was even harder. "I haven't seen her since last November. Since we sent her to the hospital with Riley."

"But that was before—" Jude paused, dark eyes narrowing. She tried again, "She went with the doctor to your hospital room. I saw her leave, after they told us you were, um, alive." She shifted in her chair, fighting not to cringe, and hastily poured herself another glass of Scotch.

"When I woke up in the hospital, Tess Foster was there," Daniel said. "She and one of her colleagues. And I was apparently under arrest."

Jude balked. "Those guys who cornered us in the alley? You said they weren't cops."

"They're not, but they had believable badges and persuasive rhetoric. Convinced the hospital staff."

"But they didn't catch Grace?"

"No." Daniel nearly sighed with the relief that still went through him. "I don't know where she and Ted went, but they hadn't found them by the time—" He stopped. "That's getting ahead of things."

He had no choice but to give them the short version of the last five months—waking in the hospital, Tess Foster explaining the terms of his new, non-negotiable employment, introducing him to Leshe.

"So, you just dove back into the bookwork?" Jude asked. Her tone wasn't laced with any accusation, but it irked Daniel anyway.

"No. I told Leshe to jump off a bridge. He threatened to send me to prison."

"For *what*?"

"Murder. The agents Joshua's wraith killed." There had been witnesses who could place Daniel at the bookstore where the attack had occurred—the clerk and probably another customer too. A prosecutor would have had a tough time proving he'd massacred the three agents with the physical strength and animal ferocity the wraith had used, but he hadn't been confident enough to call Leshe's bluff.

To his surprise, Jude accepted that answer and let him continue outlining the months of recuperation and translating Leshe's texts in the hospital. He left out his useless escape attempts and the days spent in solitary confinement as he told her about working in an unpleasant office building somewhere in Montreal, sleeping on a cot in the office. Finally, he got to the trip across the American border and down to Phoenix in the back of a truck with Marianne and her team, the dig camp, the doors in the tunnel.

"Joshua came after me last night." Daniel finally got to Jude's initial question.

"At the dig?"

"No. The dig went . . ." He paused to find a euphemism for the massacre. He couldn't. "Everybody died.

Something in there killed them." *N'ellaphalen thrace.* Bel's words rung in his head and he thought of the sinister, half-formed presence at the back of the chamber. "I ran. Joshua found me . . . after."

"How?" Jude demanded.

"He didn't say. But he could tell, somehow, that I'd been somewhere . . . he said *enchanted.* And he was interested."

"So, you just told him all about it? You need to start holding grudges again."

"I didn't have a choice," Daniel said tersely. "He's more powerful than he was last year." He reluctantly explained the compulsion her father had demonstrated, glossed over the supposed map on his phone, Joshua's sudden fury resulting in shattered glass, and moved onto Bel.

Even there, he couldn't tell them the full truth. He relayed all that Bel had said about the potential sacrifice and the Visitant, but left out the stone obelisk he'd found in her pantry—one of four lost keys to the Lower Halls. He needed to keep the story simple for now. Simpl*er,* anyway.

"Then your fiancé's minions broke in, threw a bag over my head and brought me here," he finished.

"Don't use that word." Jude poured herself a third shot of Scotch but didn't drink it. "Or that tone."

Daniel bristled. "What *tone?*"

"We ought to bring Karl in on this," Abe cut in.

"*Joshua* is not a credible source," Jude argued.

"I don't think he's entirely sane," Daniel started. "But—"

"Karl and the Ubran can judge that," Abe said, still focused on Jude. "And they're a hell of a lot better placed to handle a crazy mage."

"Oh, I don't know. I knocked him off that balcony pretty easily." Jude stretched her fingers before letting them curl into a fist.

Abe seemed to interpret her continued silence as his cue to depart. He retrieved his hat from the table and gave them both a nod before he headed out.

"You probably shouldn't be in here when he brings Karl back." Jude deflated against her chair, studying her fingers on the table. "Want me to find you a bedroom?"

"No," Daniel said, too quickly. He amended, "Can I just—Can you send me home?" The question felt awkward and pathetic.

"Where's *home*?" She didn't look up, but one side of her mouth curled in a smile of disbelief.

"I don't know. Montreal." Leshe had found and frozen his bank accounts, credit cards, even the hidden ones. He'd probably known about the handful of apartments and hideouts too. But Leshe was dead, and sleeping on the street was preferable to closing his eyes in this house.

The place felt wrong. Uncanny, like a hiss of static at the edge of his mind. Eerie and dangerous in a different way than just the memory of being tied to a post and stabbed with vicious glee by a siren with a row of shark teeth.

"I shouldn't have left you in the hospital," Jude said.

"I wasn't expecting you to be there." Daniel realized the unintentional harshness in the words too late.

"It just seemed best for everybody if I took off. For you, mostly. It was so—"

"Jude." He tried to interrupt.

"Yeah," she agreed bitterly. "Classic fucking Jude."

"You couldn't have done anything if you'd stayed." She'd have been captured too, outnumbered. And who knew what Leshe would have tried to do with her, with her powers? The thought made Daniel's chest tighten.

Voices came from outside the kitchen door and Jude tensed, her eyes going wide. She sprang up from the table and hurried over, pushing it open to interrupt a conversation between a man and a woman.

"Dee," Jude said, her voice suddenly chagrined as she held the door open to allow them entry. "How are you?"

"I'm okay." The woman was short, with olive skin and dark curls laced with bright pink. "I had this really awful dream, though. When I woke up, I was hungry and I, um, didn't know how to make drawer toast."

"It's okay." Jude gestured her inside, agitated for some reason. "This is Daniel. Daniel, Diana Garcia, my roommate. Ex-roommate? Current fortress-mate, I guess." She indicated the man behind Diana. "And that's Eli, my, uh, bodyguard."

Said bodyguard seemed not to have heard her introductions. He studied Daniel with sharp, narrowed eyes.

"Cain," he concluded in a contemptuous growl.

"Yep." Jude shot the word like a challenge, but Daniel braced himself for an attack.

Eli only frowned, darting a mildly disapproving glance to Jude before concluding stiffly, "I see."

"Hi," Diana said, casting a brief, puzzled look between Eli and Daniel as if not understanding the sudden tension. She extended a hand. "Nice to meet you. You like a . . . werewolf or something?"

Jude stifled a laugh. "He's human."

Nice that she still thought so. The memory of Abe's less-than-solid reply to his similar question earlier made Daniel suck in a deep breath to counteract a sudden tightness in his lungs.

"Oh, thank *fuck*." Diana slapped both hands over her mouth, looking startled then guilty about her relieved exclamation. "No offence," she told Jude. "Just . . . it's nice to have another normal person here?"

"Danny's not normal," Jude scoffed.

Her casual joke grated painfully against Eli's watchful, yellow-eyed glare. The unwavering scorn radiating from that side of the room made Daniel think of Raj's predatory sneer, of Joshua's off-handed violence. He didn't belong here, trying to get comfortable in the predators' lair.

Diana—whoever the hell she was—seemed clueless and Jude wanted to pretend that if she didn't notice the discomfort, that would make it go away for all of them. Like she could force her new, regal will on the whole room.

When Daniel's eyes landed on the empty spot beside the refrigerator, he broke. He shot to his feet, startling the others.

"I'll take the bedroom." He needed to be alone, even if was in this damnable house.

"Upstairs." Jude tried to hide the fact that she'd been chewing on her lower lip as she nodded toward the kitchen doorway. "Second door on the left."

26

"I DIDN'T MEAN TO scare him off," Diana said, turning to watch Daniel hustle out of the kitchen.

"Trust me, it wasn't you," I said, glancing to Eli.

"Oh, I know." She snorted. "I was trying to be polite." She moved past me to drop into the seat Abe had vacated. "You've been living like a nun the whole time I've known you. Figured you were pining after somebody."

The word *pining* made my shoulders twitch, but I couldn't tell if it was an instinct to hunch in or to throw a punch.

"Ex-nay," I hissed, given we had a small audience. Fighting warmth in my cheeks, I glanced to Eli. "Can you ask someone to, uh, summon Joshua for me?"

My bodyguard raised a dubious eyebrow, but inclined his head in agreement, so I went for broke and added, "And I need you to keep an eye on Daniel."

"On—?" He glanced over his shoulder in surprise before giving me a hard look. "You expect an attack?"

"A what? No. I just think there's a really good chance he'll try to slip out of here. I mean, it's what I would do."

Eli frowned at me but didn't blow my cover by pointing out it was what I *had* done. I didn't really know if Diana was serious in thinking the whole escape had been a dream, but he seemed to think so.

"I don't think it's in your best interest to have me protecting a human," he started.

"Sure, but of the two of us, who's the Mab?" The words came out sharper than I'd meant them. I was on edge about Diana's appearance—about being such an asshole that I'd actually forgotten about my unconscious roommate upstairs.

My bodyguard snapped his mouth shut. His icy gaze betrayed his annoyance but he didn't argue, lowering his head in an almost sarcastic bow and disappearing as he stepped backwards into the doorway.

"So this . . . dream." I hated how much I wanted to play into that fiction, but it felt shitty lying to Diana. "Did it involve us going out a window back to Tofino and then getting attacked by a bunch of tree people on Highway Four?"

"Damn it." Diana frowned at me, swallowing hard. "It was real?"

"Yeah. Sorry."

"No, it's—" She sighed deeply, leaning forward. "Not good, but, I mean—it's . . ." She trailed off again.

"It's shitty," I supplied, then words spilled from my lips almost too fast to consider. "Karl sent some guards to clean up the, uh, mess, and they brought our stuff back. I'm sorry about your car, though—I'll buy you a new one."

Diana considered that for a moment, then sighed. "Maybe I should go home. It seems like you have a lot on your hands right now."

"Dee, you can't. Your home is my home. My father knows where that home is."

"You just told Eli to 'summon' him."

"Yeah, *here*, where we're surrounded by armed guards." I took a deep breath, hating the words as they came out. It felt like they'd come from Ilse—or Eli himself. "People have probably seen you with me. Maybe the wrong people." I thought of the tree people. They were all dead, but who knew if there were more of them, if they had some way of communicating with the rest of their . . . grove?

What was a group of tree people called? "I promise," I finished, "I'll find a way to send you home safely."

Diana was quiet longer than I'd expected, and I braced myself for an argument that would make me feel like a hypocrite. Instead, she nodded and studied the kitchen cabinets.

"Does the whole house work like drawer toast?" she asked. "Like, do I just open a cupboard and find flour? I need to bake something."

"Yep, that's exactly how it works. You want help?" I'd come home more than once to Diana rolling out dough or scraping golden-browned pastries off a cookie sheet. Baking seemed to serve as a form of stress relief for her, some way to control her environment.

"I really don't." She gave me a brave smile. "I think I need to, uh, process a little bit. On my own." She got to her feet and used one hand to gesture me out by wiggling her fingers. Probably in an effort to sound less freaked out than she was, she intoned, "Begone. There'll be buns in the morning."

Then she hesitated, glancing toward the window over the sink to venture, "Is 'morning' even a thing here?"

"Ish?" I agreed.

With Diana scouring the cupboards for her baking ingredients, I headed into the hallway. I'd half-expected to encounter Eli, Abe or Ilse with new reports of catastrophes that would force me back into the kitchen, back on defence.

Two guards stood at the far end of the hallway. They didn't address me as I swung around the banister of the stairs, though both bowed their heads low.

Upstairs, I gave a hasty knock on the door to the bedroom I'd staked out and then slipped inside.

Daniel jerked to his feet from where he'd been sitting on the bed. When he saw it was me, he sank back down onto the edge of the mattress.

"What are you doing?" he asked, as I shut the door and headed around the bed to the opposite side.

"It's my room," I said. "I claimed it last night. Conjured up a TV and everything." I picked up the remote from the bedside table and aimed it at the small screen to make my point.

"But you told me to come in here. Second door on the left."

"Yep." I let him solve that puzzle on his own.

He gave me a warning look that made me suppress a smile but rather than argue further, he muttered, "How do you even get TV signal here?"

"It only plays *Law & Order*." I turned on the screen to demonstrate. A new episode was just starting.

"Why?" On the scale of 'mystified by the house' to 'so very over it,' Daniel was edging toward the latter.

"Because that's what I expect to be on?" That had been my conclusion last night after puzzling it over with my bottle of whisky. "The house seems driven by expectation. I don't really understand how it works."

"Yet you've got no problem manipulating it." He stood, and for a moment, I thought he was going to leave. It sounded like he meant the words as an insult or an accusation, but I didn't see why.

"Nope." I shrugged. Noting the torn fabric of his navy blue t-shirt, I conjured another one that was identical but intact from the drawer in the bedside table.

Daniel caught it when I tossed it to him, turning it over in his hands like he wasn't quite sure what it was.

I gestured to the ripped collar on his current one. When he hesitated, it seemed like he would refuse, toss it back to me, but after he rubbed the fabric between his fingers for a second, he gave in and started to strip the torn shirt off.

I tried to politely keep my eyes on the TV screen but they betrayed me, darting over to glimpse my ex's exposed arms and chest. His familiar body was lean but solid, and the lines of muscle seemed more defined than I remembered—probably thanks to the weeks of hard labour he'd mentioned. Four pinkish scars running across the top of his left shoulder caught my attention—those had to be the wounds from a griffin's claws in Niagara Falls last summer. Further down, another jagged blemish peeked out above the waistband of his jeans. There was probably a twin scar on his back, from the sword Gordon had stabbed through him last fall.

I'd have had a matching one just below my ribs too, if Joshua hadn't used Abe to heal me right there on the spot. I tossed my head to shake off the queasy memory and plopped down on the other side of the mattress. Settling against the headboard and kicking my feet up, I changed the channel to find the same show at the same moment in its episode.

"What am I doing here?" Daniel asked, tugging the t-shirt down. Now the only scar of his I could see was the one I knew best—the little one below his eyebrow. The one I'd given him the last time we'd slept in the same bed.

"Watching bad TV and taking a breather between near-death experiences." That answer won me the exact vexed look I'd expected, so I added, "You seem to get into trouble when I'm not around."

"Jude, this isn't a *joke*." He rubbed his forehead with one hand, looking drained and overwhelmed as he started to pace in front of the door. "This is the Court. I don't belong here."

Me either. I almost brought up the daring tale of my earlier escape attempt, but I didn't want to give him ideas. I could have mentioned the binding too, but he'd either be pissed off about it or else he'd use it as an excuse to disappear from my life again—*while* being pissed off about it. I'd tell him later. When I had confirmation that the palace mages had even gone through with casting the spell.

"Look, I can conjure up a TV somewhere else." I started to get up, feeling suddenly ridiculous. I was coming on too strong, trying to punch this weird, immense situation into something normal-sized and play it off as routine. *Fun*, even. Because being with Daniel again made things better, at least for me.

"Don't go." He stopped short, looking alarmed by his own words. "I mean, it's your room."

"Okay." I sat back down too quickly, my legs folding because they hadn't wanted to move in the first place.

He sighed and moved to sit on the edge of the bed again, still facing the door but at least within my reach now. He seemed calmer, like arguing with me had put him a little more in his element.

I had to stifle an unwelcome yawn, studying the scene on TV for a minute. Between my ill-fated escape, getting my ass rescued by Saskia and then going toe to toe with her on a few too many shots, followed by Daniel's appearance and his whole story of Joshua's bullshit, it felt like it had been days since I'd woken up here and kicked over my bottle of whisky.

Where was that bottle, anyway?

When I realized Daniel was still focused on the door, I prodded, "You want me to mute this so you can have your panic attack in peace?"

"I'm not—" He gave me a dirty look over his shoulder. At least it took his attention off the door for a few seconds.

"Look," I said, "I don't know if you noticed, but I'm kind of the boss around here. Stick with me, you'll be fine."

27

"Oh, for the love of—" Bel's dismayed voice drifted from the kitchen into the living room where Joshua had gone to regather his strength. He'd needed to put some distance between himself and her boxes of iron. Luckily, there didn't seem to be much of the damned metal at the front of the house.

He listened to her moving through the next room, probably examining the shattered window in the back door, the splintered pantry door. One of the Archduke's thugs had used enough force to pull the deadbolt directly through the wooden frame.

Bel didn't look surprised to see him as she crossed the threshold into the living room.

"I knew leaving you here was a terrible idea."

"I didn't do any of that." He didn't have the energy to be annoyed.

"Then who the hell did? Not your little tag-along." She took a quick look around as if she'd missed Daniel in the room.

"The Archduke will compensate you for the trouble." Joshua's bitter recitation nearly stirred a dry laugh in his chest, but the hint of mirth didn't catch.

"Where do I send *that* bill?" Bel snorted, folding her arms across her chest.

"Were it not for all of this damnable iron—" Joshua waved a hand toward the back of her house. "—I'd have torn those fools limb from limb and sent them back to Raj in a bloody jumble. Perhaps even before they did any property damage."

"Why the hell were you dragging Alan Cain's spawn along with you, anyway?"

"Judith's fond of him."

"That must be galling." Bel rolled her eyes. "Seems like it'd have been easier to just stick to the traditional 'shovel and a shotgun' speech, though."

"The . . . what?" Had he come into the middle of a different conversation? Joshua tried to trace the exchange back. Sometimes he lost time. Maybe he'd missed something.

"You know, that fatherly 'touch my daughter and I'll bury you' nonsense." Bel switched to an affected, gruff voice for her explanation, but it made no further sense.

Some strange human custom, perhaps.

"I have no interest in policing who Judith spends time with," Joshua said. "She's solidly mastered the art of making her own mistakes. One of which is her refusal to speak to me, hence—"

"Oh! Hence you kidnapped her boyfriend?" Bel barked a laugh as the understanding dawned on her. "Brilliant parenting, that. Ten of ten, no notes."

"I needed to get her attention." Joshua bristled at her derision. "There was little other choice. She's well-protected now."

When Bel raised her eyebrows to press the unasked question, he admitted reluctantly, "Judith has become, of late, the Mab."

Bel's eyes widened. She gaped at him, frozen. Finally, she sank into the nearest armchair, digging into her pocket to extract a thin, white stick and a lighter. She put the joint between her lips and lit it.

"Why do you insist on using that noxious weed?" Joshua snapped.

"It relaxes me."

"It numbs you."

"You should try it." She eyed him again, tapping the ash into a tray beside her. "Might help you cut down on the kidnapping and torture."

"I didn't hurt him." The baseless accusation piqued him more than it should have. "Why are you so concerned with—how did you put it—the *spawn* of a Consilium director? They were no friends of yours."

"Human solidarity." She shrugged.

"You'd claim solidarity with any creature as long as it was against me."

"Probably." Bel rested her head against the back of the overstuffed chair and regarded the ceiling.

"Were I you, I'd be less concerned with that fool's well-being than with the fact that he knows about your apocalyptic contraband," Joshua shot back.

The fear that flashed through Bel's eyes made him regret the flippancy, but he didn't apologize. She knew better, knew holding onto that stone was stupid and dangerous. She was the expert on the goddamn Lower Halls, after all.

"Damn it," she muttered, and took another drag on her joint.

"Why the hell do you *have* that thing?" Joshua snarled. "And why *out*, where anyone could find it?"

"Because not *anyone* could." She glowered at him, as if Daniel walking into her pantry had been his doing, not hers.

"You work in iron." Joshua couldn't banish the curtness from his voice but he attempted to modulate it. "You might have made somewhere more secure for the damn thing, like a *locked* box."

"Yeah? Where's the first place somebody breaking into my house would look?" Bel challenged. "The iron bloody treasure chest, you think?"

Why would she expect someone to break into her home? Joshua couldn't make sense of it. It was worthless to argue, though. She would quarrel merely to spite him.

"Where is it now?" he asked.

"Safe."

"I doubt that." He paused to see if she would offer more, then asked, "Do you have the others?"

"No." With an exhale, she studied her joint as if to avoid his eyes. "Why do you want them?"

"I don't. But there are things out there that do, and if it's not well-hidden—" Joshua's muscles twitched, trying to prompt him to his feet. He wanted to be moving, pacing, perhaps tearing this house apart until he found something she cared about deeply enough to reveal her new hiding place for the keystone.

He took a breath to relax. An ache had started at the base of his skull and his muscles felt too tight.

Bel's eyebrows quirked into a knowing expression.

"You short out the electricity in my neighbourhood again," she warned, "you'll regret it."

He winced inwardly at the embarrassing memory. She'd been his first stop after he'd left the Bie'lelhii, the only person he could think of to take him in in this strange world, fifteen years after he'd last left it. He hadn't been in full control of his power then—he'd all but shattered the nearest electrical grid.

That she could feel the frustrated power emanating from him now was concerning. He made a second effort, stronger this time, to tamp it down.

"That was an unanticipated reaction," he said.

"Reaction to *what*? Don't say seeing me, because I won't believe you."

"Freedom, then. Warmth. Life. My return to this world. Take your pick." He waved a hand to disperse the sweet smoke. "I need you sober."

She managed a laugh around the joint pressed between her lips, lighting the burnt end again just to show she could.

"You *need* me?" she echoed, exhaling and rolling the thin paper packet between two fingers. "Now that you've burned every other bridge? Well, let me drop everything."

"What do you want me to say?" Joshua snarled, teetering on the verge of breaking something. "I *heartily* regret leaving."

"I bet you do." She rolled her eyes, then reluctantly, without meeting his, conceded, "What could you possibly need from me?"

"Assuming you'll still refuse to tell me where you hid the keystone—"

"Correct."

"—at least tell me where you found it."

"Why? They were all hidden separately, far from each other. There's no clue to finding the others."

"I don't want to find the others. I want to find the creature that's seeking them."

28

Daniel flinched awake to gunshots. The bedroom came into focus and he realized the noise had come from the television on the opposite wall. A police procedural was still running at a low volume.

Jude lay beside him on the bed, asleep and breathing evenly. Her head rested on his upper arm and she'd snaked a hand across his stomach. The television remote had fallen from her grip onto the mattress.

He retrieved it and shut the TV off. The sudden silence seemed to echo but she didn't twitch. However long they'd accidentally slept, it seemed to have been enough to clear Daniel's mind so that he just felt tense, too alert.

And thirsty. Slowly, so as not to wake Jude, he extricated himself from her embrace and got to his feet. He couldn't give words to the certainty that if he left this room, the walls would shift, the space would grow or contract. The hallway might just extend forever like some demented variation on a house of mirrors.

Steeling his nerves, he retrieved his work boots from the floor but didn't put them on until he was outside the room, with the door firmly shut again.

The door across the hall stood ajar so he approached it carefully, half-expecting something to pop out at him. It looked like a bathroom, the light already on. He shut the door and turned on the faucet, letting it run and staring down at the clear water. It looked safe. He didn't have many other options.

Abe had said it was safe. Hell, Jude had conjured up a bottle of Scotch out of nowhere and downed shots in the kitchen with no ill effects. Not to mention that bizarre television, and the t-shirt he was currently wearing.

But Jude and Abe were different—they had Antagonist blood. *Faerie.* Daniel tried to loosen the admittedly pejorative Consilium term from his brain. Using that wasn't going to win him any friends here, and it had started to feel uncomfortable on his tongue.

Torn between feeling overly cautious and not paranoid enough, he put his fingers under the tap. The water felt normal, cold. Liquid. What had he expected? Some strange odour, an oily feel? He cupped his hands under the faucet and took a tentative drink that turned into three more handfuls.

He lifted his head and winced at the mirror over the sink. He hadn't seen his reflection in a while—no mirrors in the dig camp. The circles under his eyes were dark enough to be bruises. At least his short, scruffy beard hid the cuts he'd made trying to shave without a mirror in the first couple of days at camp.

He could probably pull a razor out of the nearest drawer the way Jude had summoned the Scotch, but he didn't want to risk spilling blood in this house again. Not that it had mattered—Joshua had found him without it. Raj too.

He wiped his hands dry on his jeans and returned to the hall, considering a retreat to the bedroom where Jude was probably still dozing. The thought of her warm body, that protective arm thrown over him, almost made him return. The queasiness in his stomach and his skittering heart told him he wouldn't sleep again, though, even with her assurances for his safety, so he headed for the stairs instead.

At the bottom, he stood in the foyer that had elongated since the last time he'd been here with Jude and Abe, leaping from apartment to hospital. The front door was now a good four or five metres away from the stairs, leaving room for several new, closed doors along the walls.

A human-shaped figure eyed him from the front door at the end of the hall, where it stood in some approximation of parade rest. A door guard, probably. It didn't move to approach him or call out and, better yet, didn't shout for reinforcements, so he turned as if he'd intended to head for the kitchen all along.

Someone else was already there.

"Hey." Diana stood at the table, arms streaked to the elbow with white powder, pressing dough with a long, wooden rolling pin. "Can't sleep either?" she asked.

As if reading agreement in his lack of an answer, she understated, "It's a weird place. Like, I have zero idea what time it is. I think my circadian rhythms are already screwed up."

She set the rolling pin aside and picked up a knife. "I bake when I'm nervous," she explained, running the blade through the soft, beige dough.

Daniel didn't know what to say to any of that. He felt dazed, lost in a dream. After creeping around the house expecting to be seized at any moment, here was Diana, who had probably just walked calmly down the stairs, decided to head to the kitchen and conjured up all of these tools and ingredients because she was 'nervous.'

"What?" She stopped cutting and he realized he'd been staring at her.

"Sorry." He moved his gaze purposefully, but his eyes landed on the empty wall beside the refrigerator. Even though the basement door wasn't there anymore, the thought of the dim, stale place still brought a sick wave of fear crashing over his head.

"You okay?" Diana prompted. "You went kind of . . . pale?"

"I'm fine. Tired. A little . . . confused."

"About what?"

"All of this. And you."

"Me?" She looked startled, then gave a short, jittery laugh. "Oh, you mean Jude doesn't usually bring her friends home?"

Home. That word felt wrong.

"I don't know what she does with her friends." Daniel narrowly avoided admitting that he'd never really known Jude to *have* friends. Apart from Aubrie.

"Well, I'm guessing she doesn't climb into their beds." Diana's tone turned dry, as if prodding for information by teasing. The way Gracie used to do. "Not that you guys were obvious or anything," she assured him. "I just don't think you'd be wandering around Bizarro House if you had your own room."

She drew the knife through the dough and something on the back of her left hand caught his attention. A pale, irregular scar stood out against her tan skin.

"What happened?" he asked, nodding to it.

Her expression changed when she followed his eyes, like she hadn't remembered the scar was there.

"Brushed some coral surfing in Hawaii."

"You surf?" The scar seemed familiar—why?

"I do," she agreed, her focus back on the table. "Not, like, professionally, but it helps me blow off steam. Hard to be stressed when you're trying to catch a wave. Kind of like baking, actually. Makes you pour your attention into something kind of persnickety instead of stressing out."

"I didn't know coral caused scars like that." The scar didn't look like it had come from a brush against something—more like a puncture through the centre of her hand that had spider-webbed out.

"Yeah, well, fire coral's a bitch."

"You were in Hawaii recently, then? Over the winter?"

Diana chuckled and her eyes darted over his shoulder, as if she were checking that they weren't being overheard from the door.

"Leshe was right," she finally concluded, "you *are* annoyingly pedantic."

No, she hadn't said that. He must have imagined it. Maybe he'd started hallucinating from exhaustion or the disconcerting house, or—

"Guess I should have expected you'd recognize your own handiwork." She lifted her scarred hand again to study it with a strange, disconnected interest, like it wasn't even hers.

"My . . . what?" Daniel couldn't catch his breath.

The keen animosity that came into Diana's eyes belonged to someone else. He'd seen it before—Tess Foster hissing at him in pain and rage after he'd stabbed her with a piece of iron in his apartment last fall.

"It's honestly a *lot* harder than I expected to keep track of what everybody knows," Diana admitted. Her smile widened, turning dangerous. "Especially since *you're* supposed to be dead with the rest of Leshe's little worker ants."

"You knew Leshe?" Daniel heard his own voice but the words still didn't make sense. He couldn't wrestle his thoughts into a coherent narrative that squared with this woman standing in front of him.

"Unfortunately. Such a tedious asshole, right? But he had the money and he had the army, so I had to compromise a little." She gestured her frustration with the knife still in one hand. "Dumbass wasn't even supposed to go *into* the Lower Halls, just have his little team dig up the door for me."

"But you're h—" Daniel almost didn't get the word out. Despite how wrong it suddenly felt, he managed, "—human."

"Isn't it awesome?" She grinned, running her fingers through the flour on the table. "It took *years* to master the form. Almost impossible to avoid those little shivery tingles Faeries get when they sense each other. Magic is so goddamn *touchy*."

"Who are you?" Daniel demanded.

"Not really a 'who,' but let's just say, nobody who matters to you anymore." She punctuated that by flicking her fingers at his face, sending a puff of flour into his eyes.

When he raised his hands to block it, coughing against the sudden powder in the air, she jammed the knife into his stomach.

Daniel stumbled back, colliding with a kitchen chair. He'd felt the blade's impact, the sudden pressure in his abdomen and the powerful upward thrust, but there wasn't any pain. He searched blindly for a wound, trying to understand why he couldn't feel anything where she'd stabbed him. Was he already in shock?

His hand came away from his stomach clean. No blood. He rubbed the flour from his eyes and searched the front of his shirt. No rips or tears. He didn't seem to have a scratch on him.

Doubled-up on the other side of the kitchen, Diana glared at him with a shock that mirrored his own. She still held the knife but had both hands pressed to her own midsection, where red was rapidly staining her clothing. She studied her free hand, rubbing her own blood between her fingers, then without warning, she burst into a cackle of laughter.

"That little bitch put a *binding* on you?"

Head still spinning, Daniel managed another shaky step back, shoving the chair between them as if that would ward her off.

"Goddamn it," Diana muttered, straightening her back with a grimace as her laughter trailed off. She tossed the knife down on the table, where its stained blade gleamed under the overhead light, then she examined the tear down the front of her shirt. The blood slicking her exposed skin seemed to bead up suddenly and draw back into the wound, like a video reversing. The slash in her flesh knit back together.

"Human fucking blood," she muttered, frowning at one red hand. She held it up as if expecting Daniel to commiserate with what seemed like atonally mild annoyance for the situation. "Human enough to fool anybody but an antiquated reflective spell, anyway."

Daniel dug his fingernails into the back of the chair in front of him. The room darkened and tilted. He squeezed his eyes shut, trying to bring his racing heart under control, make sense of anything. He couldn't let his guard down, not with this unknown adversary. He had to open his eyes to be sure the woman—creature—across the room wasn't coming at him.

She hadn't moved, wiping her bloody, floured hands ineffectually on her jeans. A strangely liquid ripple went through her body like a twitch, but she remained Diana.

"You know I've never actually had a scar?" she mused, still frowning down at her hand. The pale scar tissue shone through the rusty blood. "And I've had some run-ins with iron before. It's never marked me up like this. How'd you manage it?"

"You're Joshua's changeling," Daniel managed.

She started to roll her eyes as if offended by the guess, but she stiffened when he finished, "The thing that wants to open the Lower Halls with those obelisks."

Her gaze narrowed with sudden interest, making his stomach clench.

"You've seen one of the keystones," she said.

Damn it. He struggled to backtrack. "I don't—"

"*Obelisk* is such a specific word," she continued, tone still calm and casual. "And the holes in the door frame are square from the outside, so it's not an easy guess to make. How would you know the keystones are shaped that way unless you'd seen one?"

"It was in a book," Daniel stammered.

"Oh, no, those stones aren't recorded." Diana's smile widened. "The Court didn't want anyone searching for them or trying to re-fashion them. There are no drawings anywhere, no descriptions."

"Then how do *you* know what they look like?"

"Because I have a few. And I'm looking to complete the set."

29

SASKIA GNAWED ON THE side of my neck with sharp fangs like a vampire. It didn't hurt as much as it should have. Mostly, it was just annoying. The dull pain stayed with me as I blinked awake and realized it was a crick in my neck. I'd fallen asleep in a weird position, propped against something.

Against Daniel. Right, I'd been snuggling against him when I fell asleep. That was embarrassing. Not as embarrassing as him currently being MIA, though.

I rubbed my neck with one hand and stretched, then unfolded myself from the bed. The TV was off and I was alone in the room. I didn't want to go looking for Daniel right away—hello, overbearing—but I couldn't quell the concern that shivered through me. Despite my little brag about running the joint, this house was a minefield with Declan and Karl and who knew who else from the Faerie Court coming and going.

I peeked out into the hallway, then did a cursory glance into the nearest open doors. Bathroom, another bedroom, both empty.

"Eli?" I called quietly.

My bodyguard appeared one door down.

"He's downstairs." He answered my question without my having to ask it, then added thinly, "The first floor seemed amply guarded to dissuade his running away."

"Thanks."

Eli followed me to the stairs. We'd only made it halfway down before the noise of a sharp crash and scuffle from the back of the house reached us.

Eli pulled me back and forced his way ahead of me, but I vaulted over the banister. I shifted gravity to land easily on my feet and reached the floor before him but not before the two guards that surged out of a door underneath the stairs that I'd never seen before.

They tried to keep me from getting through, but I punched one hard in the shoulder and it surprised him enough to face me. As he turned, I slipped by him.

In the kitchen, Daniel stood behind a chair, his face streaked with white, one hand to his stomach, looking stunned. The kitchen table was dusted with flour and baking stuff lay all over it.

Diana stood at the back door—when the hell had *that* come back? And why was the front of her shirt stained bright red? Her expression was dark, a malicious amusement that I'd never seen before on her features.

"Talk later," she told Daniel, before she yanked the door open and disappeared through.

Eli shoved past me and the guards to dart after her, but stopped short on the threshold with a sharp gasp. He hesitated only an instant before slamming the door shut as if something in the distance were running at him.

The wall around it surged in like liquid, spilling over the frame and covering it. The door disappeared again.

"What the hell?" I managed.

"The Old Roads." Eli sounded stunned. "She's—how?" Without looking at us, he kept his back against the spot where the door had been like he might still have to brace it against something on the other side.

"Your Highness," one of the guards started, "you shouldn't be in here."

"I'm fine," I assured him. "Everything's fine."

"No, it's not." Eli and Daniel spoke at the same time.

"Somebody explain." I hated how shrill my voice got, but damn it, I was exhausted and nobody was making sense.

"She stabbed me." Daniel examined the front of his shirt, running a hand over the fabric as if he expected to find something out of place.

"*Diana?*" I choked out.

Rather than answer, he rubbed away some of the flour on his face. He studied it on his fingers before finally meeting my eyes.

"What's a binding?" he asked.

My stomach did a wild somersault. "Go back to how Diana stabbed you," I stammered. "Where? How? W-why?"

"She wasn't human." He said the words like an experiment.

"Of course she was!" I snapped. "I never felt—I mean, I would have *known.*"

"She had the scar I gave Tess Foster."

"The what? What does Tess Foster have to do with anything?" Was I losing my mind? How was some random ex-Consilium psycho related to any of this?

I tried to calm down. "Look, I know the scar you're talking about. Dee got it surfing in Hawaii. Coral or something."

"She sent Leshe and his people into the Lower Halls," Daniel said. The certainty in his voice made my throat tighten.

Eli made it worse.

"She can't have been human." He still looked winded, slumped against the wall where the door had been, wearing a thousand-yard stare. "At least, whatever ran out of here wasn't. A human couldn't use the Old Roads so easily."

"What are the Old Roads?"

"A surreptitious means of transport through the human world. Through the . . . well, the space between."

"That weird white space outside?"

"Not exactly." He grimaced. "More like a layer . . . over it. One step closer to your world. Most Faerie can't even use them anymore. They're ancient. Abandoned." Eli's eyes darted over his shoulder. "There are things on them that . . . shouldn't exist anymore."

"How would Diana know Leshe?" I asked Daniel. "You think she worked for him?"

"I think he worked for her." He still sounded dazed, as if considering the words for the first time as he said them. "She's not Diana Garcia. Just like Gracie said Tess Foster wasn't Tess Foster. It's—" He sighed, sagging against the chair. "Joshua was right. It's some kind of . . . shapeshifter. Changeling."

Joshua was right. Not words I loved, especially coming from Daniel. Couldn't we just hop back to '*I don't think he's sane*'?

"Get out," I told the unfamiliar guards.

They hesitated, eyes darting to Eli, so I spun to give him the brunt of my glare and made a pointed gesture toward the opposite door, including him in the order. "Out."

My bodyguard twitched like he might insist on staying to hold up the wall, but finally he crossed the room. He paused at my shoulder, putting his head close to mine and lowering his voice to murmur,

"This isn't safe. Those two were clearly planning something together and it went wrong."

"Nothing is clear to me," I returned, offended by the accusation on Daniel's behalf. "And I've got a better chance at *making* it clear without an audience, so GTFO. That means—"

"I know what it means." A muscle twitched in Eli's jaw and the resolute expression on his face made me think he was contemplating throwing an arm around me and hauling me out of the room forcibly.

Instead, he turned and went to the door, ushering the guards out. I'd half-expected him to try to get away with going invisible on the threshold, the equivalent of the mime feigning a walk down stairs, but he passed through and I couldn't feel his presence anymore.

Satisfied we were alone, I turned on Daniel.

"Start over."

He sighed, looking for a moment like he might prefer to just pass out rather than rehash it.

"Diana has a scar on the back of her hand," he finally said. "The scar from the iron rod I put through Tess Foster's hand last November."

"Tess was human. Diana is human."

"Then how did she jump through that door? Your bodyguard agrees with me."

"He thinks you're hatching a plot against me. Is he right about that too?"

Daniel's hiss of exasperated annoyance sent an unexpected relief through me, what with all this talk of shapeshifters and people not being who they said. At least he was acting normal.

"Okay," I agreed. "So we're not going to defer to Eli's judgment, then."

"What's a binding?" he demanded.

"Don't change the subject." But I couldn't not answer. "It's a spell that means no Faerie can hurt you unless you hurt one first."

"You put *a spell* on me?" A tremor passed through his body, outrage in every syllable of the words.

"I *had* it put on you, yes," I countered. "For protection."

"I don't need protection."

"Uh, five months in a millionaire's prison hospital, palling around with Joshua for a night then getting dumped here as Declan's captive insurance policy kind of say otherwise." I ticked each example off on my fingers. "Plus getting stabbed by a *changeling*, what, five minutes ago?"

"Take it off." Daniel didn't appreciate my pithy sarcasm.

"I can't. But if you're mad enough to hit me, that would probably do it." For an instant, I thought he was going to take me up on that suggestion, but instead his shoulders slumped and he looked toward the window over the sink.

"Why did you even bring me here?"

"I *didn't*. Your decision to punch the Archduke in the face brought you here."

"And this spell is your way of making sure I behave? Like Raj said—*training*? Control?"

The words bored into me like a spinning drill bit, the pain taking my breath away and making me growl, "I am not trying to control you."

"You put a fucking spell on me!" Daniel snapped.

"Because you're an easy target!" Too far. I struggled to walk that back as he glared at me, but I couldn't.

"I'm a prisoner, then?" he asked. "Or is it a *pet*?"

"Of course not." I didn't know how to explain, how to make him understand. My fingernails dug into my palms. "Look, all of a sudden I have power and everybody wants it. I didn't ask for this stupid crown, but I've got it, so I'm going to do what I have to do to protect the people I—"

The words caught, scraping like a rock. Everything that had washed through me when I'd forced pen to paper and written his name surged back. I steeled myself and finished, "the people I care about."

He was silent a moment and I couldn't read his expression. Finally, he shook his head and turned away, muttering, "Since *when*?"

"Don't play dumb," I said, not quite suppressing a flare of annoyance. "It's one of the things you really suck at."

"You can't keep me here."

"I'm *the Mab*, Danny. Fucking *watch* me."

The floor behind me creaked under a footstep. I swallowed hard and turned around, prepared to snap a few stern commands at whichever nosy guards were poking their heads in.

Not guards, just Abe and Ilse. That was probably worse.

30

"MISSED ALL THE EXCITEMENT." The cowboy's voice was flat. He studied Daniel with sharp eyes, probably reading his emotions before glancing to me.

Daniel brushed past them and left the three of us in the kitchen. I wanted to shout after him, threaten to shrink the house to one single room until he stopped and heard me out. Where the hell did he think he could go, anyway?

Regret rushed through me, trying to scrub away that childish desire, but it didn't succeed.

"What happened?" Ilse asked, her voice gentle.

I skipped the most recent fight and gave them the rundown of our shitty afternoon—what time was it, anyway?—as Abe retrieved a sponge from the sink and started to wipe flour off the table. I moved the chairs back into place as I talked and Ilse disposed of the dough Diana had been working.

Diana. How was any of this possible? I'd been living with her for nearly four months and I'd never felt a tingle off her, no hint of Faerie magic.

It was a total coincidence that I'd moved in with her at all. I hadn't even intended to go to Tofino, but I'd met a woman on the train outside Calgary. Her name was Pam and we'd bonded over a sneaked-on fifth of cheap whisky—hers—since we were both headed to Vancouver. We'd chatted, exchanged numbers. I'd never expected to hear from her again, but after a week burning through my cash in the Vancouver suburbs, she'd called. A friend of hers in Tofino had pulled strings to get her a job at a resort, but she'd decided to go back to Calgary. She didn't want to back out without finding him somebody else to take over. She'd thought of me.

She'd told me I could take the employer-subsidized staff accommodations she'd booked too, but when I'd reached Tofino a week later, her roommate-to-be had gone ahead and filled the space. The two friendly, Australian surfer-slash-waiters living there had let me sleep on the floor for a few nights before they'd found me Diana's spare room. Diana wanted the extra rent and somebody to look after the place while she was away half of each week for work.

It had been good luck. Hadn't it?

Yet I'd been missing the whole time I'd been in Tofino—completely hidden and off the Faerie radar. Could Diana—if she was this changeling thing—actually have orchestrated all of that? The creeping tendrils of suspicion still couldn't square with the fact that Diana was human. I'd *felt* that she was human. And not just me.

"She felt human to you too, right?" I demanded, looking from Abe to Ilse as I clarified, "Diana?"

"Didn't spend much time with her," Abe said, having the decency to look uncomfortable as he admitted, "but yeah."

I couldn't help thinking of the night Eli had attacked her in our apartment. How he'd hesitated, that strange look on his face, before conceding that he'd made a mistake.

"Daniel thinks she's some kind of shapeshifter. Joshua told him about some creature that can, I guess, become human?"

"Daniel Cain's been colluding with your father?" Ilse gave me a sharp look.

"Not by choice. How is that the most important point here?"

"Never heard of a shapeshifter who could become human," Abe started.

"I mean, Mei did." Aubrie's right-hand woman had been a dragon, not a shapeshifter, but she had been half-Faerie like me. She'd sold Aubrie out for a spell that would burn up her Faerie blood and leave her fully human, and as far as I knew, it had worked.

"That was different," Ilse said. "That was a singular spell which interacted with a part of her blood. This is—people can't just *hop* between human and Faerie." Her pitch went just a touch higher than usual. Coming from Ilse, that felt like full-on panic.

She smoothed it back to finish, "If your roommate was a shapeshifter, you would have known."

I squeezed my eyes shut, pressing three fingers into my forehead and leaning back against the wall. Nothing made sense.

Abe cut through that mire with a simple, dry—and fucking irrelevant—question.

"What's got your boyfriend so pissed?"

I shot him a dirty look, wanting to pull myself shut tight like a cocoon. What could he read off me? It didn't matter. It wasn't worth hiding.

"Danny's mad because I put a binding on him."

Ilse's eyebrows shot up in alarm, but Abe beat her to the punch. "Without his permission."

"You can't always *ask* before you protect somebody." Defensive anger flared through my chest.

"But you could have, this time."

"He'd have said no."

"That's his right." The cowboy hesitated. "You asked *me* about the binding. What's the difference?"

"You *know* the difference. Daniel's afraid of magic."

"Ah, so you *did* notice that."

"Stop being clever and just spit it out, okay?" I snapped. "I'm a bad person and a bad Faerie and I'm doing a shitty job being Mab—I get it." I kept myself from kicking over the chair that stood in the middle of the room.

"I'll make some tea." Ilse's voice was quiet as she headed toward the counter, but I heard the stiff note of judgment there too.

"None for me," Abe muttered, heading for the door. He had to slow when he reached it to dodge around Karl, who appeared in the doorway with a severe frown.

"Your Highness," they said, barely noticing the cowboy.

"Jude," I growled.

Karl hesitated long enough to make it clear they weren't going to heed my warning, then said, "Your—" some jumble of syllables I didn't understand, "—has informed us of the latest developments."

"Eli," Ilse supplied over her shoulder, for my benefit.

Traitor. Well, not really. Eli'd been the Ubran's man since he shown up. My fault for thinking I might win a single ally here.

"Given even this house is no longer safe," Karl went on, "we must insist that you cross with us on the next wave so that you can install your successor."

"Next wave, huh? Well, I'm shitty at surfing. Diana could tell you except—" I had to choke back a laugh that felt too close to hysterical for my comfort. "Yeah, she can't."

"A wave is a narrow window every few hours when both worlds come into contact," Ilse explained, as if my remark hadn't been a joke. I'd heard the word used before in this house and known it was something about the timing for Faeries crossing between worlds.

"We've devised a plan that should assure you sufficient comfort in our world long enough to perform the rituals," Karl added.

When I didn't throw myself at their feet to thank them for the concession, they added, "It is imperative that your consort swear fealty and that you in turn accept your heir."

"Imperative," I repeated with a sigh. "Declan and Saskia probably think so." Or maybe only the former, given my heart-to-heart with Saskia. 'Fealty' from the Archduke didn't suck as a concept, but now that I had proof that the binding on Daniel was working—which actually threw a lot of weight behind the 'Diana is a Faerie' theory—there wouldn't be any need for that awkward 'consort-taking' portion of the evening.

Declan was going to be furious. Good—maybe this ritual would be fun after all.

"So you found a way to sneak me in, huh?" I asked.

"No *sneaking* is necessary." Karl sounded surprised. "Your Majesty, I hope you know that the proscription against human entry into our world is purely for the human's safety. It's not due to any concern of ours. The strength of the magic tends to be more than *most* humans can bear, so we generally prefer to keep them out.

"However, we've found an acceptable location for the rite near a portal on our side. It should not affect you unduly."

Unduly. An ominously vague term, but also a fancy word that a Faerie who didn't speak English as a first language would use.

Part of me *did* dig the idea of slipping past the velvet rope to party in the Faerie realm. Who else got to do that, apart from a handful of random people throughout history and the Consilium assassin team who'd gone over to blow up the old Mab last year? Kind of an exclusive club, really.

Plus, I was going to have to do these rites sooner or later. Why not take 'sooner', given this house was filled to the brim with angry men sulking about my decisions. Then I could work on passing off the Mab stuff to Saskia, finding some way to abdicate.

"When's the next wave?" I asked.

Karl glanced to Ilse, who knitted her brows together for a moment as she did the calculations in her head.

"Thirty minutes."

"Shit." A startled shot of anxiety twinged through my bravado. *That soon?* "I don't need to change clothes, do I?"

31

I HADN'T EXPECTED TO be so nervous facing the open front door half an hour later. It was just the usual doorway, but now, unlike when I opened it to somewhere in the human world, I couldn't see what I was walking into. Just an unpleasant, murky mist.

Karl and company disappeared through it without hesitation but I couldn't make my foot move.

A gentle arm slid through mine and tightened, making me flinch and look away from the mist to Ilse's serene face.

Right. Get this over with and then I could get back to all the other problems currently mounding up behind me. Maybe I could score a little more free rein once I had an heir.

Aubrie would have killed for this chance. My old partner-in-crime *had* killed for it—become a mass murderer for it, actually—and never even gotten it. *See Jude win.*

Crossing the threshold didn't feel like winning. The floor fell out from under me and I almost stumbled, but luckily Ilse's arm kept me upright. I felt weightless, floaty, not sure how to align my next step.

The air was still, and it smelled strange. Almost flowery, but as soon as that word occurred to me, my brain reclassified it. The bizarre mix of cloying sweetness and sharp, salty acidity was more like someone had just peeled an orange full of warm blood in front of my face.

The mist dissipated but that didn't help. The world around me spun like a kaleidoscope of bright, blurry colour and repeating shapes. I tried and failed to compress whatever was in front of me into something recognizable, blinking rapidly and steeling my stomach to suppress a lurch. Good thing Ilse'd warned me not to eat anything. It wouldn't exactly look regal, puking as soon as I set foot in the Faerie world.

"Close your eyes." She stopped me, her presence still the only thing anchoring me to three dimensions.

Following her command was simultaneously the best and worst thing. It blotted out the dizzying carousel around me but it left me in the dark with the feeling that things were Very Not Right here. An irrational certainty spiked through me that something unnatural was stalking me, creeping behind me, lowering to pounce. My muscles tensed for flight.

I flinched again as Ilse applied something cold and gunky to my eyelids. It had a medicinal smell cut with a softer scent, and it banished my fears almost instantly. I felt more myself. I wasn't the prey flying into the spider's web, just the idiot half-human walking into the Faerie world.

But I was in charge here.

When Ilse gave me the okay to open my eyes, I hesitated. Part of me still didn't want to see what was out there. I widened them and blinked. The ointment she'd applied felt gooey and grainy at the same time. It blurred my vision but at least it didn't sting. I had to fight to keep from lifting a hand to wipe it away, squeezing my eyes shut and opening them again to clear things. She'd said she couldn't apply it until we were already across in the Faerie realm—the magic wouldn't work elsewhere.

The room came into soft, blurry focus, and it *was* a room we'd stepped into. I could make out the general blur of walls around us, solid and tinged purple, with natural veins like some kind of stone. The veins pulsed slightly with light but I tried to ignore that. The air felt like indoor air, a little stale and without much movement.

A distant voice came from our left. I turned toward it only to hear Ilse answer in the same melodic tones. In the human world, the Faerie tongue sounded musical, but here it *was* music. The notes of Ilse's words punctuated the air and rose above the general orchestral hum around us.

I still didn't understand the language. No magical ointment for that, I guess.

"How are you finding it?" Ilse's voice in English sounded so disjointed it almost made my chest crack open.

"Fine, good," I panted in one breath. I focused on the words, their sounds as my own throat produced them. This was my language, not the world breaking apart.

Like seeing through glamour, taking the time to squint and focus helped bring the spinning of the Faerie world to something more like a slow, languid wave. I was finally able to make out what looked like intricate, coloured tapestries on the walls. Tiny creatures on them moved in unison, swaying in some intricate dance.

"Is that wallpaper real?" I asked.

"What wallpaper?"

"Oh. Wait, are those are windows?" When Ilse affirmed it, I clarified, "Is there a party going on?"

"A public celebration of your reign. Don't worry, you won't have to go down there."

"Where are we?"

"In the Mab's private sitting room."

"And where's everybody else?" We seemed to be alone. "Weren't they just ahead of us?" I'd hesitated a moment or two after Karl and the others had disappeared through the safehouse's front door, but I'd walked in right after them.

"Time and space distort differently here," Ilse said, choosing her words gingerly as if she weren't quite sure of them. "The Ubran are preparing the ceremonial chamber."

"Thank you, Ilse."

"It's my pleasure."

"I doubt that." I managed to stifle a bitter laugh. "Especially not given the last thirty minutes. You were pissed about the binding too. Gonna side with Abe and say I'm being a tyrant?"

"No."

Even in the buzzy, undulating room I could hear her avoidance in the single word.

"Then what?"

"This isn't the time."

"Have we got anything better to do? You want to show me around the palace?" I half-expected her to call my bluff and start a historical walking tour, but instead she gave in.

"Abe believes you should have done the binding differently," she said. "I fear you shouldn't have done it at all."

"Why not?"

Silence. Soliciting Ilse's opinion felt like pulling teeth.

"Whether you know it or not," she said slowly, "you sacrifice an enormous amount of goodwill to protect Daniel Cain, and I don't believe he's worthy of it." She paused. "I realize I'm of the minority in your personal retinue, but I don't like him and I don't trust him."

Had I *ever* heard Ilse express a forceful opinion before? Despite not loving where this was headed, I stayed quiet to urge her to go on. It felt like holding painfully still to keep from spooking a butterfly.

"I was a prisoner in that warehouse for months," she said. "Trapped, surrounded by iron day and night."

"The Consilium's warehouse." The memory of the place sent an unpleasant chill through me too, and I'd only been there an hour, tops.

"Cain's," Ilse insisted. "He became their leader and *he* kept me there. Or else he didn't think of me at all, which might be worse."

"I did shitty things in the Consilium too," I said. "I hurt people, probably people just like you. Fought them, took them into custody, let them be hauled off and studied or tortured or . . ." The possibilities turned my stomach. I had never asked what happened, hadn't cared to know.

Which might be worse. "There are probably a few Faeries out there who remember me and hate me too," I finished.

"There are several powerful factions who desire that the whole of the Consilium, anyone ever to associate with it, be culled and the organization struck from memory," Ilse agreed. "Which is precisely what makes your continued allegiance to Cain dangerous."

"*Allegiance* is a pretty strong word," I started to protest.

"I understand affection for humans, Jude. I do. Mei's become a dear friend—" She caught herself as a shock of surprise went through me.

"Mei?" I stammered. "Aubrie's Mei?" How did Ilse even *know* Mei? She'd found the two of us in Niagara Falls, after Mei and I had escaped Aubrie's hotel room. Ilse had helped us get down to the falls and stop Aubrie's half-Faerie minions, but the three of us hadn't been socializing.

"It doesn't matter," Ilse said. "It was a faulty example. Mei is merely a human, unaffiliated."

"*Now*," I added pointedly, irked that Ilse was willing to give Spencer Aubrie's years-long lover and top crony a pass while attempting to lecture me about Daniel.

"Miranda let her affections sway her too," Ilse said. "You walk an even finer line in this world than she did."

Her earnest words broke my heart. Pain rang in them, grief and sorrow for my aunt, who, I was remembering way too late, had been Ilse's lover.

Ilse was *afraid* for me. I almost wished I could be as afraid for myself, but self-preservation had never been my greatest skill. I wasn't about to kowtow to some group of embittered Faerie elite who wanted to rampage through the human world and kill anybody they didn't like. To hell with that.

I didn't want to keep arguing with Ilse, though. I had other ideas to fill time while I was cooling my heels waiting for the Ubran.

"Are there libraries here?" I asked.

"Several." She headed off my next question. "I doubt they would be of much use to you, though—nothing would be in English."

"But you could translate, right? Would they have stuff about this changeling thing? Whatever it is Diana might be?"

Ilse was silent a moment before venturing, "While I don't claim to be a scholar, I've *never* heard that term before. Except in *human* stories."

"Right. The Faerie who swaps its kid with a human child." I realized I'd been chewing on my lower lip and stopped. "Joshua said this was a shapeshifter with healing abilities, though."

"That strikes me as . . . fanciful."

"This entire trippy dreamscape palace strikes me as 'fanciful,' Ilse, but that doesn't mean I'm not standing in it."

"Jude, your father is—"

"Nuts, I know." I wanted to move closer to her press my point but I didn't want to lose my balance in the shifting room. "But Diana stabbed Daniel and it didn't take. That wouldn't have happened if she were human, right?"

"Bindings are complicated—"

"Complicated or not, they still only work against Faeries."

"Perhaps Diana has a modicum of Faerie blood," Ilse said stubbornly. "Too small a percentage to sense, but still enough to trigger such a delicate spell."

"Is that even possible?" I scoffed.

"All things are possible."

"Well, if that's true, then a 'changeling' like Joshua described is also—"

Ilse cut off my bratty needling with an uncharacteristic sigh.

"I'll summon the royal librarian."

32

DANIEL RETREATED TO THE upstairs bedroom. He had nowhere else to go, not unless he wanted to fight his way out of the house. Maybe that would work now, given whatever this *binding* was.

He shut the door, cursing inwardly that there wasn't a lock on it. He spun to search the room for something to bar it with.

Stop panicking. He took a breath, holding it to slow his galloping heart. There was nothing specific worth barring the door *from* right now. Besides, if someone wanted to get into the room, they would. Jude had been right about that: he was an easy target. Especially here.

When he glanced back at the bedroom door, the thumb latch of a deadbolt gleamed above the knob. Was he hallucinating? He knew he hadn't missed the lock the first time he'd examined the door. It hadn't *been* there. Now it was.

Daniel opened the door cautiously to verify that there was indeed a keyhole on the other side of the latch now, with a key sticking out. He slid it from the lock and examined it. Nothing fancy, just an ordinary house key. He flipped the thumb latch a few times and watched the deadbolt move out and back in.

It made him think of the TV behind him, of asking Jude how they got signal here in . . . wherever the hell they were.

"The house seems driven by expectation."

She'd conjured up whatever she wanted from the cupboards downstairs. The house itself had even shifted, expanded and changed by magic.

Had he created the lock on the door? Had he willed it into existence? Was it the spell Jude had put on him that allowed him to manipulate the house the way she and the others did? Or was it the curse Joshua and Abe had mentioned, the ability to see through glamour, to break thrall?

He shut the door, flipped the deadbolt and sat down with his back against it. The key dug into his closed palm. The house was silent around him, as always. He'd half-expected Jude to follow him, chase him down and keep arguing.

A throb in his bad shoulder told him when he'd been sitting tensed up for too long. Dread had settled into his muscles. He'd been waiting in sickening anticipation for whispers restarting in his head, the buzz in his ears, the foreign syllables chiding, begging, demanding he submit to them.

It hadn't come. This wasn't like memorizing the incantation, reading the spell into his head. Even if he had created the latch on the door, that magic wasn't demanding anything from him in return. Not yet, anyway.

He couldn't just sit here, frozen in terror, waiting to lose his mind. He had to do *something*, and he didn't have many options. Tentatively, he crept closer to the bedside table, where a closed drawer waited for him. How had Jude created that Scotch earlier? Did he have to ask—? No, he hadn't done anything before but wish internally for the lock on the door.

With a sigh, he steeled his nerves and concentrated on the drawer.

"Books on bindings." He said it aloud, just in case, but winced at how uncertain his voice rang in the room.

Opening the drawer, he found a slim hardcover. *A Beginner's Guide to Bookbinding.*

The house was mocking him. He tossed the book onto the bed and tried to come up with a better way to phrase his request.

The next result was *Of Human Bondage* by William Somerset Maugham.

He wracked his brain for titles he knew from the Consilium, books that might have something to do with Antagonist spells. Diana—whatever she'd been—had called it 'an antiquated reflection spell.' He tried that too, but it didn't produce any better results.

He quickly accumulated stacks of books, magazines, papers and, oddly, a VHS tape from the drawer. He worked his way down through broad categories of 'binding' that had nothing to do with magic, through mirror construction and self-reflection, a handful of bondage pornography and then finally narrowed it down to spells. As hard as he tried to specify his ask, none of the media was useful.

Maybe something here was preventing him from finding the information, or maybe it just didn't exist. Either way, there was nothing for him here. Daniel stretched his legs, stiff from sitting. How long had he been at this? The door was still locked. Jude still hadn't come after him, hadn't sent anyone up after him. Maybe she'd forgotten about him, sidetracked by some more important Court business.

Getting to his feet, Daniel listened against the door for whatever good that would do. With a confidence he didn't feel, he threw the lock and yanked the door open. When that yielded nothing, he darted out into the hallway and back to the stairs. Luckily, they were still where he remembered them being.

He paused only an instant at the bottom before making his mind to stride to the single guard hovering beside the front door.

With a forced calm, he approached the unfamiliar, woman-shaped creature at the front door.

"I need to leave. On an errand for the Mab," he lied.

"I wasn't informed—" the guard started.

"Due to the . . . infiltration." Daniel gestured over his shoulder to the kitchen. How long had it been since Diana had fled? He fought to keep panic from leaking into his voice. "The Mab told me to—"

Footsteps from behind made him spin, expecting to see Jude or maybe Abe. Instead, Eli had emerged from a room along the hallway.

"What's going on?" Jude's bodyguard approached, a hint of doubt in his stiff voice.

"I need to leave. To pick something up from home," Daniel said, adding, "Montreal." He hesitated, not sure whether to push forward with his lie or concede. Finally, he added, "Jude knows about it."

Eli considered that, amber eyes unreadable, then cast the guard a brief nod. The relief it brought Daniel was short-lived when the other man said, "I'll accompany you."

Daniel kept his expression neutral, trying not to give anything away. One on one, he might be able to take the other man, or at least break away and run. When the guard moved aside, he recited the address of his most recent Montreal apartment the way he'd heard Jude and the others do to trigger the door, then yanked it open.

The familiar living room tightened something in his chest. It had been left in a cluttered mess from the ambush last November when Gracie had been injured. The bookshelf beside the TV had been emptied since then, and probably all the boxes in the bedroom that had contained Consilium information too, but everything else was as he'd left it.

Eli followed him in. The door closed behind them and the Antagonist said nothing, simply studied the room.

"I'll just be a minute." Daniel fought to keep from breaking into a jog as he moved past the other man.

"Is there a back entrance?" Eli put up a hand to stop him.

"Not one I would use." Daniel guessed the source of the question.

"Explain."

"There's a fire escape off the back bedroom, but we're three stories up and I don't do heights." Admitting it felt ridiculous, shameful. *Throw myself into fights with dragons and mages without a second thought, but tall staircases, well, that's a goddamn step too far.* He still had anxiety dreams about pounding down the creaking, circular stairs off his first apartment in Montreal, fleeing with Jude from a fire last summer.

Eli seemed to agree that it was too stupid to be a lie and he dropped his arm to let Daniel stray further into the apartment.

"I don't want to chase you," he added in a quiet, even tone, "but I can, I will, and I'll win."

Daniel ignored the self-assured statement of fact, heading to the bathroom. Maybe he could find a weapon there. Hitting Eli would break the binding, though. As much as he hated the thought of the spell settled over him, he couldn't help flashing back to the pressure in his gut when Diana had tried to stab him—the way it should have hurt but hadn't. That blow should have killed him.

You're out of your depth. You always were. Joshua's words rang sharply true. He *had* been surviving on luck, and a desperate, stubborn refusal to look down and acknowledge that the old ground had given way. This wasn't a feasible path any longer.

Gracie had known that. She'd recognized it first and he hadn't believed her. If he'd just given it up when she wanted to—

He ducked into the standing shower. Kneeling down on the right side of the raised lip, he counted the tiles from the bottom and from the left to find the one he wanted. If he hadn't remembered the location, he would have had a tough time picking the particular tile out. It blended in well with the rest of the wall, where most of the grout was missing. Maybe that meant Leshe's people hadn't found it when they'd gone through the apartment.

He fixed his fingernails around the edges of the tile and put some force into yanking it back. He'd pried it off last year when he moved in, then reattached it with stick-on Velcro, and the substance made a tearing sound as he freed it.

Behind the tile, he'd scraped a hole into the wall big enough to stuff a plastic bag. He pulled it out, shaking off a layer of plaster dust. The bag contained a wad of cash, a forged passport and the key to a safe deposit box that would supply him with further fake IDs, a few credit cards and more cash.

He had enough money on those cards and cash to last three months, maybe four if he was careful. He'd planned vaguely for the idea of running, disappearing, but never really thought it through. His mother had never gotten around to imparting that lesson in detail. What did you do when you disappeared? Where did you go?

Where had Gracie gone?

"What is that?" Eli stood in the doorway.

"It's private." Daniel got to his feet. *Should have gone for a weapon first.* He clutched the bag in one hand and the piece of white tile in the other.

"You're a terrorist. Nothing's private."

"I'm a *what*?" The word shouldn't have surprised him, but he couldn't help arguing, "Your side killed *two hundred* people in Toronto a year ago."

"And there were over three hundred in the palace." Eli's tone remained neutral. "I can't let you back into the house without knowing what you're carrying."

"I'm not going back to that house," Daniel said.

"We're getting off-topic." Eli extended a hand.

Daniel ran his thumb over one of the corners of the tile. Not very sharp. It might do some damage if he swung it hard at the Antagonist, but it wouldn't be enough. He relented and passed Eli the bag he'd dug out of the wall.

The other man accepted it, only checking the contents briefly before handing it back. Without a word, he left the doorway, turning toward the front room of the apartment.

Not a dangerous terrorist, though. Daniel banished the self-effacing thought. He tossed the piece of tile onto the counter and it landed with a clatter.

Since Eli hadn't demanded they leave, he seized the opportunity to continue back to the bedroom and went through the closet. His clothes and belongings were still there, so he replaced his work boots with a pair of tennis shoes—easier to run in, if it came to that—and changed his t-shirt for one that wasn't made of magic.

"Do you have a camera hidden in the living room?" Eli appeared in the doorway. He hadn't made a sound coming down the hall and Daniel knew for a fact that the old, wooden floors squeaked under weight.

"A what?" he stammered, startled. "No."

"Then we should leave immediately."

33

"Where's the camera?" Daniel asked, lowering his voice to a whisper as he trailed Eli out of the bedroom.

"In the plant." The other man stopped before entering the living room.

"I don't keep plants." Daniel caught sight of what was indeed a small, potted plant on the kitchen bar. "And if I did, they wouldn't look that healthy."

The copious, uniformly green leaves that spilled from the plain, terracotta pot all had a cheap, plastic shine. No wonder there hadn't been a pile of eviction notices for non-payment of rent crowding the front door. Maybe Leshe had kept the apartment's rent paid, hoping to catch Gracie.

"It's aimed at the front door," Eli said, sounding annoyed. "I missed it on my first sweep." He cocked his head, listening, then jerked his chin toward the front door to indicate they were leaving that way.

Instead of the hallway outside, though, he opened the door to the yellow-lit foyer of the Faerie house.

"I'm not going back there." Daniel's heart raced as he took an automatic step backwards.

"Yes, you are." Eli left the front door open and moved toward him. "You have five seconds to decide whether or not you'll be conscious when you do."

They both tensed at the sound of several heavy bodies creaking on the old floorboards just outside the apartment, somehow behind and just beyond the eerie glow of the Faerie house.

Before Eli could reach the open door, a second door that looked identical to it cut through the scene of the Faerie house, erasing it to reveal the real hallway outside the apartment, along with a group of unfamiliar faces.

"Your people?" Eli tossed over his shoulder as he turned on their new adversaries.

"I don't have *people*," Daniel snapped, snatching the first weapon he could reach—the fake, plastic plant in foam dirt. The camera tucked into it gave it a little more heft, at least.

The woman at the centre of the group had a long, thin weapon that crackled with electricity—something like a cattle prod. She swiped at Eli, who danced back to avoid the end of the weapon as the rest of the intruders spilled into the apartment. Only a few carried handguns. Whoever they were, they'd come to the same conclusion as the Consilium—that most non-iron weapons were more trouble than they were worth against Faeries.

Eli disappeared.

Startled, Daniel searched the doorway for any sign of him, any sparkle or disturbance to the air. Nothing. Had the bastard abandoned him, left him armed with a plastic plant against a group of at least five unfamiliar agents?

The crowd in the doorway had paused, too, the woman in the lead holding up a fist to still her followers. She didn't trust Eli's disappearing act either. From the way the people around her crowded uncomfortably into the doorway, there had to be more outside in the hallway behind them.

Daniel seized on their inattention to throw the potted plant. He aimed for the weapon in the woman's hand, hoping to knock it out of her grip, but Eli appeared suddenly, near the kitchen to his left.

The Faerie clutched an aluminum pan he must have liberated from inside, swinging it like a baseball bat to slam the plastic pot off its initial trajectory and redirect it at the lead woman's chin.

It hit hard enough to bloody her nose. The woman staggered back into her allies, knocking at least one off their feet. Eli and another adversary darted in to wrestle for the cattle prod at the same moment, Eli swinging the pan again.

A door slammed from the back of the apartment—the one to the balcony off the bedroom. Reinforcements coming up the winding fire escape?

Daniel darted to the bedroom door at the end of the hallway, pulling it shut in the same moment an equal force tried to haul it open. Barely thinking, he shifted back to put his weight on one leg and kicked the door with the other, sending it into the emerging agents with force.

He spun back toward the living room but didn't get more than two steps before someone grabbed him from behind, trying to snake an arm around his throat and yank him off his feet. He managed to duck and evade his captor, throwing up an arm to block the next swing.

The other man didn't have a weapon, or if he did, he hadn't drawn it. His fist sent pain twinging through Daniel's arm but didn't trigger the binding. The bigger man was human. Backed against the wall, Daniel aimed a punch at his throat.

The other man dodged but someone from the living room stumbled into him from behind and shoved him back into Daniel's second punch. The guy recovered fast, jabbing the heel of one hand into Daniel's bad shoulder with a force like a freight train.

Agony crackled down Daniel's arm, and the other man followed it up by driving a fist into his stomach. He crumpled, struggling to breathe. His left shoulder was a tangle of white-hot pain that stretched up into his neck and down through his side.

Doubled over, gasping, he had a better view of Eli, finally subdued in the living room by half a dozen people. Bound by what had to be iron manacles, he still snarled at his captors as they aimed kicks at his head.

More people poured in through the front door. How had none of the neighbours noticed, called the police? Maybe Leshe had bought the whole damn building last fall and left it empty as a trap.

"Stop!" Daniel snapped, wincing at the sharp pang the force of the word stirred in his aching gut.

Someone cuffed him in the side of the head hard enough to summon a distant ringing in his ear. The hit knocked him forward onto the worn carpet, too stunned to fight the heavy manacles that locked around his own wrists.

Iron. Maybe it was all they had. Maybe they were trying to make a point. *Lie down with Faeries, wake up in iron chains.* His father would have appreciated that.

Someone hauled Daniel to his feet. He coughed down bile as gravity reminded his left shoulder of his limp arm's weight. Head spinning, he was able to see that they'd gotten Eli upright as well. The Faerie seemed to be unconscious now, sagging in their arms.

"Don't worry," the man closest to Daniel said. "Leshe wants you alive."

34

THE ROYAL LIBRARIAN TURNED out to be a creature that looked unpleasantly like a heap of thick, black slugs gleaming with oily moisture as they wove in and out to create a humanoid form.

But she—Ilse had assured me it was a 'she'—had the spectacular ability to magically locate any piece of media from the royal libraries, then summon it out of thin air, so I was getting over her gelatinous motions fast. Besides, I couldn't stare too hard at her without the room beginning to spin around me.

Nothing useful had turned up in the royal libraries for the term 'changeling,' nor did the librarian have any suggestions for a shapeshifter that healed itself when it shifted. Just because the creature wasn't documented didn't mean it didn't exist—maybe it had stayed under the radar somehow.

"What about stuff like the Lower Halls? The Wild Hunt?" I tossed out terms I remembered from Daniel's story back in the safehouse kitchen, hoping to come at this changeling from another angle. Figuring out what the thing was after might help me pin it down—make any of this make sense.

The librarian waved a writhing hand and a stack of books appeared at her side. Every piece of media she'd summoned so far had smelled musty, close to the usual library scent of old paper, but just herbaceous enough to feel unnervingly foreign.

"Where would you like to begin, Your Highness?" The librarian's English was halting and quiet.

"Give me the gist. The Shadow Mab was a Mab cursed to become a shade because of . . . something to do with the Wild Hunt, right?"

"Shadow*ed* Mab," Ilse corrected me gently.

The books rearranged without the librarian touching them and the top one fell open, pages flipping to create a breeze that smelled like an unpleasant green smoothie.

The librarian spoke in beautiful, musical tones and Ilse translated, giving me the short version of what I remembered Grace saying last fall: the Shadow*ed* Mab and her consort had raged through both worlds with a cadre of bloodthirsty cultists, slaughtering humans and Faeries alike in some whirlwind campaign of carnage, apparently just for funsies. Ilse called them the Wild Hunt when she translated, but if I remembered right, Grace had used 'the Host' interchangeably too.

A powerful group of Faerie mages had put a stop to it. They'd trapped them both, then cursed the Mab to become a shade—renaming her the Shadowed Mab—and created a little piece of the Faerie realm to house her and her servants forever, as Faerie ghosts.

They hadn't wanted to cast the exact same curse on her consort, afraid that the two of them in an identical space could somehow rise back to power. So, the consort had been shut away in a stone cavern, buried somewhere in the human world—the Lower Halls.

"Why the human world?" I interrupted.

"It was further away from the Bie'lelhii," Ilse relayed, after putting my query to the librarian.

A *game reserve and a garbage dump* was how Daniel had put it, when he'd related bitterly to me how he thought the Faerie world conceived of the human one. Hard to argue, honestly, given they were locking their serial killers up over there.

The librarian spoke again and Ilse translated: "The Lower Halls were sealed by removing four keystones. The only way any person of Faerie blood can enter or exit is with all of these stones in place."

"Why?" I demanded. "If the consort was so dangerous, why make a way out at all?"

Ilse relayed the question to the librarian and then bounced the retort back to me: "Every lock must have a key."

"Faerie philosophy," I muttered. "Too much to hope they did more than throw away the keys, though, right?"

"The stones were hidden far from one another, ostensibly two in Faerie and two in the human world, but there's no proof of that." Ilse paused to listen to the librarian. "All details of the keys and their locations have been purged from every known record."

"Are there *unknown* records?" I returned dryly.

"I don't know how to pose that question," Ilse admitted. "She's going to say 'no.' "

"Obviously." I sighed, fighting the urge to pace. I'd inadvertently tried it a few minutes ago and it had just made me feel seasick.

If Diana *was* this changeling thing, and if she *had* been in league with Daniel's William Leshe to dig up the Lower Halls, then what was the point? She couldn't get inside. Well, if she turned human, maybe she could. But she still wouldn't be able to get the Shadowed Mab's consort *out*, which seemed necessary for whatever power-seizing scheme she inevitably had up her sleeve.

"Is there some hint inside the Lower Halls for how to find the keystones?" I asked.

The librarian answered without need of Ilse's translation. "No, that would be idiotic."

"Oh, you're editorializing now?"

That comment *did* require a translation from my water sprite attendant, and the librarian seemed uncomfortable.

She was right, though—it *would* be idiotic to leave hints or memos to finding the keys inside with the consort. If we were being honest, though, old Faerie Court regimes *had* done idiotic shit before, like recycle incantations, and we'd suffered for it.

Still, Daniel had said that nobody else came out of the Lower Halls alive except him. Unless Diana had gone down there *after* it had been uncovered, found something? I was starting to think she'd never been a doula, never attended a birth, because it was a pretty convenient cover to get her out of my sight half of each week to be whoever she wanted to be.

Why *me*, though? Why trick *me* into living with her, hide me from the Court? She'd never tried to hurt me, ransom me—nothing like that. Just pretended to be my friend. It didn't make any more sense now than it had an hour ago.

A sudden bell-like noise rang through the room. The splashes of purple wall to my left seemed to vibrate and then one section slowly lightened. A door opening.

"Oh." Ilse sighed. "The Ubran are ready for you."

In all the research frustration, I'd almost forgotten about my actual purpose for setting foot in this weird new world: the ritual to name my heir.

35

Maybe I was becoming more accustomed to the palace. This time, when Ilse led me through, the scene didn't shift quite as much around me. Things still swam a little and I had to walk carefully, unsteady on my feet when the floor danced and spiralled every few metres.

The ceremonial chamber seemed tall, maybe open on top. The air was both fresher, like a cool breeze was coming in from above, and heavy with spicy perfume. All four—five? Sometimes six?—walls around me appeared to be made of the same purple stone I'd seen in my sitting room. Its veins gleamed in what was probably candlelight. Impossible to tell since everything in the room seemed to vibrate just slightly.

The others stood around a table—at least, I thought it was them. Even after I shut my eyes tight and re-opened them, the moving forms blurred together and came apart, changing size and height until they seemed to have gone from sitting to standing as I entered. Was it actually a table they stood around? It had the requisite flat surface and some legs but the word 'table' seemed to stretch to fit the shape.

Ilse alone kept her human glamour: two arms, two legs, one head with black curls that went blue at the roots—an anchor in the maelstrom. She brought me around the table-ish form to what must have been the head.

"May I?" she murmured, and I nodded, not knowing what she was even asking until she put her hands under my armpits and, pressing her hands against the sides of my rib cage, gently lowered me into what seemed to be a chair.

Sitting was worse than standing. I'd been getting used to the room around me, almost completed a mental map of where each blob and undulating shape was, but bending my legs and lowering my body threw the whole thing out of whack. The room spun around me. I was upside down. I was underwater. I was very, very far away from the table.

A sharp tap came against the centre of my back and I drew a breath. Had I stopped breathing?

Ilse stood beside me and I fought not to reach out and take her hand, hold it like a child clinging to my mother for the duration of this ordeal. I blinked the room back into some coherent form. Tiny spots became clear for an instant—a slick, purple wall, the flicker of an oddly-shaped light bulb—electricity, then, not candlelight? The room bubbled in my peripheral vision, never wanting to settle on a single state for long.

How the hell had the Consilium guys made it through this world, even with the Faerie ointment? How had they navigated through this shifting palace to find the Mab and her inner court and blow it all up? How had they even worked explosives? My fingers seemed to elongate on my hands when I looked away from them, then snapped back into their regular form when I remembered that wasn't normal.

Music again, from ahead of me, as the shapes around me spoke. Their individual forms came into sharper focus as I looked at each one, but all of them shimmered like a mirage on hot asphalt. It didn't help that none were human-shaped anymore. One seemed to be a beam of light with teeth, and another had way too many eyes.

"The Ubran is beginning the ceremony and has informed the others that they will move quickly through it to detain you here for as short a time as possible," Ilse related quietly in my ear.

"Which one's Karl?" I whispered back. I followed her eyes to a group of forms that seemed to move in and out of each other—a three-fingered hand here, two vertical eyes there, one body towering over the others and then swallowed back into the general chaos. For a moment, there were three distinct forms, then five, then two, and seven for the blink of an eye.

My head hurt.

"You're doing better than I expected." The wry, superior tone of Saskia's voice was immediately familiar, coming from a set of sharp, dark angles beside me that occasionally resolved into a hard, gleaming body. "I thought for sure you'd throw up."

"There's still time," I returned, and her very human-sounding chuckle was annoyingly reassuring.

The top of her head pulsed with an unnerving, blood-red glow. Had the Consilium term 'redcap' actually come from some hapless human stumbling over here? I just assumed they'd stolen it from storybooks, but humans did occasionally get tricked or led through Faerie portals, if you believed the Consilium stories, so maybe one of them had come back raving with descriptions of the beings over here.

Now that I had some idea what Saskia looked like on this side of the portal, I scanned the table for Declan, assuming he'd be a similar bundle of shapes. He seemed to be seated at the far end of the table, mirroring my position.

A few musical notes came from his general vicinity and were answered back from near Karl.

"They would like to start with the contract establishing your formal relationship with the Archduke." Ilse set something on the table in front of me—a giant, green moth like the one that had been beating against my window screen in Tofino. Probably the same one, actually. Good thing I wasn't about to find out what I was supposed to do with it.

"Oh, right," I said. "I'm not doing that anymore."

"What?" A low, angry growl in English came from the other end of the table. The room fell into a sudden hush around us.

"Well," I continued, "I realized that I only owed you *one* favour for that trumped up bargain you cornered me into last year, and you were trying to slip in two." I sat back in my chair as gingerly as I could to look casual while keeping the room from tilting sideways, raising my hand to count them both off on my fingers: "Take you as my Consort, *and* adopt Saskia. I think I'm just going to do the one. Good try, though." I kept my sarcasm bright and deceptively friendly. Twisting the knife felt good.

I was tempted to mention the fully functional binding I'd put on Daniel, just to warn Declan off whatever petty retaliation plans were rolling through his mind, but I didn't want to bring it up here. I brushed the moth away and it fluttered its wings, flickering like static.

Even though I couldn't quite tell where the Archduke's eyes were in the mass of vibrating darkness at the end of the table, I could feel his icy glare sweeping down at me.

"Your Highness," Ilse started, as Saskia leaned closer to me to warn under her breath, "While I love the enthusiasm, embarrassing my father in front of this crowd isn't your brightest moment."

"Too late." The spicy, incense scent in the room was beginning to remind me of melting plastic and I wanted to be home more than I'd wanted anything in my life. I raised my voice to include the whole room again. "Let's move on, shall we?"

After a moment of startled hesitation, several voices began to sing—or speak, I guess—in unison. Probably the Ubran starting the adoption ceremony.

"Do you prefer I translate word for word?" Ilse asked.

"Just give me the gist."

"They're hailing you as the New Mab," Ilse said. "Sovereign of all that is green and holy. Uniter of the . . . houses." Apparently some words didn't have English equivalents. "Sacred vessel of the unbroken Ancients."

The song stopped in a guttural sort of hacking.

"Judith," Ilse finished. All those nice titles and my given name wrecked the flow. Maybe I could ask for a fancy Faerie name instead.

"Today we bear witness," Ilse went on, as the Ubran did, "to the Naming of the royal heir."

The Ubran speakers sung something else that sounded like:

"*Alihana-ka-ray-ka-lie—*" a low trill "*—aroon-hi-free—*" and finished with a noise from the back of their mouths that I couldn't quite categorize.

Ilse leaned in to relay: "Saskia."

No wonder they took human names.

"Lift your eyes to look upon the union of a new branch to the Lineage. By sky, sea, earth and stone, by flame, blood and bone, the exalted vessel of all that is ours—meaning, the people, the citizenry, your devotees—" Ilse added the aside, apparently struggling with how to translate what seemed to be a pretty wide concept that must have been important to her. "—adds new growth to the sacred majesty of her queue."

I stifled a laugh at that last, probably ill-chosen word and the sudden change in my breathing made me feel sick again. I regretted making the joke to Saskia about throwing up later on. I sucked in a deep breath of the sharp, perfumed air, holding it to force my stomach to relent. The spicy scent tickled my nose and made me want to sneeze.

"They're addressing Saskia now," Ilse told me, as the Ubran hummed on to my left. "Asking her to swear allegiance to the Lineage and to you as her new mother and as the representative of the sacred and ancient trust."

I could have done without the words 'new mother' but I reminded myself it was entirely ceremonial.

A new voice trilled in the emptiness the Ubran's chorus had left, then followed the sound by adding in English, "I do so swear," for my benefit.

So Saskia could brown-nose with the best of them. It didn't surprise me, but I was a little annoyed to find myself appreciating the gesture.

The seven entwined voices picked up again and Ilse said, "They're addressing you now."

I gave the shimmering shapes my full attention, willing this to be over with as my stomach snuck in another sickened twinge.

"As your chosen heir has sworn her allegiance to the Lineage in full view of the council assembled here, it's only left for you to claim her," Ilse said.

The room fell silent and the air felt even heavier, settling on my shoulders with the weight of the expectation in the multitude of eyes around me.

"Repeat after me," Ilse whispered.

I froze, expecting her to launch into a complicated, trill-filled litany that I was never going to pick up, but instead she went syllable by syllable. I formed my lips around the foreign sounds, trying to mimic her, and was startled when what came from my throat seemed like a pretty good imitation. I almost nailed one of the high-pitched, painful-sounding trills.

Good enough, apparently, because some of the tension in the room dissipated. Someone applauded—at least, that's what it sounded like. It was a sharp, fast but rhythmic noise that broke out from my right and spread to the rest of the room in some form or other. It didn't sound like everyone was clapping using hands—some sounds were squishier or harder, making me think of tentacles or claws.

Ilse put a hand on my arm, as if to help me up.

"We're done."

Before I could try to stand, an explosion of harsher, more strained musical chatter broke out, loud enough to freeze me in place.

Ilse's fingers tightened on my arm, somehow both firm and liquid.

"What?" I demanded. "What is it?"

"We need to leave quickly." She held her ground while the other shapes around us whirled into colourful tornadoes.

"What?" I huffed, squeezing my eyes shut for a moment to get my bearings. "More tree people?"

"No. It seems a . . . a protest has broken out in the celebration outside."

"Against me?"

"Against—I'm not sure." Ilse was a terrible liar. "Saskia's gone to talk them down, but as I said, we should return to the other side of the portal immediately."

A flurry of dark shapes obscured her, including one with pulsing red at the top of it. I couldn't follow the volley of conversation in the Faerie language between Ilse and the other voices, which sounded like an angry choir.

"The Ubran think it's best if I lead a decoy team, just in case," Ilse told me. "The Archduke and his soldiers will see you home."

"How close are these protesters, Ilse?" An edge of panic set in.

"We must go *now*." That was Declan. Sharp fingers grasped my shoulders and yanked me up, out of my chair. Too fast.

The room spun around me. Rather than rising from my chair, I was on the ceiling and then I stood parallel to what had previously been the floor, and finally my stomach betrayed me. Bile filled my throat. I vomited and the room went black.

36

Daniel hooked his fingers into the chain-link fence and shook it, craning his neck back to see how it moved at the top. The metallic rattle echoed in the vast, quiet basement, but the fence was set securely into the concrete floor. It seemed stable enough to climb but even then, another sheet of chain-link covered the top. No hinges or holes anywhere except the door.

"Will you stop that?" a voice grumbled from his right. "It's giving me a headache."

"You're awake," Daniel moved toward it, relieved.

"Lucky me," Eli muttered with no real venom. He lay on his side two cages away, same as he had been for an hour or more.

After an uncomfortably long time in a car with heavily tinted windows, their captors had delivered them via loading dock and freight elevator to this bizarre prison. Their cells were two of several in the giant room, both just big enough to lie down in, doors strung with a heavy chain and padlock. The room was laid out like a storage area, sectioned off into small units separated by tall chain-link fencing. No windows, probably underground.

Daniel pressed closer to the fence to try and see Eli's condition better. While someone had removed the heavy, iron manacles from his own wrists once he was in his cell, Eli's were still securely locked above his hands. They'd been looped through the drainage grate in the centre of his cell, holding him on much a shorter leash.

"Are you all right?" Daniel asked.

"Sure." Eli coughed but didn't move. Maybe he was concussed. Their captors hadn't been gentle with him. Did Faeries suffer wounds like that—concussions? Brain damage? Daniel didn't know enough about their actual physiology beneath the glamour to make an educated guess.

When he looked closer, scanning for obvious injuries, the other man's fingers became talons, like a bird's. The skin was mottled and black, nails sharp and blue, gleaming in the lights.

Daniel bowed his head as dizziness washed over him—a flood spurred by cold, visceral terror, a primal panic of the uncanny that his mind couldn't make sense of. Focusing on the solid, cement floor brought him back into his body. With another deep breath, he tried again to look at Eli. This time, the other man's legs terminated in a disconcerting mist that seemed to narrow into nothing.

He snapped his eyes shut again, clutching the fence to stay upright. The thin, sharp metal dug into his fingers, miring him in the present. In the expected, natural world. It wasn't enough.

Then Eli asked, "How long have we been here?" His solid, human-sounding voice, strained in pain but still tinged with a clipped annoyance, cut through the horrifying miasma.

Daniel focused on that note of normalcy, managing to draw another deep breath that let his instinctive terror recede.

"I don't know," he said. "An hour or two, maybe." He couldn't lift his head again, dreading what he might see this time. "Are you hurt?"

"I'll live," Eli grunted.

The bravado made Daniel smile despite himself, eyes still on the concrete. "Not very specific."

"Your friends are probably listening."

"My *friends*?" Daniel bit back a bitter laugh. "What part of this *cage* makes you think I'm tight with whoever owns it?" He rattled the chain links again to make his point, but his spite wasn't really directed at Eli.

The other man hissed under his breath, something unflattering no doubt, but didn't speak again.

Fine. They had nothing to talk about anyway.

Daniel pushed off the fence, welcoming the petty anger that surged to replace the fuzzy, distorted terror he couldn't quite reconcile. He lowered himself to the floor, moving his injured shoulder carefully. The burning pain had receded but it was still stiff.

Leshe wants you alive. That's what the man had said, before they dragged him out to the waiting car. But how was *Leshe* alive? Some narrow escape? A bargain with the creature inside that cave? Maybe Leshe had given the Visitant everyone else in exchange for his own life. It certainly fit Leshe's motives, but Daniel didn't see what the trapped Faerie creature would gain from that bargain.

A door opened and closed somewhere ahead of them. Heavy footsteps approached. The sound coaxed Daniel back to his feet.

A hulking form appeared and resolved into a giant man with stark, white eyes. He passed Eli's cage and stopped at the door to Daniel's, brandishing a key. Without saying a word, he undid the padlock and let it fall to one side. He hauled the door open and stepped inside, filling most of the space in the tiny cell so that there was no hope of staying out of his reach.

Daniel backed against the fence anyway, wincing when it rattled again.

Strange flashes of memory flooded his head, forcibly drawn up. Tendrils worked their way through his mind like fingers flipping through pages. The feeling was uncomfortably familiar, like when Abe and the mage had accosted him last November to excise the incantation from his brain.

Dread shot through him as he turned his head, fighting to avoid the eerie white eyes. His heart raced and the room spun. He was drowning, suffocating. Pressure dug harder into his skull—hard enough that it should have caused pain.

The bigger man jerked back sharply, like he'd been burned.

Daniel's legs folded without his permission and the room tilted again. He sank down, clinging to the fence to keep from sprawling across the floor as he panted and fought to stay conscious. *Reflection.* He regretted having been so angry with Jude for casting the binding on him, but even now that warred queasily with the resentment of being constrained, manipulated.

The giant, who had to be a mage of some sort, turned to stare at something outside of the cage. He lowered his chin as if speaking silently to someone, then made a wordless grunt that still conveyed annoyance.

When he grabbed Daniel roughly by the back of the neck and yanked him to his feet, Daniel clung to the narrow chain-link. It dug painfully into his fingers, but he fought. If he could make the mage pull hard enough to hurt him again, then—

Then what? He was in a cage in the bowels of an unknown building. There was no escape.

He gave in and allowed the giant to haul him out of his cell. They went through a doorway with a key card reader then into the freight elevator. The big mage hadn't acknowledged Eli and Daniel hadn't glanced at the injured man either as they'd passed his cell, still half-afraid of what he'd see.

Two floors up and then down a short hallway, they arrived at what looked like an office building's security room. A bank of a dozen small monitor screens, old hardware, lined one wall in rows.

The door locked behind them and the big mage took up a sentry position beside it.

William Leshe sat tilted back in a swivelling office chair, his fingers steepled on his stomach. He turned when they entered, kicking his feet off where they'd been propped on a desk.

"Had to try." He sounded almost apologetic. "All this memory rape stuff is so uncouth, but sometimes it works."

37

THE PERSON STUDYING DANIEL with wry amusement looked like William Leshe, but wasn't acting like him. It made Daniel think of Gracie's assertion that the woman she'd met last fall hadn't been her old colleague Tess Foster—that it had been someone else with the same face.

"You're not Leshe," he guessed.

"No." The smile that slid across the smooth, sallow features was malicious, out of character for the dismissive, confident William Leshe. "But I couldn't let his money and power go to waste, could I?"

"Who are you?"

"I already told you, I'm not really a 'who.' "

Diana had said that. This creature was Diana, somehow, and William Leshe. Human, but not. Joshua's changeling. A fetch, a creature that could become anyone or anything. How was that possible?

"You killed the real Tess Foster?" Daniel asked.

"She met with an unfortunate accident." The other creature shrugged. "Nothing against her personally, of course. Not like the original owner of *this* face." Its fingers rubbed its chin as if considering the skin it wore, flashing the pale, jagged scar on the back of its hand.

Then it shrugged and continued, "Now that we're less liable to be interrupted, you can tell me where you saw the fourth keystone."

"I don't remember." Daniel said the words slowly and deliberately, but his denial rang hollow even to his own ears.

"Then allow Victor here access to your memory so we can find out." The Changeling tipped his head sideways to indicate the giant mage at the door.

"No." Daniel took an instinctive step to the side, expecting them to rush him.

The thing wearing Leshe's face noted his reaction, brows raised in interest.

"I see," it said. "Fear rather than principle. Perhaps we can overcome that. What you know is worth more to me than merely releasing you unharmed, though clearly that's the first thing on the table."

It stood straight again, starting to pace as if it couldn't hold still. "I'll also release the holds on your finances, return your passport, clear your name of whatever pesky legal charges our friend Leshe drummed up to coerce you. Then you'll be free to keep running. Or not."

"What do you want in the Lower Halls?" Daniel asked.

"You already know that, I'm sure. N'ellaphalen thrace, the Consilium's so-called Visitant." Noting the surprise that quick answer produced, the Changeling grinned. "Weren't really ever in your father's confidence, were you?"

That taunt was almost painfully predictable.

"Just skip to the end," Daniel snapped.

"But that's glossing over the good part. Your father and I—the Consilium and I, in fact—were allies. We were going to close the portals."

"That's impossible. There's no way to—"

"There is, and it's trapped in the Lower Halls. N'ellaphalen thrace is a being of immense power. The Old Court sealed it away to put an end to the Wild Hunt, because they couldn't control it."

"But you can?"

"I don't need to. I can *become* it." The Changeling added, in a knowing drawl, "Which also means I'm the only one in either world that can kill it."

"And walk away with its power. Sounds like a bad deal for everyone but you."

"I don't care about the Wild Hunt, or the Shadowed Mab, or any of the nonsense that the Visitant would, well, *visit* upon our worlds if it got free." The Changeling rolled its eyes, becoming distinctly less William Leshe again in that moment. "*And* I have a vested interest in closing the portals. Or at least limiting the access a little more."

"Why?"

"You used to just do as you were told." The Changeling clasped its hands behind its back as the last few disappointed words came out, turning to face the blank wall of monitors.

Even as its body stopped, its flesh still seemed to move. Subtle at first, the skin and clothing melted and reformed in a viscous, fluid motion, leaving another figure of nearly the same height.

This man was stockier, with broad shoulders and a barrel chest. His blond hair was thinning, trim beard shot through with white.

"No." Daniel shut his eyes instinctively, as if that would make his father's face disappear. Blood pounded in his ears.

"I trained you better than this." It was almost Alan's voice.

"You didn't—" Daniel glared at the thing wearing his father's face, catching himself. "You're not him."

The smug satisfaction in the sharp blue eyes that sized him up wasn't Alan's. His father had never been that outwardly pleased with himself—it would have given too much away. The discordance cut through Daniel, shaking him out of his immediate shock. He could almost see another face lingering behind that familiar one—something just as cruel and disdainful, but deeply amused.

"I'm not talking to you like this," he said. "Be someone else."

"You don't give orders." Alan's snarl struck like a lightning bolt, making Daniel flinch despite himself. "Especially now, after coming up short time and again. Even against Spencer Aubrie, for god's sake."

"Aubrie's spell failed," Daniel snapped. "We stopped it."

"But he *began* it, you worthless idiot. It may not have entwined the worlds like he planned, but it nudged the doors wider." The look of disgust on the Changeling-as-Alan's face made Daniel want to sink into the floor.

He steeled himself. This wasn't his father. His father was dead. This thing was a monster playing a role for a specific purpose.

"Why do you think the Shadowed Mab's cadre of minions waited until *now* to try and free her?" the Changeling went on. "They couldn't get her through the portal before. Now this world is being overrun with Antagonists. Glamour's becoming scarcer the more of them that stream over here. The balance has shifted and powerful monsters that would never have made it across are seizing the opportunity, turning sideways and slipping through."

"Like you."

The thing's laugh seemed to come from several mouths at once, echoing around the room.

"You do take a certain pride in superiority, don't you?" it mused. "It must be so satisfying to finally *win* anything, even if it's as meaningless as a well-placed verbal barb."

Daniel felt the muscles in his hand curling reflexively into a fist. He wanted simultaneously to hit both his father and the inhuman creature gloating beneath those smirking features.

"You can still fix your mistake," the Changeling said. "Tell me where the fourth keystone is and we can close the portals, cut the Antagonists off." Mocking dripped from the key word, helping to stir the hostility that re-inforced Daniel's response.

"No."

"I suppose I respect forgoing the easy option." The Changeling picked up a remote control from the desk and used it to bring one of the monitors to life. The camera showed Eli, sprawled on the concrete floor in his small cell.

Daniel hadn't been able to see the other man's injuries before. Eli had been brutalized—both of his eyes had swollen shut under the pressure of bruises beaten onto his face. Blood stained the floor beneath his body.

"He looks bad," the Changeling agreed, then added almost thoughtfully, "I have humans who could easily circumvent that binding, do the same to you. But to be honest, I don't think it would get me what I want. Sacrificing *yourself* is always the easy part."

On the screen, another man entered the cell where Eli lay prostrate on the floor. He held a cell phone in one hand and the cord disappeared into his forearm, similar to the man Daniel had encountered in Bel's kitchen.

Aiming the phone at the broken body before him, the newcomer snapped a photo, then held the phone closer and tapped at the screen with one finger.

Eli groaned. The sound didn't come through the monitors, but Daniel heard it nonetheless when Eli's lips moved, accompanying the Faerie's twitching, pained motions as he curled into a tight ball.

"Have you heard of technomancy?" the Changeling asked. "Apparently it's all the rage in Faerie right now—integrating your innate powers into electronic, human toys. Your friend the Archduke is a big proponent of the innovation—a patron of sorts. I actually poached this curious specimen from him."

The creature studied the man on the screen, adding, "This one can just look at you and see your past wounds. Even bring them back. Apparently, the camera in the phone stabilizes his vision so he can do more at once. It's quite impressive."

With a gaze down at its own, still-scarred hand, it flexed its fingers and finished, "You'd think old injuries wouldn't be as bad as new ones, but somehow the old ones just . . . sting more."

Daniel wanted to look away, but he couldn't. Dim echoes came back to him of the brutal phantom pain in his leg, in his head, lying on Bel's kitchen floor.

On the monitor, the technomancer tapped his phone screen again. Daniel's memory of Eli's legs ending in mist warred with the sick certainty of the other man spasming in pain as the bone in his shin snapped.

"I can't tell you what I don't know!" he insisted.

"Victor can." The Changeling nodded to the mage near the door. "But you won't let him. If you truly didn't know where the keystone was, I think you'd be willing to let us figure it out for you, to save your compatriot here."

When Daniel looked away from the monitor, trying to focus on the tiled floor, the Changeling tapped another button on the remote. Sound came through speakers to the side of the monitor bank, Eli groaning and choking.

Daniel's throat tightened and he sank to his knees. He swallowed hard, trying to make space beyond Eli's hacking sobs. The sound echoed in his ears but the words he needed wouldn't come. The vision of leathery talons in iron manacles filled his mind.

The Changeling already had three keystones. He couldn't give it the last one.

Another tap of the remote and the speakers cut off abruptly. "Well done." The thing leaned down to say the words quietly in Daniel's ear. "Contrary to your pathetic bluster against this face and its prejudices, I knew you wouldn't break for an Antagonist."

Daniel glared at him but he couldn't argue, washed in shame as he fought to avoid looking at the monitor.

"Watch him die for a bit," the Changeling said, "and then we can discuss whether you'll go through it again for one of your own."

He pressed a button on the remote and brought another screen to life, a brief respite from Eli's writhing body. This one showed a plain white hallway where a figure slouched against the wall, waiting for something.

Breath left Daniel's lungs.

Zeb.

38

ABE STOPPED SHORT UPON entering the kitchen. The back door had returned, nestled into the far wall beside the sink like it always had been. He frowned at the familiar brass knob, which seemed oddly foreboding, though he couldn't figure why.

He'd seized on Jude's trip to Faerie to retreat upstairs and catch forty winks, clear his head a little. He didn't know how long he'd actually been asleep—no clocks in the house—but he felt rested for the first time in days. Like he'd finally gotten a full eight hours. Ten, even.

Hadn't helped much with making a decision about his place here, though. Jude's running out had hurt more than he'd expected, and her casting that binding on Daniel nagged at him too. Good intentions turned too easily into calculated manipulation when power like the Mab's got involved.

Nobody had finished cleaning up the mess in the kitchen. Splashes of flour and bits of hardened, cracked yellow dough still littered the kitchen table and dirty dishes lined the counters. The scene clashed with the pristine, sparkling state he expected from this room. Seemed like somebody should have stepped in to alter things already.

But the house felt different again. Quiet. Abe had become accustomed to the bustle of many unfamiliar bodies in the last day or so.

"Sir?"

He flinched. The honorific grated in an unexpected way, though it hadn't been addressed to him in sarcasm. Turning, he met the eyes of an unfamiliar Faerie guard hovering in the kitchen doorway.

The other creature looked just as surprised to be addressing him.

"Someone is asking for you," he said.

"Me?" Abe regretted the question as soon as it passed his lips.

The guard's eyes darted from one side to the other, as if he might have missed someone more worthwhile in the room.

"Yes," he concluded. "By name."

"All right." Abe started to follow him, then hesitated. "Why's the door here?"

"Sir?"

"This one." He tapped the back door lightly. "Wasn't here earlier."

"Security protocols have returned to normal."

"Since when?" Abe frowned at the honey-coloured rectangle that stood in sharp relief to the white wall. Could it be due to Jude taking an heir? Were the Ubran less worried about her safety now?

"Orders just came through," the guard answered. "We're returning the space to its former state and we'll be departing on the next wave."

"On the next—?" Abe spun to see the guard retreating through the doorway. He sighed and followed.

The front hall didn't feel as long as it had been earlier. The house was contracting, returning to its original size.

Abe forgot his concerns, recognizing the visitor from a distance. He had to steel himself to keep from spinning on his heel, rejecting this audience, and marching right back into the kitchen.

"What do you want?" he snapped.

"I'd have preferred to forgo this meeting," Joshua said. "But these idiots are insisting that Judith is not here."

When Abe said nothing, Joshua added, "She has requested my presence and I demand to see her." His tone was deceptively polite for a demand, but Abe still took too much pleasure in replying.

"Nobody lied to you. She's not here. Went across the portal."

"When?" Joshua's dubious tone snagged on an uncertainty Abe hadn't clocked in his own mind until that moment.

Too long ago. Eight, ten, twelve hours? Even with the time slippage between the realms, the rhythm of the crossing waves, she should have been back by now.

Something was wrong.

"Abe, there you are." Ilse's clear voice rang from the top of the stairs, continuing as she descended. "They've told me they're closing the hou—" She stopped abruptly when she noticed their guest, putting a hand on the banister for stability and staring wide-eyed.

"Don't mind him," Abe said. "He's not staying."

"My daughter summoned me," Joshua growled. "And I will wait."

"No one's waiting here." Ilse matched Abe's tone as she took a few more hurried steps down the stairs.

He appreciated the unified front. He moved back toward the staircase to meet her as she reached the foyer. In a low voice she demanded, "Abe, why are they closing the house?"

"Closing it?"

"Moving the regiment. I can't find Jude."

"Didn't you go over and back with her?"

"Over, yes." Ilse's violet eyes flashed. "But we returned separately."

"You *left* her there?" Surprise made Abe raise his voice more than he'd meant to. A snap of fury sizzled through him but he quelled it when he saw that the water sprite's surprise had turned to icy fear.

"There was a revolt—a minor revolt after the ceremony. It required our hasty exit. I was tasked with leading a decoy team. Jude was overwhelmed." The words were delicate, lacking judgment the way only Ilse could. "The ceremony took too much of her energy. She lost consciousness, but she had healers attending her, and a security team to see her safely back here."

Abe extended his power into the house, feeling for more emotions, more people. The place certainty wasn't amenable to helping him out—magic rarely was—but he could usually pick up on Jude's particular human mix despite the interference.

Nothing.

"What's happened?" Joshua glared at Ilse.

She twitched as if shrugging off his command. Her eyes darted to Abe but she didn't wait for his approval to venture, "The Ubran have already relayed several messages from her so I assumed she was . . ."

She stopped to gesture over her shoulder toward the room that Karl had been using as an office.

"She hasn't been here," Abe said, trying to pitch his voice low and knowing in the same instant that he hadn't achieved any sort of privacy.

"She was intercepted," Joshua snarled, turning toward the door and sweeping out so quickly that it shivered but didn't close.

The relief that flooded Abe's tense muscles when the old mage disappeared through the door was cancelled out too easily by the anxiety that took its place. Was Jude even *in* this world? Had the Ubran detained her in Faerie, taken her prisoner there now that the lineage was assured of continuing?

Dread burrowed into his chest. He wanted to ask Ilse the chances of that, given she was better versed in Faerie politics than him. She'd resent his mistrust, though, and he couldn't afford to alienate her.

"Who headed this security team you mentioned?" he asked. "Eli?"

"No, Eli stayed here." Ilse shook her head, her lips pressing into a thin line. "The Archduke took control of Jude's passage."

"Maybe she's at her consort's place, then." He didn't much like the idea but it gave him a moment of relief before Ilse corrected him.

"Raj didn't become the consort. Jude refused him."

"And you *left* her with him after that?"

"Consort or not, the Archduke isn't her enemy," Ilse said. "Even though Jude's timing was ill-considered, she was within her rights. His position depends entirely on remaining a part of the Mab's Court, so while he'll undoubtedly express his displeasure in some petty way in the future, he wouldn't let her come to harm."

"Not even with his daughter poised to take the throne? Seems like the exact right time for an underhanded power play to me."

"Well, perhaps you're talking out of turn about something you don't fully understand."

Abe wanted to argue, remind her that he'd spent years fighting and undermining the Old Court with Miranda. He'd seen first-hand how those imperious Faerie assholes would do all the harm they could plausibly deny with a shark's smile. Raj was no different, just another variation on the theme.

But he was walking a fine line with Ilse now and he was going to need her help.

"Wouldn't be the first time," he finally conceded to her accusation. "Let's just find out where Jude's gotten to."

39

DANIEL FLINCHED AS THE electronic door swung open. He'd wedged himself into a narrow spot under the bank of monitors where he couldn't watch Eli writhing in pain or Zeb tapping his foot impatiently in the empty hallway as the minutes—hours?—ticked by.

The Changeling had turned the sound back on before leaving. He didn't know how long he'd listened to Eli's weakening moans or to Zeb's increasingly sharp sarcasm as he noticed the camera and started barking at it.

Zeb didn't seem bothered by anything about the situation except the wait, and Daniel had noticed on the screen that his friend wore a key card attached to the front pocket of his jeans. He *worked* here. Leshe must have caught him too. Zeb had never actually been Consilium but he'd worked closely enough with Daniel, and maybe more importantly with Gracie, over the last year to have apparently been worthy of capture.

"And here you are, still frozen." The Changeling hadn't changed forms, continuing to use Alan's voice.

Daniel resisted his urge to snap at it, keeping his eyes fixed on the floor. He wanted to demand it take another face again, but that would only result in derision.

"Ready to do the right thing yet?" the Changeling pressed.

"Let them go." Daniel hated the strangled note in his voice.

"Don't embarrass yourself further. The Antagonist is already dead. You've failed him, though I'm not sure why you pretend to care."

Bitter shame flooded him. The thing was lying, it had to be. But he'd heard Eli's moans taper off into silence. He could hit the Changeling. It would break the binding but for a desperate instant, Daniel wanted that, if only so it would force the creature to hurt *only* him to achieve its goals.

"I don't know where the keystone is anymore!" he snapped. "*Please.*"

"Desperation. That means we're getting somewhere." The thing in his father's body lifted a landline phone on the desk, jabbing one number on the keypad and then relaying, "Go ahead," into the mouthpiece. Then it cast a glance back to the giant mage hovering by the door and made a gesture with one hand.

That prompted Victor to cross the room and haul Daniel roughly to his feet. The big man tightened his fingers around the back of Daniel's neck, squeezing tendons and forcing him to watch the monitors.

On the screen at the top right, Zeb straightened up and gave a wary nod to somebody who'd entered the room where he waited.

"What the hell, man?" he said. "You know it's been forty minutes, right?"

"Yep." The technomancer from Eli's cell approached, holding up his phone and angling it to snap a picture.

"Hey, no photos. What are you, shady goon yearbook committee?" Zeb seemed primed to say more, but the technomancer tapped his phone screen with one finger. Zeb's eyes bulged in surprise and he put a hand to his side, staring down at it as if he expected to see blood. "*What—?*"

The technomancer swiped a finger across his phone screen again and Zeb collapsed to the floor, face aimed away from the camera as he writhed in pain.

"Stop." Daniel tried to pull out of the mage's grip but he couldn't summon enough power to move his legs. His lungs had gone tight and his head spun, trying desperately to settle on any one thought, any certainty. He couldn't escape his father's eyes or Zeb's groans. "Please stop."

"Pathetic." The Changeling chuckled. "Your friend—*only* friend, probably—" The harsh, bitter twist of the knife Alan had always excelled at found its mark. "—is dying in front of you. And you hesitate, let him suffer for your cowardice? *Talk.*"

"I don't know where that key is now!" Daniel snarled. "I saw it, yes, but then she hid it!" He couldn't stop his gaze from shifting back to Zeb's writhing form on the monitor, desperate for some solution.

A third figure had appeared in the room on the screen. The newcomer didn't touch Zeb's tormentor, but the phone tumbled abruptly from the technomancer's hand. The Antagonist himself hit the floor next on his knees before crumpling.

"Who's *she*?" the Changeling asked.

"I don't know." Daniel still couldn't bring himself to look at his father's face, but he had to keep the Changeling's attention off the monitor. He drew a deep breath, tried to pretend he was considering it. He had to fight to keep from rushing his answers. "She wasn't Consilium. I'd never met her before."

"You'll have to do better than that. Her name. Location."

"She's—I don't know." He'd never expected to be so relieved by the goddamn curtain Joshua had used to transport them. He really had no idea where Bel was or how to find her. "I don't know where we were, how we got there."

"Who is *we*?"

The electronic lock on the room's door clicked. The Changeling spun with a snarl to face the interruption. Probably intent on lambasting a subordinate, its eyes went wide as it recognized the intruder.

40

Joshua dodged the first opponent that came at him, a hulking creature radiating the power of a mage. He danced out of the bigger man's grasp, dropping heavily to the linoleum floor to sweep the giant's feet out from under him.

Using his power to topple the big mage triggered the iron he wore strapped to his back. It singed his skin even through his shirt, coat and the towel he'd wrapped it in. He ignored the sting, reaching into his coat instead for the silver knife he'd stashed there.

He dealt two quick stabs, one to each of the big mage's colourless eyes, rendering the other creature truly blind.

The mage roared more in fury than pain, his cry shaking the room. It cut off abruptly as Joshua cast a whispered curse into his ear to freeze his body.

The proximity of the spell to the iron caused what felt like an electric wire to Joshua's own back. Fighting a grimace, he straightened and tugged on one of the heavy, leather gloves he'd liberated from Bel's backyard.

His true adversary waited across the room, wearing the unexpected face of Alan Cain. Strange. It was an older version of the human man than the one Joshua remembered, but familiar all the same.

The monster lifted its chin with a smile, as if catching a scent.

"You've brought iron," it said. "How old-fashioned."

It liked to hear itself talk, this creature. They'd met, possibly more than once, but it was hard to be certain. In any event, its gloating tone probably meant it leaned toward overconfidence rather than gullibility.

Joshua drew the iron rod from his back, lifting it like a bat. The iron burned through the leather glove, but at least it had no competition in the walls. This building wasn't an old Consilium hold. The walls were mere timber, concrete and plaster.

Which meant the Changeling was likely as susceptible to iron as the rest of them.

Joshua darted forward, altering the direction of his gravity to give his swing at the Changeling's head extra force.

Alan Cain's face collapsed in on itself before the iron touched him. The man's body imploded next, shrinking abruptly into something small and fast, something with wings.

Joshua's swing went wide but he recovered fast enough to strike the new creature—a hummingbird, maybe? Or a sylph?—with his other hand. His hit had enough force to knock it off-course.

The burn of the iron exploded through his hand as he altered his trajectory with his own magic and spun to give chase. Not for nothing—he caught the Changeling at the far wall.

Its tiny body burst outwards, growing instantly. It had likely been aiming to be an ogre, but Joshua's thrust of the iron rod buried the poisonous weapon in the general vicinity of its rib cage. He increased his force again to shove the weapon deeply into the wall behind it, pinning the thing.

The half-formed ogre gave a heavy groan that cracked apart into something like laughter. Its body rippled and reformed, flesh fighting to forcefully eject the iron so it could change once more.

Joshua kept both hands on the end of the rod to brace it. The iron jerked again as the Changeling shrank its form into something smaller, trying once more to force the poison out of its healing body.

Then Joshua found himself glowering at his own doppelganger pinned to the wall. It wasn't just mimicking his face—it had his magic, every iota of his power. He could feel the force oozing from the other being, everything he'd built up over fifteen years in hell.

Such a curious creature. It was almost a pity to end it, but the thing was too dangerous to live.

"You're not who I expected to stage a rescue," the creature said, a wet lungful of laughter passing its lips.

"Rescue?" Joshua snorted, then realized there was someone else in the room. A human—the one Jude favoured. The younger Cain—Daniel. Joshua had missed him on first inspection of the room, disregarded in favour of the dangerous opponents. He risked a quick glance over his shoulder to be certain the human still posed no threat.

Daniel hovered against the far wall, watching them with caution. Smart enough to stay out of the fight.

"I'm not here for him," Joshua said, though it felt unnecessary. "Where is Judith?"

"You've been misinformed." The Changeling bared red-stained teeth, its chest heaving again. "Your daughter is not—"

It stopped abruptly and Joshua quelled his disgust at watching his own eyes roll back in the thing's head.

The Changeling died in his form and slotted another one in. A young woman this time, her dark curls streaked with bright pink.

"—here," she finished.

"Turning human won't help you," Joshua said, refusing to marvel at the sudden lack of magic emanating from the woman's form. Whether or not the iron did as much good with the thing feigning human, it still had a metal rod puncturing its chest and a human couldn't survive that either.

The woman grunted, pushing forward slightly. She gained half an inch, forcing Joshua to take one hand from the rod and place it against her shoulder, shoving her back. "You're burning through glamour," he said, ignoring an inadvertent trembling that had started in his hands. The one still holding the iron rod felt like it was gripping a red-hot poker.

"Your flesh will turn to ash before I succumb," the creature hissed.

Noise from the doorway drew Joshua's attention but it was just another human stumbling in. The one he'd come across outside this room, tangling with the abomination that had worked a human cellular phone into its wrist.

Daniel tackled the newcomer, but it seemed more like an attempt to prevent the intruder drawing attention than any sort of aid.

Joshua turned his gaze on them anyway and snapped, "Bring me the knife."

Daniel froze, staring at him. The other human—another male, shorter and darker skinned—went pale and slumped back against the wall, gaping at Joshua with horror.

Had they met? He looked somewhat familiar.

No distractions. Joshua looked back to Daniel and indicated the silver knife he'd dropped beside the prostrate mage.

Then he returned to the Changeling. "Tell me where Judith is and I'll take your head off. It'll be quicker than dying through each one of these faces of yours."

"I don't have her."

"You masked her all winter. Hid her from everyone." If Judith was missing again now, it only stood to reason this creature had taken her once more and covered its tracks.

"You give me too much credit," the Changeling purred. "She did most of the work on her own, cloaking herself from *you*." After giving the barb a moment to settle, it added, "Cloaking her now, at the height of her power, that's beyond my reach. And Victor's." It gave a weak nod toward the big, unconscious mage, then huffed again against the iron in its chest.

Lifting its head with a grin that still showcased a set of bloody teeth, it goaded, "It's so obvious."

The creature's body shifted again, reforming out of the woman so that the Archduke glared down his nose at Joshua. "Who has the motive to shut your daughter away? The means?" it prompted. "She meant to take Raj as her consort, you know. He's probably walled her up in some dungeon to rule in her stead. I can get her back for you."

"Your assistance is unnecessary." Joshua glared at the stricken humans again to thunder, "Bring me that goddamn knife!"

Daniel had gotten to his feet, but not taken a step toward the weapon. His eyes were fixed on the Changeling.

"What if it's right?" he asked.

Hot revulsion coursed through Joshua at the ridiculous question. He couldn't waste energy tossing a spell at the idiot.

"If Raj indeed has Judith, I will free her," he snarled. "Help me end this monster *right now* and maybe you'll live long enough to see her again."

"You'll never get into Raj's fortress," the Changeling taunted. "Not even *you*. Fingerprints. Retinal scans."

"She's not here," Daniel said, voice tight and certain. He took another step toward them, avoiding a swipe from his human companion that seemed intended to drag him back to safety. "I know she's not, because if she were, that thing would be torturing *her* to make me tell it where the keystone is."

"And I would have deeply enjoyed it," the Changeling agreed. It shifted its attention to Daniel, coaxing, "I can get her back for you. Help me and you have my word that I will deliver her to you unharmed."

"Don't you dare try to negotiate with it," Joshua snapped, bristling as he felt the other man getting closer. The human couldn't injure him, hadn't even picked up the knife, but the impending proximity made him feel every twist of the iron throbbing into his hands. "The word of this face dies when it does."

"And, with it, your chances of retrieving Jude!" the Changeling spat. It managed to grip Joshua's wrist with a limp hand to add, "This body is your only chance."

"Lies."

"What if they're not?" Daniel was too close, a hand extended to touch Joshua's arm.

Joshua jerked up a surge of power to backhand the younger man, but found himself tumbling back in a rush of dizzying motion. His body wasn't under his own control until the shock of cold tile slapped his cheek.

He struggled for a breath, sluggish and stunned by the sudden motion that had projected him across the room. His hands still burned, but he propped himself upright as quickly as he could to glare at Daniel.

The insolent whelp didn't even bother to look at him, to make sure the hit had landed successfully. *I'll kill him.* Joshua's fingers itched beneath the burns. He would revel in taking the meddling fool apart piece by piece to learn just how the hell a human had managed that kind of power.

It had felt so much like Joshua's own, the force of the blow he'd meant to deliver, rebounding on him . . .

Damn it. Judith bound him. The subtle, sharp edges of magic curled around Daniel like smoke when Joshua focused. He'd missed it before, in disregarding the human as unimportant. He never should have told her about that spell.

Idiots, the lot of them. Leave them to their doom. He tried to part a curtain in the air but he barely had the strength to lift his hand, much less the power to slit the world open with his blistered, burned fingers.

Daniel laid a light hand on the end of the metal rod that protruded from the Changeling's chest. He didn't put pressure on the iron but shifted his weight as if to show the other creature that he could.

"Your word," he said. "You use your power to find Jude, free her if necessary and return her unharmed. You leave us—everyone in this room—similarly unharmed."

The Changeling licked the blood off its front teeth.

"Agreed."

Rather than yank the iron rod from the thing's chest, Daniel dropped his hand to his side and took a reluctant step back, leaving the creature free to dislodge the iron and heal itself.

The Changeling barked a mocking laugh that turned into a groan as it stretched its shoulders. What had been Raj's face blurred, mutating painstakingly into someone else. The slick, dark line of iron puncturing his dissolving chest bobbed up and down before finally being forced out.

The bloodstained metal rod hit the tile with a sharp, resounding clang.

41

"IF I ASK WHAT the hell just happened," Zeb murmured, "would I get an answer?"

"In this exact moment, no." Daniel had promised his friend a long time ago that he would try to be honest, so he did his best despite being mired in a tumult of anxiety and regret.

Coming down off the high of adrenaline and terror had left him open to galling doubt. It was still difficult to turn the events of the last thirty minutes over in his mind. He'd struck a deal with that monster. At least it had bought him time and space to think.

And Jude's freedom, maybe. If that had been true and not part of some elaborate trap. *For what? It already had me on the verge of giving it Bel's name.*

After freeing itself from the iron, the Changeling had shifted into Tess's form. She'd called a new set of guards into the security room to haul Joshua out, having them snap iron manacles over the old mage's ruined hands as soon as they'd dragged him across the threshold.

"*Everyone* in this room *similarly unharmed,*" Tess had gloated, repeating Daniel's hasty, ill-considered words when he had tried to argue, to hold her to their agreement. "*'Intent' only matters to spells. With bargains, precise wording is key.*"

Which meant he'd trapped Zeb here, safe from the Changeling only within the four walls of this room. Another fuck-up. Another mistake in a long line. That bitter certainty sounded too much like his father's voice in his head, and the thought made him squeeze his eyes shut to banish thoughts of Alan.

"Should we . . . *do* something about him?" Zeb ventured, gesturing to Victor's prostrate form across the room.

Daniel had almost forgotten about the unconscious mage. Victor seemed to be breathing, though the blood on the floor around his head had turned dark and tacky.

"You see a first aid kit around?" he muttered, lowering his head. "Emergency supplies for getting stabbed in the face?"

"No." Zeb fell silent, but the discomfort in his voice made Daniel wish he could find some shred of pity for the big mage. He couldn't forget the painful vise-grip of Victor's fingers on the back of his neck, forcing him to watch the technomancer torture Zeb.

The Changeling wouldn't give up on the keystone. After it fulfilled its part of the bargain that had spared its life—*if* it did—the creature would return to torturing and killing anyone that might drag the information about the stone from Daniel's throat. Zeb, Jude, Gracie, Riley. He'd seen the naked hunger in its eyes when it talked about the keystones, about the Visitant. It wasn't going to stop until it had what it wanted.

The scar on the creature's hand kept nagging him. *Your handiwork*, Diana had said. He'd stabbed Tess Foster through her palm with a piece of iron, one he'd pocketed after cutting it out of Abe's wrist. Joshua had sewn iron under the healer's skin to paralyze him.

Healer. The word caught. The iron had reversed Abe's powers last fall. He hadn't been able to help Gracie after she was injured. Maybe the residual blood on the iron had been what had scarred the Changeling?

It didn't matter. Even if that was the solution, where was he going to get enough iron-poisoned healer's blood to drown the damned thing?

How long would it have lasted with the iron buried in his chest, if he hadn't interfered? It had shape-shifted despite the poison, from the ogre to Joshua to Diana to Raj, then Tess. Could it have held out indefinitely, generating new faces, new creatures? No, there had to be a limit. Joshua had seemed to think so, and while the old mage was probably overconfident, he wasn't stupid. He knew more about the Changeling than anyone.

You're burning through glamour, he'd told it. So the creature used glamour like a regular shapeshifter. That reminded Daniel of something the Changeling itself had said in his father's voice: *Glamour's becoming scarcer*. Almost a complaint. Aubrie's spell had propped the door wider between worlds, more Faeries were coming across and, what? Over-consuming the stuff the Changeling fed on? It wanted to close the portals, limit access, to protect its own sustenance?

Glamour could be unravelled, broken, seen through—but could it be destroyed? Used up? Daniel's rudimentary studies on it at the Consilium hadn't told him enough about it to know, but the more he turned it over in his head, threads of where to start looking began to grow into a shaky plan.

"I thought you were dead." Zeb's interruption brought him crashing back into their current reality. "Tess told me you hadn't survived."

"Tess?" Daniel hadn't realized he could possibly feel worse. He'd forgotten his earlier realization that Zeb had been roped into Leshe's employ too, that that was why he'd been available to the Changeling today. What had his friend gone through these last five months?

Zeb didn't look much worse for wear, at least. Short and wiry, his black hair still buzzed close to his skull and silver gauges shining in his earlobes, he radiated annoyance and exhaustion, but no obvious abuse.

"How did they find you?" Daniel asked. "Leshe and . . . Tess?"

"Grace hustled me off to some hotel that . . . that night." Zeb didn't have to specify further. "I came to the hospital to check on you the next day. They grabbed me before I got to your room."

"I'm sorry," Daniel added, immediately hating the trite words. "I wasn't exactly allowed to text."

Zeb snorted. "Like you would have." Before Daniel could protest, he continued, "Nah, it's not a surprise. Maybe you want to trust me, but you don't. I'm not sure you ever did. I'm not sure you have friends like that."

"Please stop, Zeb." Daniel rested his head in his hands. That only made him think of the Changeling again, of pleading with it.

How the hell could he have taken the thing at its word? Joshua was probably right—its 'word' died when its face did. A pang of nausea roiled through him thinking of the thing's faces melting from one to another like a deranged flip-book.

Zeb seemed to be having the same flashback.

"What was that thing?" he asked.

"Changeling. An ancient shapeshifter that can take any face it wants."

"Asshole. You choose le pire fucking moment to be honest on purpose." Zeb swallowed hard despite his dry, bilingual sarcasm.

Daniel fought back an inappropriate laugh and lifted his head to study his friend.

"How's your side?" he managed.

"Fine."

"No lingering effects from the . . . ?" He wasn't sure what to call the technomancer's attack. A spell? A conjuring? Instead, he touched his ribs in the same spot Zeb had been stabbed last summer, the spot his friend had clutched when the Antagonist had tortured him.

"That stopped as soon as your father-in-law decked the guy with the phone," Zeb said.

The bitterness in that barb stung.

"It's not what you think," Daniel started.

"So you *didn't* abandon what seemed like an escape plan and cave as soon as that—whatever that was—*changeling* said Jude was in trouble?" Zeb challenged. "You didn't cut a deal with it and then beg it not to put her psychopathic father in irons?"

"I didn't beg." Daniel didn't know what else to say.

"What are you going to do, then?" Zeb muttered, his voice a frustrated growl. "Just head off with the new monster when it comes back and tells you where Jude is?"

"I don't have much of a choice."

"You could have let her crazy, murdering father go save her."

"He only cares about her when it suits him."

"Guess that's where she gets it."

Daniel tensed, muscles rigid enough to tweak his bad shoulder. *I deserved that.*

He'd been in shock after getting stabbed in Switzerland last November, but even reeling from the pain and blood loss, he'd heard the sickening snap of bone and recognized Zeb's strangled sob. Joshua had cracked his friend's chest like an egg, intent on removing his beating heart and offering it up to raise a Faerie demon.

He couldn't have betrayed Zeb worse today if he'd tried. He deserved every drop of his friend's vitriol, all the furious disbelief and spite.

"I have to go, Zeb, but you don't," he said. "In fact, you should get as far away from here as possible, while Tess—while the Changeling is gone."

"And go where?" Zeb snorted a bitter laugh, idly flipping the key card that still hung from his pocket. "That changeling thing is my *employer*—it knows where I live, runs my goddamn life. How are you so safe to pal around with it?"

"It can't hurt me." Daniel's throat tightened. The memory of Eli's agonized moans swallowed him before he fought them off. "Jude put a spell on me."

He winced at the heavy sigh that drew from the other man. Zeb's introduction to Faeries had been falling under the thrall of a succubus at a bar. He'd been wary of Jude and everyone like her ever since, certain they were using their magical influence to sway people.

"Is that why you have to go rescue her?"

"No. Not in the way you mean. I'm not *compelled* to go after her, but I . . . I need to." Daniel didn't know how else to explain. "You don't know Raj. If he's got Jude—"

"What? What's he doing that she doesn't deserve? Isn't she the one who beat you within an inch of your life last winter and left you to die?"

There was no easy response for that. Zeb was right, but he didn't understand everything that had happened since then.

The room's door swung open, making them both tense. Daniel got to his feet and gestured Zeb back as Tess strode in. She'd changed out of her bloodstained clothes into jeans and a bulky sweater that made her look more like the young woman Daniel had met at a Montreal university last fall.

"Time to go to Singapore," she said. "I've put a few things in motion for our devious rescue plan, but we'll need to be close to Raj's hotel, ready to roll when the time is right."

When only Daniel started to move closer to her, Tess looked to Zeb. "Come on. You too. We'll need an anchor."

"Zeb stays here," Daniel snapped. "In this room, where you can't touch him."

"Then we all do." Tess's laugh was harsh and triumphant as she folded her arms across her chest. "You didn't think to give me a timeline for rescuing your little queen, you know. I'm *quite* busy, so it might be a few more years before I get back around to it. You want to stay here with your friend, fine. Vending machines are down the hall. They're restocked on Thursdays."

"What's an anchor?" Zeb broke in, climbing to his feet. "Spell it out and don't skimp on the details. What do I do? Does it involve drowning?"

"Zeb—" Daniel started, but his friend's glare stopped him.

Tess smiled, seemingly delighted by their budding argument.

"The Archduke is very well-connected," she told Zeb. "He controls all of the magical routes in and out of not just his hotel, but almost everything on the island of Singapore. Getting out of his territory with our little Mab prize could be difficult.

"I happen to have my own private spot in the city, though," she continued. "A quiet little pied-à-terre with an escape route that's fully hidden from Raj. Problem is, the only way to hide it was to make it invisible to those magical doors everybody likes to use. Hence, I need a living anchor present in the apartment to guide us back there. That way, when I find an enchanted door, instead of saying, 'take us to my secret apartment,' I can say, 'take us to wherever Zeb is.' Makes it harder for them to track us, too, if we're quick." She sighed. "I'd hate to compromise the apartment—I've put a lot of work into it."

"You're not using *Zeb* to keep your real estate safe," Daniel told her, voice flat. "Find somebody else."

"Humans make the best anchors. Stabler energy." Tess grinned at Zeb again. "And *your* presence in particular has the added bonus of the solid, intimate bond with *this* domineering asshole—" She indicated Daniel. "—of which I got a lovely glimpse while I was having you tortured."

She cocked her head and gazed at a corner of the ceiling, miming thoughtful consideration as she avoided both of their glares.

"Make me a bargain, then," Zeb prompted. "Guarantee my safety while I'm anchoring, promise to bring me back here safely immediately afterwards, and I'm in."

"Zeb, don't," Daniel said, trying to pick through his friend's words for any obvious loopholes. "Please don't."

"He's cute when he's begging, hmm?" Tess shot Zeb a knowing smile, then conceded, "Fine. You have my word that while you're anchoring my apartment, you won't come to any harm by my hand."

"By your hand or *anyone* in your employ," Daniel added.

"What he said," Zeb agreed. "And it's a deal."

42

ABE SEARCHED THE UPSTAIRS bedrooms while Ilse 'made some calls.' He had no idea what that actually entailed for a Court water sprite, but he hadn't bothered to ask. He had nobody else to rely on, so he had to let her take point on finding Jude. He didn't really think their queen would turn up asleep in one of the bedrooms, though. He was looking for Daniel. If Jude was really missing, it couldn't hurt to have everybody on deck.

The bedroom Daniel had been using was empty, door ajar. Abe stepped inside, moving a short pile of books aside with his foot. He stooped to grab one. *Of Human Bondage.* Working his way through the tomes left haphazardly around the floor, he realized what he was looking at. Daniel had been conjuring books that had to do with bindings. He'd started too broad, obviously, and finally narrowed the books down to Faerie-related information.

Even then, none of it seemed particularly pertinent to the spell Jude had ordered. So he hadn't found what he'd been seeking. Where the hell was he?

"Eli's gone too," Ilse said from the doorway.

Abe turned to see her standing stiffly. She ran her eyes over the books without taking them in, mind otherwise occupied. Dark edges of doubt had begun to creep into her—whatever she'd found in the last thirty minutes, it hadn't increased her faith in the Ubran or the Archduke.

"It's not your fault," Abe said.

Her eyes snapped up to meet his, startled, then she managed a weak smile that didn't go beyond her lips.

"Thank you," she said. "But it was my responsibility to look after Jude and I fear I may have been found wanting."

Arguing with her'd do no good. Ilse was a stickler for decorum.

"How'd your calls go?" he asked instead.

"I could only leave messages for the Ubran. The Archduke is currently in the human world, but again, I'm being shut out."

"Joshua seemed to have an idea," Abe offered.

"That's why I believe we should follow him."

"Now?" It had been maybe an hour since Joshua had taken off. Plus, time moved differently in the house. Abe was pretty sure it moved slower than in the human world, but every now and then when he exited, he'd been gone longer than he'd thought. Seemed like the house just moved at its own speed, whatever that was.

In any event, there was no guarantee Joshua was even still wherever he'd headed, or that they'd be able to find him.

But they had no other leads, so he followed Ilse back downstairs to the front door. Part of Ilse's 'making calls' had apparently been tracking down Joshua's current location, or at least a last known one. She had better command over the house than he did and she brought them out at the base of a loading dock.

Tall buildings rose on all sides of them. Some sort of urban downtown. Probably Montreal, given the parking restriction signs in French on the nearby street.

Abe let out a low, slow breath and let his power fan out, seeking any sharp, distinct emotions that would indicate someone held against their will. Jude's emotions were usually strong, hard to miss. She wasn't here.

But Joshua had been. Faint remnants of fury hung in the air like a blood trail. Abe had never felt emotions linger in space like this. It should have been magic hovering, the traces of Joshua's deeply cultivated power, but his abilities seemed to be inextricably tied into his state of mind.

Yeah, that tracks. Doesn't bode well, though.

Ilse headed for the door of the loading dock, throwing Abe a glance over her shoulder. She was clearly set on barging into this building whether he backed her up or not. When she reached the presumably locked door, she shimmered and shrank, melting rapidly into liquid that slid through the opening at the bottom.

Abe glanced over his shoulder, scanning for witnesses, but the place seemed empty despite the mid-afternoon sun.

After a minute, the door opened and Ilse let him in. Two human men lay sprawled on the floor, breathing evenly. Without touching them, Abe could see the calm, golden cast of their blissed-out state. The water sprite had calmed them to sleep.

"This way, I think," she murmured, heading toward a door at the far side of the inside loading dock. She was following Joshua's signature—she must have felt his magic too.

They crept down a blank, deserted hallway, then around two corners before Ilse stopped in front of a nondescript door. Without waiting to be asked, she smoothed into liquid form again and seeped under the door.

Abe tipped his ear against it. He heard what sounded like a muffled exclamation of surprise. It cut off sharply, then the knob at his elbow suddenly turned. He jerked back, preparing to fight, duck or run—but it was only Ilse.

She stood back to let him in and then shut the door gently behind him.

Abe stopped short at the puddle of blood on the floor. His eyes travelled up to the bulbous man swaying upright just above it. The cloying, cramped crackle in his skin told him it was a mage—a mage with blood on his face and pain pulsing from his eyes. They'd been gouged by a blade.

"He says Jude isn't here. He requires your assistance," Ilse said.

"He—" Abe trailed off. Had she promised the mage his healing power in exchange for something?

It didn't matter. If she'd made some bargain with the mage, that should be good enough for him. Besides, he couldn't stand idly in the room while the other man's pain tugged at him. He still hesitated, asking the mage, "You armed?"

I am not. The thought came telepathically, reminding Abe that the bigger man probably didn't actually need to see in order to do damage.

He still reached up to press his thumbs gently on the mage's wounded eyes. The other man didn't flinch at his touch, leaning in. Abe barely had to summon much energy to knit the delicate tissues and flesh back together. Faeries came so easily to his power.

Once he'd finished, the bigger man gave an appreciative nod and stepped back.

Abe left him, taking in the rest of the room. It looked like some type of security office. Two of the monitors in a bank of maybe twelve were on. A splatter of blood accompanied a hole in the wall to one side. More blood on the floor, along with what looked like a short section of iron rebar. The tableau gave the impression that somebody'd been run through with the iron but there were no other bodies in the room.

Ilse's sharp intake of breath caught Abe's attention and he joined her in front of the monitors. He followed her eyes and recognized Eli on the black and white screen. He lay sprawled on the concrete floor of a chain-link cage, hands manacled together. The puffy, swollen bruises on his face indicated more of the same beneath his torn, bloody clothing.

The only other illuminated monitor screen showed Joshua huddled in the corner of a make-shift cage similar to Eli's. His hands were manacled in front of him, probably with the same kind Eli wore—almost definitely iron. He stared directly into the camera with a hateful, unwavering glare.

"Hell," Abe muttered.

"Agreed," Ilse returned. She turned, looking to the big mage. "Do you have access to the dungeon?"

43

When the mage failed to understand Ilse's term, Abe tapped the monitor to indicate the chain link cages.

"Know where this is?"

Yes. The big man's voice flooded his mind along with a dim sort of map, making him wince at the intrusion and the volume. He immediately felt the apology and the other man added, *Storage. Freight elevator. Here.* The last word was accompanied by the offer of a key card, presumably to get them more easily through the electronic doors.

Ilse put a hand to her head as if she'd heard and seen the same—maybe the mage had broadcast it to both of them.

"Least we know nobody's watching the cameras but us," Abe muttered.

"For now," Ilse agreed.

"Your hair's leaking, darlin'."

She ran a self-conscious hand back over her hair, which had turned damp and was starting to tinge blue further from the roots. The gesture restored her human glamour with a snap like an icy wall going up.

They left the big mage in the security room. Abe knew he should have been more concerned, but he'd healed the creature. They'd come to an understanding. It wasn't exactly trust, but it was close enough.

Ilse took the lead again outside of the security room, moving casually as if she had every right to be there. They followed the mage's telepathic instructions, which were fast disappearing from Abe's mind like dissipating smoke.

He started when he kicked something small, sending it skittering a few feet down the hall ahead of them. It was a cell phone, its screen smashed, and it trailed a short, black cord that smeared what looked like dark, reddish blood on the floor.

Abe glanced to the spot where it had originally been and saw fingers peeking through an open doorway. An unconscious man lay on the floor in the empty room, blood leaking from a ragged hole in his wrist where it looked like the phone cord might have been joined to him.

"Abe, don't—" Ilse started, just as he'd crouched to touch the man's hand. A flicker of pain shot down the inside of his own wrist, sharp and sudden enough to take his breath away. He tumbled backwards, breaking contact.

"There's something wrong with him." Ilse held the phone by one corner between her fingers.

"You don't say." Abe examined the inside of his wrist, half-expecting to see a distention of mottled purple and red, the way it had looked after Joshua had sewn iron rods under his skin last fall.

His arm looked fine. His body had healed those wounds months ago. Didn't even hurt now. Almost like he'd imagined the shock of unnervingly familiar pain.

"I *did* say—" Ilse stopped when she saw his expression, recognizing the sarcasm a beat too late. She flung the phone away. "It's some sort of . . . modification," she said, frowning sourly at the man. "It feels warped, unnatural. I don't like it."

Abe didn't feel anything different than another Faerie, but Ilse was clearly more attuned to the power. He did another cursory check of the man without touching him. Whoever'd assaulted him had torn the phone from his wrist, knocked him out with a solid blow or two, but he seemed to be breathing evenly. He'd probably wake up, though what state he'd be in would depend on what the phone had been hooked into his body for.

"Leave him." Ilse took a step back. "I'm starting to forget the map."

Abe realized the big mage's telepathic aid had fled his own mind entirely. He shoved himself up off the floor and followed Ilse at her quick pace.

She sighed with relief when they finally reached a large elevator, then hesitated, looking to the key card clutched in her fingers.

"Swipe it." Abe nodded toward the black, electronic pad beside the direction buttons on the wall.

Ilse did as he demonstrated and tapped the key card to the pad before hitting the down arrow. When it turned green and the arrow lit up, she allowed a small smile.

"Just like in the movies."

The elevator doors slid open and a tinny, recorded voice announced, "Going down. En descente."

The wide freight elevator took them down two floors to B, and stepping off, Abe knew they'd come to the right spot. The room was large and shadowy, but broken up into small cages by the same fences he'd seen on the monitors upstairs.

"Not much iron," Ilse said with a touch of relief. "None in the walls or the fences."

They found Eli first, sprawled on the floor like a battered doll, the same way he'd been on camera. He wasn't breathing. Abe could feel the chilly lack of emotion, the lack of life from outside the cage. The man had been dead for a few hours at least.

"Hell," he muttered, swiping his hat from his head in a futile gesture of respect.

"He smells like the one upstairs." Ilse's voice was brittle with fury.

"The phone guy?" Abe opened his mouth to ask if 'smells' was really the word she'd meant to use, but Ilse gave a quick shake of her head.

"We might not have much time," she said.

Abe followed her deeper into the maze of cages—storage, the big mage upstairs had called it. Ilse'd been closer to the truth in calling it a dungeon.

They found the cage where Joshua huddled. Just like with Eli's cage, a padlock joined two ends of a heavy chain to hold the door closed.

"Not very sophisticated." Ilse touched the padlock gingerly, lifting it to see the keyhole. The fingers of her free hand merged and elongated into liquid, flooding the tiny lock with enough pressure to move the pins. Then she yanked the chain free.

"Are you just going to stand there or do you plan to get me out of here?" Joshua snapped, when Abe didn't immediately pull the door wide.

The complete lack of gratitude made him feel less guilty about the instinctively petty response that rose to his lips.

"Kinda enjoying the 'standing' right now."

"I told you before, my assault on you was nothing personal," Joshua grumbled. "It was to put my daughter out of harm's way."

Abe balked. "When'd you tell me that?"

The older man hesitated, a shadow of uncertainty passing over his face. It was gone just as quickly, and his lips twisted into a sneer.

"I have all day," he said. His eyes flickered in the direction of the camera he'd been staring at. "You may not, if you'd prefer not to end up next door."

The bastard didn't know nobody was watching the cameras. Abe suppressed the urge to tell him, '*Nah, we'll wait*,' because Ilse made a noise in the back of her throat.

She was right. They still had to find Jude, and they had no idea when whoever ran this place was coming back.

44

Daniel followed the Changeling across the opulent hotel lobby. The creature strode with an easy, casual grace like it actually did own the hotel that went along with the face it wore. At what seemed to be somewhere around midday, the place was peopled but not crowded. A few travellers stood at the check-in desk with luggage and several others had taken up sleek wing-back chairs near the front windows to pull out a laptop or phone. No one paid them any attention, which seemed odd given the Archduke was some kind of celebrity.

He remembered the placid, round-faced man who greeted them at the desk in front of the hotel's private elevator. Same concierge as last November. The man's eyes slid past him with no recognition, fixing on the Archduke.

Daniel braced himself for some realization of the façade, for armed guards to descend on them.

"Welcome back, sir," the man said. With only a slight tilt of his head toward Daniel, he asked, "Should I have this taken to the sixth floor?"

"No." The Changeling-as-Archduke said the word with a wry twist, resting a hand lightly on the back of Daniel's neck.

Daniel twitched, muscles tensing, but fought not to shrink from the touch. As if playing into his instinctive reaction, the fingers tightened on his neck and Raj's voice purred, "I intend to keep this one a while longer."

The creature really had the Archduke's self-satisfied amusement down pat.

"Very good." The concierge didn't seem bothered.

The Changeling tilted Raj's chin up and widened his eyes just slightly at what looked like a camera at the top of the elevator. After a second, the doors opened automatically. The creature gave Daniel a slight push forward and then followed in the usual languid manner that suited his current face.

Daniel slowly let out the breath he'd been holding as the doors closed without the Archduke's servant joining them.

He could help asking, "What's on the sixth floor?"

"How should I know?" The Changeling smiled a lazy Raj smile, eyes half-hooded. "Harem? Abattoir?"

Daniel suppressed a shudder. *We're here to get Jude and get out.*

The elevator went to the thirtieth floor without either of them pressing a button. When the door opened, the hallway outside was empty and quiet. Daniel knew this walk. He'd come to this same hallway with Jude and Abe last fall.

"He's keeping her in his private suite?" he asked, trying to shove down a flare of protective anger.

The Changeling's smile indicated that he hadn't succeeded.

"Close at hand," it agreed.

Buildings glittered in golden sunlight beyond the giant windows, stretching out for a fantastic distance. The doors to the suite were unlocked.

The Changeling-as-Archduke entered with a flourish, ushering Daniel inside. Closing the door, the creature went to the desk nearest the entryway, opened a drawer and removed what looked like a small, black remote.

Aiming it at one corner of the room, it pressed a button and then set the remote aside. "No need for cameras."

Daniel scanned the corners of the open, airy room but didn't see any of the aforementioned cameras. Most of the room was taken up by a cushy yellow sofa, two plush, navy armchairs and a large flat-screen television. Like outside in the hall, giant windows ran along one wall. Despite being Raj's base of operations and, ostensibly, his home in the human world, the suite was pristine and generic. The only personal touches were a vase of flowers on the desk by the front door and a large oil painting over the television that was done in too much red and black splatter to be sedate, hotel-standard art.

"You've been here before?" he asked.

"Once or twice." The response was sly, inviting further questions.

For an instant, he couldn't help wondering if the Changeling had set him up, actually sent him in here with the real Raj. It made him snap his response more sharply than he'd intended.

"As *what?*"

The other creature only offered a knowing smirk and inclined its head toward the hallway at the far end of the main room. Colourful guitars were mounted on the walls here, some pristine and some clearly well-worn, but most were elaborate and probably expensive.

Checking the closed doors in the hallway, the Changeling faltered. It opened one to an empty bathroom, then the next to an empty bedroom with a hiss of annoyance.

Daniel looked past him and had to blink. For an instant, he'd seen a door at the far end of the long hall, but he must have imagined it, because it was just a blank wall. Odd, actually, given the spacing of the guitars along the other walls—

"There," he said, understanding in another instant.

"I see it." The Changeling sounded annoyed, shouldering past him toward the glamoured door.

The door materialized as they got closer and appeared fully when the Changeling put a hand on the knob and turned it. They entered a small bedroom that contained a bed against one wall, perpendicular to the same floor-to-ceiling windows that ran along the side of the whole suite.

"Nice of him to give her a view," the Changeling chuckled.

Jude lay in the bed on her back, soft blankets pulled to her chest and her hands folded over them. Her hair was loose, smoothed away from her face, and she wore a blue pyjama top. She breathed evenly, expression serene and lashes dark against her cheeks. She looked like a posed doll. What the hell had Raj done to her?

Daniel couldn't keep his hands from clenching into fists. He scanned for anyone else in the room, trying to pick out any telltale glimmers that might indicate magic or glamour. Had she really been left alone, unguarded?

He crouched beside the bed and touched her hand, then shook her shoulder gingerly. When neither stimulated even a twitch, he brushed her cheek and said her name. Her skin was warm but her body seemed too still for this sleep to be natural. Nothing he did altered the slow rhythm of her breath.

"How do we wake her?" he asked.

"You could kiss her," the Changeling returned.

Daniel ignored the thing's smirk. Seeing Jude helpless and fragile like this brought a new, painful clarity to her casting the binding spell on him. Right now, he'd use any spell, do anything, and fuck the consequences, just to see her awake—colour in her cheeks, that wry smile and the challenging glint in her eyes.

But it couldn't be as a simple as a kiss, could it?

"Ah, here we go." The Changeling spoke again before he'd made up his mind, nodding toward the wall above the headboard.

A small, silver mirror hung there, but the other creature's calm tone hadn't taken into account the horrific presence of a human-shaped hand that had been messily amputated partway down the arm and nailed to the wall beneath it.

A hand that held a cellular phone with the cord snaking into the vein at the wrist.

Below it, the mirror reflected another blurry hand on the opposite wall. Stomach shifting, Daniel turned to follow the sight-line and found a piece of polished, black stone the same size as the mirror. The hand above this mirror didn't have a cell phone, probably the partner of the first one.

"Told you, technomancy is trendy right now." The Changeling smirked at the gory tableau. Studying the two polished surfaces that reflected each other, it murmured, "Caging the spell between an infinite mirror is clever. Identical mirrors create too strong a feedback loop to hold magic forever, but obsidian and silver—that's an atonal minority that would probably even keep this poor bastard's flesh from decaying. Honestly, I'm impressed."

"You would be," Daniel muttered. If the technomancer who'd unwillingly donated his arms to Raj's project had been the same one who'd drawn up his previous wounds in Bel's kitchen, maybe he'd brought back Jude's coma from last spring. Then Raj had used the mirrors to trap her in that state indefinitely? That sick bastard.

A door slammed open from the front room. The Changeling grimaced.

"Raj must have had some code to the cameras I didn't catch."

"Can we move her?" Daniel snapped. "Will it hurt her?"

Several heavy sets of approaching footsteps answered that question. Someone battered the wood of the hidden door with what Daniel imagined was probably the butt of a large gun.

"I've never seen this before, so I don't know." Raj's lips curled into a bitter smile but the Changeling winced as the door shook under another blow. "Have we got another choice?"

They didn't. Daniel snatched a decorative lamp from the bedside table and the Changeling seized a small end table from beside the shuddering door. With a glance, they synchronized. Daniel swung the lamp into the mirror as the Changeling smashed the obsidian plate.

45

I woke with a gasp, yanked abruptly out of a dream I couldn't remember. My racing heart and the sweat soaking my clothes made me up my classification from dream to nightmare.

"Hands on your heads!" someone snarled.

Vision came back slowly as I blinked, resolving out of darkness. I was lying on something soft but firm—really comfortable, actually. Why was someone barking out orders?

"On your *heads*." The voice came sharper, slower.

"This is as high as it goes." That terse, furious response stirred a warm affection in my chest. *Danny?*

"What's going on?" I rasped, forcing the room into focus. My body felt blurry, like a mild hangover.

"Get on your knees!" The more distant voice barked again.

"I'm already sitting down!" I snapped, realizing in the same moment that I rested on a giant, cushy mattress, with buttery soft sheets tangled around my legs. Why was I wearing silky, blue pyjamas in an unfamiliar bed?

"Jude." Daniel stood beside the bed. He hissed my name like an aside, but he wasn't looking at me, eyes fixed at something in front of us. He'd moved his right hand to the back of his head but his left arm was only raised halfway in surrender. He couldn't lift it higher, thanks to the griffin's claw wounds.

I followed his gaze to three unfamiliar men bearing—was this some movie-induced section of my nightmare?—shiny, black, semi-automatic weapons. Their bodies filled the doorway in front of us.

Where were we? The last thing I remembered was passing out in the shifting, dreamy Faerie world. Right after throwing up. Ugh.

This room felt stale and generic, and it smelled . . . *real*? The word came unbidden to my brain, either in response to the thought that this might be the Faerie realm or still my nightmare. I touched my eyes to make sure they weren't still smeared in ointment. My face was clean.

The man closest to the end of the bed lowered his weapon when I met his gaze. He twitched like he'd considered bowing.

"Your Highness," he said, his voice slightly strangled. That made the other guys lower their guns slightly, looking at him in horror.

"Could you ask 'em not to shoot us?" Another familiar voice came from the other side of the bed. Abe.

"Nobody shoot anybody," I managed, blinking and swivelling my head to take the whole thing in. Daniel stood closest to me, at my right. He stared past me at Abe in amazement, as if he hadn't expected the cowboy to be there either.

My heart pounded hard enough in my chest that it was probably visible through the thin pyjama top. How had I gotten here, into somebody's bed? Why didn't I remember? Vomit burned my throat and I forced a slow breath out through my nose.

"Where are we?" I asked.

"Singapore," Abe answered.

"The *hell* we're in Singapore!" I sat up straighter, but recognized the decor of the Archduke's hotel fortress with a jolt. Ilse had said Declan would get me safely home—why the hell had I been sleeping over here? "What happened?" I demanded, digging my fingers into the soft sheets as if that might keep my head from spinning off my shoulders.

"The important thing—" Abe's drawl was still annoyingly calm. "—is that we get out of here *now*."

"Why wouldn't we?" I hesitated, eyeing the armed men in the doorway, at least one of whom was Faerie, since he'd recognized me as the Mab. I put my next question to them, keeping my voice as hard as possible. "Are we prisoners?"

"Of course not, Your Highness," the lead guard said, keeping his eyes lowered.

"Cool. Then we're leaving." My head was too fuzzy to deal with this, but I trusted Daniel and Abe. The former moved closer, lowering his hands as if he expected he might need to support me, but my legs held as I climbed out of the bed.

"We'll need an enchanted door," Abe told the guards.

"Yes." The lead guard still sounded uncertain. "Uh, this way."

He led, and the other two let Abe, Daniel and I follow him. They brought up the rear through what looked uncomfortably like the Archduke's lush hotel suite and out the set of double doors into the hallway I hated recognizing.

The lead guard took us down the hall to a plain-looking door just shy of the elevator. He stopped and gestured for me to open it. An enchanted door, Abe had said. Had to be like the safe house—a door that would take me anywhere I wanted. I couldn't help hesitating at the unpleasant memory of the woozy, dreamy Faerie realm being on the other side. It wasn't, though—not here.

"I don't want to go back to the house," I warned Abe under my breath. "Not yet." Maybe not ever.

The cowboy put a hand on my arm, sliding gently around me to take charge of the situation.

"I got it, Majesty." He said my shortened title like a term of endearment, maybe for the benefit of the guards around us, but it still sounded weird.

He stepped close to the door and whispered something, probably an address he didn't want the other guys to overhear. When he shoved it open, I followed him through the door and Daniel brought up the rear, closing it behind us.

Then we were in an empty apartment with filmy paper curtains on the windows to diffuse the light.

"Where are we now?" I managed.

"Still Singapore," Abe started.

"Who are *you* now?" Someone appeared suddenly from my left, cutting off the cowboy's explanation.

I jumped, inadvertently letting out a shriek of surprise that I wanted to regret when the newcomer gave me a smirk. What the hell was *Zeb* doing here?

"It seemed wiser to appear as someone she trusted," Abe answered him. His voice was a mix of annoyance and amusement.

"But you're not?" I stiffened, automatically studying his familiar face. His dark eyes held a wry glint that was very un-Abe. He'd dropped his usual folksy drawl.

"I suppose that remains to be seen." The cowboy's weathered face reformed in ripples until I met the glittering, disdainful eyes of a Black woman a few years older than me. Tess Foster, the ex-Consilium traitor who'd roped Daniel into William Leshe's employ. No, scratch that—Tess Foster, supposedly a face of my father's fabled changeling.

"Fuck." I stepped back and collided with Daniel. He tried to put an arm around me, conceivably to pull me back or shield me, but I shied away, putting distance between myself and the three of them. "What the hell is going on? You guys shapeshifters too?" I snapped at him and Zeb.

"No," Daniel said, as Zeb rolled his eyes. "Jude, you were in Raj's hotel—"

"Yeah, I figured that out." Asleep in a bed in Declan's private suite. A shudder ran through me and I braced my shoulders to keep from letting it show. I couldn't banish the tremor from my voice but it didn't stop me from challenging, "Why? How?"

Daniel's eyes darted to Tess as if he expected her to explain, but I got his attention and added, "Not her. You." I kept my eyes on his face so as not to miss a single twitch in his expression that might betray that he wasn't who he appeared to be.

"Raj has thugs that call themselves technomancers," he said. "Some of them can apparently visualize your old injuries, make them manifest again in your brain—make you feel them like they're actually happening again. They take your picture with a cell phone that's . . . connected to their body, and they using that to pinpoint your memories somehow. We think he got one of his people to summon back your coma from last spring and trapped you in it."

There were so few words in that sentence that made sense, but the overall gist did sound like shit Declan would pull.

One word bugged me more than the others, though.

"We?" I inclined my head toward Tess, who had just been Abe, and—if I'd heard Zeb's initial question of 'who the hell are you now?' correctly—somebody before that. Maybe Diana.

"She's Joshua's Changeling," Daniel agreed.

"I will tear out your lungs if you call me that again." Tess glared at him, then seemed to realize her mistake and jerked her chin toward Zeb instead, correcting, "*His* lungs. Damn binding."

"You promised no harm would come to him by your hand," Daniel warned.

"What a time to find out Joshua was right," she shot back with a menacingly cheerful grin. "Constraints on harm by my hand are entirely dependent on *whose* hand I'm wearing."

"How do you know any of this is true?" I couldn't follow the conversation as it veered off, still half-mired in the bizarre idea that I'd just been pulled out of the exact same coma as last year. How the hell did that *work*?

"Because Zeb and I both experienced it too," Daniel said, eyes darting briefly to his friend. "When Raj grabbed me and brought me to you, to the house, one of his goons used the same kind of power on me to bring back . . . injuries from last year." He left that vague, shifting uncomfortably before nodding at Tess to finish, "And *this* had one of them torture Zeb."

"Changeling Tess has Terminators too? This just keeps getting better." Why the hell was Daniel cooperating with her?

"Technomancers," Tess herself—or not—corrected me with a withering sigh.

"I need to sit down," I mumbled, glancing around the empty apartment, half a second away from just collapsing into a heap on the floor. Declan had spirited me out of the Faerie realm and used some kind of cell phone magic to trap me in a Sleeping Beauty spell, a goddamn coma rerun? Why—to put his daughter in charge now that she was officially my heir? Or was this just retaliation for my breaking our 'engagement' so publicly, refusing to sign his little contract in front of all of his friends?

It didn't matter why. The fucker would pay for this. As soon as my head stopped spinning.

"Don't fall apart yet, Your Highness—we're not out of Raj's reach." Tess shoved the door open to reveal what looked like a tunnel of some sort. It was pitch-dark with rough, earthen walls. A line of smooth, grey stones had appeared across the threshold when she'd opened the door. "He won't follow us here."

"Hell if I'm walking into the dark with a bunch of shapeshifters," I said, shaking my head and managing a step back.

"*She's* the only shapeshifter," Daniel said, indicating Tess again.

"Then why are *you* with her?"

"I needed her to get you out of Raj's hotel."

"Prove it." Now that we'd left the Archduke's armed guards behind, I didn't feel the tingle in my skin at all, from any of them. But I hadn't felt it from Diana either. "Prove you're not shapeshifters."

"I'd have left you in the tower growing your hair out," Zeb muttered, "but I was overruled."

Okay, Zeb checked out.

I turned on Daniel, making my voice as hard as I could to keep from sounding like I was begging him. "Say something only you and I know."

He struggled for a moment to think of something, then finally offered, "When you were high on painkillers last fall, you were filling out a magazine quiz at the hospital and you asked me if you were 'scrappy.' "

His words stirred a dim recollection that made my cheeks start to burn despite my hazy, high-alert state. The embarrassment intensified to 'fire of a thousand suns' when Zeb stifled a laugh.

"And now I *really* regret that," I said.

"The answer is yes."

"I'm convinced you're you. Literally shut up now."

46

CROSSING THE LINE OF stones in front of the door sent me spinning into darkness, falling. Then I landed on solid ground in a dimly lit space. The circle pressed in tight around me, squeezing my body until I stumbled across another line of stones, gasping.

The air felt only slightly better outside. I closed my eyes tightly as a wave of vertigo crashed against me. Daniel sank into a crouch and put his head between his knees. Zeb was prostrate with his forehead pressed against the ground.

"Any better this time?" Tess asked, in a chipper, mocking tone that said she already knew the answer.

They'd done this before, then, coming with her to find me. To rescue me. What the hell had Daniel promised this changeling in return?

"Where are we?" I managed. Light came from somewhere above the circle of stones we'd stumbled out of, but it was dark otherwise and I couldn't make out any walls. The space around the stone circle was open and empty. No breeze pushed the air around us and it smelled earthy, stagnant and stale, like an unfinished basement. The silence made my ears ring.

"We went through a Faerie Ring," Tess said. "We're on the Old Roads."

My body ached—I hadn't realized until now that all my muscles had been tense and alert for a while—since going through the unfamiliar door in the hallway of Declan's hotel, maybe. It was something more now, though. For how dim and empty the place around us looked, it vibrated with a hum of electricity that made the hair on my arms stand at permanent attention. Like being surrounded by a crowd of Faeries—dense magic.

"We shouldn't stay here," Tess added. "Can you walk?" She eyed us warily, and we all pulled ourselves to our feet, managing to stay upright now that we weren't in the heavy pressure of the Ring.

We made it about five metres before Tess threw up a hand. "In the name of the Mab, we demand safe passage!" she shouted. Then she glanced over her shoulder to tell me, "I use that all the time down here, but I'm sort of curious to see if it changes anything that you're actually *here*."

"That'll keep things from attacking us?" Zeb asked dubiously.

"Make them think twice about it, anyway."

"What are *things*?" I asked.

"Whatever's been living down here, keeping the Old Roads in use." She hesitated, darting a look to the left as if she'd heard something, then said tersely, "Let's go, quickly."

"These roads only exist because something lives down here?" I hissed, striding to keep up with her.

"They're woven from glamour. Glamour only comes from living beings. Hurry up!"

We reached another circle of stones with a phantom light illuminating it from somewhere above, and Tess paused, gesturing to it. "Inside."

Something skittered behind me—something that sounded too big to be skittering. I spun, muscles primed to fight. The next sound that came from the gloom in front of me stirred a sense of terror I hadn't known existed. A weird chittering, the sound of a hard shell vibrating. It made me feel intensely human, soft and vulnerable.

Daniel started to say something, but I shoved him away. I'd meant to just push him across the stone boundary and into the circle, but when my hand made contact with his chest, a force erupted between us. It sent me sprawling to one side and I coughed at the stale dust I'd stirred up.

"I wasn't even trying to hurt him!" I snapped to no one. Goddamn binding.

Wait, where was everybody else? Swivelling my head showed that they'd all disappeared, and so had the circle of stones we'd just been standing beside. The binding's retaliation had knocked me further away than I'd realized.

I got to my feet, the immensity of the darkness around me making me want to draw into myself, stay as small as possible. Light still came from somewhere above but didn't seem to cast any shadows, leaving the open space around me a murky grey.

Parting my lips to call out, I couldn't bring myself to make a sound. My ears still rang with the stillness. Nobody else was here. I was alone.

Not quite. Something emerged from the darkness ahead of me with the flutter of too many tiny feet.

My body reacted instinctively, without waiting for my brain to catch up, and I sprinted in the opposite direction.

A circle of stones resolved out of the amorphous space, laid out on the ground like the ones where I'd just been. The place seemed empty except for my footfalls and the horrifying scuttling of a few dozen soft feet behind me.

I wanted to leap across into the circle to safety, but I stopped short, suddenly remembering how Eli had melted the safehouse's back door back into the kitchen wall and then pressed his body so protectively against that space. He'd been afraid of something *here* darting through the door's opening. *Things that shouldn't exist*, he'd said. What if I went through the circle and this creature on my tail followed me?

I turned to see my pursuer. It gleamed gold and brown under the sickly light—a giant beetle, as tall as me when it reared up on two sets of back legs and waved its front legs at me. Its face—head?—was oval and almost human, except it had eight eyes that blinked in unison and shone with intelligent malice. No mouth.

Oh, no—there *was* a tiny, pulsing mouth, between the oversized, jagged pincers at the bottom of its head.

Yeah, I couldn't let this thing follow me home.

47

THE SHIVER OF THE bug's antennae sent a jolt of reflexive revulsion through me. My muscles screamed to shift gravity and leap safely to the ceiling—but was there even a ceiling in here? Usually I had a pretty good awareness of surfaces I could jump to, but the Old Roads just seemed to stretch up forever.

I sucked in a breath and tried to be diplomatic. Just because it was a bug didn't mean it wasn't a Faerie. I couldn't rely on my usual skin tingle to reassure me because the whole place pulsed against my body in a charged, stuttering heartbeat.

"Hi. We haven't been introduced, but I—yeeeagh!" The syllable trailed off into a gag without my permission when the creature's face gave a sickening twist. It rotated like a clock, all eight eyes studying me intently as it spun in a series of jerky motions.

"I'm the Mab," I finished, with as much authority as I could muster given my skin was currently trying to squirm off my bones. "Your, uh, queen." I'd tried not to make that a question, but even I didn't believe it.

The bug's face clicked back into place, having gathered whatever information it needed. Then it moved in a blur, its hard-shelled body slamming into me with a shocking impact.

Breath left my lungs in a huff when I hit the rough dirt of the Old Roads with the thing on top of me. Its paralyzing weight triggered a flashback to sitting up, shocked and hazy in the tangled sheets in Declan's hotel.

Fury ripped through me, electrifying my muscles. I wanted desperately to lash out, not just to protect myself but to crush something in my bare hands, to tear flesh with my teeth—to bring fierce, bitter pain.

I managed a wild punch to what I thought was the bug's head, and it screamed. The pitch of the sound made me wish I didn't have ears. Using one hand to shove its razor-sharp pincer away from my face, I groped with the other over my shoulder for one of the stones that made up the circle. My fingers closed around the solid, smooth weight, and it came free of the dirt easily.

I slammed the rock into the side of the bug's rotating head. The stone almost slipped out of my fingers when it hit the hard shell, but I managed to get a second, lower hit to the side of the thing's face. This one cracked one of its sharp pincers.

With a grunt, I closed my free hand around the broken, jagged appendage and wrenched it off.

The bug jerked back with another scream that made the blood boil in my brain. It freed me long enough that I remembered my new power. Whether or not there was a ceiling up there didn't matter for me if I aimed my gravity at the bug.

I hauled myself up and tried to summon the heat into my hands that I'd felt when I'd knocked Joshua off the balcony in Tofino, when I'd tried to fight the tree people on the highway. I shoved the bug back, channelling my anger and fear into a dense force that I aimed at its centre.

The creature jerked up as if pulled by a string, dragged away from me, but it didn't go as high into the air as I'd hoped.

Exhaustion flooded me as the heavy thing crashed back to the dirt. I couldn't call the energy back into my trembling arms.

I'd dropped the bug's liberated pincer, but I snagged it from the dirt just as the thing leapt on me again. I lifted a knee, intent on driving it into the creature's underbelly, but I let out a strangled shriek when my kneecap cracked audibly against its hard exoskeleton. My arms faltered long enough for the bug to snap its remaining pincer within millimetres of my nose.

The bug laughed—fucking *laughed*—a hard, wheezing sound that sounded mammalian. The reaction made its layered body twist, showing that its shell was formed of several layers of plating.

Bracing one arm against the creature, I pulled the liberated pincer back and buried the sharp end in the bug's side, aiming for the space between plates. My second swing sank into something soft.

The bug screamed again and I had to clench my teeth to keep them from vibrating out of my head. I shoved the pincer in deeper. Thick, hot liquid slipped over my hand, coating my fingers. I flipped my gravity to press my weight forward, burying the jagged piece deeper into the thing's abdomen and fighting to rip it across the bug's width.

Warmth seeped through the fabric of my filmy pyjama top. The bloodcurdling scream that had been rattling my skull choked off into silence. The bug's weight collapsed on me.

I gasped, mind reeling in the dark, stale air. The lifeless weight pressed me down, too heavy to shove off. I managed to wriggle out from under it, hauling myself away on trembling arms. I got to my feet covered in something sticky that was either blood or guts, and flung the torn pincer to one side before stumbling across the circle of stones.

Nothing happened. I still stood in the dim, stale cave with the dead bug lying to one side.

A hole in the circle at my feet gaped like a missing tooth. I'd torn one of the stones free and dropped it after hitting the bug with it. It was within arm's reach, just outside the circle.

I bent forward to grab it and pop it back into place. The ground fell out from under me with enough force to suck the air from my lungs.

Should have gotten *out* of the circle, replaced the stone, *then* gotten back in.

That realization was lost as darkness flooded my brain, then light—way too much light. A vast, yawning sky gaped open to suck me in, tearing me upwards.

Hands stopped me, fingers digging into my sides, then my arms, jerking me upside down then upright with a speed that made me hack and double over.

"Jude?" Daniel's voice. The blurry form above me, the arms wrapped around me, had to be him. Fear and concern coloured his words, enough to stir a desperate relief in me. "Jude, are you okay?"

Gentle, cautious hands searched me again from somewhere beyond my consciousness, fingers easing their way down my body looking for wounds.

Reality crept in. Oxygen inflated my lungs with a painful spark, triggering the familiar rhythm of breath. The air was fresher, cold and crisp like impending snow.

"Yeah," I managed, straining the muscles in my abdomen to sit up despite the weakness that warned me it wasn't a good idea. "Giant bug."

Brushing my own limp, ineffective fingers at the yellow, sticky substance that coated my chest and stomach, I muttered, "Ugh. I guess sometimes you really *are* the windshield."

Daniel choked out a laugh. His hand stayed warm on my cheek, his relief almost palpable through my skin. The closeness of his body struck me, the warmth, the faint soap and sweat scent. I felt safer and steadier than I had in a long time.

For an instant, I just wanted to tap out, preserve the moment, but another voice snapped me back to reality.

"Yes, yes, very touching."

Daniel's fingers tensed on my arm. The pressure made me aware of the protection his body put between me and the creature that had spoken. Had he ever protected me before? On purpose?

Probably not since throwing himself into the bar fight that had put him in my path and ruined his life.

"She could need medical attention," Tess added pointedly.

"Abe," I started.

"You run a risk going back to the Court," she said. "You have an heir now. Do you really think the Ubran didn't know what happened to you? Where you were? Or is it more believable that they were willing to let the Archduke leave you in an enchanted sleep and take the throne?"

Karl and Saskia had said my life was sacred, but that didn't mean there weren't workarounds, like Declan's tossing me back into a coma I hadn't liked the first time around. Tess was right. The Court didn't need me alive and conscious; they just needed me breathing. Until they didn't.

"I offer sanctuary," Tess continued. "For all of you. 'Hospitality' is how we used to put it. Shelter, medical assistance, a meal."

"Nah," I said, staggering to my feet with Daniel's help. It was dark here, though brighter than the Old Roads, with bluish streetlights casting a glow on everything around us. We stood just outside the circle of stones in what seemed to be an empty, overgrown city lot. "A little coffee," I added, "full hangover breakfast poutine, and maybe pointing some cannons at the goddamn Archduke and I think I'll perk up just fine, thanks."

"Give us twenty-four hours," Daniel said. "In lieu of your 'sanctuary.' Twenty-four hours in a location we don't have to disclose, ever. Not to you or anyone. No one you coerce, command or *ask fucking politely* is allowed to be present, to watch or to listen to any of us during that time. At the end of it, I'll bring you the keystone, but I'm your partner. I'm along for every move you make. We go to the Lower Halls together."

Keystone. The word snagged on my brain. Those things the palace librarian had said allowed access to the Lower Halls? Not so good and lost after all, apparently. How the hell did Daniel have one? What else hadn't he told me?

"Fully absorbed the lesson about precise wording, I see." Tess rolled her eyes, then her expression turned calculating. "And if I demand one of your companions as a guarantee for good behaviour while you're gone?"

"Then take your pick." Daniel's calm, indifferent tone gave me whiplash after the protective way he'd cradled me.

I couldn't help glancing at Zeb, relieved to see my surprise mirrored back at me. At least the loyal idiot didn't like that cool, callous answer anymore than I did.

Tess sighed, looking annoyed.

"Hostages are always more trouble than they're worth," she concluded. "I'll give the three of you six hours instead."

"Twelve," Daniel countered.

"Eight. *Fully private*, to your stated specifications, after which you will give me the keystone or *his* life is forfeit—" She indicated Zeb before returning to Daniel to finish, "—as is yours. You can ride shotgun to the Lower Halls, but any and all previous agreements between you and I become null."

I jumped in. "Except for the binding."

Daniel tensed but Tess turned an amused glare on me.

"That spell of yours is old magic. I can't trump it with a bargain," she said.

"Well, just in case you're lying, it's in the contract now, right?" I returned.

With another dramatic sigh to show how irritating she found my quibbling, Tess repeated, "Eight private hours to yourselves as previously laid out, after which I come to you and you turn over the stone or else, blah blah blah. Then I'll allow you to act as my sidekick, but all other bets are off."

She cocked her head at me to finish pointedly, "with the *unnecessary* exception of the already irrevocable binding currently placed on our Mab's precious pet."

"Don't be a bitch," I muttered.

"That's not part of the deal. Timer starts now."

48

I jumped when Zeb pulled his phone from his back pocket and started typing something into it with one thumb.

"What are you doing?" I risked a glance around for Tess even though I'd just watched her disappear like a stage magician without the smoke, leaving us in the same spot where we'd come through the stone circle.

"Setting a timer," he said. "You want her popping out of thin air in eight hours like a demented genie?"

"I do not," I concluded grudgingly. "Good idea."

As soon as Zeb had finished and lowered the phone, Daniel asked, "Can I borrow that?" and took it from his hand without waiting for an answer.

Zeb gave it up without a fight, but an uncharacteristic twinge of annoyance crossed his face.

Same, buddy.

"Where are we?" I asked, shivering as I looked around to take better stock of our surroundings.

"Home. Montreal." Zeb pointed past me and I turned to see the familiar downtown skyline in the distance.

"And how, exactly, do *you* have a keystone to the Lower Halls?" I put the question to Daniel, who had dug his wallet out of his back pocket and had what looked like a business card in his hand.

"I don't." He kept his attention on Zeb's phone.

"Nice dodge, real cute. I did a little bookwork over in the Faerie realm and those stones are bad fucking news. I guess it's no surprise the Consilium managed to steal one somehow."

Daniel tensed. "You sound like your father."

"And you're *acting* like yours." I mimicked his indifferent tone to mutter, "*Take your pick.*"

"That monster gets off on screwing with us," he snapped. "It thrives on drama and emotional manipulation. I called its bluff and it worked. You're both here."

We were back to our usual tango: seemingly mutual attraction to knives out in two minutes flat. I didn't know whether to laugh or stalk away so I split the difference and glowered.

"I'm here because the Changeling wants me here," I pointed out. "I don't know if you noticed, but it forgot to say *my* life was forfeit if you didn't bring the stone."

"I did," Daniel said, because of *course* he had.

"Well, I want to know why." This creature had inserted itself into my life, pretended to be Diana for four damn months. It had shielded me from the prying eyes of the Faerie Court, hidden me away and fooled Miranda into an inadvertent murder-suicide. "So I guess I'm in this 'til the final villain monologue."

"We have eight hours without her—*its*—interference." Daniel's tone lost some of the sharp terseness. "We need to make some decisions, and—" He frowned down at the screen of Zeb's phone. "—I need to go see a blacksmith in Kingston."

"What for?" I snatched it from his hand before Zeb could.

He'd pulled up a browser and done a search for 'Isabelle First blacksmith' that had resulted in the website of a place called Furst Forged in Ontario.

Zeb's text app indicated that it had been used recently. Thinking of the business card Daniel had tucked away again, I tapped the icon to bring up a brief conversation with a number I didn't recognize.

-*It's Daniel. I need to come by.*

—I can only assume that you know what ungodly time it is and that I'll have to accept the intrusion because the world is ending.

Danny had texted somebody who typed full, sarcastic sentences. Who the hell was he setting us up to visit at 4:30 in the morning? The number had a Montreal area code, so it wasn't the Kingston blacksmith, whoever that even was.

"There are a few things I didn't tell you yesterday." Daniel apparently meant that to pass for an answer to my earlier question.

"Oh, only a *few*?" I shot back. "How refreshing."

"Welcome to the club." Zeb snatched his phone from my hands.

"Well, Kingston's, what, four hours away?" I said. "You'll have plenty of time to fill us in on what we missed."

"Three," Zeb corrected me. Looking thoughtful, he added, "This time of night, I bet I could make it in two and a half."

"And is there alternate transportation for those of us who don't want to die in a fiery crash on the 401?"

"Can't you just fly, Queenie?"

I gave Zeb my best withering look but another concern surged into my brain and drowned him out.

"Damn it," I said, looking down at my body. "I'm probably radiating some magic Mab beacon."

"Now she tells us," Zeb muttered, but Daniel didn't look quite as concerned.

"The Changeling—Tess—implied you'd glamoured yourself before," he said. "In Tofino?"

"*She* did that. Well, Diana did."

"She told Joshua otherwise. It could have been a lie, but . . . you *are* the Mab."

"When did she—?" There was so damn much he hadn't covered that he was going to be explaining himself the whole way to Kingston. I sighed, forcing myself to focus. "I don't know how to glamour."

"Have you tried?"

Fair. Mab-hood had already come with a lot more fire-power than I'd anticipated—why wouldn't I be able to cloak myself away from my enemies? And I *had* spent the last five months living with a black cloud over my head, mired in the faint hope of disappearing off the grid from everybody who knew me. Maybe that had somehow contributed to Diana's cloaking me, to Miranda being certain enough I was dead that she'd risk her own life taking another heir.

I tried to summon that same feeling, the queasy dread of having my aunt pop up in a mirror or one of her minions knocking on my door. When I replaced Miranda with Declan and Karl, the dread surged into a wave of red-hot rage. The emotions roiled through me together, hard and fierce enough to take my breath away.

No. I reined it in with as much force as I could muster, trying to channel the rush into something else—a shield, a cloak. I fought it down, compressed it until only a faint warmth of the anger and fear tickled me. It felt a little like when the power had surged down my arm to knock Joshua off my balcony, like when I'd flung the bug away.

Daniel twitched as if something had startled him.

"What?" I pressed, and Zeb glanced from me to him, puzzled.

"We're wasting time." Daniel avoided my eyes. Avoided looking me in the face at all, actually. He usually did that when I used my power in some way he didn't like. He gestured to the yellow smears across my front. "It's freezing out here and you're covered in—"

"Pounds of bug guts." The reminder made me shiver despite the unnatural warmth under my skin.

"So I'm not leaving you here," he finished. "Whether you're cloaked from Raj or not."

Well, I'd definitely done *something* with my magic. If it wasn't glamour, and if Karl and Declan showed up with an army and tried to drag me off somewhere, they were going to be sorely disappointed. I was still the Mab. I was still in charge. That was why Declan had kept me unconscious in the first place. They couldn't take me on awake and in full possession of my faculties. *Bring it.*

49

I TRAILED DANIEL AND Zeb across the sparse grass, wincing at the cold mud under my bare feet until we reached the nearest sidewalk. The concrete was colder, but at least it wore some of the flaky dirt from the soles of my feet. My right knee throbbed from hitting the bug's armour. It was the same one I'd injured last fall, but luckily it didn't feel more than bruised this time.

"Can you get a car?" Daniel asked.

"We'll borrow one." Zeb was already on his phone again, starting to move toward the sidewalk.

As we passed a sixplex under construction, I stooped to pluck a brick from a pile beside the street. The area around us was dark and empty, no lights in the windows. I stopped beside a plain, black sedan, but before I could smash my brick through the window, somebody caught my wrist and yanked me back.

"Not that kind of 'borrow,' chiquita," Zeb said. "What are you, twelve?"

"Still holding a brick," I warned.

"Si j'allais voler un char, I'd do it with a little more finesse."

"Décâlisse." I didn't know much French but I had picked up a few important phrases living in Montreal, like how to tell someone to fuck right off.

"We're gonna miss the bus." Zeb inclined his head toward the busier cross-street up ahead and I tossed the brick aside.

Navigating from his phone, he led us to the corner of two streets that served as a bus stop. Daniel got himself and me on the next vehicle by swiping his plastic pass and having a long talk in French with the driver. The exchange made me ultra-aware that I was barefoot and wearing a pair of silk pyjamas plastered to my body with wet bug guts, which showed how very little I had on underneath.

"Ça va?" the driver asked me dubiously, inviting me to contradict whatever Danny had told him.

"Bien," I replied, then added, "Weird night, man. Pour vrai."

The driver snorted a laugh in response, then gave me one more sharp-eyed look. When I passed his second test, he tapped the button that closed the doors behind us and I followed Daniel and Zeb to a set of empty seats.

"Where are we borrowing a car?" I asked.

"My uncles run a body shop," Zeb said. "They'll have a beater we can use."

"At five in the morning?"

"I've got a key to the shop."

"Your life makes so much more sense to me now." No wonder he drove the way he did and always had a new, shitty car to bang up.

"I need to make another stop," Daniel broke in. "To see Mei."

"*That's* who you were texting?" I balked. "*Mei?*" If you'd have quizzed me on the top ten people I'd expected Daniel to drag us to see, I wouldn't have come up with more than two, and Mei wouldn't have even been on the list.

First Ilse, now Daniel. How did the ex-dragon keep popping back up into my friends' lives?

"Who's Mei?" My outburst had made Zeb pull out his phone and check his texts, as if to bring himself up to speed.

"Good question," I agreed. If she was who Daniel had texted, that meant he carried her number in his wallet. Why? An odd defensive rage surged in my core and I swallowed hard to fight it down.

"She's a—" Daniel stopped, not certain about whatever he'd been about to say. "She's got something I need to borrow. I can explain it all on the way to Kingston."

"I'm coming with you to see her," I said, adding hastily as I nodded to Zeb, "The less time I'm in a car with this maniac, the better."

"Feeling's mutual, chiquita," Zeb promised, but his smirk made me think he'd seen past my excuse.

We rode the bus in silence for several more stops, then Daniel and Zeb had a quiet conversation that ended with Danny and I descending onto what would have been a busy rue Notre-Dame in Griffintown were it not too early for the sun to be up. Zeb didn't join us, off to get the car.

I trailed Daniel to the locked glass doors of a high-rise, which opened when he buzzed the intercom. Seventeen stories up, Mei was waiting for us.

She wasn't someone I'd ever expected to see again. Wrapped in what was probably an expensive beige cotton robe printed with indigo flowers, with her raven hair swept up into a clip at the back of her head that left strands escaping to frame her beautiful face, she sized us up at her door.

"I like the beard. Suits you," she told Daniel. Then her dark eyes darted to me. "Company, how nice."

Did Daniel normally show up here alone? He'd known right where to come without her giving him her address in a text.

Mei took in my yellow gut-splattered pyjamas with thin-lipped disapproval. "What happened to you?"

"Fought a giant beetle."

"Please don't sit down anywhere." She sighed and shoved her door open wider to allow us entrance.

Her apartment was swanky, giant windows on one wall facing the lights of the downtown skyscrapers. The furnishings were all modern, a calming mix of white, cream and chrome.

"We don't have much time," Daniel said. "Does your amulet work?"

"If I say 'no,' will you leave?" Mei's weary tone indicated she already knew the answer, so she conceded, "Yes, it works."

"What's the radius?"

"Two metres, maybe."

"Do you still have the book?"

"It was a loan." Mei's hand went to her chest, clutching something hidden beneath her robe. Then she dropped her arm and her shoulders in the same motion, drawing up to her full height which was still a few inches short of Daniel's. She looked for a moment like she might try to deck him. "You can't have it."

"I'll get a new one made. Mei, I wouldn't ask if it weren't important." His voice was quiet and apologetic. Something in his cautious tone made me tense, fighting a new surge of jealousy even before he offered, "I can show you how to make a ward instead."

She sighed. After another few long seconds, her hands went to the back of her neck and she released the clasp of a chain. She retrieved a necklace from beneath her robe and delivered it reluctantly into Daniel's hands.

A brief, bitter taste on my tongue accompanied a shudder that told me, whatever else her necklace was, it was probably made of iron.

"I'm holding you to that ward business," she said. "*Now*, not later. Before you martyr yourself at whatever stupid thing you're doing. I'll make coffee." She glanced at me. "And you need a shower."

No argument there.

50

"The Ubran haven't returned." Ilse strode into the kitchen of the Faerie house, vibrating with enough anxiety Abe didn't need to be empathic to see it.

"How are you surprised?" Joshua growled. He was struggling with his iron-damaged hands to fit a key into the manacles around his wrists, since Ilse couldn't transform to undo the lock the way she had on the steel padlock of his cell. He'd had no trouble conjuring up an appropriate key from a nearby drawer, as if he'd been in the house before. Or maybe just worked out its power by some innate knowledge. "You haven't realized yet that they're involved?"

Cynicism was the only thing Abe and the old mage agreed on at this point.

"Karl's not coming back, darlin'," he said, sagging into his chair at the kitchen table. "He and the Archduke are—"

"We don't know that yet." Ilse pressed her lips into a thin line. The disappointment in her eyes made him certain he'd played into her worst human stereotype. "There are still too many questions."

She looked to Joshua to ask, "What happened to Eli? Who killed him?"

When the mage returned a disinterested shrug, Abe prompted, "The other man in those cells with you."

"Dead before I arrived, I'm afraid."

"And Cain?" Ilse added. "Daniel? He and Eli disappeared around the same time. Was he there too?"

Joshua darkened at the human's name, turning his attention back to his manacles.

Big yes, Abe thought. Too bad that got them no closer to knowing what had actually gone down, or why.

Joshua succeeded in unlocking the cuffs and they fell to the floor with an audible clank. He kicked them to the opposite side of the room. The floor seemed to sag beneath them but he didn't notice, examining his ruined hands with a grimace.

Several voices came from the front hallway, and a new exhaustion flooded Abe as he recognized the Archduke's sharp tones.

"I demand to see the Mab." Raj appeared in the kitchen doorway, flanked by a couple of his guards.

"Demand all you like," Abe returned. "She's not here. We were under the impression that she was with you."

No hint of guilt flickered across the Archduke's face. He drew his phone from his pocket and presented the screen to them.

"I know she's here." It showed what appeared to be a screenshot of surveillance video—probably from the Archduke's hotel in Singapore, given the familiar hallway. A group of people walking—Jude, Daniel and . . .

Abe balked at his own image, face tilted up to gaze fully into the camera under the familiar hat currently resting on his head.

"That's not me," he stammered.

"Of course it is," Raj snapped. "You've absconded with the Mab. Helped Cain and the Consilium take her captive."

"The *hell* I have!" Abe got to his feet fast enough that he knocked a chair backwards.

Ilse caught it before it hit the floor, guiding it back into place as calmly as she said, "That's impossible. Abe's been with *me* all afternoon."

"Then perhaps *you* were also aiding your human friends." Raj's gaze swept the room and settled on Joshua. "I suppose it's no surprise to find you sheltering this malignant, unregistered mage too."

Joshua finally looked up from his hands, but it appeared to be merely from curiosity. When he realized he was the subject of Raj's laser focus, he threw back his head and laughed.

"You're a stickler for regulation now, are you?" he returned, adding a long word in his mother tongue that Abe didn't know. Despite the delicate, melodic syllables, Ilse looked scandalized and one of the guards beside Raj shifted in clear discomfort.

"Take them into custody," Raj growled at the men flanking him. "And search the house."

"You will do neither." Ilse stepped between them. "I'm not convinced there's been any such foul play. What was Ju—the Mab doing at your hotel in the first place?"

"She consented to return with me to discuss our future plans."

"I wasn't informed of that."

"Maybe she didn't trust you."

"She was *unconscious* when I left her in your care." Ilse's voice lowered to a warning pitch.

Abe shot a look to Joshua, half-expecting him to jump in again merely from boredom, but the other man only watched the exchange.

"It should be easy enough to locate her," Ilse continued.

"Do you think I haven't tried?" Raj cast her a disdainful look, as if the sprite were something he'd inadvertently stepped in. "Someone is hiding her. Again." He glanced again to Joshua, who pointedly ignored him.

"I must speak to the Ubran and the Heir," Ilse said. "And I want to see this surveillance footage of yours in its entirety."

"You're in no position to make demands," Raj snapped.

"It's my right as the Mab's chief attendant."

"She never appointed you." Surprise flashed through the Archduke's body too fast to actually reach his face, but Abe caught it. As they argued, the sheer helplessness of the situation washed against him like acid, burning his nerves.

"Tell them," he hissed at Joshua. "You know what the hell's going on, speak up."

"I have nothing to say," the old mage returned.

"Tell them about the Changeling, you spiteful bastard!"

"The *what*?" The Archduke stared at them and Abe realized he'd raised his voice. "Are you actually attempting to advance some racist, human mockery to cover your misdeeds? As if any Faerie would be stupid enough to leave its own, superior offspring for some lowly human—"

The derisive doubt in the Archduke's voice seemed to trigger Joshua in a way that nothing else had so far.

"While I quibble with the term and the resulting myth, the creature's real," he said.

"You've spent too long in the Shadowed Mab's realm," the Archduke sneered. "Internalized folktales."

"Or you're a terrified child who doesn't want to hear that his boogeyman truly exists." Joshua got to his feet with a grace and speed that surprised them all, resting his wounded hands lightly on the table.

"Boogeyman?" Raj tried to hide the fact that he'd flinched away. Disdain dripped from the word.

Joshua said something in Faerie, something Abe didn't quite understand. His slow translation had to do with 'a thousand faces' but he hadn't caught the noun, the subject of Joshua's response.

"I've met it," the older man added. "Watched with my own eyes as it died and revived itself."

"Surely this is a step too far, even for you." The Archduke turned on Ilse.

"I demand to speak to the Ubran," she repeated, "and the Heir. Now."

The Archduke's lips twitched but he didn't exhale the frustration that flashed across his features.

"Very well," he said, inclining his head to her in a mocking facsimile of respect. He raised his voice to address his guards again. "Take the other two—"

"No." Ilse cut him off again. "They'll remain here, unmolested, until I'm satisfied."

"And if you're a part of this conspiracy?"

"Then you'll need to levy a formal accusation against me, which will involve both of us going before the Ubran and the Heir. Shall we?"

Abe suppressed a grin at Ilse's measured response. For the most placid person he knew, the water sprite could really pack a neutral statement full of disapproving annoyance.

Uncertainty rang in the Archduke's hesitation, but he finally acquiesced. He lifted a hand to the far wall, erasing both the back door and the window above the sink, gave a clipped instruction to one of his guards, then spun on his heel and left the room.

Ilse cast Abe a brief, reassuring smile and followed, presumably headed to the giant mirror in the living room. Having the situation taken out of his hands felt better than merely pacing the kitchen, but not by much.

51

MEI'S BATHROOM WAS MODERN and pristine, done in black and white tile with shining, silver fixtures so spotless they must have been cleaned by a weekly service.

I stripped off the wet, stinking pyjamas. Mei had sniffed that she could probably dig up something better for me to wear but I didn't know what that meant, given she was at least two sizes smaller than me. I couldn't exactly walk around in this nasty mess, though, so I balled up the pyjamas. The slippery silk brought me rocketing back to waking in that unfamiliar bedroom and my stomach lurched.

I'd been undressed and redressed unconscious, manipulated like a doll. The idea of faceless hands on my body made me want to crawl out of my skin. I'd have preferred to set the silk rags on fire, but I settled for stuffing them into the wicker trash can lined with plastic.

Then I hopped into the narrow, standing shower and practically melted when the warm spray hit. The heat made my skin sting, especially my hands and feet, letting me know just how cold I'd gotten on our journey without noticing. My knee throbbed again to remind me it was still bruised, but the hot water helped.

A bunch of coloured plastic bottles and jars sat in the shower niche. I scrubbed some shampoo into my hair, loosening any lingering bug entrails, then let the suds rinse away the rest of the noxious stains from my skin.

Shutting off the spray, I grabbed a towel from a folded stack in the alcove beside the shower and wrapped it around my torso. I poked my head out the door, expecting to have to call for assistance. Mei and Daniel had probably gotten caught up in their common interests—wards, amulets, how great it was to be fully human. Maybe I'd just have to parade out there naked.

Dial it back. I swallowed the raw, unsettling resentment that tried to squeeze my throat closed. Could I be riding some heightened wave of emotion from popping out of a magical coma? Seemed like I should have built up a tolerance, given it wasn't the first time that had happened to me.

A folded stack of clothing waited on the floor: a lilac-coloured sweatshirt that was oversized on me and would have swallowed Mei whole, along with a pair of leggings that had probably started life long and black but since been cut off into faded, greyish shorts with a small hole on the left thigh. Underneath sat a pair of pink flip-flops.

I tugged the clothing on in the bathroom, then eyed the cutesy, cartoon kittens dancing across the front of the sweatshirt in the mirror. Unless I'd really pegged our ex-dragon hostess wrong, this wasn't Mei's.

An aroma wafted in from somewhere, probably the kitchen—the sharp, acidic scent of fresh coffee. It beckoned me back out.

Daniel and Mei sat at her kitchen table, both focused on something Daniel was drawing on a piece of paper.

"—sprinkle it with the salted mistletoe ash, then you have to weave the rowan between the copper like this," he was saying, as he moved the pencil. "Knots on the outside, or it'll catch fire."

"And this actually worked for you?" Mei's voice was flat as she tilted her head to one side.

"I'd do it for you if I had time," Daniel started. He sounded resigned and tired but there was an earnestness in his voice too that made my chest tighten.

They both tensed, as if becoming aware of my presence in the same moment, and glanced toward me. They seemed embarrassed and the way Mei leaned back slowly in her chair felt calculated.

Dull irritation radiated beneath my skin, thorns prickling. I gritted my teeth to fight the thoughts off, saying, louder than I'd intended:

"Thanks for the clothes."

"I'm the floor captain for our building's monthly shelter donations," she replied.

Fuck you very much too. "You know it's March, though, right?" I gestured to the shorts.

"No one donated any pants in your size. You'll have to come back in a month or two—the winter clothing will be available then."

"You should be careful about issuing invitations," I said, revelling in the way her face fell even though I didn't have anything on deck to back that threat up. Instead, I pivoted to, "Coffee smells amazing."

"She's really the Mab?" Mei shot Daniel a dubious look.

"Yep." I answered her before he could. "Life's funny, huh?"

"That's a word for it." She lifted her mug with both perfectly manicured hands and took a sip, then nodded toward the coffee maker on her polished marble counter. "Help yourself, Your Highness."

"Haven't heard *that* one a hundred times in the last forty-eight hours," I muttered, snagging one of the blocky, generic, white mugs from a stacked holder.

I hadn't realized how hungry I was until the scalding, bitter liquid touched my tongue. Another look at Mei's pristine kitchen told me she probably cooked as much as I typically did. I wasn't about to beg to warm up whatever delivery leftovers she had in her fridge, even though I kind of wanted to.

"All the doors and windows," Mei muttered, running her eyes around the open concept apartment as she went back to considering what she and Daniel had just covered. "How long did it take you?"

"Fourteen tries." The answer came from me as I caught on that they'd been discussing making wards.

Mei arched a skeptical brow at me and Daniel looked startled.

"She's right," he said. Apparently he'd forgotten that he'd told me that last fall when I'd noticed the copper wire and iron nails around his door. And the scorch marks from the first thirteen attempts.

What he hadn't mentioned was where the hell he'd turned up the spell to make a ward, which kept a Faerie from entering somewhere uninvited. The one he'd made at his apartment had worked, though—tearing a sylph off my neck and keeping Joshua out, even though my father had threatened to tear it apart like smoke.

"Probably six hours," Daniel added, a more precise answer to Mei's question. "But I was still working some of this out as I went. Though my place was smaller than this."

I couldn't help but look from one of them to the other, scanning for little tells, evidence that they were closer than I'd thought. Then I remembered how fondly Ilse had started to speak about Mei. Did she know about this? Was that part of the reason she'd come down so hard on me about Daniel?

I downed another sip of coffee before starting, "How long have you two been—?"

"Where am I supposed to find mistletoe at this time of year?" Mei leaned forward again to study the paper. She didn't acknowledge that she'd talked over me, but Daniel's eyes lingered on me another moment as if expecting me to erupt.

Mei's phone buzzed beside her on the table and lit up with a message. She consulted it and relayed, "Your friend's almost here."

Zeb must have been texting her, since neither Daniel nor I had a phone anymore. That put the kibosh on their warding session. They covered a few final questions, then Mei showed us out of her apartment with little fanfare, just a chilly goodbye.

"You missed your calling as a wizard," I told Daniel as soon as we were back in the elevator. It had been intended to make him laugh, but it seemed to have the opposite effect. He was still thinking of Mei, probably. Her safety without the amulet.

I kept my voice as light as I could. "What were you guys talking about while I was in the shower? Just ward stuff? For twenty minutes?"

"It's a touchy formula."

"So, when did you start seeing Mei again?"

"She called late last summer and asked for my help."

"With what?"

"A *book*, Jude." His tone thinned with annoyance as we reached the ground floor. "She'd dug up some old Faerie book and she wanted me to . . . basically to authenticate it. Verify a translation for getting that amulet made. She was getting hassled by some of Aubrie's former collaborators."

"So, naturally, you had to ride to her rescue."

He'd already stepped off the elevator, aimed toward the front door, but my sarcastic tone made him stop and turn to face me again.

"You don't get to be jealous," he snapped. "You've got a *husband*."

"Consort," I corrected. "And, no I don't—I didn't go through with it. Why do you think the asshole kidnapped me and put me in a magical coma?"

"I can think of a few reasons." Daniel crossed the lobby, shoving the front door open with more force than it needed.

Son of a bitch. I followed as fast as my stupid, pink flip-flops would carry me.

"Yes, I'm jealous, okay?" I managed to catch him at the curb, swinging around to plant myself in his path. "Just like you're jealous of Declan. Which is ridiculous because *I loathe him.* Not like you and Mei, all cozy up there—"

I caught myself with a wince, saying, more for my benefit than his, "The point *is,* I get it."

"This is just some kind of nostalgia for a time when things . . . made sense," he said. "When this—" He gestured between us. "—was simpler. Easier."

"I told you that I'm into you," I cut in. "*Now,* not way back when. And you ran away."

He balked. "You mean when you made some vague reference to trapping 'people you care about' with magic spells—?"

"Oh, that's why you bailed? I was too vague?" I closed the distance between us, dropping my sarcasm. "Let me be clear, then. I'm not pining for those 'good old days' when I saw you as a mark, some good-looking guy who had a nicer apartment than mine and paid for our drinks. I don't miss that me. She was stupid.

"I like being with you. You're annoyingly smart and fucking heroic and you adapt to the most bizarre shit without blinking. You give the benefit of the doubt way more than you should and you'll do anything to protect the people you love. If I'd realized *any* of that last year, I might not have blown up your life, and mine, and . . . everybody else's."

The night around us was as silent as five a.m. in the city could be. A siren wailed somewhere to our right and the dull, quiet revving of a semi's engine floated over from the distant freeway.

Daniel made a sound that might have been a laugh. He pulled away from me and retreated a few more steps before finally saying,

"Eli's dead."

"Are you—? What?" I tried to rewind the conversation in my head to find where he'd made that jump. "When? How?"

"The Changeling had a—it doesn't matter. It had someone torture him to make me tell it about the keystone and I . . ." His voice broke. ". . . didn't."

His hot and cold streaks during the last hour made a little more sense given he'd been carrying this news this whole time. I didn't know what to feel. Eli had protected me, helped me. Shown up out of nowhere and thrown his body between mine and danger. Because of what I was—the Mab—not because of *me*. We hadn't exactly been friends. Not yet, anyway.

He'd been loyal, though, followed my orders against his own better judgment. I'd told him to keep an eye on Daniel, and he had. Damn it.

"I didn't realize how much the Changeling wanted it." Daniel added, voice still low. "Or maybe I did and I just let it—I don't know. I let it kill him. Because he wasn't human."

He considered his own words then flashed a wan, bitter smile. "Really fucking heroic."

"You're not responsible for some monster killing Eli," I insisted. "No more than I am for telling him to tail you."

I believed that as little as Daniel probably did, but I forced myself on. "If you'd told the Changeling how to find the keystone, it'd have probably killed Eli anyway, then you. Then the whole world—maybe both worlds?—with whatever it's trying to break out of the Lower Halls. Instead, we're here to fight another day and you've got some brilliant plan to kill this goddamn shapeshifter with Mei's fancy iron amulet, right?"

There was a reason I hadn't gone out for cheerleading in high school.

"Not so much a brilliant plan as a desperate one."

"My favourite kind."

52

"Take the next right." Daniel relayed directions from the map on Zeb's phone as his friend eased a foot off the accelerator. They'd been speeding down empty, two-lane country roads for the last ten minutes, since leaving the 401 just south of Kingston. The sun broke golden across the frosty farm fields to the left.

It was just after eight. He hoped Bel was an early riser.

On the drive down, he'd given Zeb and Jude a rundown of his last twenty-four hours—and the last five months, for Zeb—and told them about Bel and the keystone.

Jude had related the few pieces of information she'd uncovered digging into the palace library. It didn't shed any more light on the Changeling's motives for freeing the Visitant, only made clearer how deeply the strange creature was invested in opening the Lower Halls, given the trouble it had gone through to find the other three keystones.

The idea of Jude visiting the Faerie realm invited more questions than Daniel felt comfortable asking, especially after she'd curled up in the backseat with her knees pulled under her oversized sweatshirt and her seatbelt stretched around them. She'd informed them that she didn't intend to ever sleep again, then spent the last couple hours staring out the window as the sun came up.

He tried not to think about their conversation at Mei's curb before Zeb had shown up. He hadn't wanted to tell her about Eli right then, but he couldn't just let her go on insisting that she wanted him, that she knew him, inventing jealousies and trying to force a world where they had any chance of a relationship.

"On the left. Here." He lifted his eyes from the phone screen as they reached a familiar driveway. He hadn't noticed the sign in the yard before: *Furst Forged, Appointment Only.*

The car tires hummed on the gravel and Bel's house came into view, same as before. Daniel had half-expected it to have been some illusion Joshua—or Bel herself—had put on the place.

Zeb pulled the car into a wider, gravelled area in front of the house, a small parking lot.

"This place feels weird." Jude shivered as she climbed from the backseat in her shorts and flip-flops. She seemed to realize the reason in the same moment, wrinkling her nose. "Iron."

"There's a lot of it out back," Daniel warned. "And in the kitchen."

"You were in her *kitchen*? Why?"

"Making tea." Daniel mounted the steps to the front door. He knocked on the door while Zeb and Jude hovered behind him. A minute went by before he knocked again, louder. Had Bel left, abandoned the house? They could go around back and break a window to check. In fact, she probably hadn't even had time to fix the pane the Archduke's men had already smashed.

Daniel raised his hand to knock once more but eyes appeared in the glass opposite him. He took a step back as Bel unlocked the front door.

She opened it just a crack to whisper something he couldn't hear.

He stepped closer to better make out the words, only to find the tip of a sharp, wicked-looking knife pressed against his stomach.

"We're closed." Bel lifted her voice, her tone both ironically saccharine and weary. "And you and I have nothing to say to each other."

"I haven't told anyone about the—" Daniel nodded toward the back of the house, steeling his legs to keep from retreating. "And I won't, if you let me in."

She put enough pressure on the blade to make him raise his hands in surrender. "Just me." He inclined his head toward Jude and Zeb behind him. "They'll stay outside."

"The hell—" Jude started, and Zeb huffed in agreement.

"I knew I should have run Joshua off the moment I laid eyes on him," Bel muttered, flicking the knife back into shadow beside her. She told the others, "Stay out front where I can see you."

Once Zeb and Jude had stepped off the porch, back onto the gravel, she pulled the door open wide enough to let Daniel inside. She kept him at a distance with the knife still gripped in her free hand.

"The Changeling has the other three keys," he said.

"Joshua's changeling?" Bel snorted. "You realize he's basically been in hell for the last fifteen years, yeah? He's lost his shit. That changeling story isn't true."

"It's real. I've met it—a few of its faces. It already tried to torture your key's location out of me and it's coming back in three hours."

"You look fine." Bel cocked a dubious eyebrow at him.

"It wasn't bleeding *me* to get the information."

"Not sure if that should make me feel better about you or worse."

"I don't really care how you feel about me. How do you feel about closing the Lower Halls for good?"

She blinked in surprise, studying the firm set of his expression as if to confirm. Then she leaned forward, waiting what felt like an awkward amount of time before asking, "Why should I believe you? You're Alan Cain's successor."

"His son, not his successor." Daniel kept his voice as even as he could. "The Changeling is vicious, ancient and *bored*. It's nobody's ally, nobody's ticket to power. I think it would burn both worlds down just to see what the fire looks like."

"Well, you're right about one thing. You're not your father." Bel sighed. "How do you plan to do away with the Lower Halls, then? And, I imagine, this bloodthirsty changeling?"

"I have half a plan. I was hoping you'd fill in some blanks about glamour."

"You want me to teach you how to use it, I suppose."

"No. I want to destroy it." Daniel retrieved Mei's amulet from his pocket and held it out to her. "I have it on good authority this will burn glamour up within a certain radius."

"Symbol's familiar." Bel accepted the iron piece, turning it over in her fingers to study the interlocking circles etched into it.

"I don't have resources anymore," Daniel said. "I need a rogue scholar."

She snorted a laugh, then her expression turned wary again as she looked him up and down.

"You've got a weird shimmer about you. Like an aura." She tensed, palming the amulet and lifting the knife again. "Are you spelled?"

"A binding," Daniel admitted. "It apparently keeps any Anta—Faerie from injuring me unless I strike first."

Bel balked. "Who in their right mind bound *you*?"

The question may have been rhetorical, but her tone irked Daniel enough that he gestured to her front door.

"Jude."

"That's Joshua's *daughter* out there?" She froze, staring at him with wide eyes. "You let me banish the actual *Queen Mab* to my driveway?"

"It's just 'The Mab.' "

"Fuck off, Consilium." Bel brushed him aside with an almost comical annoyance to open the front door again and poke her head out. She barked, "You two, get in here."

Jude and Zeb scrambled inside. After a set of somewhat awkward initial introductions, Bel reluctantly led all three of them upstairs to what had probably been intended as a second bedroom, but was instead crowded with books, papers and boxes. One shelf also held a jumbled collection of glass jars containing what looked like dried flowers, herbs and mushrooms.

"What are you, a witch?" Jude asked, surveying the jars. "Are witches even a thing?"

"Hard to believe *you're* really the Mab," Bel returned.

"It's the kitten shirt," Jude said.

"Keep telling yourself that," Zeb muttered.

As Bel zeroed in on the bottom of a distant shelf, Daniel cocked his head to read the titles on the one nearest him. There were a handful he'd heard of, most that he hadn't. It seemed like an impressive collection.

"Are there a lot of symbols out there for diffusing glamour?" Zeb peered into a jar that looked to be packed with dead moths.

"Destroying," Daniel said. "Not diffusing."

"That's it." Bel attacked another section of her bookshelf. She ran a finger over the spines of books until she dug out a narrow, stapled sheaf of papers from between two hardbacks.

Flipping through them, she said, "There was supposedly a stash of candles that could burn up residual glamour. Made by . . . I want to say monks? Few centuries ago, maybe. Limited edition, pricey as hell because—yeah." She waved a piece of paper. "The Mab got pissed and burned down the whole bloody monastery."

Daniel accepted the paper. It contained what looked like a photocopied telegram in Portuguese and a blurry photograph of a ruined, stone building.

"This is an internal Consilium report," he said, recognizing the pattern of filing numbers that ran along the top of the sheet. "Where did you get this?"

"Rogue scholar," Bel reminded him, putting emphasis on the first word as if that were enough of an answer. "That's the symbol you've got." She pulled another book from her shelf and thumbed through it. "Two circles, one beginning to eclipse the other."

She tossed that book aside and snatched another, flipping the pages in a stream and then narrowing her focus to one location. With a triumphant smirk, she presented the open book to him, setting Mei's amulet on the page beside it.

"Devorator praestigium," she said.

Devourer of illusions. The page was hand-written in blocky Latin instead of the graceful, delicate strokes of the Faerie language like the book Mei had brought him last summer, but the icon was the same. The rest of the text laid out instructions, methods of use and warnings Daniel didn't remember from Mei's version, but that made sense—this one looked to have been written by humans wanting to use the mark rather than Faeries meaning to discredit it.

"Well?" Zeb prompted. "Is it going to work?"

"It should." There were no further instructions for using the amulet. He didn't remember any from Mei's book either—it just . . . worked. Devoured the glamour in its vicinity.

Daniel handed the book back to Bel and pocketed the iron. Even with the written confirmation that the symbol would do what he'd thought, it didn't feel like enough to hang a plan on. Not that they had another choice, or time to find one.

"We're going to need that keystone," Jude reminded their host.

Bel was silent a moment, fixated on the book in her hands. Finally, she turned a glare on the three of them.

"If you lot mess this up and release the Visitant on this world, I *will* hunt you down, grind your bones to dust and cast them into bloody teacups."

"Weirdly specific," Zeb remarked.

"I think you'll have bigger problems to worry about if the Visitant gets out," Jude said, then hurriedly assured her, "But don't worry—I don't mess things up."

Her eyes darted briefly to Daniel then away before she finished, "Anymore."

53

Joshua reclined in the wooden chair, letting the sharp angles dig into his back. It provided a welcome spike of discomfort every so often that eclipsed the throbbing ache in his hands.

Across the room, Abe paced like a caged tiger, rubbing the back of his neck with one hand. He'd left his large hat sitting on the table. For someone who'd always seemed completely at ease following Miranda, the cowboy had fallen to anxiety quickly on his own.

One of the Archduke's personal guards hovered near the door. He'd been watching his charges intently for a good ten minutes, then gotten bored and cocked an ear toward the hallway as if to see what he could overhear.

Joshua wished he could cast a barrier spell, keep the Archduke's goon from listening to them. If he could guide the situation to his preferred end, though, he was going to need his strength for other things.

"You're angry with me, I suppose," he said, "for not spilling my guts, as the humans say, to that idiot Raj."

The cowboy stopped and cast him a disparaging look.

"Who's the empath here?" His drawl was thick with bitter sarcasm.

The Archduke's guard glanced at them, then away. They weren't important.

"Damn right I'm pissed." Abe gestured to the closed room around them. "You got us sealed up in here when we could be—I could be—helping."

"Helping with what?" Joshua scoffed. "Better that self-righteous ass—" He inclined his head toward the doorway, indicating not the guard there, but Raj himself. "—burn his boundless army out against our adversary than we do."

"Sounds like a lot of unnecessary deaths."

"We have different definitions of the term. I suspect the carnage *will* be necessary to impose the gravity of the situation on all of the powerful parties involved."

"You're a damn sociopath, you know that?"

"I can't imagine you're the first to make that observation, but it shouldn't surprise you to hear that I don't care."

Abe glared at him, more astute to the sarcasm than Joshua had expected. Then he dropped into the chair across the table.

"Tell me about this critter," he said, adding, "Changeling," in a voice sharp with warning when Joshua was tempted to pretend he didn't understand the rough vernacular.

"A term coined by humans. It means nothing, just like *fetch*. The Consilium called it *cambiatus*. Or *Innōmināta*. *Puer mendacem*, too. They loved Latin, found it so antiquated and dramatic."

"You said you'd met it." Abe eyed him dubiously. "Seen it do its changeling thing?"

"I drove an iron rod through its chest." Joshua put his hands up to remind the cowboy of the blisters on his palms.

"You knew what it was before you did that. I imagine that's what made you desperate enough to try." The other man continued to be annoyingly astute, but Joshua twitched at the word *desperate*.

"I met her—it—before my imprisonment in the Bie'lel-hii." He didn't even recall what name she'd been using, just wisps of a female face. "We crossed the portals together, but she betrayed me to the Mab, turned me in. I cut her throat just before the soldiers caught us—watched her bleed out and die." A cold fist of anger squeezed his chest. He still remembered the fury bearing down on him, helping him shift his weight to press the blade deeper. Her body falling still with that beautiful, satisfying finality.

Then her flesh melting, changing. "She shifted into the guise of a Mab's guard, one of my captors, and escaped."

"Maybe you didn't actually kill her."

"I did." Joshua had given the cowboy enough. He leaned closer, darting a glance to the guard and then lowering his voice. "If you heal my hands, I can create a door and get us out of here."

Abe followed his lead, tilting his head nearer, but murmured, "Sneaking out's bound to make us look guilty."

"You'd prefer to be *innocently* executed for treason? Be my guest." Joshua could tell the words piqued the other man, even through the dark look Abe gave him. This part-human creature couldn't possibly trust the Archduke or the Ubran. Even the water sprite who'd gone off with them was likely to betray him if she needed to.

"Where do you mean to be rushing off to?" Abe asked.

"Judith's in danger." Dull anger tightened Joshua's chest thinking of the shapeshifting monster mocking him, the way that stupid human—Cain—had used that damned binding as a weapon against him.

"What danger?"

"A pertinent question I'm happy to answer once we're free."

The cowboy shook his head, refusing to accept a vague answer. Thoroughness was typically an asset Joshua appreciated, but right now it was taking up precious time. "The Changeling—" How he hated that term, wished he'd never used it, "—has designs on Judith. I tried to warn her.

It's been trying to get close to her for some time. Cain will give it the means."

"Not *trying*," Abe said. "Jude lived with the thing for a few months and nothing happened."

"She wasn't the Mab then." Joshua extended his blistered palms in what looked like a submissive gesture of surrender, putting them within the healer's reach.

Abe seemed to bite back his next argument. He risked a glance toward the kitchen doorway, then reached out and rested his fingers on Joshua's injuries.

The cowboy had a light touch but the healing still stung. At least it was an improvement over the iron burns. Joshua gritted his teeth, forcing his attention onto watching his ruined flesh knit back together under the healer's fingers.

It didn't restore his spent power, but that would only come with time. With the iron dispersed from his blood, at least he could work magic again. The instant the cowboy withdrew his hands, Joshua flicked his wrist and sent a burst of energy toward the distracted door guard.

Abe bolted out of his chair to lower the man's unconscious form to the ground, glaring at Joshua as he did so.

Joshua got to his feet and pressed his will into the shifting, malleable wall of the house, summoning the shape of a door up through the plain, plastered wall. It was easier than cutting a curtain but still strained his energy.

He gave the skeptical healer a smile anyway, feigning ease. "Shall we?"

54

I FELT QUEASY LEAVING Bel's place. The iron stashed in the house had done a number on me, more than usual—almost like the Consilium's warehouse but even worse. Residual coma effects, maybe. I threatened Zeb with my iron-induced carsickness and convinced him to hit a Tim's drive-thru on the way. Two double chocolate donuts *did* help to ease my stomach.

It took us another hour's drive and then a twenty-minute ride on a little car ferry to reach the island marina in the St. Lawrence river where Bel said she'd stashed the keystone. Running water did something to mask magic, or powerful items. I hadn't really listened to the full explanation.

The marina wasn't open for the season yet, but according to Bel, some of the floating docks had already been put in and she'd convinced a friend of hers who ran it to let her stow the rock in a waterproof bag attached to the bottom of one by a chain—iron, of course, probably handmade.

She'd called ahead to tell him we were coming, which felt surprisingly helpful. Helpful enough to actually be a trap, as I'd suggested, but Daniel had disagreed and since Zeb was an unfailingly loyal idiot despite our brief, shared moment of camaraderie when the Changeling had been choosing a hostage, I'd been overruled.

No reason for all three of us to get snared. While the guys walked down to the docks, I perched on the hood of the car and hunched forward against the chill. I cradled a now-lukewarm coffee in my hands but it didn't help.

"Didn't you used to be a queen?" An annoyingly familiar voice came from my left. "Now you're just a lookout?"

I tensed but tried to play it off. "Breaking your word early, aren't you?"

"I'm five minutes late, actually." Tess leaned against the car beside me, a canvas backpack hanging off one shoulder. It looked heavy. "Per my bargain with your boyfriend, I wasn't allowed to determine his location until the eight-hour mark."

"And you found us in five minutes?" Zeb's phone alarm must have gone off down there on the dock, then. No wonder I hadn't heard it. "How?"

"A girl needs to keep some secrets. Where is he?"

"Getting your stone." I nodded to the marina, half-expecting her to take off after them.

Instead, she hopped up uninvited to sit on the car hood beside me. She ignored my side-eye and relaxed, tilting her face up to the warm sun and closing her eyes.

"You're awfully blasé about this rock you were so hot for," I remarked. "Aren't you going to turn into a fish and go down there and snatch it?"

"Fish don't have hands."

"Water sprites do. And those—what are those guys that turn into seals?"

"Selkies."

"Can't you be whatever you want?"

"I can take any form I've seen," she agreed. "Gaining a particular creature's innate power requires a certain . . . deeper understanding."

"Like what? Shaking hands? Five-minute convo at a party? Spending a night killing a bottle of whisky and watching B-movies together?"

The edges of her mouth quirked into a smile but she didn't lift her head.

"Are you asking if I can mimic your power?"

"I wasn't, but sure, can you?" When she didn't answer, I prompted, "Why aren't you wearing Dee's face?"

"Your father killed her."

Nice try. I didn't rise to that the way she probably intended. Daniel was right, this bitch really did like to stir the drama pot.

"But *you* killed the real Diana Garcia?"

"You never met the real one. As far as you're concerned, I was Diana."

"That's a 'yes' on the murder, though? What about Pam?"

"Who?" She opened her eyes, blinking against the sunlight.

"Pam. The woman I met in Calgary. The one who called me once we were in Vancouver to tell me she wasn't going out to her job in Tofino and did I want it?" It sounded so contrived when I said it aloud.

The Changeling considered my description and then nodded slowly. "Oh, yes. Pam."

Her cold, distant tone told me what I needed. Maybe I'd met the real Pam in Calgary and the Changeling had killed her in Vancouver to get me the job out there. Had Pam sounded different on the phone? How would I have known? I'd known the woman for a few hours on a train.

"I've learned that it's too difficult, logistically, to imitate a living person for a serious length of time." The Changeling's voice became disgustingly earnest. Murder was a simple fact to her, something performed routinely. She'd killed Eli too, and who knew how many others. So many that she couldn't even remember their names.

"Then why mess with it at all?" I propped my feet up on the hood, resting my folded arms on my knees and trying to keep my voice casual, as if my next question weren't the very thing that had driven me to this exact spot. "Why play my roommate for four months?"

"Oh, that was just sort of . . ." She considered her words and settled on, "fun."

When I glared at her, she shrugged. "It wasn't even about you—not at first," she said. "Miranda was actually starting to pull the Court back into shape after all the murder and mayhem last year—" She waved a hand as if to gloss over the Consilium's attack. "—much quicker than I'd anticipated, honestly. A distracted Court was more useful for me, since I was so close to opening up the Lower Halls. Hiding you was the easiest way to send them back into a tizzy."

"I was a distraction?" Why did that feel so disappointing?

"Yes, but I genuinely liked hanging out with you."

I couldn't help but roll my eyes. "Right. Is this the part where you apologize and beg to be friends for real?"

"Nah, I have enough friends."

"Doubt that."

She barked a laugh at my childish retort, but I continued, prompting, "Then why are you hanging up here talking to me?"

"How much did he tell you about the Lower Halls and the Visitant?"

He meaning Daniel, obviously. I bit back my first answer of '*everything*' because she was probably just itching to call my bluff, ready and waiting to lob a surprise bomb and sow mistrust between us.

I settled on, "Enough," and didn't bother to tell her I'd done some of my own research.

"The Visitant has a deep affection for the Mab's power," she said. "It started out as a Mab's Consort, you know. Storybook romance. The Shadowed Mab and the Visitant ravaged both worlds together as the Wild Hunt and had a great time doing it."

Noting that my expression hadn't changed, she added, "I need you to be a distraction again."

"Pass."

"Would it help if I say you're the only one who can do this for me? The Visitant won't notice anybody else. Sure, it'll wake up to kill a few humans that wander in, might even take a swipe at me, but for you, for that power in your blood, it'll manifest completely."

Her voice almost sounded dreamy with desire, but she moved on in a brisker tone. "Then I'll know its power. I'll understand it, mirror it and kill it. Very little risk to you."

"What the hell does 'manifest completely' entail?"

Tess's smiled widened. "Does it really matter?"

I caught sight of Daniel and Zeb trudging up from the marina. Daniel was carrying a navy blue bag he hadn't gone down with. He had the keystone. The Changeling wasn't going to let him or Zeb out of her sight alive now. She was probably two seconds from telling me exactly how she could break his binding if I refused to play her distraction.

So, no, it didn't matter. I was walking into the Lower Halls with this imposter, this parasitic, lying mass murderer—but she sure as hell wasn't coming back out.

55

ABE BREATHED AN UNANTICIPATED sigh of relief as he and Joshua stepped out of the kitchen-between-worlds and onto what looked like the lawn of an unfamiliar property. They'd emerged from a side door in a free-standing, one-car garage. The back of a two-story house sat to their left and most of the space ahead of them was taken up by an impressive blacksmith's forge under a wooden canopy.

That explained the new, strangling feeling tempering his relief. Iron.

Joshua paid no attention to the heavy, metallic scent, sweeping with a determined air toward the house.

"No." A woman planted herself in the open back doorway, folding bare arms corded with muscle across her chest. Dark-skinned, with short, grey hair and a fiery glare, she faced the old mage down. She had an accent, maybe British. "Go away. I'm moving house and I'm done with all of this."

In an effort to be polite, Abe swept his hat from his head as he followed Joshua, straying closer to her.

"Cain's been back here, hasn't he?" Joshua snapped. He seemed to read something on the woman's face because his body tensed. "You didn't give him the keystone?"

"Go away." Her voice was less forceful this time, which seemed like an answer in the affirmative.

"Was that creature with him? The Changeling?"

"No." The woman tilted her chin up to level a challenging stare at him. "But your daughter was."

Relief surged through Abe, heavy enough to blot out the nagging pinch of the nearby iron. Jude was safe. She'd been here.

"Where have they gone?" Joshua wasn't placated. "Back to the creature's lair, I suppose."

"You *hear* yourself, right?" The woman cocked a sarcastic eyebrow at him and Abe had to stifle a laugh.

When her attention shifted to him, he gave her a quick nod and greeting, "Ma'am."

"Bel," she corrected.

"Abe. Sorry about this."

"Stop your damn quips." Furious energy crackled off Joshua's skin and they all tensed when the glass in Bel's large back window gave a sharp crack.

"All right." Bel unfolded her arms to raise her hands in surrender. Her tone turned gentler, more cautious. "How do we stop this, then?"

"Don't placate me like a child." Navy tendrils of resentment flooded through the already blood-red fury whipping through Joshua's body.

"I'm placating you like a ticking time bomb, which you are." Bel flinched when another crack snaked through the glass.

Abe laid a calm hand on Joshua's upper arm, letting his own power fuse into the mage's. It didn't feel like when he'd healed Joshua's hands a few minutes ago—the pain spiking out of the other man now was deep and visceral, playing out physical manifestations of his emotional trauma through his magic.

Not much chance of assuaging something like this, but Abe couldn't help trying. He managed to skim off the sharpest peaks of pain and Joshua sucked in a breath. It wasn't so much 'healing,' not in the way Abe usually practised it, the restoration of skin and bone, but it seemed to do something and it left him winded.

A tremor ran through Joshua's body too, and he came back under his own control. He edged away from Abe with a quick, surprisingly half-gracious nod.

"Piss off now," Bel said, reaching down to retrieve a narrow, blunt piece of raw iron that had probably been stood beside her just inside the door. "If I have to replace these windows—"

"I'll shatter every inch of glass in this house," Joshua growled. The brittle fury and desperation swirling around him didn't seem hooked into his powers, at least for the moment. "I'll turn them to sand and *bury* you."

"Guess it's good you're speaking in complete, patronizing sentences again." Bel rolled her eyes, hefting the iron into both hands.

Abe took a step back, not wanting to be in the centre of this standoff. He shouldn't have freed Joshua in the first place. He didn't relish the idea of trying to diffuse things by tackling the other man to the ground, siphoning more of his power if he could, but the option wasn't off the table.

"Jude's fine," Bel said, in what seemed like a last-ditch effort to talk Joshua down. "Safe. Happy . . . ish. I saw her, spoke to her."

"With Cain," Joshua muttered. "Retrieving the keystone for that . . . that *abomination*."

"Why would Daniel help the Changeling?" Abe asked, startled.

"He's his father's son," Joshua growled. "He's Consilium, he's the product of an exhaustingly long line of humans seeking to exterminate us. Take your pick."

"Bullshit." Abe inched closer to the other man against his better judgment, half-expecting he'd soon need to grip Joshua's arm again.

"You're not human to him," Joshua snapped back. "You realize that, yes?"

Abe winced. Daniel *had* said something like that, but he'd been trapped in the Faerie house at the time, rightly pissed off and afraid.

"Doesn't matter," he concluded. "World's not black and white like that."

"Yours may not be. His is." Joshua lifted his eyes to Bel, as if challenging her with the same accusation. When her expression didn't change, he growled, "And Judith's the Mab. He'll let that monster use her any way it wishes."

"First off, no, he wouldn't," Abe said. "Second, Jude wouldn't stand for it."

"She's infatuated with him."

"Doesn't preclude that she's still got a mind of her own," Abe shot back. "Stubborn as hell. Give her some credit."

"*Oi*, My Two Dads—shut it." Bel looked from one of them to the other with annoyance. "Yeah, I gave them the key. They're going to trap the Changeling thing in the Lower Halls. Now piss off and bother *them*."

She took a step back and slammed the door shut, all but daring Joshua to smash the glass in the four window panes. Three, actually—one was already broken, covered in cardboard and tape. She hovered behind the door, peering out at them and probably clinging to the iron, but Joshua had gotten what he wanted, and he lost interest in her presence.

"Perhaps we can head them off," he said, turning back toward Bel's garage.

"How?" Abe frowned. "Daniel said the entrance to the Halls is somewhere in the southern U.S." They couldn't go back through the house. The Archduke would know they were missing by now.

"She'll have a Faerie Ring," Joshua murmured. "Likely one near the Lower Halls and another somewhere in that damnable office building she frequents. Where was that?"

"Montreal, I think." Abe remembered the French parking signs.

"I should have enough energy for a curtain, if we move away from this mess." Joshua sneered at the forge and the iron.

"Well, lead on, then." Abe didn't really want to know what a 'curtain' was, but no way was he letting Joshua chase Jude down alone.

56

I shivered in the dim, grey light of the Old Roads. The place was no more welcoming than the last time we'd been here, and still unnervingly empty. *Until it's not.* I swallowed hard and forced myself not to listen intently for clacking or skittering echoing out of the gloom. My flip-flops made an annoying rhythm as I walked that was probably drawing every spooky monstrosity around.

"It's not far." Tess took the lead with the confidence of somebody who'd never been bowled over by a giant bug. She didn't toss up a hand and demand safe passage this time because we reached another circle of stones in less than a minute.

"How do you know this is the right place?" I hadn't gotten all the details about navigating the Roads coming out of my enchanted nap.

"It's a route I've taken a lot."

Another leap through a Faerie Ring was just as fun as it had been a minute ago, but at least I felt like I was starting to build up a tolerance. We all were—neither Daniel nor Zeb collapsed when we stumbled out of the stone circle, though Daniel put both hands on the hard-packed dirt wall to steady himself.

We'd emerged somewhere very . . . orange. A tunnel. String lights hung from ceilings the colour of rust, dirt reinforced with planks of wood. Nice that there was a ceiling again.

Tess led us down the narrow tunnel until it widened, bringing us face to face with a stone doorway and inky blackness. A pile of similar-coloured, shattered stone had been roughly dumped to one side, but pieces still littered the space in front of the void.

The area felt rotten. Wrong. I had to steel my legs to keep from retreating.

"No henchmen?" I asked Tess. "No extra goons?"

"We're all friends here, aren't we?" She dropped her backpack heavily on the ground then nodded to it, telling Daniel and Zeb, "Slot the stones in and we'll head inside."

"We?" Daniel repeated.

"Mab's coming with me." Tess flashed him a knowing smile. "Do you really think I'm stupid enough to walk into the Lower Halls alone and let you pull the keystones out behind me?"

Right. Nobody with Faerie blood could walk in or out of there with the stones removed.

"Here I thought I was the critical diversion," I said, kicking off my awkward footwear in case running became necessary.

"Oh, dream big. Hostage *and* diversion." The sarcastic edge in Tess's voice reminded me of Diana, and I dug my fingernails into my palms to keep from smacking the grin off her face.

Daniel touched my elbow, making me flinch, then startled me further by pulling me fully against his chest in a sudden embrace.

"You don't have to do this," he said in my ear.

"What's the worst that could happen?" I whispered back. The vibration of his reluctant laugh against my ribs lightened my dread. I half-expected some last minute advice, a piece of information he'd been holding back.

Instead, he kissed me. The electricity that sparked through my body when his lips touched mine washed out the rest of my immediate anxiety.

"Just be careful," he said, having the decency to look a little shaken himself when he let me go.

Tess wasn't paying attention to us, facing into the looming darkness contained by the rectangle of carved rocks. She looked almost excited, shoulders twitching to move her forward, eyes bright.

Zeb had unloaded four long stones from the backpack, but he kept his eyes averted from Daniel and me. He'd clearly noticed our moment, and was probably holding back some choice words on account of me being the lucky bitch who got to walk into the black hole with the shapeshifting monster in search of the *other* monster.

The guys each took a side of the door. One, two, three, four obelisk-shaped stones ground into place as they shoved them into the corners of the frame, completing the pattern.

Tess reached back for me, intending to lead me inside like a sacrifice.

Screw that. I was a queen. I refused her hand and we stepped through the doorway as equals. My skin prickled in a new way, like I'd walked through a sheet of ice. I had no magic ointment here to help my eyes adjust to the absolute darkness.

Wait, why was the darkness absolute? I spun despite realizing that the door we'd just walked through had disappeared. A shudder ran through me but I quelled it, swallowing hard against a suddenly dry throat.

"Mab." A soft hiss came from somewhere to my left.

"Hey, hi." My voice came out bolder than my legs felt. Where the hell had Tess disappeared to?

Another whisper came from my right, then one behind me, overlapping and repeating. I couldn't make out the words, but I was about ninety-percent sure they weren't in English.

Something butted up against me gently, like a giant cat rubbing against my leg—up to my ribs, then disappearing. At least it wasn't the hard exoskeleton of a bug. I held my ground, muscles taut and ready to run. It nudged me again, this time lapping my body in soft waves. Pushing me a little, testing me? The whispers sounded closer.

"I don't speak Faerie," I said, voice loud and sharp in the stillness. Where the hell was Tess?

Sudden cold caressed my shoulder through the sweatshirt, like a chilly mist, but in distinct, pointed traces. The Changeling? No, this wasn't entirely solid and it felt cautious, almost . . . curious? The tendrils ran gently along the skin on the back of my neck. Fingers? The vaguely moist feeling made me think, *tongues?*

Repulsed, I dropped my shoulder. Pain raked my back, the frigid tendrils turning solid to rip through the lavender fabric into my skin. I screamed, spinning to swing blindly at whatever stood behind me, but there was nothing there.

Something scraped against me again from behind and I flipped my gravity, spinning weightlessly through the darkness. I searched for somewhere safe to land, something firm, a ceiling to the chamber. Nothing, just like on the Old Roads. I was falling—up, down? Terror flooded me, the same I'd felt being half-blind and off-balance in the Faerie realm. But there was no Ilse to guide me here.

I tried to reverse my course and hit the ground *hard.* The way the impact rattled my jaw, I couldn't have been hovering more than a few inches above it to start. The shock knocked the breath from my lungs and the air pressed around me like thick liquid.

Agony tore through my back again, icy needles digging into the left of my spine. I couldn't move, couldn't scramble forward or make myself fall up again, away. My muscles refused to respond.

Strips of flesh tore away from my back and arms along with shredded fabric as the pain worked up to the base of my skull. Fire flared through my head.

A sudden force hefted me upright, off the ground, and whatever was out there flayed a strip of skin from my chest this time, ripping a line from my throat to my sternum. Tears burned down my cheeks. I still couldn't move.

Something resolved out of the darkness, something massive. It gave off its own light, starting as a sputtering, dim glow and growing in brightness until my eyes stung. The Visitant loomed over me, one appendage still resting on my chest, pressing against the raw spot. It stood upright like a person but with a few too many fingered appendages coming off its enormous, shaggy core. Vivid blue eyes peered into mine—maybe more than two, or maybe that was my vision doubling.

"Stop," I tried to say, summoning all of my energy to a tiny movement of my lips. I felt the vibration in my throat but no sound came out.

"Mab." The voice was in my ear again—literally inside, rumbling in my head.

The eyes receded, sucking backwards in streamers of bright green and blue that morphed into teeth. So many teeth. They glittered in the thing's inborn light, lining the enormous jaws that had yawned open in front of my face to swallow me whole.

"Not yet," Tess's voice sang from the darkness somewhere behind me.

A horrific shriek exploded through my skull and the pressure holding me vanished. I swayed on my feet. Suddenly free to collapse, I tried to lock my knees instead. It half-worked and I staggered, then hit the hard-packed floor again in a heap. The spots where the skin had been torn from my back and chest throbbed with searing pain, but the worse feeling was the things behind me: the Changeling and the Visitant.

By the light leaking out of the Visitant, I saw them all too vividly, circling each other and attacking. The Changeling was smaller, deft and quick, flickering between forms like a TV picture out of whack, a tug of war between channels. The Visitant turned into a bright, oil-slicked wave, arms multiplying too fast to comprehend. It screamed again, light pouring from its mouth and banishing the darkness to tiny corners.

A rush of heat seared my aching back. My arms gave out and my body begged me not to move, not to twist the raw, open wounds crisscrossing my skin. Coughing on the dust made stars explode behind my eyelids. I lost track of the giant creatures doing battle around me, pressing my forehead tightly to the ground and wanting nothing more than to sink into it. Become part of it. Just black out and lose touch with the agony running in rivulets across my body.

I couldn't. I had to get up, do something. *Fight.* I forced myself up on my elbows in time to see the Visitant swell to twice its original size and then slam down on the tiny, shifting body of its adversary with another triumphant roar.

Something exploded from its middle—a smaller version of the shining creature erupting through the original, puncturing it. Blinding light flooded the room again and I clamped my eyelids shut, hunkering down and gasping at the pain that washed through my body.

The air stilled too suddenly into silence. I could only hear my own ragged breathing again. My wounds pulsed in time with my heartbeat.

"You've done beautifully." A voice pooled on one side of me and then slid to the other.

Had to be the Changeling, given the Visitant probably didn't speak English. Had it won?

"That was *affection*?" I spat the words, struggling for a full breath against the burning that radiated down my back and chest.

"It tried to crawl inside of you." The voice sounded human again, cruel and amused. "To join with you." It sounded like *me*. "Lonely little bastard."

Something caressed my shoulder blade again, firmer than the misty fingers. I winced away, sending another crack of pain through my skin and hacking out a wail.

"What are you doing?" A burst of hot lava exploded through the spot where my neck met my shoulder. My fingernails broke against the ground as I tried to claw into it and haul myself away from the new, brutal pressure penetrating my raw skin.

My own voice came back to me out of the darkness.

"Knowing you."

57

"Here." Joshua stopped at what seemed to Abe like a random door in the nondescript hallway full of similar ones.

He'd hardly noticed the unsettling experience of stepping through the shimmering tear in the air that Joshua had called a curtain. It had brought them back to the office building in Montreal, though they'd entered via the front door this time. Joshua had directed the same furious power that had cracked Bel's window into tossing the human guards in the lobby around like puppets.

One had still managed to set off an alarm. The whine of the siren ought to have reassured Abe that the mage hadn't done permanent damage to the more or less innocent humans, but right now it just annoyed him.

Joshua had barely noticed, tearing a path further into the building. Now he gripped the knob of the door he'd chosen, then employed some of his unnatural gravity's weight to snap it open. The lock gave with a groan, and they faced what looked like a large supply closet. The overhead fluorescent was already on, illuminating two sets of empty shelves set against the walls and a maybe two-metre wide circle of stones in the centre of the floor.

"There you are," Joshua whispered, moving inside. "I knew she'd have made her own Ring."

"Hang on," Abe started. He'd heard stories about the Old Roads—they couldn't just rush into this with no weapons, no defence. There were things in there that couldn't be reasoned with, that wouldn't even respond to cold iron. Not that they even had *that*.

Joshua swept a hand back and the accompanying surge of power knocked Abe against the door frame hard enough to press the breath from his lungs.

The old mage stepped across the stone circle and disappeared.

Abe blinked. He'd seen all kind of crazy things—a man disappearing into a circle of stones wasn't anywhere near the strangest—but something about the place froze his muscles.

No, it wasn't the place. It was something else, something coming up behind him . . .

"Foiled your escape, I see." The Archduke's voice floated over his shoulder in the same moment that someone clapped a hand on it, fingers digging in hard.

That touch broke the spell and Abe jerked away, spinning to see Declan Raj and his guards crowding into the doorway.

"Abe." Ilse ducked under the arm of one and dodged the swipe of another in order to approach him. Her shimmering body became a welcome shield between him and the mass of the Archduke's soldiers that spilled around their master into the supply closet.

With a jerk of her chin, she thrust a warning hand at the man who'd tried to grab him. Abe didn't know what kind of power she intended to threaten with, but whatever it was, he loved her for it.

"Where's Jude?" she asked.

"In the Lower Halls." Abe nodded toward the stone circle. "If you believe Joshua."

One of the unfamiliar men whispered, "That's a—" His eyes were fixed on the circle with horror.

"Joshua made this?" The Archduke bent down to study the stones without touching them. He and his posse had stopped short at the unassuming circle, no one bold enough to cross it.

"No," Abe said. "It was already here." He tensed his legs to throw himself across the circle of stones, but a sudden warm wave of calm stayed him.

Ilse's fingers were still on his shoulder and she bled his strength from him. The room swam before his eyes, an excruciating serenity flooding through his body.

"Please don't," she said, voice quiet.

He didn't have to look at her to know using her power on him was difficult for her, but her stubbornness shone through. She considered him a friend, wanted to protect him. He hadn't even realized.

"We'll be blind in there," she said, still trying to talk him down even though her touch had already done it. "None of us knows how to navigate the Old Roads."

"Neither does Joshua," Abe grunted.

"He's a fool," Raj muttered.

Abe wanted to laugh at the realization that the lofty bastard was listening to them, even felt compelled to reply, but it took too much energy.

"He's more powerful than any of us," Ilse said, deftly making the innocent fact a sharp dig.

She let out a soft, startled gasp and her calming touch disappeared, leaving a weary coldness to spread through Abe's chest. He staggered on his feet but Ilse's hand was quickly replaced by two more, gripping him tighter as they hauled him back toward the door.

"How dare you?" Ilse fumed, being held by a guard wearing gloves, who'd pinned her arms tightly behind her back.

"For your own safety," Raj told her. "I'd never forgive myself were the Mab's *chief attendant* pulled accidentally onto the Old Roads by a raving human on my watch."

"Goddamn coward," Abe growled. The Archduke clearly had no intention of sending anybody through after Joshua, after Jude. Better for him if she never came back.

58

I GROANED AND TRIED to pull away from the creature pressed uncomfortably against my back. My shoulder screamed in pain as I dropped it to throw us both off-balance. I tangled together the last weak threads of my power, shifting gravity just a few degrees to swing myself back around and slam a bare foot into the Changeling's side.

Freed from its grasp, I shoved myself upright on shaky legs. Darkness descended and I shook my head to dispel it. That motion had me back in a heap on the ground, huffing in pain.

Have to find the door. Have to get away.

Something stabbed though my hand, splayed on the ground in front of me to hold my body up. I shrieked, my vision snapping back into focus. I stared at my own face in front of me—eyes narrowed, mouth twisted in a mean grin.

The other me—the Changeling—had gouged sharp fingernails into the back of my left hand. Then she raked them down the back of her own hand, leaving bloody tears through the pale, webbed scar that marked her as Other.

She thought she was going to walk out of here as me?

Hell, no.

I managed to coil both my legs back under my body. My muscles wanted to give up, collapse, but I sucked in a quick breath and leapt, forcing my legs into a sprint before they knew what they were doing.

Where was the damn door? I'd been spun around during the fight—left, right, up, down. Maybe I was running deeper into the chamber, not out of it. At least I'd left the other me behind . . . somewhere.

I had to stop moving to have enough energy to call out.

"Daniel?" I coaxed my voice into a shout, and added, for good measure, "Zeb? Hello?"

My name echoed back from somewhere—or did it? Maybe Daniel's voice. It sounded so far away I might have imagined it. What if it was the Changeling? Could it do Daniel's voice while it was still wearing my body? Or had it just turned into him, lurking somewhere in the darkness, waiting to fool me?

No. Stop. I forced my thoughts into one narrow focus. *Find the exit.* A noise echoed in the wide, dark room—a sharp, raspy staccato that filled my ears.

It was my own breath. The short, tight gasps pierced the silence around me in a painful rhythm. My adrenaline started to leach away, but I took a trembling step forward and reached deeper into myself, into my power, trying to find whatever traces of Mab magic I had left.

I could alter the gravity of other things—could I *pull* the door to me somehow? I didn't have the energy to lift my hands the way I'd always done before, so I focused on taking another step forward and used the motion to dig deep, drawing the hot, furious vibration of power I'd used before.

It felt distant, chilly and weak, but I poured myself into it. I compressed the space between me and the exit, turning gravity sideways to let the door drag my taut, trembling legs toward it.

"Jude?" Daniel's voice was louder now, closer. There was light ahead.

I blinked and pushed through the darkness, forcing it to part like drapery until a sliver of dim, yellow light peeked through. The lanterns in the tunnel.

The air around me seemed to gain mass suddenly, or maybe I did. I hit the ground on my hands and knees, wincing as the impact snapped my teeth together. Fire raged from my shoulder to my throat and swirls of black danced through my vision.

I crawled forward through the thick heaviness, bracing my elbows to keep them from dumping me onto the hard dirt. It turned redder with each centimetre I gained toward the lantern-light but the chamber tore at me harder, bearing down on my head and screaming shoulders.

Fingers closed around my ankle.

59

Daniel wedged Mei's iron amulet into a narrow slot between two of the stones in the door frame, using the metal's edge to dig out some of the compacted earth as he did so. Having found no information in Bel's book to the contrary, he had to go with Mei's guess that the amulet's radius was around two metres.

In its spot tucked into the door frame, it should be burning up all the available glamour across the whole opening. *I hope.*

A scream echoed out of the black doorway. His blood ran cold. *Jude.* She was in pain—terrified, furious.

He tore one of the lanterns from the wall, turning for the doorway, but Zeb caught his arm before he could get through it.

"It's a trick," his friend insisted.

"It's not." Daniel jerked away. When he reached the door again, the chamber had gone silent. He lifted the lantern high but the light seemed sallow and weak, unable to hold its own against the living darkness. His heart raced, torn between the fierce desire to leap into the chamber and sift the darkness for Jude, and the terror of the open void just out of his line of sight.

"Jude!" he shouted.

"Hey!" Zeb joined in. "Jude—over here!"

They shouted for another few seconds and then listened. Nothing.

He could go in after her, but the idea that he could navigate that space successfully was ridiculous. Seeing through glamour was one thing, but this wasn't glamour. Whatever this chamber was made of, it was heavy magic he didn't understand. He shouldn't have let Jude cross into that yawning void.

As if anyone ever *let* her do anything.

"There." Zeb released Daniel's arm and crouched down, waving both hands into the darkness as if he might dispel it. He withdrew his hands just as quickly, shaking them with a shudder. "I thought I saw something."

Daniel leaned in further with the lantern, ignoring the rush of vertigo that chilled him. The light fell on a body this time—Jude on her hands and knees, half a metre in. He started to reach for her, but the memory of Marianne Nguyen's empty, glazed eyes, her body flung across the threshold like bait, froze him.

Something moved behind Jude, clinging to her—holding her back. A doppelganger, an identical Jude. Same wild, dark curls matted around her face, same shredded clothing, same gaping, red wounds across her back and arms. This one gripped the first's ankle, and her left hand was a mass of orange-red blood and dirt. No trace of the silver spiderweb of the Changeling's scar.

The one in the lead didn't have it either. Both her hands were pressed flat against the chamber floor to haul herself forward. She lifted her head, blinking at the doorway, and seemed to see them.

"Help," she managed, trying again to yank herself forward.

"Danny," the second one gasped. "Don't touch her!"

"Get your own face!" The one in the lead grunted and kicked weakly backwards. The motion looked too slight to shake off her captor's hand, but desperate energy sparked off her, creating a fierce, sudden push that flung the other her backwards with a furious wail.

Daniel reached in and grabbed Jude's elbow, trying to bring the lantern closer with his other hand to search her face for a shadowy image of the Changeling's cruel, mocking eyes beneath the surface of her familiar features. He didn't see anything—just Jude.

"You sure this is the right one?" Zeb grunted, gripping her other arm.

"Décâlisse," Jude hissed weakly.

They hauled her back over the stone threshold, lowering her gently back to safer ground in the lantern-light.

Angry, red strips crisscrossed her back, arms and throat where pieces of her skin had been flayed off. They oozed under the tatters of her sweatshirt. She had a deeper, penetrating wound near the base of her throat that had stained both the front and back of her shredded clothing a dark, slick crimson.

Daniel couldn't help running his thumb over the skin on the back of her left hand as he helped set her down, trying to feel through the blood and grime for the raised, mottled skin that would mark her as an imposter.

A shudder ran through Jude's body but she resisted yanking her hand away. "I'm *me*," she managed through terse, pained gasps, "scrappy as hell. Get the stone."

Damn it. How had he forgotten for even an instant? Daniel turned to hastily lever the nearest keystone out of the doorway, but something slammed into him, sending him sprawling into the rough wall of the tunnel.

Pain flared through his ribs when he hit a wooden support beam, but it was forgotten as fingers closed around his throat.

"I should end you here." Joshua's furious glare filled his vision. The tense lines of concentration on the older man's face betrayed the fight he was putting up to keep from tightening his grip around Daniel's windpipe hard enough to activate the binding's response.

He'd used Zeb's body like a weapon, slamming him into Daniel to knock him off balance without triggering the reflective spell. Over the mage's shoulder, Zeb was picking himself up with a hand to his head, looking dazed.

"Keystone," Daniel rasped, trying to nod against Joshua's steel grip to the closest corner of the doorway. The Changeling must have recovered from Jude's last blow by now. They had to pull the stone or it would escape.

He stretched his left arm toward the nearest keystone, still resting in its place in the top right corner. The strain burned the scarred muscles in his shoulder.

Zeb lurched forward on his hands and knees, reaching for the keystone in the lower corner of the door frame. His fingers scrabbled against the block, trying to find purchase.

Daniel lost sight of his friend as Joshua shoved him harder into the tunnel wall, but a moment later, the old mage grunted in pain and faltered.

Zeb had successfully pulled the keystone on the lower left side of the door. He must have slammed the heavy obelisk into Joshua's ankle as soon as he'd freed it from the door frame, because he wielded it in both hands like a cudgel from his spot on the ground.

Daniel pulled out of Joshua's grip as the older man spun toward Zeb, growling.

The tunnel shuddered around them. Daniel reached Jude as she tried to surge up from her knees. She swayed and dug her fingernails into his bicep to get her balance, then her eyes fixed on the doorway and widened in horror.

An identical pair of eyes gleamed out of the darkness there, shining with bloodthirsty malice. The rest of the Changeling came into view in the doorway. It had mimicked Jude from the placement of the fresh wounds tangled into her shredded shirt, to her bare, dirty feet. The eyes were wrong, though—dark, furious, empty. No spark of Jude's sly deadpan or twinkling skepticism.

"The Mab's power." The Changeling squared its shoulders and shook its head, seeming to delight in its current body. "*And* the Visitant's. Should be a *lot* of fun, don't you think?"

It started to reach out, then stopped. With a hiss of surprise, the thing stared down at its own muddy hand as if it had never seen it before. It pressed its fingers against an invisible wall across the door, then made a fist and slammed it into the barrier.

"What have you done?" it thundered.

It twitched, trying visibly to change its form, but it couldn't. The amulet had worked, sucking up all the available glamour around the door and trapping the Changeling in Jude's form. A form that couldn't cross the threshold while the keystones were missing.

Zeb scrambled to his feet to put more distance between himself and the doorway, still gripping the loose keystone—one-handed now, but ready to swing it like a weapon.

"Clever," Joshua murmured, eyeing the frustrated Changeling with a modicum of appreciation. His eyes slid to his daughter and he flinched, shedding his trench coat. He tore a sleeve from his coat and started to press it against the gaping wound near her collarbone.

"'S fine," Jude mumbled, grabbing the fabric weakly and dabbing it against the puncture with a grimace. When Daniel put a hand over hers to increase the pressure, she choked out a groan and insisted, "I'm okay!"

"Get the other stones." Joshua shifted his daughter away, wrapping the remains of his coat around her shoulders as he took over pressure on the most critical wound.

Daniel bristled at the command, but gave in and joined Zeb retrieving the other three keystones. Zeb took the two on top without being asked and Daniel dug the tips of his fingers into the narrow space around the stone on the bottom right. It came free easier than he'd expected.

Jude's doppelganger growled inside the chamber, the noise increasing incrementally as if it felt each keystone being extracted. Its fingers raked the impenetrable doorway again.

"This trick won't hold me," it hissed, craning its neck as if trying to see what barred it inside the Lower Halls. "I have the power of the Mab and N'ellaphalen thrace. I'll hunt you all down and skin you alive, break you into tiny, wailing pieces."

"Knock yourself out," Daniel muttered.

"Is there another way out of here?" Zeb asked, stuffing the stones back into Tess's backpack. "Or do we have to go back through that screaming vortex?"

60

I FORCED BREATH OUT through my nose, snarling as I fought the pain that seemed to come from everywhere in my body. The jump back through Zeb's aptly-called 'screaming vortex' was worse than before with open, oozing wounds. Joshua had tried to do some kind of spell to help us avoid using the Old Roads again, something he called a 'curtain,' but had concluded he didn't have the energy for it, so we were stuck with the stone circle.

I tried to hold the balled up sleeve of my father's coat against the sticky hole under my collarbone as I staggered forward.

"Anyone remember where we came from?" Zeb huffed, frowning into the gloomy darkness.

"Give me the keystones," Joshua said, "and I'll direct you."

"Absolutely not," Daniel started, as Zeb took the words out of my mouth: "Fuck that."

"Two of them, then." My father glared at each of us in turn. "They can't be kept together as a set."

He had a point, though as soon as we got out of here I was definitely going to send some Mab firepower down to blow up that whole tunnel and bury the Changeling and the Lower Halls in rubble.

Zeb and Daniel exchanged a wordless conversation, then Zeb sighed and unzipped the backpack. He removed two of the keystones and tossed them so that they landed heavily at my father's feet.

Joshua frowned down at the dust they stirred up, but deigned to stoop and pick them up, tucking them both under one arm.

"This way." He started ahead without waiting to see if we would follow, limping a little on the ankle Zeb had smacked with the keystone but still steadier than the rest of us in this dizzying place.

I had intended to stumble after him, but my legs took an extra few seconds to respond and I found myself sagging against Daniel.

"You okay?" He propped me up, brows furrowed with concern as he studied my face.

"Yep." My eyelids felt heavy and his features swam in front of me. The throbbing pain in my body had started to fade, a chill taking its place. My limbs trembled without my permission.

"She doesn't look good." That was Zeb, somewhere to my right.

"*You* doesn't look good," I muttered, wincing as my words slurred together. I tried to take a step forward, just to prove that I could, but my body felt so much heavier than usual.

My feet left the ground and I tilted at an angle. I wasn't falling. How?

Daniel had lifted me into his arms, was carrying me.

Yeah, okay. But just this once.

The Old Roads blurred into a mass of shadows and faded into the background. A sudden, sharp sound drilled into my brain. My eyes flew open and I rocked in Daniel's arms hard enough that he almost dropped me.

"I hear it," he hissed.

The echoes of the clacking and chittering of sharp pincers and dozens of tiny legs were getting closer.

"Crisse de câlice de tabarnak," Zeb muttered, always game to show off his Quebecois profanity.

"They're attracted to the blood." That came from Joshua, somewhere ahead of us.

The black spots had crowded into my vision again and I couldn't see him. "The circle you want should be just ahead," he said. "Break it as soon as you're through."

"Can't fight them." The words were out of my mouth before I'd thought them through, and I belatedly noticed the lack of a subject. "*You.* You can't."

"I could, but that wasn't my intention." I practically heard Joshua's chilly smile in his voice. "Go."

"Don't," I told Daniel, since I wasn't in control of my legs.

"Jude." My father's voice was suddenly closer. "I can't heal you. You need to get back to your world."

Had he ever called me by my preferred name before? Hell of a time for him to get sentimental.

He spoke again, but not to me. "If you bring her to any harm—"

"Go to hell," Daniel returned. Then we were moving. I sucked in a breath, trying to wake myself up, find more words to argue. Joshua's voice rang out somewhere—behind us this time? Growing fainter. I couldn't make out the words but there seemed to be a staccato repetition, a tune . . . ?

"Is he *singing*?" I whispered, not willing to trust my addled brain on that one.

"Sounds like it." Daniel sounded just as mystified.

A minute later—maybe?—Zeb's voice reached me down a tunnel.

"He didn't say where it would take us."

"It's got to be better than here," Daniel answered. Then to me, "Hold on."

The words hadn't made it through my sluggish brain when the tornado sucked us away. I spun helplessly through the air, trying to cling to the distant sensation of Daniel's arms. I was suffocating.

Then I was standing.

Then I was sitting down heavily on a hard floor when my legs said 'screw that' and gave out.

Something yanked Daniel from me. My wounds stung all over again as cold air flooded them.

"Take them into custody." The irritatingly familiar tones of the Archduke's voice stabbed through my brain.

"No." I said the word with as much force as I could muster, putting all my effort into the muscles in my legs. Something slipped off my shoulders and pooled around my legs—Joshua's coat.

The room came into focus. I was upright again, some-how. We'd come through a Faerie Ring into what looked in my swimming vision like a large supply closet. There were way too many people here. Declan, for one, and the others seemed to be a bunch of his unfamiliar goons, crowding around me. Around *us*—Declan's guards had grabbed Daniel and Zeb, holding them to one side.

"No," I repeated, forcing my voice into a stony com-mand loud enough that the soldiers would take notice. "Danny and Zeb are *mine*. Let them go."

I managed to focus on Declan's face. His eyes burned into mine and his upper lip curled in disdain.

"She's dazed," he told his guards.

"She's in *shock*," Daniel spat. "Get a fucking doctor or a healer or a—"

A sharp, meaty thump and a groan cut him off. It took me a second to equate the two but as soon as the realiza-tion hit, I staggered forward, making the threads of pain throbbing through my body surge into one.

"Don't *touch* him!" Those words burned down my throat. I tried for more as the room spun into a mass of dim colours, but they blurred into the rushing in my ears. Why the hell was it so cold in here?

"Jude." Daniel was suddenly next to me, his warm hands on my shaking body. "It's fine. I'm fine. The binding—just sit—"

I wanted to melt into his arms but I couldn't feel him anymore. A distant rasp of metal echoed in my ears, then Daniel's voice again, directed away from me this time, growling, "*Try* it."

Darkness swept back in with a thunderclap.

61

Abe fought his way out of his captor's grip, twisting to one side and locking the heel of his boot around the other man's heel. He yanked his foot forward and threw his weight in the same direction, sending his adversary to the ground in a heap and breaking away.

Jude's voice came from beyond the row of Raj's soldiers blocking the doorway. It was wrong, off—strained and broken even as she snapped what sounded like commands.

He darted out of the grasp of another man, then shoved his way through the Archduke's stupefied battalion hard enough to knock at least one of them off their feet. He pushed past Raj himself, standing frozen with his sword drawn.

Jude lay sprawled on the supply closet's floor, her head and shoulders cradled in Daniel's lap. Narrow, bright red wounds ran down her arm and chest, and a thick spill of dark blood stained her shirt under the younger man's hands, oozing from a wound at her clavicle that had probably punctured a vein.

Abe batted Daniel's fingers away from the wound and put his own against Jude's sticky skin. He pushed his power into her, stirring her cells and ordering the torn, damaged tissue to knit itself back together.

Her pulse was faint and erratic. She'd lost a lot of blood. She shivered and her eyelids fluttered, then she went still.

Damn it all. Abe searched Jude's throat for the thrum of a pulse and found nothing. The cold, lifeless void swelled under his hand, tugging at him hard enough to tighten his lungs.

She's gone. It'll suck me in.

"Abe," Daniel managed, voice pleading.

Mind already made up, Abe grabbed the younger man's nearest hand and slapped it over his right shoulder.

"You hold on," he ordered. "Ground me. Do not let go."

Daniel's fingers tightened on his shoulder. Another touch pressed on his left shoulder and the gentle, steady presence of Ilse's magic streamed through him.

Balanced between the two, Abe took a deep breath and laid both hands on Jude's chest, over the hollow where her heart was silent. He closed his eyes and focused on the centre of the darkness, narrowing the black tunnel until it became a string.

A rope, leading down. Him clinging to it. Strong wind pummelled him, circling and pawing with a ferocity meant to shake him off, make him fall. Something swelled in the darkness nearby, a maw gaping open.

Abe tightened his grip on the rope. A pulse of calm throbbed through him in response. Ilse. Daniel. Holding him steady.

Slowly, he began to descend the inky rope, tilting his head to call her.

"Jude? Darlin'? Come on, come back."

Nothing. The darkness dug into his skin like tiny hooks, burrowing along his arms and legs. It filled him with a painful exhaustion and heavy apathy. The sudden overwhelming feeling of being torn from everything he knew, everything he loved, told him he ought to be sad, but he couldn't summon the strength.

Floating alone, listless in nothing.

Something yanked both him and the rope off-centre.

Abe couldn't catch his breath, swinging, flailing, spinning. He came to a stop upside down. Was he upside-down? There was no up or down here but he felt dazed, off-centre, not sure where his limbs were.

"Hey." A face appeared out of the blackness, resolving into Jude's features for an instant before blurring. Her voice glitched in and out. "What are . . . doing here?"

"Come to get you," Abe huffed, reaching for her hand. "Have to go back."

Her flesh dissipated into mist, dancing away into the darkness like shifting shadows.

"Jude," Abe growled, desperation leaching into his voice. "Goddammit!" He'd never come this far before, never felt the freezing void so close to hauling him in as he did now.

Fatigue deflated his muscles, constricting his body into a tight ball of agony. He wanted to let it still him, let it loosen his fingers, give in and let go.

Can't.

He did the only thing he could think of, hollering her full name. "Judith Sylvia Waldron!"

"I'm here." Fingertips brushed his knuckles.

Abe grasped them tightly, willing with all his might for her flesh to solidify. Then they were both clinging to the rope, spinning through the emptiness.

"Hey, darlin'." He tried to smile despite the shallow, panting breaths wracking him. He couldn't quite focus on her face but he felt her, the dim beacon of her emotions. He refused to let go of her ice-cold hand. "Think home's behind us," he gasped, "but I'm falling down."

"There's no 'down,' " she said.

"Is." Abe could only get the single syllable out against the sucking, screaming abyss that surged around him. He struggled to focus, reaching out for Daniel and Ilse back in the real world, tightening his fist around the rope. His fingernails dug into his palm, sparking pain around the warm lifeline. A tug on the rope spun his internal compass back to true north.

"It's ahead of me," he said, but now they'd reversed positions without moving. He really was falling, flailing against the weight that fought to tear him from his connection. "Gotta flip over. Can't fight gravity."

Jude chuckled and the chill of her hand on his started to warm as her voice came through the roaring blankness.

"I've got a little trick for that."

She nudged the void that gaped below them. Her nudge became a push, became a shove. Threads of colours shot through the darkness and they both spun together, ass over teakettle, as the abyss coalesced into a dizzying tumble.

62

"How the hell could you do this to me?" Saskia glared through a full-length mirror. "I told you two years, *minimum*! I'm not ready."

"So sorry for literally dying," I shot back, sprawling across the bed behind me. I'd tried to take the call standing up, prim and proper, but the hell with that if Saskia was going to go on a tirade over there.

"Don't try to play on my sympathies." She paused her angry pacing to flash me a dirty look. "I should have known you'd weasel out of this and leave me to clean up your mess."

"Since when do you have sympathies?" I snapped, "And *I died*. Trust me, it wasn't exactly my plan." I bit back the details that stirred in my throat about the misty nightmares that came with having skimmed a hand along death's surface. About waking with a ragged gasp and the sick certainty that there shouldn't be breath in my lungs. About the bitter shame when Abe, somebody dearer to me than I'd realized, had gone off to camp in the desert rather than look me in the eye after he'd torn me from the jaws of death.

The cowboy had said he just needed time alone to work out the mess in his head, as if he'd died and returned right along with me. Maybe he had. I didn't know the nuts and bolts of what had actually happened, just the few stilted sentences he'd given.

And the way Daniel sometimes twitched and moaned in his sleep.

Maybe Ilse was getting aftershocks too. I hadn't seen much of her, but the three of them had messed with something primal to chase me into death. They'd made the choice, and I wasn't allowed to say that I hadn't deserved that kind of gift.

"Stop whining," I muttered, pushing myself back into the current conversation. "You're not even fully Mab yet." Uncomfortable power still echoed in my veins. My adopted heir had most of it, yeah, but even death hadn't managed to cut me completely off from the quagmire of Faerie royal blood.

"How are the Ubran taking it?" I asked.

"They're not acknowledging it," Saskia said. "For all intents and purposes, I'm now the Mab and you're . . . well, you're best forgotten."

"Can I get that in writing?"

"Absolutely not." She tried to suppress a smile I didn't like. "Have you heard from your father?"

"Nope." I winced but I should have expected the question. "With my luck, he's living on the Old Roads. Probably made himself King of the Bug People."

"Well, no one over here is particularly keen to declare him dead again."

"Me either." Given I'd managed to kill one of those bugs, Joshua could probably have handled a whole swarm of them without breaking a sweat. He would definitely turn up again when I least wanted to see him. "So, the reason I called—"

"I called *you*," Saskia interrupted, flashing a streak of the imperiousness that suited her so well in her new role.

"Whatever." She was right—I still didn't know how to use the mirrors for inter-dimensional chats. "We need somebody to blow up the Lower Halls and make sure that goddamn Changeling is buried for eternity. Cement the amulet into the doorway first, though."

I'd already tossed one of our two keystones into the Gulf of Mexico yesterday from a hired boat, several miles offshore. Abe had taken the other with him to stash in some lonely, inhospitable desert spot.

"And I'm going to need to borrow a shapeshifter to pretend to be William Leshe and disband that new Consilium," I added. "Daniel and Zeb liberated all the unwilling employees, but there are still some, uh, die-hards hanging on."

"You allowed your . . . your *paramour* access to Leshe's people?" Saskia's glare seared me. "Of *course* you did. Why *not* hand an army over to a war criminal? How could that go poorly?"

I swallowed my first reaction. I was getting better at this diplomacy shit.

"Did you have somebody *else* sitting around who can relate to a group of pissed-off, defensive humans? If there's drama or bloodshed, you're just going to make Consilium two-point-oh stronger."

She balked. "Says who?"

"Says me, your current co-Mab and human ambassador."

Saskia stared at me long enough that I thought the call was frozen. Could Faerie calls through mirrors freeze like Internet video calls?

"Hello?" I finally tried.

"Human ambassador," she repeated. "I'll take you up on that." Before I could protest, she added, "I'll send you a shapeshifter. Don't get me in either world's tabloids."

Weird but honestly not a surprise to know they had tabloids over there. I reluctantly returned a made-up salute that made her roll her eyes, then Her Co-Highness ended the call and I was left staring at myself in the full-length mirror.

Human ambassador. Damn it. Why couldn't I just keep my stupid mouth shut?

I hadn't dressed up for the call, still wearing the plain, black tank top and a pair of running shorts I'd rolled out of bed in this morning, but Saskia hadn't noticed. The dark circles under my eyes seemed lighter in my reflection, but maybe that was just the extra bronze in my skin from the tropical sun.

Embracing the positives, I left the mirror to saunter back into the cabin's main room and announce to the aforementioned war criminal,

"I won."

"Congratulations?" Daniel sat against the arm of the wicker sofa, a laptop propped on his legs. He'd wedged a pillow behind his bad shoulder to prop it up but the position still looked slightly uncomfortable.

There had been some awkward talk of him and I taking things slow, since we still had a lot of violent, painful history to dig through. But when I'd demanded a tropical vacation from the Court to recover from being Mab, I'd invited him along and he hadn't hesitated. We weren't great at 'slow.'

"Any news?" I perched on the sofa arm.

"Hasn't been long enough." He'd been trying to get in touch with Grace for the last two days: writing to her old email addresses and hoping they'd get forwarded, putting coded posts up on sites she might frequent, leaving messages with people Ted knew. I didn't know the exact details and hadn't asked, because it seemed to stress him out.

"Saskia's going to send a shapeshifter who can pretend to be Leshe," I said. "I figure that'll help disperse all his rabid fans. She's being a bitch about turning over the new Consilium to you, though."

"Why would you ask her to do that?" Daniel started hard enough that the laptop tilted sideways on his knee and he gaped at me. "I don't know how to deprogram a cult."

I seized the moment to dump the laptop gently to the floor so I could take its place, wedging my body onto the sofa beside him and resting my head on his chest.

"You can read up on it," I said.

"Jude." His tone was disapproving but I felt the muscles in his arm tensing as if he was fighting not to wrap it around me.

"You're the one who said we can't just leave a bunch of people going to a defunct office full of stolen Consilium shit day-in and day-out because eventually some rando's going to stumble onto a dangerous Faerie artifact and, like, start a spell to burn out the sun, remember?"

"That's not *exactly* what I—"

"Anyway," I continued, "the only candidates I see heading that up are you, me and Zeb, and congratulations, it's *your* birthright."

I'd fully expected the heavy sigh I got in return, but I chided, "If I still have to be royalty, then so do you. It'd be tacky for me to shack up with a commoner."

Daniel pinched two fingers to the bridge of his nose and closed his eyes, but he was definitely trying not to laugh.

I fought the urge to slide my hands under his t-shirt. After my argument with Saskia, I was the wrong kind of wired. Instead, I sat up and said, "Let's go swimming."

"I'll stay where there's AC, thanks."

I rolled my eyes, then put a hand on his cheek and leaned in to kiss him. He wrapped one arm around my waist, hugging me closer, then twined the fingers of his other hand into my hair to keep my mouth on his.

I postponed my swim.

The pale stretch of sand outside our beach cabin's front door was blazing hot under my bare feet when I finally poked my head out. It had been baking all day in the sun, making me dash on tiptoe for the relief of the ocean. Palm trees shaded the cabin behind me, but once in the water I was exposed to the full power of the heavy, orange sun lowering on the horizon behind me.

The gentle rhythm of the waves lapping the shore reminded me of being on the beach in Tofino. I glanced back to the brightly coloured surfboard planted upright in the sand near the cabin door. I'd almost managed to stand up on it this morning during the private lesson with my very handsome, encouraging Latino teacher, but eastern Mexico wasn't quite the paradise for surfing that west coast BC had been. Smaller, calmer waves here.

The water was warmer, though. Wading in up to my shins felt like walking into a tepid bath. I missed the cold shock of the Pacific, but I stood still in the gentle Gulf waves to let the sand settle. A crab scuttled away from my feet beneath the rippling water. I hadn't changed into a bathing suit, but given the completely private beach that the deep pockets of the royal Faerie treasury had afforded me, I could have easily gone naked here with no one the wiser.

No Faerie tabloids. The thought made me chuckle to myself. I waded far enough to let the water lap at the hem of my shorts and my fingers dangled into the ocean. My feet sank a little deeper into the soft, velvety sand with each incoming wave, but I didn't mind. Part of me still couldn't believe I was finally here, breathing in this humid, salt-perfumed air with no looming threat to the world hanging over my neck. I was supposed to be dead.

Not in some noble, self-sacrificing blaze of glory, just by having been dumb enough to get flayed and stabbed by two ancient monsters in tandem. I didn't deserve this reprieve, but merit wasn't everything. Sometimes you just did your best and took what came back, whether the scales fell even or not.

Another incoming wave swept the earth from under my feet and I fought the weight of the water, shifting my gravity to level my body between the two opposing forces.

It would have been nice, given I'd had to inadvertently condemn my friends to life with my flickery, black-and-white horror movie nightmares, to at least have slipped the tethers of the Faerie crown in the process of coming back to life. But no, here I still was, straddling two worlds—and not even in a fun way.

At least I was good at keeping my balance.

Indie books like this one rely on word of mouth and reviews to make their way in the world.

If you enjoyed the "Gravity's Daughter" series, please help other readers find it by leaving a rating and/or review on your favourite review site.

My deepest thanks to all the readers who've discovered and enjoyed the "Gravity's Daughter" series—bonus appreciation points if you've left a rating/review or hopped onto my mailing list for my infrequent updates, but honestly, thanks just for reading the books. It can be hard out here for us indie authors but the readers—both dedicated and curious—make all of this possible.

Thanks as always to my wonderful editor, Julie Kay-Wallace, whose knowledge (or mad research skills) on smithing tools and arterial wounds, along with the usual grammatical stuff, helped keep the story tight and kept me from looking like an idiot. (The lagomorph bit didn't make it into the final copy, but I'm personally bettered by knowing that jackrabbits are not rodents.)

Thank you also to my wonderful beta readers Samia and Brianna. Your comments helped greatly with the final tweaks that strengthened the story and made this book shine.

Finally, thanks to my sister Ronnie for your encouraging pep talks and unwavering enthusiasm. (Not that kind of borrow.)

Stephanie Caye lives in Montreal with her partner and two furry supernatural beings disguised as cats.